WHAT MONSTROUS GODS

WHAT MONSTROUS GODS

ROSAMUND HODGE

BALZER + BRAY

An Imprint of HarperCollins*Publishers*

Balzer + Bray is an imprint of HarperCollins Publishers.

What Monstrous Gods

Copyright © 2024 by Rosamund Hodge

All rights reserved. Printed in the United States of America.

No part of this book may be used or reproduced in any manner whatsoever with-out written permission except in the case of brief quotations embodied in critical articles and reviews. For information, address HarperCollins Children's Books, a division of HarperCollins Publishers, 195 Broadway, New York, NY 10007.

Library of Congress Control Number: 2023937524

ISBN 978-0-06-286913-5

23 24 25 26 27 LBC 5 4 3 2 1

FIRST EDITION

For my grandmother Dolores "Dee" Ramirez

1933–2021

Painter, homemaker, iconographer, and mother of readers

The Gods of Runakhia and Their Shrines

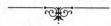

ITHOMBRIEL, KING OF WISDOM AND THE NIGHT

A dark, faceless god. His head is a ring of pale flesh around a void.
The moon and the stars and the night are his domain, and all the
wisdom contained therein. His saints grow an ever-widening hole
in the center of their foreheads until they die.

Shrine: Anazyr, the capital city

JUNI-AKHA, QUEEN OF VICTORY AND THE DAY

A glorious, terrible goddess. Golden horns grow from her head and a
golden plate covers her face, which no mortal has ever seen. Power and
victory and daylight are her domain. Her saints have golden horns, and
slowly a plate of bone covers their faces until they starve.

Shrine: Anazyr, the capital city

NIN-ANNA, LADY OF SPRING AND HEALING

A gentle, dawn-bright goddess. She has golden hands, and flowers
spring from the earth where she walks. Springtime and healing and
new life are her domain. Her saints have golden hands and die of a
burning fever as they whisper of flowers.

Shrine: Ir-Atsakha, a center of pilgrimage

ZUMARIEL, LORD OF SUMMER AND PASSION

A ferocious, yearning god. Ten thousand red ribbons wrap his body, and with them he binds the hearts of men, inflaming lovers with desire and soldiers with courage. Love and war and the heat of summer are his domain. His saints grow red ribbons from their bodies and die vomiting them.

Shrine: Nan-Darakh, a university town

NEM-UNA, LADY OF AUTUMN AND SECRETS

A silent, watchful goddess. She has one hundred eyes and no mouth, and she knows all secrets that have ever been kept. The whisper of falling leaves is her holiest hymn. Her saints grow eyes upon their palms and cheeks and waste away as visions of her secrets consume them.

Shrine: Zal-Enda, a vast monastery

SARRIEL, LORD OF WINTER AND ENDINGS

A grim, inexorable god. His arms end in stumps and a blindfold covers the bloody sockets of his eyes; he has no tongue. He rules over all endings, the dead of winter, and the hour of death. His saints die after losing first their hands, then eyes, then tongues.

Shrine: Undanna, a factory town

THE TWO WHO HAVE NO SHRINE
OR APPOINTED TIME:

IM-YARA, LADY OF DEVOTION

A burning, faithful goddess. Flames wreathe her hands and heart, and her eyes are made of fire. Every form of purity and loyalty and devotion is her domain. Ghostly flames dance over the bodies of her saints until at last they burn alive.

MOR-IVA, KNIFE OF THE GODS

A dark, bloody goddess. Her chest is a bloody chasm, and she holds her heart in charred, clawed hands. She is the knife of the gods and slays those she deems unworthy. Her saints have clawed hands with skin charred black; they die when their hearts burst under her judgment.

1

THE GODS ARE SILENT.

The gods are always silent.

We know this, in the Convent of St. Eruvaun, better than anyone. The gods no longer touch our world. They do not make saints who can work miracles. They do not speak, and perhaps they cannot even hear us.

But that doesn't stop me from praying silently, desperately, as I half trot to keep up with Sister Zenuvan's long strides, my boots slipping against cobblestones that are slick with the morning's rain.

O Nin-Anna, lady of golden hands and healing, I pray to the goddess of our convent, *please let Mother Una say yes this year.*

I've asked on every birthday since I was twelve, and every year Mother Una has shaken her head and told me I'm still too young. But tomorrow I'll be seventeen—old enough to take vows as a nun—so surely she can't make me wait any longer.

Let this be the year that I avenge you. The year I kill Ruven. The year I bring back your saints and end the plague.

The next moment I smack face-first into Sister Zenuvan as she stops abruptly. I stumble back, gasping, "Sorry!"

"Daydreaming again?" Sister Zenuvan looks back at me. "Awful danger, to walk and dream at the same time."

Her voice is solemn, but she softens the words with a wide smile that dimples her pale cheeks and reveals all her missing teeth. Sister Zenuvan is only thirty-two, hearty and strong and six feet tall, but she lived on the streets for years before she entered the convent. She sold her two front teeth and lost three more to infection.

She's one of the few nuns who's never doubted me. Last year—the first time Mother Una ever thought it over for an entire day before telling me no—I overheard Sister Zenuvan saying, *She's not too young. I'd gutted three men by her age.*

Because you were running with a gang of thieves, Mother Una replied. *Lia is softer than you ever were. Softer than the last girl who tried and failed to kill Ruven too.*

"I'm sorry," I say aloud.

Sister Zenuvan pinches my cheek. "Just stay alert till we're back behind convent walls, hmm?"

I almost laugh. We're standing on Highmarket Street, the second-fanciest shopping lane in the whole city. The crowd bustling past us is all plump matrons, grim-faced businessmen, and peaky young apprentices. There's a policeman with a round blue hat leaning against a nearby lamppost; they patrol this street twice daily for beggars and pickpockets.

But I remember what Mother Una told me last year: *You're still so dreamy and easily distracted. In five hundred years, this convent has found only seven girls with the power to enter the briar and try to kill Ruven. None ever returned. You have to be better than all of them.*

So I nod obediently and follow Sister Zenuvan into a shop whose polished brass sign reads AKHARYN & SONS: HERBS, TINCTURES & RARE EXTRACTS.

Inside the air is filled with an intoxicating mix of scents: herbs and spices, varnish and preservatives, the softness of an herb garden and the sharpness of a hospital room all at once. I draw in a greedy breath. This is my favorite of all the shops we visit; if Ruven were to make an illusion to trap me, it would surely smell like this.

The herbalist, Mr. Akharyn, is a short, pale man with eyes that bulge behind the little gold spectacles perched on his nose. A lot of the nuns don't like that we get so many of our medicinal supplies from him, for he's one of the heretics who worship the dead god preached by the Magisterium. A crucifix hangs shamelessly at the back of his shop; it's carved of pale wood but painted with crimson rivulets of blood that flow down the heretic god's twisted corpse. Beside it hangs a faded little painting of some heretic saint, a young woman robed in white and blue.

But Sister Zenuvan insists that he has the best herbs of anyone in the city, so we always come here. And while I know I should hate anything to do with heretics, I can't help loving Mr. Akharyn's shop: the rows of glistening herb jars, the narwhal horns hanging from the ceiling, the odd specimens displayed in the window.

There's something new this time: a glass case that holds two dead scorpions, one bone white and the other soot black, posed with their tails raised at each other in silent threat. A shiver crawls down my spine as I stare at them, their jointed limbs and bodies, their delicate pincers. I've never seen a scorpion outside a picture in a book before, and they're a kind of monstrous that makes my skin crawl, yet strangely beautiful. They almost look as if they're dancing.

A hand falls on my shoulder and I jump, but it's only Sister Zenuvan.

"Wanting a few more pets?" she asks.

"No!" I protest, my face heating in embarrassment as I remember all the creatures—from cockroaches to kittens—that I used to try to adopt.

Sister Zenuvan laughs softly. "I'm only teasing. I know you've outgrown it." She raises her basket to show the restocked jars of herbs. "We're done here."

Silently I follow her out of the shop and through the streets. Most times when I go out with one of the nuns, we stop at half a dozen shops, and my job is to carry all the purchases. This time, all we were sent to buy was herbs, which Sister Zenuvan likes to carry herself. I've come along because we're also going to visit several patients who were recently discharged from our hospital, so I'm carrying a satchel full of medical supplies and the little wrapped packages of oats and bacon and candied nuts that we give to people who have left us.

Our convent is dedicated to Nin-Anna, the goddess of spring and new life and healing. Not only do we care for all the sick and wounded who come to our hospital, we visit them after they leave, until we're sure that they are completely healed and their new life begun.

It's one of the things that I'm most proud of: we don't care for people out of love for money or even duty, but because we love healing. Because we set things right.

That's why I belong in the convent, no matter how many times I doze off at prayers or lose myself in fancies when I'm supposed to be cleaning.

Because I'm going to set things right.

I'm so busy thinking about this—Mother Una would shake her head in disappointment—that I don't notice where Sister Zenuvan is leading us until we're walking out into the great square before the royal palace.

It's not the first time I've come here. Everyone in the city of Anazyr does, sooner or later. The great square has become half marketplace, half carnival, with stalls selling meat pies and dried fruit and little pop-up paper models of what (they think) the palace once looked like.

Nobody has seen the palace itself in five hundred years. At the far end of the square, beyond the massive wrought iron fence, stands the briar: a vast, ever-shifting mass of thorny, shadowed vines, tall as a factory with smokestacks, completely engulfing the royal palace.

When the briar first appeared, hundreds of people tried to find a way through the thorns to free the royal family. None were ever seen again. These days, nobody believes it's possible to break Ruven's curse. Parliament built the iron fence so that no more people could lose their lives trying. Only the nuns of my convent still hope.

Only *I* can prove them right.

"Surprise," says Sister Zenuvan, smiling at me.

For one wild, hopeful moment I think that maybe it's time—maybe I'm going in right now, maybe she's decided to disobey Mother Una and believe in me when nobody else does—

"I thought you might like to look through one of the telescopes again," she says. "For your birthday."

It's the only thing I should have expected, but a strangely resentful disappointment curls in my stomach. Sister Zenuvan did this for my birthday when I was *twelve*. I'm older now, can't she see that?

But I still manage to smile and say, "Thank you."

We go to the little booth at the edge of the square, where Sister Zenuvan pays two coins for me to look at the palace through a miniature telescope. Sometimes the briar opens up a little, and people glimpse a fraction of an arch or window, but today I only see exactly what I saw last time: dark vines winding over each other like a swarm of ants on a piece of rotting fruit.

For a nightmare moment I imagine that's exactly what lies beyond the briar: a palace rotting and dead and gnawed by insects, the bodies of the seven girls who went before me piled in a putrefying mound at the doors.

Then I push the thought away and step back from the telescope. I'm not a child anymore. I've set broken bones and stitched torn flesh and helped saw off gangrenous limbs. Whatever Ruven has waiting for me inside the briar, I'm not afraid of it.

I will talk to Mother Una tonight.

We go on our way. But when we get to the first house on our list, there's a crowd gathered. As we start to push our way through, I hear the whispers. *"Plague. Death."* When they notice Sister Zenuvan's white veil, they start to pull away from us—but from fear of contagion rather than respect, judging by their expressions—and then we reach the rope barrier the police have strung across the street.

Icy dread winds through my stomach. The house we were going to visit, where the stonemason had gone home to once his broken leg was mostly healed, has a red plague flag over the open door.

There's only one sickness we don't treat at the hospital: the Red Death. The law won't allow us, and I don't think Mother Una would either. Everyone who gets it dies, and almost everyone who tries to take care of somebody infected gets it too. The only thing that can be done is to lock afflicted families in their houses until the plague has run its course with them.

It has already finished with this family. A policeman stands watch by the door as two corpse collectors carry out a sheet-wrapped body and heave it into their cart.

"Wait here," Sister Zenuvan says, and slips under the rope to talk to the policeman.

I squeeze my hands around the handle of my basket, a cold ocean of grief inside my chest. There are no more miracles. We know this in the convent, and I know it better than anyone else.

I was eleven when Papa staggered home from a long day at the factory, shivering with fever. My mother said it was no more than a touch of worker's lung, that he'd be well again with a day or two of rest. But the next morning he vomited blood, and I was already old enough to know what that meant. Mama tried to go for help, but she was dragged back by policemen who nailed wooden slats across the door.

"Fourteen days," Mama told me, her eyes bright with tears as she stood at the foot of the narrow stairs. "That's how long the quarantine is. Lia, you keep Colan downstairs with you. Don't come up for any reason."

Then she vanished up the stairs to care for Papa, and I never saw her alive again. When I finally dared creep up the stairs—five days later—they were both already dead, curled together in their narrow bed, puddles of congealed blood around them.

Colan, my little brother, was only five. He didn't understand what was happening, and I couldn't bear to tell him what I'd seen. I thought I'd have time to explain it all to him later. But on the tenth day, his eyes started bleeding. He didn't know what it meant, but I did.

I held him as he shuddered and vomited blood onto my skirt and died. I dragged him up the stairs to rest with Mama and Papa, and

I washed myself as best I could, and then I sat down with my back against the front door, waiting to sicken and die myself.

But when the fourteen days were up, and the police broke down the door, I was still alive. I'll never know why. It wasn't a miracle; the gods can't heal anyone now, not with the shrines asleep and no more saints being created. Mother Una explained that to me in my first days at the convent, clearly enough for me to understand even through my haze of grief.

I'm so caught up in memories that I don't notice Sister Zenuvan returning until she's right at my side.

"Anyone?" I ask softly. The words *like me* hang unspoken between us.

She shakes her head. "No," she says grimly.

Without another word, she marches away, and I have to run a few steps to catch up. Most of the nuns would have mouthed some platitude to me, but Sister Zenuvan understands grief better than most. It's one of the things I like about her.

There are five more people on our list to visit. They're all healing well and happy to see us, and I smile at them in return. But inside the ocean of my grief is slowly turning to a storm of rage.

If I'd gone to kill Ruven a week ago, that family might be alive today.

As we walk back to the convent, I practice argument after argument in my head. I have to convince Mother Una to let me go.

But in the end, I don't need to say anything. As soon as we arrive back at the convent Mother Una finds me, looks me up and down, and says, "Wash up and get ready to pray, child. You're going to the palace tomorrow."

2

THIS IS THE STORY, AS I learned it from the nuns.

Of all the countries in the world, Runakhia was once the most blessed. For here alone, all eight of the gods were fully known and worshipped rightly: wise Ithombriel, victorious Juni-Akha, gentle Nin-Anna, passionate Zumariel, silent Nem-Una, inexorable Sarriel, devoted Im-Yara, and bloody Mor-Iva. Their shrines were open doorways into the divine realm through which the gods could hear the prayers of the faithful, and they would choose saints from those who came to worship, granting them the power to work miracles.

Nor was that all. Since ancient days, the kings and queens of Runakhia had been so loved by the gods that they were granted the Royal Gift: they could walk through the shrines into the realm of the gods and survive standing in the presence of unveiled divinity. They used this gift to make pacts with the gods, and to wield divine power even more mightily than the saints.

Thus it was that no plague ever touched Runakhia, for the saints could heal it, and no foreign fleet ever landed on its shores, for the royal family would call down storms to destroy it. Such was the blessing of our kingdom's golden age.

But even in Runakhia, there were those who fell to the lure of foreign heresies like the cult of the Magisterium. Rejecting the eight gods, they worshipped only the corpse of a dead and broken false god . . . and dreamed of someday bending all Runakhia to their will.

And then five hundred years ago, upon a summer's day, a stranger came to the royal court. He strode into the palace wearing a dark cloak, shadows lapping at his feet. Standing before the royal throne, he declared his name was Ruven, a servant of the Magisterium, and that he had come to break the rule of the royal family and end the age of saints. He boasted that he would do it before their eyes, using such powerful sorcery that the whole royal family together could not stop him.

The queen said he was welcome to try, and all the court laughed with her. None of them had any fear, for the gods' ancient blessings assured that nobody could ever harm the royal family within their palace.

But raising his hands, Ruven called upon the unholy powers of sorcery to cast unending sleep upon them all, and that power answered.

He spared only one person, a minor duchess, whom he commanded to tell everyone what he had done. He proclaimed that the palace was his domain forevermore, that he had silenced the gods and ensured there would be no more saints made ever again. For the same sleep that had taken the palace had also fallen upon the shrines, breaking the link between the human and divine worlds. Only somebody with the Royal Gift could breach his spell, and he had already captured the entire royal house beneath his power. As the duchess fled, a dark briar sprang up behind her, walling off the palace from the rest of the capital.

And so the golden age of Runakhia ended. With no more saints to work miracles of healing, the cities grew clogged with disease. The shores of the kingdom were no longer protected by the magic of its kings and queens, so other countries began to cast greedy eyes upon it.

At first, the people of Runakhia did not forget their gods, nor their beloved royal family—not in the first years after Ruven, when the Red Death killed a third of the entire population, and not in the bitter century that followed, as they fought for freedom against Zémorine invaders. Nor did they give up hope, for now and then somebody of entirely common blood would be born with the Royal Gift. That person would go to the briar and attempt to enter the palace, defeat Ruven, and break the spell.

But none succeeded, and none ever returned. And as centuries wore on, and Runakhia grew strong and glorious again—as Parliament negotiated treaties and built a navy that could defeat any foe before they reached our shores—

Runakhia forgot.

The holy shrines changed from centers of pilgrimage to mere tourist attractions. Fewer and fewer people vowed their lives in service to the gods. Instead of remembering that Runakhia was favored beyond all other lands, they chased the fashions and technology of Zémore, an atheist nation that had abjured all gods.

Until at last only one convent of nuns still hoped that things could be set right. Every time they found a girl born with the Royal Gift, they raised her and trained her and sent her into the briar to kill Ruven. Seven girls they had sent, and none ever returned.

The eighth girl is me.

I spend my seventeenth birthday, from sunrise to sunset, kneeling in the convent chapel and praying. The gods may be silent, but that doesn't mean we should cease to honor them.

We remember that, here in the convent, even if nobody else does.

When I started the vigil, in the pale, cold hours of the morning, those thoughts were enough to keep my heart racing. The last notes of Lauds, which I had chanted along with the nuns, still rang in my ears. My heart thrummed with excitement.

Now the chapel is full of a bone-dry silence. A shaft of afternoon sunlight falls through one of the windows, hot and heavy on my hair and shoulders. I'm hungry and tired, my heartbeat a sluggish trudge.

Wearily I raise my eyes to the painting above the altar: Nin-Anna, the goddess of springtime and healing—and of our convent. *My* goddess.

She looks like a young woman, barely older than me. Her warm brown skin is flushed as if she's just finished dancing, and her jet-black hair swirls around her as if caught in the wind. She stands in a forest glade, holding a sheaf of flowers in her golden hands, and flowers blossom in the grass around her feet.

Her eyes, staring out of the painting at me, are a shimmering, luminous gold.

I remember the first time I saw those eyes. I had just arrived at the convent; I was still numb with grief and could still feel Colan's fevered weight in my arms, still hear the echoes of Mama's agonized retching. Several of the nuns fussed over me with mugs of tea and whispered comfort, but none of them seemed real. Nothing *was* real, except the Red Death.

Then Mother Una took me into the chapel, and I looked up into Nin-Anna's golden eyes.

My left eye is brown, but my right eye is gold. It used to make other children call me cursed and Mama frown in concern, but Papa told me it was a sign of good luck, and I'd always believed him. When I sat alone in our house, waiting to die, I wondered if my eye really was a curse, and that was why the Red Death had come to us.

There in the chapel, Mother Una explained to me the truth: my golden eye was a sign that I had the Royal Gift. "You belong to the gods as no one else does in these degenerate days," she said, and then she started to explain how I might kill Ruven and save us all— but that part was too much for me to take in just then.

All I could think about, as I stared up at Nin-Anna's golden eyes, was simply that I belonged to her. And she was mine. She understood my grief, and she hated the Red Death as much as I did, and she wasn't going to let me be alone anymore.

A rush of gratitude fills my heart, and I lean over, pressing my forehead to the ground in a full prostration.

"Thank you," I whisper. "Thank you, *thank you* for giving me a new home. Please . . . let me pay you back. Let me serve you."

The words shiver out of me, tiny and yet frighteningly bold. I swallow, and then take refuge in the words of ritual: "O lady of the golden hands and healing, grant me thy strength. Give me thy blessing. Help me to avenge thy people and set them free."

And then I rest.

I don't mean to. But the tile against my forehead is cool, and the sun is still warm on my back, and the air feels peaceful and holy around me. I think, *Surely Nin-Anna is pleased with me*, and it's such a sweet comfort that I rest in it. I don't sit up, and I don't pray; I listen to my breathing and think that I will move in a moment, just another moment . . .

I am kneeling in the convent garden, sunlight on my neck and the hum of bumblebees in my ears, the scents of lavender and rosemary heavy in the air. Little wisps of white clouds fleece the blue, blue sky, and it's such a beautiful day that I could stare up at the clouds and smell the air forever.

But I know there's something important buried in the garden, so I begin digging. The damp, dark earth crumbles easily under my fingers, and with every handful my heart pounds a little faster, because I'm so close, so close, I'm going to find it—

I scrape away one more handful and there it is: a pair of hands that stretch as I free them from the dirt, pale fingers reaching up toward the sky.

It's the most beautiful thing I've ever seen. Impulsively, I reach down and clasp the hands. The strange fingers tighten around mine, dirt gritting between our skin, but the roughness only makes me want to weep because that means it's real, this comfort and relief and promise of future joy is real.

I know I must keep digging. There's a whole person lying buried, waiting to be free—but I linger because this moment is too sweet to relinquish, this feeling that I have claimed somebody who is claiming me in return—

The sound of a door opening startles me awake.

I bolt upright, my head still fuzzy with sleep but my heart

14

pounding with fear and shame. What am I doing, falling asleep at a vigil like some spoiled child? Half the nuns already don't think I'm strong or brave enough. What if this is the final straw that makes Mother Una decide to have me wait another year?

I dare a glance back over my shoulder, and the fear curdles into something sourer. It's Anabekha, wearing the dove-gray veil of a novice.

We came to the convent within a few months of each other: the only two foundlings the nuns have raised in decades. *She's just two years older than you*, Mother Una said when Anabekha arrived. *You'll be playmates. Like sisters.*

But those two years might as well have been ten. We never played together, not really; Anabekha was too busy learning everything the nuns taught, just a step faster and a little better than I ever could. When she asked to take the veil six months ago, nobody expressed a single doubt.

"Don't worry," she says, smiling at me. "I won't tell."

I nod mutely. I should say thank you, but instead I want to hiss and spit like a cat. I know it's just my jealousy that makes her kindness feel like condescension, but I still feel it.

Another way she's better than me: she's never been the slightest bit jealous that I have the Royal Gift and she doesn't. Even though so many of the nuns think she would have been the better choice.

Maybe they're right, I think glumly as I watch her walk forward to light the candles ringing the altar. Even her stride is perfect: quiet yet confident, graceful and measured. When she halts by a candle, her slender hands make lighting it into a dance.

The dream rushes back to me suddenly: the pressure of those

fingers wrapped around mine, the hard lumps of the knuckles. I realize they must have been the hands of a man—they were large enough to cover mine—and my face heats, but for a few moments I can't stop turning the memory over in my head.

Nin-Anna requires her nuns to be celibate. I never thought of that as a sacrifice before; the pimple-faced errand boys I saw in the marketplace hardly seemed worth more than a goddess. So it's foolish to feel that way now, just because I had a dream of feeling wanted, chosen—

You are chosen by the gods, I remind myself. *You are wanted by Nin-Anna, and you are needed by the kingdom. Not Anabekha.* You.

So I drag myself into perfect posture, fix my gaze on the painting of Nin-Anna, and try my best to pray as Anabekha lays out the psalters and the nuns file in to sing Vespers. I don't look away from the goddess's golden eyes until I hear the heavy *step-step-thump* of Mother Una approaching with her walking stick. Then I can't help glancing back.

Mother Una's hair is all white, and the dark skin of her face is lined with wrinkles, but her eyes are bright as ever. She smiles at me like I've done well, and I feel a glow of nervous pride.

"Lia Kurinava," she says in her deep, husky voice. "Have you kept the vigil?"

"Yes, Reverend Mother," I say, because I have stayed here, I have prayed, I have not eaten or drank. Surely that is good enough.

"Then rise and join us in the praise of Nin-Anna," says Mother Una. "And avenge us."

But I don't go to avenge them immediately. At the convent, nothing is ever allowed to interrupt either prayer or meals. So when we have

16

finished chanting Vespers, we all file into the refectory for a dinner of cold beans and bacon.

Usually it's the most cheerful meal of the day. Breakfast is all silent, predawn efficiency, and lunch—the largest meal—is when one of the nuns reads aloud from an old sermon or the life of a saint. If there's time left over for conversation, it's supposed to be discussion of the reading. But at dinner we are allowed to talk as much as we like, about whatever we like. I never have much to say, but I like listening.

There's no chatting tonight though.

At first I'm too busy wolfing down my beans. But as I scrape the last of the sauce from my bowl, I realize that none of the older nuns have reprimanded me for eating too fast. The room is ominously silent, and when I look up—

A lot of them glance away instantly, but I can still tell: half the room is staring at me.

I drop my gaze down to my spoon. The beans and bacon—delicious after a day of fasting—feel like a heavy lump of clay in my stomach. All those eyes and all those faces are scorched into my mind.

It's not the skeptical, worried gazes that bother me. Or rather, they do bother me, but I've been hearing people say it was a pity Anabekha hadn't been the one born with the Royal Gift for years now. I'm used to it.

But some of those gazes were soft with reverence and hope, and those ones haunt me. Even today, after all I've done to prepare, I fell asleep at the vigil. I dreamed of a man holding my hands—a thing forbidden to nuns of Nin-Anna—and I treasured that thought for a few minutes after.

I won't fail, I promise myself, promise all of them. *Nobody will die like my family ever again.*

After dinner, I go to my rooms and dress in my very best white blouse and dove-gray skirt. Then I return to the chapel.

Mother Una stands waiting for me before the altar, holding in her hands a knife with an ivory blade. When I see its pale gleam, my heart starts pounding with fear and eagerness at once.

"When I was younger than you are now," says Mother Una, "I watched another girl walk into the briar. The thorns peeled back before her as she strode forward. But she was barely inside when she tried to turn back. Instantly the thorns closed in on her and she died screaming before us."

I have heard this story a hundred times before. The thought of needle-sharp thorns stabbing through my whole body used to keep me awake at night, and Mother Una's words still send a chill through my stomach. But now I also feel a flicker of resentment—why can't she trust that I remember?

"I know, Reverend Mother," I say. "I won't hesitate. I won't turn back. I won't stop for anything until Ruven is dead at my hands. I swear it."

Mother Una nods with austere satisfaction. Another nun comes forward with the leather sheath, and Mother Una herself kneels to strap the knife onto my leg.

And then, accompanied by Anabekha and Sister Zenuvan, I go forth to face the sorcerer who silenced the gods.

When we visited yesterday, the square in front of the palace was practically a carnival. Now it's dark, lit only by the glow of the few gas lamps at its edges. Most of the vendors have already left, and the few that remain are hastily packing. Nobody likes to be near the briar after nightfall. There are stories that once the sun sets it sings to people, luring them to their deaths.

The people of Runakhia have forgotten their love for the royal family. They are starting to forget their faith in the gods as well. But for all they've turned Ruven's sorcery into a tourist attraction, they still respect its danger.

I don't hear any song now as I stride into the square, just the soft whistle of the evening breeze as it sends an old newspaper and a few scraps of trash dancing across the cobblestones. Before me, the briar is a mountain of shadow, rearing far above the great iron fence that has been put around it to stop girls like me from going to their deaths.

Shivers run up my spine and down my arms as I walk forward, faster and faster, until I come to the padlocked iron gates. I put my hands out, grip the bars, and feel their cold metal edges cut into my fingers.

Now, I think. *I'm going to do it now*, and I feel a strange impulse to sob, at once nauseous and exultant.

A hand touches my shoulder, and I look back. It's Anabekha, her eyebrows drawn together in concern.

"Are you all right?" she asks.

"Yes," I say, for once meeting her gaze without wanting to bristle.

I'm about to do something she cannot. And when I'm done, we'll finally be sisters. Equals. Nobody will ever compare us again.

I will be worthy of you, I think, *and you will be proud of me.*

"I'm sure Ruven won't stand a chance against you," says Anabekha.

"Just remember," says Sister Zenuvan, "if he's too much on his guard for immediate stabbing, you can always charm him as Saint Dinakha did with the Zémorine general."

The memory of my dream—bare hands touching mine—shivers through me again, and my face heats. "No I can't!" I blurt out.

"Why not?" Sister Zenuvan grins crookedly. "I'm sure you're just as pretty."

"Dinakha was a saint of *Zumariel*," I mumble. Seducing an invading general to kill him in his sleep is the perfect way to serve the god of love and war, but it wouldn't be holy to a goddess who loves everything fresh and new, dewdrops and springtime and virgins alike.

"I'm going to be a nun of Nin-Anna," I remind Sister Zenuvan. She will accept me killing Ruven for the same reason she allows her nuns to amputate gangrenous limbs—but she won't accept unchastity.

Sister Zenuvan's grin gets wider. "All the more reason to enjoy yourself while you can."

Suddenly, from halfway across the square, a man calls out, "Hey there! What are you doing?"

We've been noticed. In a moment somebody will try to stop us.

"Go," says Sister Zenuvan. "Now."

"Help me up," I say, and they both drop to their knees and clasp their hands, making a foothold. I step onto their hands and clamber up in a wild haste. For one instant I teeter on the top of the gate, gasping for breath—

And then I swing my legs over, heedless of the spike that catches at my skirt and rips it, and I drop down into the darkness of the briar.

3

HALFWAY THROUGH THE BRIAR, I NEARLY lose my mind.

I don't know how long I've been walking through the dense, overgrown darkness, step by careful step. The briar presses in on every side, like a cage molded to fit my body. Branches slide through my hair without tangling to scrape at my scalp. When I reach forward, shadowy thorns press through my sleeves without piercing the fabric, to prick at my skin and draw blood.

With every step I take, the briar silently unfurls itself ahead of me, remaining just inches away from my face. Behind me, it closes up again, dark and dense as death. Not a single ray of moonlight pierces the interwoven thorns. I only know I'm still on the red-and-gold mosaic path because of my little oil lantern.

The dim, flickering light makes the thorns even sharper, their movement uncannier. There's a terrifying vastness to the briar, as if I haven't stepped *into* a place of thorns and darkness but *out*. As if I stand in the shallows of a vast ocean that might at any moment turn to storm.

And it whispers.

That's the worst part, what makes fear writhe in my stomach and crawl shivering over my skin. At first I thought it was just an echo of the wind, filtered down through the thorns, but with every step I grow more certain: the briar whispers to itself. Or maybe it whispers to me.

I've heard stories of how the briar can sing bewitching songs. As I force myself deeper into it, step by step, I suddenly wish that it did. Because then it would be a thing that willed and wanted. I could defy it and thwart its plans.

But this quiet meditation echoed from thorn to thorn?

The briar wouldn't care if it killed me. If the dark vines suddenly wrapped around my limbs, and the thorns grew to spit me like an animal, it would happen as calmly and inevitably as the winter rains.

I remember Mother Una's story about the girl she watched die on the thorns. I think of all the stories I've read about people who tried to enter the briar and never returned. Most of them were marked with the Royal Gift, just like me, and it didn't save them.

Are you so different? Do you think you're so much better than all of them?

I don't. But if I turn back now, I will die.

Slowly, carefully, I take another step forward, and the briar unwinds itself to—

A skeleton.

It is bleached white, all traces of skin and hair and clothing scraped away. Yet somehow it looks almost alive, because it doesn't hang peacefully in place, like a relic in a church. The bony hands claw at the thorns as if still trying to escape; the skull is thrown back, jawbone stretched open in an endless scream.

I can't help it. I flinch from the horrifying thing. Instantly I remember that going back will get me killed, and I try to lunge forward without touching the skeleton—I wobble, grasping at the air for balance—

And I drop the lamp.

It doesn't even hit the ground. The briars catch it first.

I grab for it, but I'm too late. Vines have already wrapped over the handle, and they don't shrink back from my hand. I try to pull it free anyway, scrabbling for a grip, but the thorns bite into my skin. With a gasp, I let go.

The lamp hasn't gone out. Its flame dances just beyond my reach, like a mockery. I can still see the skeleton hanging before me—

The skeleton has moved.

Or rather, the briar has moved it, pulling it apart limb from limb to make a constellation of bones framing the path I have to take.

Horror crashes down on me. For an endless, sickening moment, it's all I can do to hold still. This is what the briar will do to me, how it will rend me apart and reshape me, if I make the least mistake. If I'm imperfect as I've always, always been.

I want to scream. I want to *run*, to turn around and claw my way out of this waking nightmare.

But that will get me killed.

A bleak, cold despair washes over me, drags me down into its depths. I can't do this. If I turn back, the thorns will rend me apart. If I want to live, I have to walk face-first into darkness and a labyrinth of bones—and I'm not brave enough. I'm not, I'm not.

O Nin-Anna, I think, but can't get any further in the prayer.

I don't know how long I stand in that spot, my breath coming in shuddering gasps that are almost sobs. But finally a thought enters my head, sounding like Mother Una's strict voice: *Did you ever really love the gods or not?*

Did you ever love your family or not?

I have vowed so many times that I will avenge their deaths by killing Ruven. That nobody will die like Mama and Papa and Colan did ever again. And the only way to make that happen is to keep going forward.

I force myself to take a slow, deep breath. Then another. Fear churns in my stomach, but I bend down and strip off first my shoes and then my stockings. If I'm to go forward without a lamp, I'll need to be able to feel if I start to edge off the path.

The mosaic is unrelentingly cold beneath my bare feet. I shiver, flexing my toes. Then I square my shoulders and close my eyes.

Silently I pray to Nin-Anna: *O dawn-bright lady, help me. Guide my steps. Give me courage. Bring me out of this place.*

Help me. Help me. Help.

Eyes still shut, I step forward, hands held out in front, sliding my bare foot carefully across the mosaic path.

The first step feels almost impossible. The next is easier.

On the third step, my fingers brush against the smooth curve of bone.

I snatch my hand back instantly; at the same moment there's a clatter in front of me. Even with my eyes shut, I know exactly what's happened. The briar has melted away around the skeleton, and all the bones have fallen to the ground.

I can't help the little moan of horror that forces its way out of my throat. For a few moments, I'm unable to move, my mind stuttering through a desperate prayer: *O lady of golden hands and healing,*

O lady of golden hands and healing, O lady of golden hands and healing—

But eventually the horror pinching at my stomach starts to fade. I slide a cautious foot forward; bones jangle softly against the mosaic as my toes push them out of the way.

They're only bones, after all, clean and cool to the touch. I have helped dress the bodies of the people who died in the convent hospital. The sores and rashes and tumors—the stinking flesh of the poor man who died of gangrene after he refused to let the nuns amputate his leg—they were all far more terrible to touch, and yet I could bear them.

The nuns of Nin-Anna are sworn to heal, and that means they must also tend to those they failed to heal.

I was born to save the royal family, and perhaps that means I have a debt to all those who have tried before and failed. I whisper a prayer for the soul of the nameless bones.

And then I go on, deeper into the briar.

Renewed determination doesn't make the journey any easier. When the briar finally—*finally*—parts to reveal wide open air and pale moonlight that dazzles my eyes after the darkness, I manage only one step forward before I fall to my hands and knees.

For a little while, all I can do is gasp for breath, ribs straining against my normally well-fitted corset. I can't believe it's over. I can't believe I lived. My body still shakes with the memory of the briar's whispers. My skin itches and stings where it clawed at me.

But I'm alive.

I sit up and look at what I've reached.

In the old histories, it was called the Palace of Ten Thousand

Arches. Staring up at it now, I think the name must be literally true. Arch upon arch rises above me, each piled atop the other—some blind, set into a flat wall; others hugging doors or windows; still others forming open doorways onto balconies.

Before me stands the main entrance: the huge, gold-plated doors through which Ruven strode on that summer afternoon long ago, still slightly ajar.

The left door is carved with the image of a tall, majestic man who has no face, only a great ring in place of a head: Ithombriel, god of starlight and wisdom. On the right door is an imperious lady with horns curving out of her head, and a plate of bone sheathing her face: Juni-Akha, goddess of daylight and victory. They stare down at me blindly, silent as all eight gods have been for five hundred years.

They will not be so for much longer.

I surge to my feet and stride up the stairs and into the palace.

4

SUNLIGHT DAZZLES MY EYES.

It's so unexpected, it takes me a moment to realize that's why I'm squinting, my eyes watering: there's sunlight pouring through the tall, narrow windows of the hallway and spilling buttery and bright across the floor.

In a daze of wonder, I walk forward into one of the sunlit patches. The marble is warm beneath my feet, as if it's been lying in the sun for hours. I can't understand how it can be a spring midnight outside the palace, and a summer afternoon within—

And then I do.

Five hundred years ago, upon a summer's day.

Ruven didn't just capture the court in his spell, but time itself. That hour of summer afternoon when he worked his magic is caught here in the palace like a fly in honey. The air I'm breathing now was blown into this room by summer breezes five hundred years gone. That is why it smells so sweet, without a hint of the garbage stink and factory smoke that cling to the whole city of Anazyr.

The feeling of wonder turns to a prickle of fear up and down my spine. I am standing in the very moment of Ruven's triumph.

I survived the briars, I tell myself. *I can kill him.*

So I continue on. In the next hallway, I find the first sleepers, a pair of what must be servants, for both their tunics are plain. One is a middle-aged woman, kneeling in a corner of the room, her head leaning against the wall; the other lies sprawled in the center of the room, a young boy with a milk-pale face and carrot-colored hair.

I kneel and touch his cheek. He feels warm and soft and healthy, nothing like the cold stiffness of a corpse. But there's no breath stirring in his half-open mouth, no pulse beneath the skin of his throat.

Again my skin prickles at the knowledge of how vast and uncanny Ruven's power is. It's not sleep that holds the inhabitants of the palace; it's a stillness so absolute that it halted them between one breath and another, one heartbeat and the next.

I wander through more than a dozen rooms before I hear the noise. It's just a soft clatter. In the convent, surrounded by the bustle of the nuns and the noise of the hospital, I would never have noticed it.

Here, in the stark silence of the sleeping palace, it rings through my head like a gong.

Now. Here. I am going to meet him now.

I follow the noise. I turn a corner. I see—

A small dining room so richly decorated that it must be for the royal family. There are gilt chairs, and a long table of dark, polished stone.

At the far end of the table sits Ruven.

My stunned first thought is, *He's just a boy.*

Because the man drinking from a jeweled goblet is barely a man. He looks no more than a year or two older than me; his long, pale face still has a boyish softness to it, and there's a sulky twist to his lips.

And he's handsome.

I'd always imagined Ruven looking like the effigies of him that we burn every year on Bonfire Night: a hideous old man, withered and scarred by his dark magic, perhaps covered in boils and pustules.

Instead he looks very like I always imagined the princes of old must have: the aristocratic lines of his nose and chin, the lordly set of his shoulders.

The golden iris of his right eye, glowing in the dim light.

It's just like mine, and with that I shiver back to the awareness that he's not a prince any more than I'm a princess. We're both commoners born with the Royal Gift, but I'm using it to serve the gods, while he used it to become a sorcerer.

I've been staring at him for several heartbeats now, but Ruven just takes a deep, lingering gulp from his goblet. Then he finally looks at me over the rim, half disdainful, half bored.

"Ah," he says. "They finally found one."

His voice is deeper than I expected, and he says the words with a strange, overprecise enunciation that, after a moment, I recognize.

"Are you drunk?" I demand.

Of all the things I had thought I might say first to the heretic sorcerer who ruined my kingdom and killed my family—it wasn't this.

"Not nearly enough," says Ruven, biting off each word. "Do you think there's any wine left in this palace? I drink on dreams and find not nearly enough oblivion."

"You're terribly, terribly drunk." I shake my head, not even afraid now, just revolted. "You—how *could* you?"

The goblet rings as Ruven slams it down on the table, and wine slops over the rim. "*That* is the crime for which you're going to reproach me? After climbing through my briar and surviving what no others have in five hundred years, you're going to lecture me on the evils of wine?"

"It's bad enough you made this palace into a tomb," I snap, "but then you decide to—to *carouse* in it?"

He flings his head back and laughs. "Convent-bred, aren't you? Angrier at a little vice than you are at the destruction of your kingdom."

I bite my lip, thinking of Mama and Papa's bodies lying together in a bed slick with blood and vomit. I think of all the people lying sick in our hospital who cannot hope that the power of the goddess will bring them healing, and I think of the skeleton in the briar, a nameless person who tried to set things right and died in agony, bones twisted into a monstrous display.

"I'm not angry," I say, my voice strangely calm. "I'm *disgusted*. You had the power to humble Runakhia and silence the gods—and you used it for what? An extra cup of wine?"

"Power." Ruven's voice turns sour. "That's what you think I have, little mouse?"

My stomach roils with the familiar shame of being dismissed—*too quiet, too dreamy, she'll never succeed*—

"I'm not a mouse," I say.

"Well, you don't have enough claws to be a cat." Ruven rises from his seat, moving toward me with a feline grace that I've certainly never had. "Or at least you don't have the wits to pounce from the shadows."

My body sparks with terror as he approaches. And yet there's a knife strapped to my leg. A hundred times over, I have stood in the convent morgue, one or another of the sisters scrutinizing me as I practiced fatal cuts from a dozen angles on the unclaimed bodies of paupers. And Ruven has no idea about any of it.

A fire that's half resentment and half glee kindles in my stomach. He thinks I'm a harmless mouse, and that's how I'm going to win.

"You have more than enough spells to call yourself a sorcerer," I reply. "Or are you going to pretend you didn't come here to destroy Runakhia of your own free will?"

His face twitches with an emotion I can't recognize. And then he's in front of me, looming over me, and I shudder as his palms slam against the wall on either side of my head.

"Who promised you?" he asks, and his voice is almost gentle.

"What?" I gasp.

His mouth twists. "Somebody made you a promise. If you tried hard, if you were obedient, if you did the impossible thing, you would be a hero. Everything would be worth it. Don't lie to me. You and your golden eye can't be here for any reason other than to destroy my spell upon the palace. Who made you that promise?"

I'm too stunned by the strange gentleness in his eyes to think. So I answer his question.

"The nuns of Nin-Anna," I say. "They found me, they saved me, they—"

I realize what I'm doing and snap my mouth shut, choking off the treacherous stream of words. Ruven has no right to my past, to my hopes and fears.

"Did someone make a promise to you?" I demand, hoping the question burns.

But he only draws back and straightens up, smiling faintly. "Didn't they teach you? I was born a monster. Same as you."

Suddenly I don't feel helpless anymore. Because Ruven is wrong. His eyes may look gentle and knowing but *he does not know me.*

I'm not a monster, and the nuns never told me that I was one. They told me that I was blessed by the gods with a special mission, and once I completed it, I could take my vows and have a place with them.

If I kill Ruven, I will have everything I ever wanted. My family will be avenged and nobody will ever have to suffer and die like they did again.

The nuns love me and I love Nin-Anna. So I can face anything.

My heart skipping strangely, I look up into his eyes. "Of course we're monsters, but—can't we be good ones?" I ask him, falteringly and falsely.

But he believes me; I see it in the softness of his eyes and mouth.

"No," he whispers, "we cannot."

He leans back over me, and for an insane moment I think he's going to kiss my mouth, then that he's going to kiss my forehead. But he doesn't. His hands tighten on my shoulders, and he rests his chin on the crown of my head, and he sighs.

I stiffen in his grip, but he does nothing terrible, and I start to relax.

"It's not too late, you know," says Ruven, his voice soft and rumbling. "You're not bound like me."

My mouth is dry, my heart rabbiting, but after a moment I manage to control my voice to ask calmly, "What do you mean?"

He draws back, his eyes meeting mine. "Surely you know."

I shake my head, genuinely confused.

Ruven curses under his breath. "What absolute bastards raised you?"

"They were nuns," I say warningly.

"Excuse me, what absolute *bitches* raised you?"

I bite back the reply that wild dogs would be better family than a sorcerer, and the nuns were better than either. Ruven is angry on my behalf, and it makes absolutely no sense, but it's a weakness I can exploit.

"What do you mean?" I ask again.

He laughs hollowly. "You wonder why I drink? The sorcery I worked to bind the royal family binds me as well. While they sleep, I wake. Without rest or hope of death. I have . . ." He stares into the distance, eyes going unfocused. "I have gone mad so many times."

My throat tightens at the grim resignation in his words. In all the times I've heard the story of Ruven's promise to rule over the palace forevermore, I never imagined that he might not want to.

"But you," says Ruven, and he catches at my chin, tilting my head up. "Whatever they've trained you to do, you haven't done yet. You still have a choice. You can go."

His fingers are gentle on my skin, yet I shiver. He is a monster, but in his mind he's trying to save me.

And I am here to save everyone.

I meet his eyes, and I say calmly, "Who says I'm going to do their bidding?"

He is stronger than me in every way. I can't kill him in a fair fight. But if I can deceive him . . . perhaps that makes me too much like Saint Dinakha, but she *was* a saint. And I cannot allow myself to fail.

Ruven laughs hollowly, stepping back. "If you're not, then you should go."

Without him looming over me, I feel strangely exposed, and I step forward to catch at his hand. A shock runs up my fingers—I didn't expect him to feel so warm, so solid. So real.

I didn't expect to feel like I was holding the hands from my dream. Like that grasp is somehow my only hope and comfort.

That doesn't matter—it can't. I think of what Ruven has said and what he clearly means, and I visualize my strategy like a surgeon finding the best route to a tumor.

"What if I want to stay?" I ask. "At least a little while. I've . . . never met somebody else like me."

My stomach turns over at the truth in those words. I was so alone as I sat in my family's house, wondering why I hadn't yet died. And though I wasn't alone in the convent, I was still set apart.

For an instant I look into Ruven's eyes with unfeigned hope as I imagine a world in which he is not a monster, and I am not going to kill him, and neither one of us is alone.

Then Ruven wrenches his hand free of mine, strides jerkily back to the table, and drops into his seat. I find myself following him as if drawn by a string; I stand less than a pace away, staring at the loose black waves of his hair as he buries his face in his hands.

He's not watching me. Carefully, I slide my hand through the slit in my skirt and ease my knife from its sheath.

I could do it now: grab his hair to hold him, slide the knife into the side of his neck. Quick, deadly. A holy service to the gods; an act of justice for my family.

My heart thuds, a strange hot wave working through my body. I could do it now. I should do it. I *will* do it now—

But my hands don't move.

"If you've never met someone like me, then you're lucky," Ruven says wearily, without looking up. "Please go."

I feel suddenly sick. He's a monster, but he doesn't want to hurt me. He's trying to save me. How can I kill him?

But how can I not, when he is the gangrenous limb slowly poisoning Runakhia? When he is the reason my little brother died in pain and fear?

Ruven lifts his head, and his face has gone strangely bloodless. "Go," he says, and there's a new timbre to his voice, a more-than-human echo. "Or I will not let you leave, and *you will not like it*."

The floor vibrates under my feet, a buzzing hum that sets my teeth on edge and rattles the cutlery on the table. In the corners of the room, shadows are clotting and swirling.

I remember, all over again, how much power Ruven has in this place. How he has never stopped being dangerous. My knife hand, pressed into the folds of my skirt, is trembling.

And then Ruven's eyes shift, and I know he is looking at my hands.

"Why are you waiting?" he asks, his voice low.

He's not a fool. In another moment, he'll realize what I'm hiding, that I do have claws and I'm here to kill him—and then he'll kill me.

White-hot terror flashes through my mind, and I do the only thing I can think of to distract him.

I sit in his lap.

The motion knocks the breath out of both of us. We gape at each other; I can feel my face blushing a bright, boiling red as I realize that I am sitting in a man's lap, and I can see an answering flush on his cheeks.

"What are you doing?" he asks hoarsely, and in that moment, he sounds like a boy again. A boy who's been lost and alone for far too long.

I was that lonely too, sitting in a house of dead bodies.

I will not weaken, I think. *I cannot weaken.*

"Only this," I say.

With my left hand, I touch his cheek. He leans into the touch, his breath warm against my wrist.

And then I cut his throat.

5

IT'S OVER SO FAST IT HARDLY feels real. One slash of the blade.

Then comes the blood.

So much blood, and it's everywhere—my face my hands my mouth—

I shove a hand against Ruven's throat, trying to hold the blood in, but it's still welling up beneath my palm. His life running out between my fingers, slipping away like my family did, and all I can think is, *What have I done?*

Our eyes meet.

For years I've imagined this moment. When I was emptying bedpans in the hospital, or scrubbing floors, or yawning my way through midnight prayer vigils, I would picture Ruven's death and find the strength to go on.

But now . . . He isn't a wraith snarling blasphemous curses, or a looming monster begging for mercy. He's just a boy choking on his own blood, gurgling as he tries to breathe through the ruin of his throat, which *I* slashed open.

And his eyes are still so lonely.

Suddenly his hand locks onto my wrist, his grip painfully strong. I flinch but don't pull back.

My eyes are the last he will ever see. My hand on his throat and my wrist beneath his fingers are the last human touch he'll ever feel. For one endless moment, nothing else matters—not what he did five hundred years ago, nor how long I've dreamed of killing him for it. Nothing is real but the two of us holding on to each other.

Then his hand goes limp. His eyelids droop. No more air whistles through the gash in his throat.

He's dead he's dead he's dead.

The thought rattles through my mind and I'm a little girl all over again, my parents' corpses upstairs and my little brother newly dead in my arms, mired in the stink of blood and the cold knowledge that nobody will come, and the gods are silent as I gasp and sob with infinite, aching grief.

The gods are always silent.

But now that Ruven's dead, shouldn't that all change?

"Nin-Anna," I whisper between my sobs. "Nin-Anna. *Please.*"

I don't know what I'm begging for, except maybe a sign that I'm not alone.

But there's no answer. I can't hear anything except my own harsh breaths.

Shouldn't I hear the sounds of the palace waking?

A terrible dread clutches at my heart as I realize that even though Ruven is dead, the timeless summer sunlight still shines through the windows.

I leap to my feet and rush from the room in a panic. It has to be all right, I tell myself as I run down the corridors of the palace, hunting for someone, anyone. Maybe the spell simply takes a little while to fade. Maybe I've already been in here long enough that it's daylight in the world outside again. Maybe—

Then I stumble upon the throne room.

The great hall is vast, the arched ceiling high as a second sky, sunlight pouring through the windows to glitter off the gold and silver traceries that adorn the walls with the symbols of all the gods. Courtiers lie slumped in a rainbow of richly embroidered silks, like all the flowers in a garden have dropped their petals.

And at the head of the room, atop the red-tiled dais, is the great golden throne of Runakhia, with a red-haired woman slumped upon it. Two great golden horns, shaped like those of a cow, grow from her forehead—a sign of the pact she made with the goddess Juni-Akha.

I know who she is: Queen Imvada, the last true ruler of Runakhia. I killed Ruven so that she would wake again.

In a trance of horror, I walk forward through the hall and climb the steps of the dais until I stand only a breath away from her.

Heavy golden rings cluster on Queen Imvada's fingers. On her head—fitted with straps that clasp to her horns—she wears the Holy Crown, a great halo made from beaten-gold rays of light, with a circlet encrusted with rubies and pearls. She is the ancient glory of Runakhia incarnate.

Hoping against hope, I reach for her shoulder, to see if I can wake her—

Her eyes snap open, and she seizes my wrist. I yelp and try to jump back, but her grip is iron.

"Why did you weep for him?" she asks.

Both her eyes glow bright gold, as if she is not a queen but a goddess.

My breath rushes in and out of my lungs, but my mouth is leaden. I try to answer her, to say that I was only thinking of my family, that I would never weep for Ruven himself, but the only sound I can make is a soft moan.

From behind me comes a soft chorus of voices: "Why did you weep for him? Why did you weep for him? Why?"

I look back. All the nobles have woken, and they are all staring at me with golden eyes, a vast crowd of divine judgment—

And gasping for breath, I wake.

For a few confused moments, I don't know where I am. Then I see the gold-embroidered blue of the canopy over my bed, and I remember: I am in a bedroom of the royal palace. I killed Ruven one week ago.

I've dreamed about it every night since.

Relief washes through me like an overflowing tide as I remember what really happened. I did realize there was daylight streaming through the windows after Ruven died, and I did panic. But it was only the morning sunlight; when I stumbled into the throne room, everyone had begun to wake. The guards seized me, but then Queen Imvada herself came forward to question me. And once I showed her Ruven's body, she believed me.

Nobody knows I wept for him.

With a cold ache in my chest, I sit up. Pale morning light streams through the windows, glittering off the blue-and-gold mosaic that swirls across the floor. It's a beautiful room, but it's starting to feel like a prison. Queen Imvada declared that I was an honored guest and brought me to this room herself, but she hasn't come to see me since that first day. For the past week, I've been utterly alone except for a quiet young maid who comes to bring me food and help me dress.

I'm used to the busy rhythms of life in the convent, where the bells are always calling us from bed to chapel to hospital to chores and back again. The maid has brought me a psalter and needle-work, but the long hours still weigh uselessly on me.

It's not a prison, I remind myself. *You're an honored guest.*

Nobody has told me that I cannot leave my room. But nobody has told me that I *can*, and the need to prove myself good and obedient weighs on me like a chain.

If they wanted me, wouldn't they send for me? If I were welcome, wouldn't they let me know?

It doesn't matter. I won't be here much longer anyway. Because tonight—the maid told me this yesterday—Queen Imvada wishes me to attend a feast with the royal family and all the court as they welcome Parliament to their ancient halls.

I'm sure this is the reason she's kept me here so long: to display me at the feast, so that everyone will know it was neither political conniving nor Zémorine inventions that broke Ruven's power, but only the will of the gods working through a simple girl. She must plan to send me back to the convent once the evening is done. And if she doesn't, at least tonight I'll have the chance to ask her. I'll explain how much more useful I will be there, how bad the scourge of the Red Death has become and how much we need the hospital, and surely she will agree.

And yet I remember the queen's face in my dream—the ruthless judgment in her glowing gaze—and the cold behind my ribs does not go away.

"There," says the maid to me that evening. "All done. Aren't you lovely?"

I open my eyes and look into the mirror. For a moment, I hardly recognize myself.

My face is the same as always. Pale, round, with a pointed nose and chin. Brown hair, neatly combed back. Nothing like Anabekha's beauty, but not ugly. And I've had a whole week to get used to wearing dresses in the ancient style—a kirtle and sideless surcote—since there was no washing the blood out of the blouse and skirt I wore into the palace.

But for tonight, my dress is all shimmering white silk, the surcote stitched with silver embroidery and tiny opalescent glass beads. My hair is braided into a crown on my head, woven with white ribbons and pale pink roses. I look like a princess.

No, that isn't quite right. I look like a doll dressed as a princess, perfect and helpless.

When I was a child, the Emporium on Highmarket Street had a whole window of dolls like that, standing in row after row. All their dresses were the same, but their silk ringlets ranged from gold to red to black, their porcelain faces from cream to mahogany, so that every rich man's daughter could own a princess who looked like her twin. I used to stare at those dolls through the window, longing for one, and then tell myself that saving and meeting a real princess would be better.

Now I don't care about dolls or princesses. I just want to go home to the convent. I want to roll bandages and clean bedpans and do all the worst, most boring jobs in the hospital, and know that I'm helping to heal people.

I want to forget that I ever felt pity for a heretic sorcerer. I want to see the new world I created by killing him, a world where the gods make saints who work miracles every day. I want to be there the first time we bring patients with the Red Death into the hospital, and I want to see them walk out alive and well, and I want to know that what I did was worth it.

I want to feel like *myself* again.

6

I MEET THE ROYAL FAMILY IN a small antechamber outside the great feast hall. And despite all my fears over the past week, when I step through the doorway and see Queen Imvada with her red hair falling in gold-laced braids to her knees, her miraculous golden horns glittering in the candlelight, with Prince Araunn and Princess Varia beside her . . . the first thing I feel is simple relief.

They're human and alive, the champions I dreamed of as a child made real. Surely now everything will be all right.

I step forward and curtsy carefully. "Your Majesty," I say, proud of how steady my voice is. "Thank you for everything."

As I straighten, I dare a glance up, and our eyes meet. The queen's golden right eye sends a jolt down my spine—I remember her glowing, merciless gaze from my dream—

"We are surrounded by enemies," she says. "Do not disappoint me."

I gape at her, but she's already turning away. "Araunn, you will escort her this evening."

"Of course, Mother," says Prince Araunn, stepping to my side. His square face is colorless and plain, but his smile is beautifully warm. "Don't be frightened," he says softly. "Mother always has to worry about politics, but we'll take care of you."

I manage to find my voice. "I'm not afraid," I say, darting a glance at the queen. "I—"

"Then try not to look like it," says Princess Varia. She's as beautiful as her mother, but far less severe: her cheeks are round, her hair a mass of soft golden curls that fall only halfway down her back.

"You'll shame us when we have to call you our savior," she adds, looking me up and down.

Anger sparks behind my ribs. "I *did* save you," I snap thoughtlessly.

The next moment my hand flies to my mouth as I realize what I've said. But to my surprise, Princess Varia nods approvingly.

"Good," she says. "Try to keep at least a little of that spirit through the feast."

Trumpets ring out below. "It's time," says Queen Imvada. Araunn takes my hand, and the warm touch startles me into silence as we walk down the stairs.

The great feasting hall is even more glorious and intimidating than I expected. Great marble statues of the gods, each the height of ten men, hold up the roof; candles and flowers ring their feet with pools of light and color. The crowd swirls among the columns, women in hoop skirts and corsets nodding to ladies in kirtles and surcotes, members of Parliament in somber black suits shaking hands with lords in brightly embroidered tunics.

As we descend, they all turn to face us. The vast sea of faces makes me dizzy, so I look instead at the dais that waits for us at the bottom of the stairs. The floor is covered in red velvet, the tables draped in black silk and laid with gold plates and cutlery.

When we step onto the dais, there's another blast of the trumpets, then silence. I dare a glance up to see all the men in the room sinking to one knee and all the ladies curtsying, with no distinction between those of the old Runakhia and the new.

It's exactly what I dreamed of as a child in the convent, listening to the nuns complain about the creeping atheism of Parliament and how no one reverenced the old ways anymore.

I did this, I think, staring at the kneeling crowd, and suddenly I can't stop smiling. *I did this*.

The exultation clings to me throughout dinner, and I eat with relish. It's a strange feast: deer that were hunted and eggs that were pickled five hundred years ago, and cakes with sugar-spun icing that were bought this morning in the city. I can see some of the old court laughing about the new foods, and some Parliamentary guests wrinkling their noses at the strange spices in the old.

Every bite is delicious to me, and not just because the simplest dish is far more elegant than anything we have at the convent. Every drop of almond-and-saffron sauce, every crumb of the sweet-spicy pork pastry, is proof that the impossible has happened. The golden age of Runakhia has returned.

Because I brought it back. Not Anabekha, not Mother Una—*me*.

When the feasting finally ends, the tables are cleared away to make room for dancing. As musicians begin playing in the niches between the great statues, Prince Araunn finds me in the sheltered corner of the hall where I've settled to watch.

"Lia," he says, smiling so brightly and earnestly that he's like the rising sun, "dance with me?"

I blink stupidly at him for a moment before I realize that, yes, he really did say that.

"Why?" I ask finally.

"This feast is for you," he says, holding out a hand.

I shake my head. "No. It's for you." He looks strangely disappointed, and I scramble for words. "I'll be back in the convent next week. The nuns of Nin-Anna don't dance. It wouldn't be right."

"You . . ." He looks briefly horrified—surely it's not *that* terrible to give up dancing?—then shakes his head. "I'm sorry. I'll leave you in peace."

He leads the first dance with his sister. After that, the two of them dance with partners from Runakhia old and new—but they're the only ones. Members of the old court only dance with others from the old court; members of Parliament and their wives only dance with each other.

After several dances, I notice that there are little clumps of men in their dark suits standing to the side, muttering to each other with solemn faces. I see the uneasy, unhappy looks that so many people give Queen Imvada.

We are surrounded by enemies.

My stomach feels cold and hollow. I've known since I was little how many people have forgotten the gods. Even most clerics claim that they have never heard our prayers and never worked miracles. I'd expected that even after I awoke the royal family, some people would not want to serve the gods.

I hadn't thought that they might not want a queen either.

But now I remember the few times I stood in the great square and listened to the drumroll as Parliament started their winter session. For five hundred years, they have been the only power in Runakhia.

I've read about the revolutions that have happened across the sea.

I always thought that could only happen in countries like Zémore, where the rulers were never blessed by the gods, but what if—

Suddenly the room is far too noisy and crowded; the music jangles on my nerves. I slip through the crowd until I find a door to one of the gardens.

Outside the night air is wonderfully cool. There's no moon tonight, but lamps glimmer among the tree branches. Close by me is a little pool—reflected stars twinkle in the dark water—with a marble bench beside it.

I sink onto the seat of cool stone and draw deep, greedy breaths of the sweet night air. But the peace of the garden can't drive the tangle of worries out of my head.

It's not your business, I tell myself. *If Parliament doesn't like the queen, what can you do about it? You're just an orphan who was briefly blessed to carry out the will of the gods. You're going back to the convent as soon as they let you.*

And oh, I do want to go back. I want to be there the first time Nin-Anna chooses one of us as a saint, and the first time that saint heals the Red Death. Maybe—the hope curls close to my heart—*maybe* Nin-Anna will even choose me as that saint, and I can work miracles of healing myself.

But even if it's not me who does the miracles, even if it's Anabekha, I'll still have a place in the convent that nobody can doubt. I'll still be able to serve Nin-Anna for the rest of my life.

And yet . . .

I had thought it would be so simple, to set right everything wrong in Runakhia. That as soon as I shed Ruven's blood, everyone would start to love the gods the way our convent did.

"Well, then, you were a fool."

Ruven's voice is soft and low, his breath tickling the back of my neck. With a strangled shriek, I surge to my feet and try to spin around at the same time. I end up stumbling back several steps, wobbling for balance.

There's nothing behind me but soft grass and a little stone arch wrapped in roses.

He's dead. And the dead never speak, I know this for certain, because if they could then surely Mama and Papa would have comforted me all those nights I cried myself to sleep.

But I can't help remembering the legends I've heard about restless ghosts that haunt the living because no god will accept their souls.

My voice shakes as I say aloud, "In the name of Nem-Una, lady of secrets, I command you to show yourself."

The wind rustles in the nearby trees. But Ruven does not reply.

I wait, my blood pulsing ready to fight or flee. But there's no reply . . . and slowly, I start to feel comfortingly foolish.

It wasn't real, I tell myself. *It was just a fearful fancy. Like your dream last night.*

Even so, the garden no longer feels like a refuge. I square my shoulders and start back toward the door into the great hall. Maybe I can't do anything to help the royal family, but at least I can stop hiding.

As soon as I step back into the hall, a terrible feeling of dread grips me. I try to tell myself that it's just my imagination, the same impulse that made me think I heard Ruven in the garden—

But something has changed. I'm not quite sure what it is, but as I look around the hall, I can see there is something different in the way people are looking at each other, murmuring. Something sharper and more uneasy.

Then I see Queen Imvada. She stands on the steps of the dais, talking to a tall, dark man whose close-cropped curls have turned salt-and-pepper with age. There's a gold star pinned on his chest, and that's how I know him.

This is the prime minister, Leo Akhanti. Until a week ago, he was the most powerful man in Runakhia.

The door I slipped through is near to where they stand. I can't help lingering in the shadow of the nearest pillar and listening to their voices.

"I have sat in meetings of Parliament since I was a child," says Queen Imvada, her words cool and measured.

"I mean no offense, Your Majesty," says the prime minister in a soothing tone that seems calculated for offense. "But much has changed in five hundred years. You will find Runakhia more foreign than you think."

"All the more reason," says the queen, "to reacquaint myself with the kingdom at once."

"Hm, well, there is also the matter of reacquainting the nation with *you*," says the prime minister. "Of course I am glad for your return—you and all the royal court. But the people have grown rather accustomed to parliamentary government. They do not know you or your children, so they do not yet trust you."

His voice is quiet, but the way he clasps his hands and leans ever so slightly toward Queen Imvada looks like an attack.

You mean you *don't want to lose all the power you have gained*, I think.

I know all about Leo Akhanti. I know that he vowed fidelity to his first wife in the name of the god Zumariel, and then divorced her. I know that he has made a fortune working with godless

Zémorine inventors to build us railways. I know that no matter what he believes about the gods, he speaks of them only when he thinks it will increase his power.

"Oh?" says Queen Imvada, her voice not much louder but quite clear. "Then they will be glad to hear this." She turns away from him and calls out, "Lia Kurinava, come forward."

My heart jolts in my chest. I realize it's going to be dreadfully obvious that I was eavesdropping, but I can't refuse the queen. So I walk forward, trying to keep my head high, wondering what the queen thinks *I* could possibly do about the prime minister.

"Your Majesty," I say, dropping into an awkward curtsy.

For one moment, the queen looks me up and down—not with hostility, but a sort of cool examination.

Then she grips me firmly by the shoulders and turns me around to face the crowd.

In a loud, ringing voice that instantly silences all the chatter, the queen calls out:

"Know that I am aware the world has changed. In two days' time, I will send my son and daughter on a Royal Progress to awaken the shrines and turn the gazes of the gods back upon this country. As they bring back saints and divine favor to our land, they will learn the shape of this new era. With them will go Lia Kurinava, the girl born in this age who saved us from the heretic sorcerer, and who will wed my son Araunn in recompense for her service."

7

SILENCE BLANKETS THE ROOM. SUDDENLY EVERY eye is turned on me in shock and surprise.

I'm vaguely aware that I should say something. React somehow. But I still can't believe the queen actually said those words.

It makes no sense. I'm nobody. The gods gave me the Royal Gift, but I haven't a drop of royal blood in me. Nor am I of the slightest importance by the standards of modern Runakhia.

Not to mention that I'm about to become a nun.

Surely when I was explaining to Queen Imvada how I came to save her, I mentioned that?

Prince Araunn breaks the silence. He seizes my hand—the gesture feels bold, in a way it didn't when we were walking into the hall together—and declares loudly, "Nothing could give me greater joy."

I should speak up just as loudly. I should declare that I can't marry any man because I'm going to vow my life to the goddess Nin-Anna. But Prince Araunn's smile is just as bright and beautiful as when he told me not to be afraid, and for a moment I can't bring myself to contradict it. Then the crowd breaks into applause, and I don't think I'd be heard even if I screamed.

After that, everything happens with dizzying swiftness: the

prime minister's congratulations, Queen Imvada laying her hand on my forehead in an official blessing, and the betrothal ceremony itself, where Prince Araunn holds my hands as Princess Varia pours a jug of wine over our clasped fingers and the queen recites a prayer to Zumariel, the god of love and war.

I stumble through it all, feeling as if I'm barely there, like this is all some bizarre dream and at any moment I'll wake up to the tolling of the convent bells.

When we finally leave the feast, Prince Araunn wants to speak with me, but I can't bear it. "Tomorrow," I tell him, and flee to my bedroom.

As soon as the maid has helped me out of my dress and into my nightgown, I tell her to leave, then fling myself down on the bed. I'm ready to burst into tears. But my eyes are dry as I stare into the darkness, and as I gasp for breath and clench my fingers into the coverlets, I am—I feel—

Angry.

I belong to Nin-Anna. I have always belonged to her. And now they're going to marry me off?

No.

I am not the first girl to face this challenge. Saint Eruvaun, for whom our convent is named, wanted to become a nun, but her father was a heartless nobleman who dragged her out of the convent before she could take vows. When she would not marry the man he chose, he hanged her like a common criminal, but Nin-Anna made her a saint as she died so that even in death she was victorious.

As I remember her story, my anger turns to a cold determination. I will follow Saint Eruvaun. I will give myself to Nin-Anna, and not even the queen herself will stop me, because I'll take my vows before they even know I've left.

I write a letter by candlelight and leave it on my bed.

Your Majesty,

I am honored by the offer of betrothal, but I already belong to Nin-Anna. The goddess chose me as a child, and I cannot forsake her. By the time you read this, I shall be vowed to a life in her service.

Then, as the sky turns pale with dawn, I slip out of the palace alone. Perhaps I could have spoken to the guards and called a carriage, but I'm too afraid that they've already been instructed to keep me here.

I won't let anyone stop me.

By the time I reach the convent door, the sun is well up, and the water between the cobblestones—it rained in the night—glitters blindingly. I'm hot and winded from the long, brisk walk, and I pause for a moment before the familiar door to rub sweat off my face. Then I grab the knocker and bang it as loud as I can.

After a moment, the door opens to reveal Anabekha.

"Lia?" she says, her face and voice all baffled amazement. "What are you doing here?"

The words catch me by the throat. *I live here*, I want to say. But Anabekha seems to think I belong at the palace.

Has she already heard about the engagement?

Her forehead creases with concern. "Is something wrong?"

I gulp. "Yes," I say. "Please, I must speak with Mother Una right now. It's an emergency."

"Come with me," says Anabekha, and leads me to Mother Una's

study as if I'm a visitor who doesn't know the way. "Wait here and I'll fetch her."

The door swings shut behind her, and I look around the room. It's just the same as I remember: the little desk covered in papers, the fireplace grate molded to look like flowers, the mural of Nin-Anna on the wall.

I've stood here once a month since I came to the convent. Mother Una would always begin by saying, *Tell me what you've learned*, and I would clasp my hands and tell her everything.

She would nod as she listened, and when I was done, she would gently tell me all the faults I had displayed that month. There were always so many. But at the end of the list, she would smile at me and say, "Despite all your failings—little by little, you are growing into what Nin-Anna wants of you."

In that moment, I always felt like I was glowing from every inch of my skin. Mother Una's study seemed as glorious as a palace.

Not today.

I look around the room, and even though nothing's changed, it feels small and drab. Confining. And *I* feel—

"Bloody," Ruven breathes in my ear.

I whirl, my heart pounding. But once again, there's nobody behind me.

Ruven is dead. I don't like to think of how it happened, but *he is dead*. And the restless dead, even *if* they wander the earth, have no power over the souls of the faithful. I have to keep that in mind, or I'll go mad.

The door opens, and Mother Una glides in.

"Whatever are you frightened of, child?"

Her voice is comforting, and yet instantly I feel two feet tall.

Nin-Anna may be a gentle goddess, but we serve her in the hospital and the surgery; there is no room for fear in any of us.

"Reverend Mother," I say, bowing. "I have returned."

"So you have," Mother Una agrees, sitting down at her desk. "Why?"

The word is like a splinter of ice jabbed between my ribs. For a moment I can't speak.

"Because I have accomplished my task," I manage to say finally. I stiffen my spine and raise my chin, trying to look like a grown woman who deserves to be a nun. "I killed Ruven. The royal family awoke. It's time for me to take my vows."

I wait through the silence that stretches out between us. This is when Mother Una is supposed to say, *Yes, of course*, and lead me to the chapel. But she only looks at me, and finally I go on, "Last night, the queen said I will marry Prince Araunn. I think she wants a political alliance, somebody to tie her family to the modern age, but—I can't. You know that. So you must let me take vows right now, before they can drag me back. It's the only way."

Mother Una was there, my first day at the convent. She helped scrub the stench of my family's sickness and death off me, and she held me the first time I cried. She knows how much it means to me to serve Nin-Anna and to heal people.

Now she sighs, the wrinkles in her pale face looking even deeper than before.

"Perhaps I should have told you earlier," she says, a terrible regret in her voice.

The splinter of ice is everywhere, piercing every part of my body.

"Why?" I ask breathlessly, and the next moment my voice is loud, furious. *"What did you not tell me?"*

"You had a common birth, but by the grace of the gods, you have the Royal Gift." Mother Una's voice is soft and sad and implacable. "There's an ancient law, for the good of all Runakhia. Commoners who bear the Royal Gift must join the royal family or die."

"What?" My voice cracks. "That's not . . . I've read all the histories—there was never such a law."

"Few outside the royal family have heard of it," says Mother Una solemnly. "It would not have been easy to explain to the common folk, who thought that simply to bear a golden eye was to be holy. But I assure you, this law was ruthlessly enforced for centuries, lest pretenders to the throne arise and claim they had the blessing of the gods. The last time the law was *not* enforced, we had the Upstart's War."

"But that was eight hundred years ago," I protest.

Mother Una raises an eyebrow, as if to say, *Our queen was born five hundred years ago.*

My face heats with embarrassment, but I plunge forward. "Anyway, I've studied the history of the Upstart's War, and I'm not going to seduce a count and bear him three bastards. I'm going to vow myself to the service of Nin-Anna. I'll never hold rank or have children. Surely that's good enough?"

"I am sorry," says Mother Una. "The service of the gods is not always easy. Give thanks that they have blessed you to suffer nothing worse than this."

"But," I say, hating how my voice wobbles, "Nin-Anna chose me. You—you told me that." Tears have started trickling down my face and I scrub them away.

"She chose you to save and serve the royal family," says Mother Una, the words a gentle rebuke. Then she sighs. "Indeed, we should have told you. But you loved the convent so much and wanted to stay here so badly. We thought—*I* thought—that you would only doubt your mission if you knew."

"My mission," I echo numbly. "But—serving Nin-Anna is *also* my mission."

Mother Una gives me a severe look. "You can serve her just as well at the palace. Don't dress up your childish longings for a place here with fancies of a divine command."

All I can think of, all I can see, are the faces of the nuns as they raised me. Sister Inuvi, showing me how to prune the roses in the garden. Sister Zenuvan, showing me the stroke I would need to kill Ruven and letting me practice on corpses. Mother Una, listening to my stammered hopes.

Anabekha, smiling indulgently each time I said that someday we would wear the veil together.

A wave of humiliation sweeps over me, hot and horrid and furious. They knew. All of them, they always knew that I didn't belong. And yet they lied to me.

Somebody knocks on the door.

"Yes?" says Mother Una.

The door swings open, revealing Anabekha. "I'm sorry, Mother," she says, "but—"

Prince Araunn pushes past her. "Your pardon, Reverend Mother. I don't want to disturb you, but my betrothed—"

He sees me, and his expression is one of desperate relief.

"You're here," he says. "I hoped you would be."

Mother Una, already on her feet, bows deeply. "Your Highness."

Prince Araunn turns to her. "You raised Lia, didn't you? And taught her how to save us. We are in your debt."

"It was all for love of you and the gods," says Mother Una.

There's a delight in her eyes that I've never seen before. She's staring at Prince Araunn as if he's all the hope in the world, and the only thing I can think—horribly, shamefully, selfishly—is, *Why couldn't you ever look at* me *like that?*

"You will be well rewarded for your faithfulness," says Prince Araunn. "May I speak with Lia alone for a moment?"

"Of course," says Mother Una. She looks back as she closes the door, but only at Prince Araunn, and it feels like a knife between my ribs.

Better than a knife to the throat, the voice that cannot be Ruven's whispers in my head, and I shudder even as I try to ignore it.

"Your serving maid came to me first," says Prince Araunn, breaking into my thoughts. His forehead is creased with worry. "Nobody but me read your letter." He holds it out to me, a crumpled piece of paper that holds all my lost dreams. "I'm sorry, but I think there's something you don't understand. The law—"

"I know," I interrupt. "Mother Una told just me."

He relaxes a little—and I realize that he was *afraid* when he first came into the room. More than anything Mother Una said, that is what makes *join the royal family or die* finally real to me. Prince Araunn was afraid that I wouldn't come back.

Because I would die if I didn't.

I know that I should be still thinking first of Nin-Anna, but I am suddenly afraid as well.

"Please come back with me," Prince Araunn says gently.

Dread and death are pulsing through my veins, but I manage to keep my voice level as I say, "You knew we'd be engaged at the feast. Why didn't you tell me?"

He licks his lips, hesitating. Then he says, "I thought you knew. I thought everyone alive today still knew what it meant to have the Royal Gift. But after we parted last night, Varia said to me—" He draws a shaky breath. "You weren't raised to be one of us, were you?"

"No," I whisper, resentment like a thousand centipedes crawling down my throat.

"I'm sorry," he says, so simply and honestly that I startle, wondering if I really heard it. But he meets my eyes and continues, "I'm sorry, Lia, truly. I wouldn't wish this burden on anyone . . . but to have the Royal Gift is to bear it." He holds out a hand. "Please come back with me?"

I remember how *The Chronicle of the Saints* described Saint Eruvaun's death: "To keep her from the service of Nin-Anna, her father had her hanged; but before the light had left her eyes, the power of Nin-Anna came upon her, and flowers sprouted beneath her dancing feet, so that she died a saint of the goddess she loved."

I've always found those words beautiful. But now I think about what they really mean: Eruvaun strangled to death in slow agony, her feet straining for the ground she would never feel again.

I should be that brave as well. I should love Nin-Anna that much.

But now that I'm facing the same choice, I realize—

I want to live.

Not so I can serve the gods, not for any noble purpose. My body is shaking with simple animal desperation to keep breathing.

Slowly, helplessly, I take Prince Araunn's hand.

"Take me back," I whisper.

8

IN THE WEEK SINCE HE WAS raised from five hundred years of enchanted sleep, Araunn has apparently learned how to summon a cab. When we walk out of the convent—his hand still gripping mine—there's a glossy black horse and carriage awaiting us.

Araunn opens the door for me, and I step inside, feeling like I'm climbing into my own hearse. But this is how I'm going to live. This is the only way I *get* to live.

It's also my duty. I tell myself this as the cab jerks into motion, carrying us back to the palace. Because I have the Royal Gift, it's my duty to leave the convent and join the royal family.

But I know I'm only embracing that duty to save my life.

Araunn doesn't ask anything of me as we drive back. He only smiles and keeps up a soft, cheerful monologue about how marvelous the modern system of cabs is, and how he's made fifteen trips in them already.

"And the gas lamps!" he says eagerly. "I never imagined the streets could be lit that way. Last night I went to the river after dark, and the city lights reflected in the water . . . it was magical."

I try to smile and nod, but the expression feels stiff and awkward on my face; I'm afraid I've managed nothing more than a grimace.

And yet I'm grateful that Araunn is filling the silence. I don't think I could bear to talk just now.

I don't think I could say a word without it turning into something I'd regret.

When we reach the palace, Araunn helps me out of the carriage and leads me back in through the front gate. Then—finally—he meets my eyes and asks quite solemnly and earnestly, "Lia. Is . . . there anything I can do for you?"

Set me free, I think. But I know he can't. So I swallow down the words and my grief.

"No, thank you," I say, proud of how calm my voice sounds, and then I flee.

I take refuge in the gardens, in a little ring of birch trees and rosebushes, where I can't see the graceful arches of the palace or hear the chattering of servants and courtiers awake after five hundred years.

I will never go home, I think, expecting to cry. My eyes burn and my throat aches. But the tears don't come.

The convent was never truly my home. I was fooling myself, all those years, and the nuns let me be a fool.

Humiliation washes over me again in a wave. How many times did I say *when I'm one of you* to Mother Una or Sister Zenuvan? How many times did I comfort myself that while Anabekha might outshine me in every way, someday we would both be nuns alike?

How many times did all the nuns of Nin-Anna secretly scoff at my delusions?

For the first time since Mother Una told me of my purpose, I wish I had been born without the Royal Gift.

"That certainly would have been convenient for me."

Ruven's voice, low and smooth and indubitably clear, steals away my breath. For a moment, I can't move. I stare at the sunlight dappling the grass, too bright and crisp for a dream, and I think, *He's dead, he's dead, he cannot—*

"But you," says Ruven, "what do you think would have happened to *you*, in that world?"

Slowly I turn and face him.

Because he's not just a voice now, not just a bloody memory in my dreams. He stands two paces away, and he casts no shadow on the grass, but in every other way he looks as solid and real as when he lived.

Only now there's a bloody gash across his throat. The strange gentleness is gone from his face, replaced with grim, unyielding hate.

My heart pounds against my ribs. I force myself to look him in the eye.

"What are you doing?" I whisper.

He rolls his eyes. "I am haunting you, obviously. You murdered me and now you have to face the consequences."

Even now, I want to turn away and ignore him, to pretend this isn't happening, convince myself it's impossible.

Then the word *murdered* sinks into my head.

"I defeated you," I say, trying to shut out the memory of his blood spilling across my hands, my lap.

"Two words for the same thing," Ruven replies.

The memories are too strong for me to hold back, and it's like I'm living it all over again: his cheek beneath my palm, the warmth of his breath against my wrist. The cold handle of the blade in my hand, the whites of Ruven's eyes as he realized he'd been betrayed, and then the hot, sticky blood everywhere, everywhere—

I stumble back a few steps, hugging myself as I try to get control of my breathing. It's over. It's done. Ruven's ghost is at least proof of that.

"Oh, it is far from done," Ruven says silkily.

"At least your *power* seems completely done," I snap, almost grateful for the distraction. Then a horrible idea strikes. "You can't hear my thoughts, can you?"

"I'm dead," says Ruven. "Do you think I still have physical ears that need to wait for your mouth to shape words?"

The thought of him knowing everything about me sends a horrible, nauseating shiver through my body.

"You seem awfully confident about your knowledge of the dead," I say, refusing to give in to the fear. "Is that what you studied as a sorcerer?"

"I studied how to be a weapon," says Ruven. "As did you. And now, just as I did, you're learning the fate of weapons in peacetime."

I stiffen. "What do you—"

"Let's return to that thought," he goes on implacably, "of a world where you had no golden eye, no Royal Gift. Do you think those nuns you love so much would have raised you then? And if they had raised you, do you think they would have shown you half so much favor?"

And I can't answer. The nuns of Nin-Anna are sworn to care for all who come sick and wounded to their hospital, but they don't usually raise children, no matter their need. Anabekha received a place only because she was the bastard daughter of a rich man who paid for a new hospital wing. If I had not had the Royal Gift—if I had not been able to save Runakhia—

I would have grown up in an orphanage and been lucky to find backbreaking work at a factory when I was old enough, if I hadn't ended up on the streets. The nuns would have cared for me only if I limped into their hospital, bleeding and beaten by thieves or factory overseers or pimps.

Ruven laughs, a low, dry sound. "You loved those nuns as a dog loves its masters, begging for scraps, licking their feet after they kicked you. And they loved you as a man loves a sword or a spade."

His words slice through me, exposing my deepest fears, and they leave me feeling raw and gutted.

I think of Sister Zenuvan pinching my cheek and smiling, and I wonder if that was only the kindness you would show to a well-trained pet.

Then I remember gazing into the painting of Nin-Anna's golden eyes and knowing she hated the Red Death as much as I did. I remember the holy wrath of the nuns against every kind of sickness as they worked in the hospital. And I remember who I am.

I lift my chin and stare Ruven down.

"The nuns love Nin-Anna," I say, "and so do I. Whether I'm a dog or a weapon, what does it matter? I'm still proud to serve the gods and the royal family."

"Lia?"

I whirl around to see Prince Araunn entering the grove.

"Your Highness," I say, wondering, *Did he hear me talking? Does he think I am mad? Does he know that Ruven—*

He smiles ruefully. "I think you're allowed to address me a little more familiarly, under the circumstances."

Because we're going to be married.

A strange thrill runs through me as I look at his thin lips and tousled, light brown hair. For the first time, I think of my engagement as not just something that pulls me away from the convent, but that binds me to a future husband. To this boy, standing right here before me.

"Yes," Ruven says right into my ear, "very troublesome if you had to call him His Royal Highness, Crown Prince of Runakhia, Protector of the Living Gods, and Duke of Im-zuri when you took him to bed."

I remember the dream I had, of warm hands wrapping around mine, and my face goes hot. I know that I'm blushing terribly, that Araunn can see it.

Stop it, I think desperately at Ruven.

"If you didn't want me haunting you," he says, "you shouldn't have killed me."

"Are you all right?" Araunn asks, stepping closer.

"Yes," I say quickly. "I'm sorry. I just—"

"No," Araunn interrupts, "It was my fault. This past week, I've seen how much the world has changed. I shouldn't have assumed you knew all the duties of the Royal Gift." His hands hovers over my shoulder and then drops away. "I'm sorry," he says.

I feel a sudden flicker of resentment as I remember the week I spent hiding in my room at the palace, feeling like a prisoner.

"If you thought I knew," I ask, and can't keep a tiny edge out of my voice, "why didn't you come to see your future bride?"

My words startle him. "I—" He falters, and then falls silent. For a moment there's no sound but the rustle of the wind in the leaves. Then he sighs, licks his lips, and says, "I was afraid. Because I felt that somehow, seeing you . . . would make it all real."

For the first time, I imagine what the past seven days must have been like for Araunn: his world and whatever future he'd expected gone in the blink of an eye, replaced with a country that has forgotten him and a wife he never expected.

Guilt seeps through my chest. "I'm sorry," I say. "Not just for this morning. I'm sorry that you don't get a choice about marrying me. I—I never wanted to do that to you."

"And I never wanted to take you away from your convent," says Araunn, sounding genuinely wretched, and that makes the weight of guilt in my chest even worse.

"It doesn't matter," I mumble.

"No," Araunn says urgently. "It *does* matter." He catches a finger under my chin and tilts up my face so I have to meet his eyes again. "You risked your life to save us. You've given up the life you could have had to join us. We owe you, Lia."

I swallow, unable to move. He's dropped his hand, but I still feel the soft pressure of his finger under my chin.

"And I want to pay you back," he says. "I don't want you to lose anything more than you must. There's still so much you can have. As a member of the royal family, you can make a pact with Nin-Anna and wield her healing powers yourself."

Sudden hope catches me by the throat. He's right. I'd planned to spend my life praying and hoping Nin-Anna might choose me as a saint—but if I approach her as one of the royal family, she will definitely give me her blessing.

And then I can end the Red Death with my own hands. I can be Nin-Anna's wrath against sickness incarnate.

"Whatever else you want," Araunn goes on eagerly, "a private

67

shrine in the palace, your own hospital . . . my mother can make it happen. And if this Royal Progress is a success, I know she won't refuse us."

Us. He says it so easily, as if choosing me is the most natural thing in the world.

"Really?" I ask, barely daring to hope. "You'd help me?"

"Of course I would." His forehead creases. "You saved me. You're my betrothed. And . . . I was hoping that we could also be friends." He holds out his hand. "Can we?"

"Yes," I say, and take his hand.

His fingers wrap over mine, warm and soft, and I think of my dream again: that ghostly sensation of being warm, wanted, *chosen*.

Perhaps Araunn didn't choose me to begin with, but he's choosing me now. As I stare into his eyes—one robin's-egg blue, one golden like mine—I feel a sudden, dizzying rush of gratitude and warmth. I've lost so much, but the gods have given me at least one thing in exchange.

Ruven makes a disgusted noise in his throat. "Will I have to watch this nauseating sentiment all day?"

Anger sparks inside me. *If you don't want me nauseating you*, I think furiously at him, *you shouldn't haunt me.*

Then I open my mouth and say to Araunn, "Will you kiss me?"

"What?" he asks.

My heart gives a jump, but I can't back down now, not while Ruven is watching. "I always wanted to know what it was like," I say. "And we're going to be married, so . . . I mean, nowadays girls are allowed to kiss their betrothed."

"Are you serious," Ruven says flatly.

Araunn laughs. "In my day too," he says. "And you more than deserve it."

He leans forward. There's a moment where our noses brush and I feel his breath against my mouth. Then his lips find mine, and it is—

Nothing.

Not bliss, not desire, just a slight pressure, warm and soft. Nothing like what I used to imagine sometimes, guiltily wishing that Nin-Anna permitted her nuns the same delights that Juni-Akha and Zumariel did.

I make a confused little noise in my throat, and Araunn seems to take that as an invitation. He slides his hands into my hair and kisses me more deeply—

And it still isn't the bliss I used to imagine, but suddenly there's a shiver in the pit of my stomach. Nobody has ever touched me this way before, and the excitement goes straight to my head like wine. Clumsily, eagerly, I kiss him back, my heart pounding faster and faster—

Araunn breaks the kiss and I reel, catching at my breath and my balance.

He grins. "So? Was it all you hoped?"

From somebody else, the words might have felt like mockery. But Araunn's smile invites me in on the joke: that we are two children forced to kiss each other, who have just discovered that we like it.

So I smile back at him. "It's a good start," I say.

"I have to go back and speak with my mother," he says. "I'll see you later?"

"Obviously," I say, and treasure his soft laugh as he leaves the grove.

Then I finally look back at Ruven. He's still a pace behind me, looking at once bored and revolted.

"Please lay me to rest before your wedding night," he says.

"Nothing could give me more pleasure," I snap.

His grimace twists into something like a smile. "Not even your prince's kiss? My, what a boring marriage bed."

The reality of my future crashes down on me again. I am going to marry Araunn. There will be a wedding night. And Ruven will be standing over my bed and sneering.

Unless I can find some way to lay him to rest.

9

❧

I DON'T KNOW MUCH ABOUT GHOSTS.

I've always known they were possible. Those who do not please any of the gods enough to enter that god's realm after death spend all eternity wandering the dark, barren land of shades. Some of those lost souls crawl back into the waking world to haunt the living. Mother Una explained this to me when I told her I was praying for my family to come visit me: *Only those abandoned by all the gods come back. Pray you never see your family again while you draw breath.*

But no one at the convent had ever seen a ghost, and no one ever talked about how to make one stop haunting you. Maybe it's something that Mother Una knows but simply never bothered to tell me because she didn't think it mattered for my mission. For a few minutes I consider asking her, but the thought of crawling back to the convent again makes my stomach curdle.

Asking someone at the palace for help seems like a better idea. I'm surrounded by people from the golden age of Runakhia, who know far more about both sorcery and divine power than I do. Surely that means they also know what to do about a sorcerer's ghost.

But I can't tell Araunn that I kissed him while Ruven was watching—that half the reason I asked for the kiss was *because* of Ruven. And when I think of going to anyone else in the palace and admitting that I didn't completely vanquish Ruven—that he's still here and I don't know what to do—I feel sick with shame.

Then, late that afternoon, Queen Imvada sends for me.

As I follow the maidservant leading me through the palace corridors, I tell myself that this is a sign of what I should do. Queen Imvada wields the power of Juni-Akha, queen of the gods; surely she can banish a mere ghost.

"If you think the queen will show you kindness," says Ruven, sounding annoyed, "you're a fool who never learned any history."

Strangely, his words bolster my spirits. It's less frightening to think about telling the queen my problems when I know I will be defying Ruven.

Your briar killed seven girls from my convent, I tell him silently. *And dozens of other men and women. I'm not taking judgments on kindness from* you.

"It's not my fault they chose to walk into a maze of sorcery," says Ruven.

I remember the skeleton I found, preserved in its last agonized contortion, and I wish there were a way to slap ghosts.

Thankfully, Ruven remains silent as I walk the rest of the way to the queen's solarium. It's a strange and beautiful place: dark stone walls carved to look like mountain crags, with a ceiling of glittering glass. Little fountains burble, sending streams of water through slender channels carved into the floor, tiled in red and blue. The air is warm and damp, and everywhere are huge pots filled with flowers and fruit blooming out of season, rare vines and trees brought from halfway across the world.

On a silver seat in the heart of the solarium, Queen Imvada sits embroidering. Her head is bent over her work as I approach, and I suddenly wonder if the horns that Juni-Akha gave her are heavy. Does her neck ever ache with the strain of holding them up?

I'm thankful that Nin-Anna will only dust my hands in gold.

Queen Imvada looks up. "Lia," she says. "Thank you for coming so quickly."

I remember my manners too late and drop her a curtsy. "Your Majesty," I say. "I'm honored."

My heart is beating wildly, even though her face is all kindness.

We're going to be family, I tell myself. *She has to help me.* But that just reminds me of how I'd thought the nuns were going to be my family.

Instead I try to think of how I should begin explaining. *There's something I haven't told you* is too ominous. *Ruven isn't really gone* is too alarming. *I need your help* is too—

"Araunn told me those nuns hadn't taught you the duties of those with the Royal Gift," says the queen, interrupting my thoughts. She sets her embroidery aside, and though there's no anger or suspicion in her eyes, I panic.

"No," I say quickly, "but I'm eager to learn. All I ever wanted was to serve the gods."

"Anyone can do that," says Queen Imvada. "But this kingdom lives and dies by the favor of the gods. So those of us in the royal family, we *please* them. We delight the gods when we enter their realm, and when their wrath kindles against Runakhia, we win their favor back."

My stomach lurches with yearning and dread. To please Nin-Anna—to know that she's looking back at me, that she loves me the way I love her—is all I've ever wanted. But the thought of the whole country depending on my being good enough is terrifying.

"I can do that," I say, hoping the words are true. "I can do anything, if Nin-Anna will love me."

Queen Imvada smiles. "That's a beautiful piety," she says. "I can see the nuns trained you well, whatever their failings. But there's something else you must know."

"What?" I ask.

Her smile fades a little. When she speaks again, she measures out each word carefully and precisely. "You saved us, so I and all my family are in your debt. Please don't think I do not feel it." Her mouth flattens. "But thus far you have proved yourself only as a hero, not as a princess."

I stare at her a moment, feeling slightly off-balance. "Of course I haven't," I say. "I know that I must make a pact with a god before I am truly one of you. The nuns taught me *that* much."

Queen Imvada fixes me with a stern gaze. "Did the nuns tell you of my brother and sister?"

"No," I say, suddenly uneasy.

She sighs, her eyes growing distant. "I was the oldest of three. My brother did not want to serve. He had to be marched into the shrine by force. So when he tried to make his pact, Nin-Anna rejected him and branded him with the mark of judgment. I had to kill him, lest his curse infect our entire country. My sister . . . she was devout, but not brave. After seeing our brother's fate, she tried to flee the kingdom before facing the same test. So it became my duty to kill her as well. And I did."

She recites the story so calmly, it takes me a moment to understand the words. To realize that yes, she said that, and she didn't weep, didn't beg me to keep it a secret.

She is not ashamed at all.

"You killed your brother and sister," I say numbly.

"Before the assembled court," says Queen Imvada, picking up her embroidery again. "I told you: to please the gods is our greatest duty. We must be prepared to pay any price for it." Then she looks back at me. "I *am* grateful for what you did. Very much so. But I can only allow you to live if you can serve as one of us. If you can't, then Araunn and Varia . . . they know what to do."

I can't speak. I feel reduced to scraps of disconnected sensations: my fingers trembling. My tongue, heavy in my mouth. My heart pounding inside my chest.

Queen Imvada has started embroidering again, as calmly as if she hadn't threatened murder.

But it's not murder. It's punishment, the normal punishment for any member of the royal family who cannot or will not perform the royal duty of delighting the gods.

They'll kill me, I think wildly. *If I tell them about Ruven, that a heretic ghost is clinging to me and I can't dismiss him, they'll think I'm defective, and they'll kill me.*

I think of Araunn, of his promise to be friends and how he already hid my attempt to run away—surely, *surely* he would not be able to—

But surely Queen Imvada had once loved her brother and sister. And she killed them.

Something moves behind one of the potted trees. I glance to the side and see it's Ruven.

"You see what I mean," he says, and now there's no scorn in his voice, only a strange pity. "They're all monsters, every one of them."

They're not monsters, I think at him.

The words sound weak and pathetic, even inside my own head. But I know they're not. I've read the ancient tales of what happened when kings and queens did not fulfill their duties, and the gods were angered. I've seen the sickness and misery that exist now because we do not have any saints.

Too many lives are at stake. Of course the royal family can't show mercy to anyone, even their own kin. It is a terrible yet beautiful virtue that they do not.

And yet . . . that means I cannot trust them to show me kindness. Not any of them.

10

AFTER MY TALK WITH THE QUEEN, all I want is to hide somewhere and never come out again. But this evening there's a farewell dinner for everyone who will be going on the Royal Progress. As I stand in front of the mirror and watch the maid braid flowers into my hair, I feel like I'm preparing for my execution.

When my hair is done, I walk slowly down the winding stairs from my bedroom. Nin-Anna is still my goddess and Runakhia is still my country, and I am still obedient. If nothing else, I am that.

Araunn meets me halfway down the stairs, and his smile melts a little of the chill from my heart. I can't forget Queen Imvada's promise that he and Varia are ready to "take care" of me if I fail, but looking into his eyes, I can't quite believe it either.

"Don't worry," says Araunn, taking my hand. "It's all right. Nobody's going to eat you."

My laugh feels like broken glass. "Are you sure there's no ancient law about that?"

A moment later I want to snatch the words back. But miraculously Araunn isn't hurt or offended. He chuckles softly, as if this were an old joke we'd always shared together.

"Only at the most formal dinners," he says. "This is a private farewell, very simple, for the queen and the members of the Royal Progress only."

It turns out that *simple* means dining in a chamber not much larger than my bedroom, but with a ceiling of gilded vaults and arches, hung with a dozen gold and crystal lamps. The queen and Varia are the only ones there when we arrive, but just moments after we've sat down, the prime minister and his wife are ushered into the room.

I'd already known that Prime Minister Akhanti was joining the Royal Progress—doubtless to make sure that he gets as much glory from it as the royal family does—but I hadn't expected that his wife would be coming with us too.

Hézoraine Akhanti is just as beautiful as the gossip says: a living doll of a woman with spun-gold curls, huge gray eyes, and flawless porcelain skin. Her Zémorine accent is just strong enough to be charming, without ever making her difficult to understand. It's easy to see how she dazzled the prime minister into abandoning his first wife practically the moment he set foot in Zémore when he went there as ambassador three years ago.

If I'd known she was to join us, I would have expected to hate her just as much as I do the prime minister. But when she smiles at me and says, "I've heard so much about you," I realize with an uncomfortable lurch that she's hardly older than myself. Suddenly it's impossible to believe she's the brazen atheist seductress the nuns always made her out to be.

"Why not?" Ruven whispers in my ear as Hézoraine squeezes my hand. "You were old enough to sit in my lap and cut my throat."

I stifle a shudder as I take my seat. *Why would you want to*

make me hate a woman who hates the gods as you do? I ask silently.
Shouldn't you wish you were haunting her instead of me?

"Didn't you tell me that the Zémorine are all gods-hating atheists these days?" says Ruven. "What is a heretic like me to do with
one such as her?"

That is a strange thought, one that silences me as I try to absorb
it: that those who hate the gods of Runakhia are not united into a
single army. That they might hate each other as much as they hate
Nin-Anna.

The next moment, every thought of Ruven and Hézoraine and
even the gods themselves is driven out of my head, because the last
two members of the Royal Progress come into the room.

One of them is a slender, bespectacled young man with light
brown skin, and dark hair slicked back from his forehead. He wears
the white clerical collar of a vicar, one of those modern religious
posts that the nuns have always raged against: a clergyman who
preaches and leads prayers without making vows to any particular
god. He immediately starts smiling and bowing as he introduces
himself, but I don't hear a word he says, because I'm too busy staring at the person beside him.

Anabekha.

She looks just the same as always: graceful, half smiling, perfect.
Her gray dress is immaculate, the lines of her white veil crisp.

"Lia!" she says, stepping forward, then drops into a curtsy.
"What a blessing to see you again."

Shame crawls through my stomach. I was never good enough for
the convent, and yet now perfect Anabekha is curtsying to me. It
doesn't feel like an honor, but a reproach.

"Likewise," I manage to say weakly.

Dinner begins with soup: a delicately spiced broth with leeks and chunks of fish floating in it. Hézoraine picks up her spoon and instantly, effortlessly takes control of the table. She compliments Queen Imvada on the cuisine of her era, and then tells a story of how she laughed at the prime minister for being afraid to eat snails in Zémore, only to be afraid herself of blood sausage when she came to Runakhia. She promises Varia that they will visit a modern dressmaker together, and she asks Araunn about his favorite thing about this era. She asks Anabekha how the hospital is doing and tells the vicar—Reverend Coldren—that she has a donation of knitted hats for the orphanage he oversees.

She asks me how I find staying at the palace compared to the convent, but I can barely string two words together. I'm too distracted by my excruciating awareness of Anabekha sitting beside me. Why is she here? I thought I was afraid of Araunn and Varia killing me for failure, but the thought of Anabekha *seeing* me fail is a thousand times worse.

Hézoraine gives up on me and turns the conversation to the Royal Progress. There are four great shrines besides the one here in the capital: Ir-Atsakha, Nan-Darakh, Zal-Enda, and Undanna.

"I've been to Nan-Darakh," says Hézoraine, "when the university there gave my dear husband an honorary degree." She flashes a smile at him. "But never any of the others! I can't wait."

"Neither can I," says Reverend Coldren. "I wrote my dissertation on the Royal Gift, and now I'll get to see the royal family create saints with my own eyes!"

I know what Reverend Coldren is implying: he's one of the faithless clergy who say the gods have never heard or answered prayers, and all the wonders of the golden age were accomplished by the royal family using their "natural affinity" for the divine realm to wield its power.

"It's the gods who create saints," I say indignantly. "Not the royal family. How could mortals ever do such a thing?"

"By the power of our divine pacts," says Queen Imvada.

"*What?*" I say, and then cough, choking on my own spit.

At the head of the table, Queen Imvada takes a sip of her wine, apparently unaware that she's stepped into the middle of a theological debate that's raged for centuries.

"It's one of the most important duties you will have," she says, "creating more saints when our people need them. It's why we dare to enter the divine realm and forge pacts with them. Runakhia cannot exist without saints, so when the gods do not supply enough, we must act in their stead. Didn't your nuns teach you that?"

"Much can be forgotten in five hundred years," says Reverend Coldren.

He gives me a pitying smile, and in that moment I hate him as much as I've ever hated Ruven. Queen Imvada can't mean what he thinks she does: that the gods have no power to touch our world at all. She killed her brother and sister to avert divine judgment.

But cold fear won't stop pulsing through me. I didn't think it was possible that I could be forced to join the royal family either.

I flee the table as soon as etiquette permits, just minutes after the stewed pears have been served for dessert. It's only after I'm two turns down the hallway that I hear footsteps and look back.

Anabekha has followed me.

She meets my eyes, smiling that perfect smile, and dull loathing pounds inside my chest.

"What is it?" I demand, hating how angry the words sound yet also wishing I could be angrier.

"I won't keep you," Anabekha says gently. "But I just wanted to say that I can't wait to see the first time you make a saint for Nin-Anna."

"Is that another thing Mother Una told you but not me?" I snarl.

Anabekha flinches back, her face puzzled and hurt. "No? I was as surprised as you were just now. But that's half of why I asked to come along—so I could learn all the things we've forgotten and tell the rest of the convent."

My rage is starting to crumble into guilt, but I still demand, "What was the other half?"

Anabekha smiles tremulously. "To make sure that you were all right, of course."

Of course her reasons are pure and good. Anabekha would never try to run from her duty, and she'd never keep secrets out of fear. She's better than me, always and forever, and I hate her for it.

"I don't know why you would bother," I say bitterly. "We've never been friends before and we certainly won't start now."

And then, before I can think about what I've said, I flee.

11

WE LEAVE AT DAWN THE NEXT morning. The prime minis-
ter wanted us to travel by one of the trains that have made him his
fortune, but Queen Imvada insisted on a stagecoach, so the people
can see us on our pilgrimage.

The stagecoach is beautiful: extravagantly spacious, with glistening black paint and gold leaf on the outside, polished mahogany
and red velvet on the inside. Varia, Anabekha, Hézoraine, and I sit
on one side; Araunn, Reverend Coldren, and the prime minister sit
on the other. Ruven haunts the empty seat beside the prime minister; he sits slouched, his arms crossed and his lips pressed into a
haughty, baleful grimace.

If Ruven's glare were the worst thing about the day's driving,
I could still enjoy it. But Anabekha keeps shooting me concerned
glances that are worse than any scorn. And whenever the prime
minister isn't lecturing us in dry, condescending tones about the
agricultural output of the fields we're passing, Reverend Coldren is
telling Araunn and Varia how they're wrong about the gods.

"You see, Your Highnesses," he says brightly, "with all due respect to the clergy of your time, and the devotion at which your
generation excelled—there are ways in which we have come to

understand the gods much better than the 'golden age' ever did. Your time was the flowering of piety, but ours is the flowering of theology."

I feel a hot rush of furious, helpless embarrassment. Coldren is nothing to me—nothing *like* me—and yet hearing him say such clownishly pompous things to children of the royal house, who are born to walk into the realm of the gods, makes me want to writhe out of my skin.

I know I should say something—for the honor of the gods, and also to let Araunn and Varia know that our generation isn't entirely faithless. But the memory of last night holds me hostage. Every time I think of a rebuke I could give Coldren, I wonder, *What if Araunn and Varia tell me that's wrong as well?*

While I'm hesitating, Anabekha plunges in.

"You mean the flowering of *doubt*," she says hotly. "Everybody knows that the theologians at your university say the gods are helpless abstractions, blind and deaf and dumb to our prayers."

Coldren blinks as if seeing her for the first time. "That is not a fair representation of divine transcendence as taught by—"

"I have read their essays! Has even one of them read the whole psalter?"

A new kind of shame washes over me. Because I've never read a single essay from any of the modern theologians—the idea never even occurred to me—but now Anabekha is debating each of them with Coldren, point by point, as I never could.

"Yes, her training is beyond compare," says Ruven. "The prize hound of your kennel, who can sit and stay and hunt on command."

I hunted you *well enough*, I think furiously.

He chuckles. "That you did," he says, and there's a note of wry admiration in his voice.

Our eyes meet, and for one moment, it's as if his death is nothing more than a private joke between us. As if his blood hasn't haunted my nightmares, as if he hasn't been the ghost lurking between me and happiness. As if he's just a boy, and I'm just a girl he thinks is clever, and in this moment I notice all over again the beautiful lines of his face.

"You sat quite nicely too," Ruven adds, and my face heats with the memory of sinking into the warmth of his lap, of his breath upon my wrist—

And then I cut you most exquisitely, I think. Without meaning to, my gaze drops to my hands; when I look up, he's gone, and the seat across from me is empty.

A hollow feeling spreads through my chest, but I ignore it.

The first day of our journey is supposed to be short: by two o'clock we will reach the town of Imbazi, where many of Runakhia's wealthiest citizens live so they can be near the capital without enduring the city's smog. Hézoraine chatters with great excitement about the celebration they will hold for us, and though Araunn smiles and says he can't wait, Varia is grimly silent.

It will be a party thrown by our enemies, I realize with growing dread. The "friends" whom Hézoraine is so excited for us to meet are people who don't want gods or the royal family to change their world. I should be eager for the chance to call these people back to the gods, but I don't want to face them.

"Don't be so bashful," says Ruven. "You had no trouble sitting in my lap, after all."

Must you keep mentioning that? I ask him, hoping I'm not blushing hard enough for any of the living people in the carriage to see.

"Well, I'm still dead because of it. So yes."

But when we're only a mile away, a messenger rides out to meet us, and my heart sinks as I see the red plague flag pinned to his shoulder.

"You must go on," he calls out when he's close enough for us to hear. "The Red Death is in Imbazi."

"Oh no," Hézoraine cries. "Who is sick?"

My first, horrified thought is, *Everyone*. The Red Death is always in Anazyr, after all, but it's been decades since it spread widely enough that anyone even thought of closing factories or theaters. For an entire town to be closed—

"It's just among the servants so far," says the messenger. "Gods willing it stays with them. But there are three households touched already, so the mayor does not believe it safe for the Royal Progress to stop here."

Relief and resentment twist together inside me. A true plague spreading unchecked is the nightmare that the nuns fight to prevent. I can't be angry that the mayor of Imbazi is trying to prevent that—but I loathe how the world stops when the rich are in danger, but not for anyone else.

"He sends his deepest apologies," the messenger continues, "and he's sent messengers ahead to Limakh and ordered them to prepare a welcome for you."

"Of course," says the prime minister. "Please relay our earnest good wishes."

"Has he told the queen?" Araunn demands.

"Ah—no, Your Highness," the messenger says, clearly surprised. "He did not wish to trouble her—"

"She'll want to know," Araunn interrupts, more firmly than I've heard him speak before. "Immediately."

"Of course," says the messenger, but he looks at the prime minister as if for permission.

"I'm glad to hear our queen has such concern for her people," says the prime minister.

"Don't worry," says Araunn, smiling at the messenger. "Everything will be all right. She can help."

"Are we going to sit here all day?" Varia demands, giving Araunn a sharp look.

Something seems to pass between them, and he settles back in his seat. In a few minutes we are on our way, and as Anabekha and Coldren start arguing again about whether prayer is any use against plague, I wonder why it is that Varia sounded like she was warning Araunn.

Limakh is small and dirty, a town that's little more than factories and narrow streets lined by tenements where the factory workers live. Their hastily organized welcome is respectably sized: the mayor and what must be the whole town council stand in the main square with a little choir of six flower-crowned young girls. But the crowd that's gathered to watch our arrival is strangely sullen.

"They don't look happy to see the Royal Progress," says Anabekha, frowning as our carriage rolls to a stop.

"Ah, that's because most of them follow the Magisterium," says Coldren. "I had my first post here, so I know the town quite well. Good workers, most of them, but wretchedly stubborn and ungrateful."

On the other side of the carriage, Ruven rolls his eyes. "Yes, how insolent to dislike the boot stamped into their throats."

I grimace. I don't want to agree with Ruven, but Coldren is pompous enough to make a saint resent the gods.

"Then they will have to learn better," says Varia, her voice all calm determination. "Just like the rest of this kingdom."

They hold a feast for us inside the town hall. There are two kinds of meat pie and not much else besides; I can tell that Hézoraine is disappointed, and Varia also looks unimpressed. To me, it's still exciting to have any dinner fancier than cold beans and bacon.

But what I really love about the feast is that the sullen crowd of factory workers is gone. The people seated with us are all from the leading families of Limakh, and *they* are absolutely delighted to host the Royal Progress. There's a continual hum of excitement—people staring at us in wonder—and perhaps they are only excited that something important is happening to their small town, but this is the first time I've seen people greet the royal family with the joy they deserve.

After the meal there are toasts for nearly an hour. My glass is very small, carved of cut glass, but every other minute a servant is at my side, refilling it with cherry-red wine. I'm careful to take only tiny sips, but by the time I go up to my bedroom at the inn, my head is fuzzy, my cheeks are hot, and all my joints feel slick and loose.

So when my serving maid leaves me, and my head falls back against my pillow, and then I open my eyes and see Ruven looming over my bed—I don't feel frightened or ashamed. I sit up, staring him in the eyes.

"Why are you haunting me?" I ask, though not in anger. His crimes and my hatred both feel very far away right now.

Ruven snorts, crossing his arms. "Bold of you to assume I *wanted* to haunt you."

"Nothing forces you to appear to me," I say. "Does it?"

He grimaces. "No. But I cannot leave you, even when I hide myself, even when I close my eyes. As I was bound to the spell on the palace, I am now bound to you."

Something twists in my stomach as I remember his bitter desperation when we met. He didn't want to be bound to the palace for five hundred years. He doesn't want to be bound to me now.

"Why did you *do* it?" I burst out. "I've studied all the histories. Before you, the royal family treated heretics kindly."

That's why, for the past five hundred years, we've had the penal laws—because when the heretics were shown kindness by the royal family, they used it against them. So now as punishment they are barred from public office and the universities, limited in how much land they can own, and levied with extra taxes.

I always used to pity heretics, even though I knew I shouldn't. Not Ruven and whoever trained him, of course—but the people who scuttled into the shabby heretic church half a mile from the convent. They were poor people mostly, over half of them foreigners taught to revere the Magisterium from birth, and it seemed a hard thing that their ancestors had used up all the possible mercy.

"You only made things worse for your people," I say. "Was it so bad to be ruled by a family that worshipped the living gods?"

Ruven looks at me, and my breath catches in my throat. Maybe it's just the wine, but for a moment I feel—again—as if there's no enmity between us, and worlds of possibility are shimmering all around—

Then Ruven's mouth flattens in ferocious disdain. "Yes," he says. "Because this country was infected with an endless plague of saints. Because your gods are monsters, and your royal family, by serving them, had become monsters as well."

I sigh, strangely disappointed. "In other words, because you're a raving heretic and that's all there is to it."

"Oh, yes, I am a heretic and I do rave with anger," says Ruven. "But that does not make me wrong."

"You heretics worship a mutilated corpse," I snap. "I don't think you have a right to call anyone else's gods monstrous."

Ruven has been snarling heresy every chance he got, ever since he started haunting me. It makes no sense for me to be suddenly so furious at him now. But I am.

"I'm tired," I say. "Leave me alone."

Ruven shows his teeth. "Make me."

When I sat in his lap, it was fear for my life that made me so shameless. Now the wine is my only excuse for looking him straight in the eyes and starting to undo the top buttons of my nightgown.

In a moment, his expression of haughty disdain shatters into embarrassment, and he vanishes. I huff out a soft laugh, giddy with knowing I can make him flinch. There's at least one way in which I'm not helpless.

If only there were some way I could be free of him forever.

And then suddenly the solution comes to me—

Nin-Anna.

Once I make my pact with the goddess, I will be filled with her holy power. Surely no heretic ghost would be able to abide that. Whatever power binds Ruven to me, Nin-Anna will dissolve it.

I only have to endure him for a few days, until we reach Nin-Anna's shrine. I am strong enough for that.

I have to be.

12

THREE DAYS LATER, THE STAGECOACH FINALLY crests the last low, rolling hill, and I see the white spires of Ir-Atsakha: the shrine of the goddess Nin-Anna.

My goddess.

A thrill of fear and exultation runs through my stomach. Varia and Araunn have agreed to let me enter the divine realm first and awake Nin-Anna. I will speak face-to-face with the goddess I've loved all my life and make a pact with her. She will banish Ruven and secure my place in the royal family. I will use her power to end the Red Death. Everything will be all right.

As long as Nin-Anna accepts me.

It all seemed so simple, that first night in Limakh. But over the last three days, I've found myself thinking more and more of Queen Imvada's brother, whom the gods branded with the mark of judgment because he had to be forced into the shrine.

I've told myself again and again that I *am* willing. That I only tried to run back to the convent because I wanted to serve Nin-Anna in a different way. And yet I did try. I did have to be forced into this carriage, on this journey.

The mark of judgment is a punishment that the gods give only to the worst of blasphemers and apostates, but I can't stop fearing it.

The queen's brother must have refused because he hated the gods, I tell myself. *And while I am unworthy, I love them. I do.*

"Yes," Ruven murmurs from his seat, "you love the goddess of life so much that you killed a man in cold blood."

You're not a man but a monster, I think at him, absurdly glad of his spite. It's so much easier to be angry at him than to fear what lies ahead.

The town that's grown up around Ir-Atsakha is small but prosperous, clearly well used to pilgrims and tourists. There are countless shops selling little statues of Nin-Anna, engravings of the shrine, and bottles of "holy water" that people are clearly meant to think come from the sacred pool in the shrine, even though they could not possibly. All across the town, Nin-Anna gazes out from countless statues and paintings, her golden hands spread wide to scatter healing upon the people—upon *her* people, for of all places in Runakhia, this one is truly hers.

As we roll through the streets, I find that for the first time in my life, I can imagine loving a place as much as the convent.

We come to a halt before the steps of the shrine. There's a crowd of townsfolk turned out in the main square to watch us, and a crowd standing on the steps of the shrine to meet us: a mayor and town councillors who babble with delight at seeing the prime minister, clergymen who greet Reverend Coldren like a long-lost brother, and nuns who are thrilled to welcome Anabekha.

And everyone, *everyone* stares at Araunn and Varia with delighted reverence. I know at least some of them must be think-ing about how after this visit, even more tourists and pilgrims will come to spend their money in the town. But this is still the way that I dreamed of people greeting the royal family, and seeing it happen before my eyes gives me hope that everything will be all right, that the golden age I dreamed about as a child really will return.

We enter the shrine together. The long nave has a colonnade running down either side, white pillars painted with traceries of gold. Through the arches, I see glittering mosaics, pictures of not only Nin-Anna but also her saints—the common folk touched and transformed by her power. Their hands turned to gold like hers, and they used those hands to heal the people around them; then, consumed by the divine power that only those with the Royal Gift can survive, they died, flowers sprouting from the ground about their corpses.

Then we come to the sanctuary of the shrine, and we all fall silent—even Reverend Coldren, who was trying to lecture Anabekha about the lives of the saints.

Because here hang the saints.

Our convent chapel had a single bone, and we thought ourselves blessed. Here in Ir-Atsakha, seven full skeletons of the saints hang from the ceilings, gilded and bejeweled and holy.

As we step into the sanctuary, a wave of incense-heavy air hits me. I draw a breath, knowing that countless women have stood in this space, singing the praises of Nin-Anna. For a moment, I don't care at all what Ruven has done, or how much power clergymen like Reverend Coldren have. Here, in the home of Nin-Anna, the lady of golden hands and healing is all that matters.

Her statue sits at the back of the sanctuary, an ancient thing crudely carved from wood and blackened by centuries of candle smoke, dressed in silks and draped in chains of jewels.

Behind her, in the wall of the sanctuary, is a single narrow door.

It opens onto a stairway that curls down, down into the ground.

Aside from me and Araunn and Varia, only Anabekha—because she is a nun of Nin-Anna—is allowed to pass through.

What we find at the bottom of the stairs is not exactly a room; clearly it was once a cave. But every inch of the pale stone walls has been carved into delicate, frothy filigree. The floor has been covered in a swirling pattern of black and gold mosaics. A thousand candles light the secret heart of the shrine and fill it with warmth.

At the center of the room is a round pool of water: the gateway to the world of the gods.

The gateway to Nin-Anna.

O dawn-bright lady, I think, staring at the flat black surface of the water. A shiver runs down my spine: this pool is as strange and uncanny as Ruven's briar.

"Lia." Anabekha's voice makes me jump; I whirl to face her, wondering if she knows I'm so shamefully afraid.

But Anabekha smiles almost shyly at me. "Tell our goddess how I love her, please?" she says.

It's the first time that Anabekha has ever asked me for anything, and it goes to my head like wine.

"I will," I say, smiling, and turn back to face the water. My bare feet tingle as I walk forward.

On the other side is Nin-Anna: the goddess I have loved all my life, who will kill me if I am not worthy.

I think, *I was born for this*, and I plunge into the water.

For one moment, I feel like I'm falling. For the next, like I'm choking. Then I am standing upright on my own two feet, cool, sweet air shuddering in and out of my lungs as I gasp for breath.

My dazed first thought as I gaze upon the divine realm is, *It's broken.*

I'm standing on a vast plain of verdant grass and little white flowers, riven by fissures through which I can see blue sky and wisps of cloud. Before me rises a mountain, but it too is in shards. Great chunks of white stone and dark earth, lushly overgrown with moss and vines and flowering bushes, hover in the air. They gather to a point like a flock of birds flying to an unknown goal. Streams of water cascade down the pieces of the mountain, falling through the air from one floating rock to another. Fluffy clouds drift between the mountain pieces, strangely small—or is the mountain larger than I first thought?

My next thought is, *I know this place.*

When I used to imagine Nin-Anna's realm, it was not like this. I pictured woodland glades or fields of flowers—something gentle and comforting. Yet as I gaze at the fractured glory of the landscape, the austere invitation of the broken mountain, it has the inevitable familiarity of a half-remembered dream.

But where is everyone?

The souls that Nin-Anna chose for herself should be here, rejoicing in their goddess. Nin-Anna *herself* should be here, arrayed in glory like the dawn.

The air hums against my skin with a sense of waiting power, but I see no gods and no saints. I realize with a horrible lurch that I had never asked Araunn or Varia what I should do when I reached the divine realm. Maybe there's something else I'm supposed to do besides just get here.

Maybe I've already ruined this.

I clench my teeth, forcing back a wave of panic. *You hardly knew more when you walked into Ruven's briar*, I tell myself.

Instantly I brace to hear his voice. He always has something to say when I think of him.

But there's only silence. I glance back over my shoulder, but I see only the impossible riven plain stretching away to the horizon.

A fear I hadn't realized I was holding trickles away. He didn't follow me. I didn't commit the sacrilege of bringing him here.

Surely that's proof that once I belong to Nin-Anna, he'll be driven away completely.

All I have to do is find the goddess I have loved all my life.

I start toward the mountain. I don't know if it matters where I walk, or if the simple act of searching will be enough, but the lush peak of the mountain seems strange and glorious enough to be her throne.

At first it's easy. The gaps between the chunks of ground are uneven, and with a little searching I can find a place where the gaps are small enough for me to leap across them. The first few times, I have to work myself up to each jump, and a pang of white-hot terror jolts through me when I'm in the air and I see the infinite blue emptiness beneath my feet. But soon I get used to it. The air has a cold, bright sweetness like nothing I've tasted before, and before long I realize that I've been running and jumping for longer than I ever could have managed in the human world, and yet I'm not the least bit tired.

As I go, I silently pray the litany of Nin-Anna: *O dawn-bright lady. O sweetness of spring. Give me strength. Show me the way.*

It gets more difficult when I start scaling the mountain, for the surface is craggy and uneven. I may not tire as easily as I would in the human world, but I still can't leap up twenty feet to span the gap between two levels. I have to keep circling around, working back and forth to find places where a lower piece is level with a bit of one that goes higher.

Halfway up the mountain, I finally start to tire. Sweat runs down my back and the air rasps in my lungs. When I stop to catch my breath my legs shake, and I'm suddenly afraid that I won't be able to start moving again. So I press on, sometimes gasping and staggering, still praying to Nin-Anna.

I can't stop wondering why I'm alone here. It makes sense that Nin-Anna would want to test me before I see her glory. But where is Saint Eruvaun, and the seven girls my convent sent to die in the briar, and everyone else who ever loved Nin-Anna?

Where is Mama?

I know it's unlikely that my family's souls were all taken by Nin-Anna. Colan was so bright and brave, I can't imagine him with any god but Zumariel. Papa I'm less sure about . . . perhaps Ithombriel? But Mama's hands were so gentle as she nursed me through childhood sicknesses—surely Nin-Anna would have wanted her.

But surely if Mama were here, she would help me. She would at least embrace me for one moment and let me feel her love again.

Why am I still alone? I wonder, tears mixing with the sweat on my face.

Finally I reach the top of the mountain. It's very small; at the center, grass and flowers give way to a circle of flat, pale stone.

I'm trembling with exhaustion and excitement at the same time. I kneel, pressing my palms and forehead to the welcome coolness of the stone.

"O sweetness of spring," I say aloud, my voice soft and shaking. "O breath in newborn lungs. O fire of life. Hear me. Please hear me."

And she finally does.

There's a strange, resonant sound, at once like ringing bells and stone grinding against stone. It's not loud, but I shudder, feeling as if my bones are going to crack apart.

Then I look up, right into the eyes of Nin-Anna.

I've seen paintings and statues and mosaics of the goddess all my life. And they were all, in a way, accurate: Nin-Anna is a young woman, faultlessly beautiful, with warm brown skin and night-black hair and hands as golden as her eyes. She wears a dress that seems to be woven of the dawn sky, ever-changing shades of rose and gold and cream. Around her feet, flowers sprout from the stone.

And yet no picture has prepared me for this moment. All my life, even as I've known that Nin-Anna was powerful and mysterious and exalted, I'd still always imagined her looking like a *person*.

But there is nothing human about her. Every line of her face and body is shaped like a woman's, but there's no mistaking the terrible, alien power behind her golden eyes. She stands no taller than I do, yet there's something impossibly *vast* about her presence that makes me want to press my face to the ground and tremble.

Then she speaks, and her voice is like her face: beautiful and infinitely inhuman.

Who comes before me, after all these years?

And I remember that it's not my duty to abase myself, but to bargain.

I swallow dryly and find my voice.

"My name is Lia Kurinava," I say. "I am here to awaken—I am here to *beg* you, please return to your shrine. Listen to our prayers.

And . . . I am also here to make a pact with you, as a daughter of the royal house."

Nin-Anna gazes down at me without smiling, her face as remote and heartless as the stars.

"I love you." The words burst out of me in a rush. "I have never loved any god so much as you. Please, *please* let me belong to you."

I believe you, says Nin-Anna after a moment, and I feel a sudden rush of pride, of *hope*—

"Hail, dawn-bright lady."

Ruven's voice rings out, loud and clear and the closest to respectful that I've ever heard it. Sudden horror clutches at my stomach as I look over my shoulder. Ruven stands a pace behind me, looming against the bright sky in his dark robes. Blood streams from the gash in his throat, dripping down his neck in rivulets and soaking his chest.

No! He can't be here—

"This girl is not worthy of you," Ruven goes on. "She has killed in cold blood, and you are a goddess who accepts no murderers."

"I'm not—" I whirl to face Nin-Anna. "I'm not a murderer," I plead, trying to ignore the memory of hot, sticky blood on my face and hands. "He's a heretic who attacked your people, I was trying to save them—"

You brought bloody hands into my kingdom, says Nin-Anna. *There is no pact I can make with you.*

"But—but—"

My judgment is upon you, says Nin-Anna. *Begone.*

She vanishes. Numb with horror, I stare at the empty spot where she stood.

"No," I whisper. "Please come back."

Then I gag, and the next moment I'm vomiting—not bile but *blood*.

With a soft moan, I look at my hands and arms. They're already crosshatched with red lines: the mark of judgment.

I've read in ancient histories what will happen next. I will vomit more blood, and the red lines will spread all across my skin, then split open. By the time Varia cuts my throat to prevent the curse from spreading, I'll be grateful for the pain to end. But what comes after will be even worse: no god will touch my soul and take me to rest. I'll never see Mama or Papa or Colan again. I'll be left alone in the shadows of death forever.

I stagger to my feet, turning around, and I see Ruven's face. His mouth is open, and there's stunned horror in his eyes.

Then his mouth snaps shut into a grim line, his expression shuttering.

"You're only reaping what you've sown," he says flatly.

I try to answer but vomit more blood instead. I'm trembling now and sweating; my skin itches and stings, droplets of blood sprouting along the red lines. With horror, I realize that I won't live long enough to return home and be executed. I will feel the full pain of the gods' judgment right here.

I wonder if this is how Mama felt when she first vomited blood and knew she'd never live to see our front door open again. I remember her being so calm and brave, while it's all I can do not to whimper.

"At least I'll die by the hand of the goddess I love," I tell Ruven, my voice shaking. "*You* only died to me."

The next moment, my knees give out. Ruven catches me—here in the divine realm, his ghostly hands are solid and warm—and he lowers me to the ground in a strange mockery of tenderness.

"I should have known your gods would have no sense of justice," he growls, and there's something dark in his voice that I've never heard before.

I gurgle and choke on blood before I manage to cough it up.

"Regretting that my death isn't slower?" I rasp.

He tucks a strand of hair behind my ear, his face like a marble statue. "Infinitely."

I can't hold back a soft moan as I feel the red lines burning their way across my face. But I manage to steady my voice enough to say, "Araunn and Varia will awaken the shrines. My people will know the gods again. I don't regret killing you."

That, says another divine voice, *is a thought worthy of me.*

There's a sudden chill in the air. A harsh smoke-and-salt scent. I blink—something, sweat or blood, is running into my eyes—

A hand touches my face. Fingers cup my chin, curve up behind my ears. Needle-sharp claws prick at my skin.

The pain fades a little as I look into a death-pale face and golden eyes.

Sitting up, I shudder and shrink away, not caring that I'm pressed against Ruven's chest. Because the one who stands before me is so much worse.

Like Nin-Anna, she has the form of a young woman with long black hair. But her face is pale as a corpse, her hands are charred black, and her long, spidery fingers are tipped in claws. Her white dress is ripped open to show the bloody ruin of her chest, ribs snapped to expose her heart.

This is Mor-Iva, the goddess of death and killing and judgment. She has no shrine, because no city has ever wanted to draw that much of her attention.

Mor-Iva reaches into her chest and takes out her heart. The scent of her blood is thick on the air, curling around my tongue; I breathe it in, and the pain eases a little more.

If you'll make a pact with me, says Mor-Iva, *you can live.*

But what kind of life would I have with her? To make a pact with a god is, for the royal family, the same as becoming that god's saint: they are filled with the god's power, and work that god's particular miracles.

With Mor-Iva, the only miracle I would work is death.

"She's a monster," Ruven breathes in my ear. "Don't listen."

"She's a god," I say bleakly.

And I want to live. Because I must see Runakhia filled with saints, because I can't let Ruven win, and because I *do not* want to die.

"Yes," I tell the goddess of death, of everything I've ever hated.

Lay your hand on my heart, Mor-Iva says and kneels down, holding out the bloody scrap of flesh.

I stare dizzily at her charred fingers, her talon-like claws. Her beating red heart. I want to cringe back and say, *No, no, I don't belong with you.*

But Ruven is right about one thing: I'm already covered in blood.

I reach out. Mor-Iva's heart is warm and velvet soft; it feels like a caress as it beats against my palm.

Lia Kurinava, I claim you. Mor-Iva's other hand grips the back of my neck. *Kill in my name and be mine.*

Her lips press against my forehead. A sudden wave of pain runs down my body, and everything goes dark.

13

I'M DIGGING IN THE CONVENT GARDEN, my fingers burrowing into warm, damp earth. With a strange feeling of familiarity, I uncover a pair of pale, slender hands reaching upward. Their fingers wrap around mine, sending a shock of warmth and being wanted up my arms, through my spine, and straight to the base of my skull. Tears prickle at my eyes, because this feeling is all I've ever desired.

Suddenly the hands clamp down on mine, a burning pain blossoming under the pressure. I jerk back but I can't pull free, and I watch in horror as my hands change, fingers growing longer, skin charring and cracking, a dark infection that flows up my wrists—

And I wake.

I'm trying to sit up, to escape the weight of the blankets—my hands sting and ache horribly—but somebody is gripping my shoulders, holding me down.

"Lia. Lia! It's all right."

It's Anabekha, her voice worried as I've never heard it before.

I sag in relief as I meet her eyes. "What happened?" I ask, the words cracking in my dry throat.

"You made a divine pact," says Anabekha. She smiles weakly, holding out a cup of water.

My parched throat aching, I reach out to take it—

With monstrous hands.

I've always had small hands with short fingers, pale skin, and stubby nails bitten down to the quick. Now my fingers are so long and thin they make me think of spider legs. Their skin is cracked and charred black, as if roasted in a fire. My nails have turned into birdlike claws, curved and sharp.

Memories crash back down on me: the realm of the gods, Ruven's betrayal, Nin-Anna's rejection.

Mor-Iva's offer. And my choice.

Kill in my name, the goddess said to me as her warm, wet heart beat under my hand.

"Gods and saints," I whisper in horror.

All the saints of Mor-Iva have been killers, their miracles necessary but always dreadful. They are feared and reverenced but never loved, just like Mor-Iva. And now I'm going to be one of them.

I realize that Anabekha is talking again, but I can't hear her words over my own heartbeat. When she touches my shoulder, I shove her away, my claws raising welts on her skin.

"Get out." The words scrape at my throat.

"What?" For the first time in all the years I've known her, Anabekha sounds unsure.

I swallow, not daring to meet her eyes. "Please. I need to be alone."

After a moment, Anabekha sets the cup down on the bedside table. "I'll tell them you're all right," she says gently, and leaves the room.

The moment the door closes behind her, tears burn in my eyes. I ignore them as I seize the cup of water and gulp it down, but as soon as I'm finished, the sobbing starts. The grief is so vast, it doesn't even feel like *my* grief, just like something that's happening to the whole world.

Nin-Anna doesn't want me. The only goddess I've ever loved *doesn't want me*, and now I belong to the goddess who is her opposite.

"Yet still holy," says Ruven. "Isn't that right?"

My head jerks up. He stands at the other end of the room, leaning against the wall, his arms crossed, his throat still marked with the bloody gash that condemned me to this fate.

Fury curdles behind my ribs. "You," I growl.

I push back the coverlets and stand. Instantly a wave of dizziness washes over me, and I drop back to the bed with a thump, gasping for breath.

"Yes," says Ruven. "Me." His mouth twists bitterly. "Still trapped here with you."

He says the words as if he were the one injured.

"You failed to kill me," I growl. "Though you did defile me. Aren't you done yet?"

"Aren't *you* done worshipping monsters?" he snaps back. "You've been hated by the kindest of them, and loved by the cruelest—don't you see how there's no difference between them?"

My charred, monstrous hands curl into fists, claws pricking the burnt skin of my palms. There's a world of difference between Nin-Anna and Mor-Iva.

"And yet both are divine," says Ruven, hearing my thought as always. "Why say that I defiled you? I *hallowed* you to a goddess you call holy."

He looks and sounds so sure that for a moment I'm left speechless. But then I remember the look of shock—almost horror—on his face when Nin-Anna rendered judgment on me.

"You had no idea what Nin-Anna would do," I snap at him. "Admit it!"

Ruven's expression twitches slightly, and that tiny sign of weakness makes my flicker of anger flare into a blaze.

"You're right," I go on, "you weren't defiling me. You were just tattling, like a spoiled little boy who thinks that if he's in trouble, everyone else should be." I see him flinch, and I press on furiously, "That's all you are: a boy who worked one sorcery and then spent five hundred years sulking that he had to bear the consequences of his own work!"

There's a horrible bleakness in Ruven's eyes. "And you," he rasps, "you're the girl who came to me with pity in her eyes and touched me with tender hands, only to murder me."

The next moment he's gone, and I'm alone, shaking with righteous fury and also—also—

Guilt.

"I had to," I whisper to the silence. "There was no other way."

Pity in her eyes. With tender hands.

I betrayed Ruven first, as grievously as he ever betrayed me.

"It was my holy duty," I say, but then my gaze drops to my charred, ruined hands, shedding ash across the coverlet.

Murder isn't holy to Nin-Anna, only to Mor-Iva.

Maybe I deserve this.

The next moment Araunn bursts into the room. "Lia!" he says, smiling in relief. "You're all right!"

I can't speak. And I can't meet his eyes. Because I can't look away from his shimmering golden hands.

"We were so worried," says Araunn. "When you didn't come out again, we thought—I was so—"

He cups my face in his hands and presses his forehead to mine. His touch is tender and warm and holy. I should be delighting in his affection, but all I can feel is a cold, bitter ocean of jealousy.

He's made a pact with Nin-Anna—with *my* goddess. And right now I hate him more than I've ever hated Ruven.

"Araunn!" Varia hauls him back from me by the shoulder. "Stop fawning over her until we know if we have to kill her."

A sudden chill runs down my spine. Varia is staring at me with gimlet eyes, her mouth a grim line.

"Just look at her hands!" Araunn protests. "She made a pact with Mor-Iva. It's all right."

My last tiny hope for mercy snuffs out. Araunn didn't say *we can't kill her*, he just said that I passed the test. If I ever fail in my future duties as a princess, he won't save me. He might not wield the knife, but Varia will make sure I die just as Queen Imvada promised.

"I did make a pact," I say, my voice shaking only a little. I raise my right hand, stretching my charred, clawed fingers to the sky. "You have eyes, don't you?"

"I do," says Varia, crossing her arms. "And I saw Araunn drag you deadweight from the realm of the gods, bleeding in the mark of judgment."

"I'm sure it wasn't—" Araunn interrupts, but Varia keeps going.

"I know my duty as a princess. I have the strength for it, even if my brother doesn't. So tell me: do I have to destroy you?"

If you think I might be an accursed blasphemer, then why would you expect me to tell the truth? I think wildly. But at least she's giving me a chance to explain.

"Nin-Anna rejected me for having blood on my hands," I say. "Because I killed Ruven. And yes, she did put the mark of judgment on me."

The words make resentment curdle in my stomach.

She judged me for setting your family free, I think. But I have no right to begrudge that, and anyway, it's no use thinking on might-have-beens. Right now I have to survive.

"But then Mor-Iva offered me a pact," I go on, meeting Varia's gaze as confidently as I can. "So I am alive and blessed by the gods— and at the moment, more royal than you. Any more questions?"

Araunn looks slightly shocked by my outburst. But Varia, strangely, loses a bit of her stiffness and smiles.

"Not so long as you can keep doing your duties," she says. "It's seldom gone well when one of us makes a pact with Mor-Iva, but you seem to have kept your sanity so far. You'll want to start practicing how to hold a fork with those hands, though. There's a banquet for us tonight."

It turns out that *tonight* pretty much means *at once*, for I've slept away most of the day. As soon as Varia and Araunn leave the room, my maid slips in and bobs a quick curtsy.

"Ready to dress, miss?"

She's not the tall, willowy servant who attended me at the palace, but a plump, pale girl my own age with mousy brown hair and blue eyes. Hézoraine presented her to me the morning we left for

109

the Royal Progress, saying that I needed a modern woman to dress me. She introduced the girl as "Jaríne"—a Zémorine name that I doubt she was born with, since her accent is pure Runakhian.

For the last three days, Jaríne has dressed me quietly and confidently. Now, however, her eyes grow wide as she stares at me.

"I—I mean," she stammers, "Your Holiness."

That's the proper title for a member of the royal family who has made a pact with one of the gods. I should be pleased, but instead my lungs feel like they're shriveling up inside my chest. Jaríne isn't looking at me as if I'm holy, but as if I'm dangerous.

As if I'm just as deadly as Mor-Iva, as much a monster as Ruven.

Impulsively, I raise my right hand as I did for Varia. "Are you sure you want to keep dressing someone with that title?" I ask.

Some emotion twitches across Jaríne's face. Then she lifts her chin.

"You mean a princess who could have me whipped or killed at a moment's notice? Because that's the lady I dressed *yesterday*."

I can't stop a sudden, almost hysterical bleat of laughter. Jaríne's words are horribly disrespectful of Mor-Iva and the royal family. But all I can feel is a vast, desperate relief that in just one person's eyes, I'm no different than I was yesterday.

"I'd never hurt you," I tell her, dropping my hand.

"How comforting," Jaríne says dryly as she steps to my side. "Please tell me you can retract those claws. No? Then we'll have to be *very* careful changing clothes."

It takes a while to dress me, and not just because of my claws. Jaríne is still learning the ins and outs of the five-hundred-year-old gowns—donations from ladies of the palace—that are all I have to wear. The worst part is when she pulls off my long-sleeved kirtle, and I see that not only is my skin charred several inches past my wrists, but the veins running up my forearms have turned black, only fading to ash gray near my elbows.

I want to stare at my arms in dumb horror forever, but Jaríne clucks her tongue and says briskly, "Curl those claws or you'll tear the dress." The next moment she's pulling a vivid crimson kirtle over my head, followed by a black surcote. As she goes to work combing and pinning up my hair, I look at myself in the mirror and feel grateful that I have nothing to wear but ancient clothes. The only place for me is the Runakhia of five hundred years ago, when all people loved the gods, and royal pacts were a normal part of life.

But that is not the Runakhia that waits outside my bedroom.

The banquet is held in the town hall, where the guilds usually meet to discuss business with local factories and businessmen. The crepe-paper streamers and flowers hanging from the ceiling have obviously been hastily tacked up, making it into a space that's just barely fit for celebration. It's packed from wall to wall: not only are the mayor and the town councillors here, but most of the local clergy, as well as a crowd of ordinary folk—it seems like everyone with enough money or a halfway decent suit or dress has made their way into the hall.

None of them want me here.

Oh, the mayor and some of the clergy babble their gratitude and admiration to me, but they excuse themselves as quickly as they can to talk to Araunn or Varia instead. And I can't fail to notice the way people in the crowd fall silent as I pass them, the

111

way they turn to stare at me and quickly look away again when they realize I have noticed.

Anabekha stays by my side as the crowd swirls around us, but she says nothing. Her gaze keeps drifting to Araunn, and I'm certain she wishes she could be attending him instead. He's the one who pleased Nin-Anna, after all.

"Your Holiness," Reverend Coldren says brightly, pushing his way through the crowd. "So good to see you recovered!"

I remember what Varia said about Araunn dragging me dead-weight from the realm of the gods, and embarrassment burns across my face.

"Good evening," Anabekha says sharply. "Prepared to admit the power of the gods now?"

"You know I have never denied the Royal Gift," he protests, then turns back to me. "In fact, I was hoping you might grant me an interview about your visions of the divine realm. It would be most helpful for my research."

Fury sparks in my chest. "Visions," I say flatly. I can already tell how he will twist my words: he'll say that neither goddess ever spoke to me, that Nin-Anna's judgment and Mor-Iva's mercy were only a fever-dream allegory of my own soul, and all my agony meant nothing.

I hold up my right hand, fingers curved like claws, and I feel a nauseous satisfaction when Coldren flinches. This is one thing he cannot deny.

"Nin-Anna branded me with the mark of judgment," I tell him flatly. "Then Mor-Iva healed me and told me to kill in her name. What else do you want to know?"

Coldren swallows nervously, but he pulls a pen and a little note-pad from his pocket. "When you, ah, encountered the goddesses, did their appearance match the traditional iconography, or—"

"What does it matter?" I ask bitterly. "Why do you care? You've never worried a moment in your life whether you have pleased them or not."

To my astonishment, Coldren seems hurt by my words. "Of course I care about the gods. Do you think I don't love them simply because I don't fear them?"

Before I can think of a reply, the mayor announces it is time for us to eat. A moment later Hézoraine is at my side and bustles me away from both Anabekha and Coldren—despite being part of the Royal Progress, the mayor and town councillors outrank them in seating.

The prime minister makes a lengthy speech, and then the mayor follows with an even longer one, but I barely hear any of their words. I'm too busy trying to ignore the strange length of my fingers, the itching of my cracked, charred skin. Too busy trying to avoid meeting the eyes of anyone in the room, and too wretchedly conscious of their stares.

On my right hand, a thick flake of charred skin lifts up from the surface of my forefinger. I stare at it in revulsion, and then—carefully keeping my hands in my lap, below the level of the table—pick at it with one of my claws. There's a sharp sting of pain, and then the flake of skin comes free, crumbling into ash.

I'd hoped to find pink, living skin underneath. Even red blood would have been a relief. Instead I stare at a patch of gray flesh that oozes droplets of black liquid.

This is the power of Mor-Iva, I think. *This is holy.*

But all I can feel is disgust.

The toasts take nearly an hour. I'm excruciatingly careful, lifting the narrow stem of my wine glass, but my fingers are no longer the same shape and my claws make everything clumsier. The glass wobbles and sloshes, and after the first sip I don't trust myself to drink again.

The meal is a little easier. Even my monstrous hands can wield a knife and fork well enough—something Araunn and Varia still struggle with, and that makes me feel a little less horrible.

But then I see how easily Araunn laughs at himself when he drops his fork and has to pick it up again, and the way the nearby people smile at him, and I feel the same poisonous jealousy I did before.

Abruptly, I can't take it anymore. I stand, and instantly the room goes silent.

"Your holiness," says the mayor with fear in his eyes. "Are you—"

"Thank you for the meal," I say, cutting him off. "It was delightful. But I must pray to my goddess now."

There's at least one thing I'm still good for.

14

EVEN LATE AT NIGHT, THERE ARE still lights in the shrine of Ir-Atsakha.

I step inside and find a celebration greater than the one I just left. Candles and flowers are clustered before every image of Nin-Anna and her saints. The air rustles with the murmuring of prayers and hymns as people throng to greet the goddess who can finally hear them and answer. At least a dozen people have been dragged in on stretchers, and every single one has a face alight with hope.

I did this, I think, halting just inside the doorway. *I made this happen.*

For one moment, nothing else matters: not Ruven's blood on my hands, and not Nin-Anna's rejection. Everything I've done and suffered is utterly worth it. Because after years of watching people die in the hospital despite all that the nuns could do, now I will get to see every single sick person healed.

Nobody will have to die like my family did, not ever again.

The crowd stirs. People are turning to look at me, more and more of them, and though the attention terrifies me I still step forward as if drawn by a string. These are my people, who love my goddess, and I—

I am not one of them. I see the disappointment in some faces, the fear in others, as they realize I'm not Araunn, not someone who can work miracles of healing. That I'm a servant of Mor-Iva instead.

"Your Holiness."

I start and turn to see a nun of Nin-Anna at my side, bowing deeply. The reverence is more salt in the wound, a reminder that I'm not one of them anymore.

"Yes?" I say, my voice wavering a little.

"Is there anything we can do for you?" the nun asks.

Nothing that Nin-Anna will allow, I think gloomily.

But I'm not the one who really matters, am I? It's the sick and the suffering who need Nin-Anna's help, and I can still be part of that by supporting the royal family.

I breathe deeply, straightening my spine. Time to stop mourning what I do not have and start being a princess of the royal house.

Time to serve the goddess who chose me.

"I need to speak with Mor-Iva," I tell her. "Do you have a place for private meditation?"

"Of course," says the nun. "Follow me."

She leads me down the nave of the shrine and through a narrow door into a side chapel, a small room paneled in white and black stone. At the far end is a small altar, and behind it hang paintings of all eight gods, rendered in white and black and gold.

"We will sing Lauds here at dawn," says the nun, "but until then you can keep vigil in private."

"Thank you," I say, a wave of homesickness crashing over me as I remember the last time I kept vigil in a chapel, and how different things were then.

As she leaves, I kneel on the cold, hard floor—that much, at least, is still the same. I draw a deep breath.

And then I press my charred, monstrous palms together in prayer.

"Oh, Mor-Iva," I whisper. "O lady of—of death." I stumble, realizing that I can't remember any of the titles from her litany.

"Knife of the gods," says Ruven. I start, and turn to see him leaning against the wall behind me, his arms crossed. "Judge of hearts. Bloody silence. Final word. Breath of night." He recites the names in a low, grim voice. "That's what your people called her five hundred years ago. That's what you're planning to worship."

The bloody gash in his throat feels like more of an accusation than ever, and I swallow uneasily. "Didn't you say I belonged to her?"

He doesn't respond, just stares at me with grim eyes—one gray and one golden—until I give up and turn away from him again.

At least he's finally quiet, I think, trying to settle myself into the right frame of mind for prayer.

And that's when Ruven speaks again.

"You were right." His voice is very soft, but something in the tone sends ice up my spine and holds me in place. "I was just a boy who spent one hour as a weapon and five hundred years sulking."

I hear . . . nothing, maybe, or just my own breathing—but I still feel sure that he's stepping toward me. When he speaks again, he sounds close enough to touch my hair.

"But that's how I know what it means to give your life and your soul away just because somebody smiled and promised you sainthood."

My skin prickles at his closeness, and I wonder wildly if he's about to grab me by the throat and strangle me, but somehow this moment has turned into a contest of wills where I must not turn around.

"If I don't serve Mor-Iva," I say flatly, "Varia will kill me. My life is already given."

He sighs, the sound cracking at the end into a dry chuckle. "And you don't regret it, do you?"

"No." It's a truth and a lie at the same time, and I have the horrible feeling he can tell. But I clench my teeth and say, "Thank you for telling me how to address my goddess. Please leave me alone with her."

"As her holiness commands."

He vanishes—I know that too, without looking. I'm alone now.

Except for the presence of Mor-Iva, who surely hears every breath I take.

Somehow this moment feels the same as letting myself sink into the sacred pool. But there's no danger. I already have a pact with Mor-Iva. I just have to speak with her.

"Hear me," I whisper, "O knife of the gods."

Then I wait, my skin prickling with anticipation. Any moment I will hear the sound of Mor-Iva's inhuman voice, perhaps smell her blood or see her pulsing heart—

Any moment.

Surely now.

But the moments go on and on, and still there's only silence.

I've stopped praying, I realize. What goddess would be pleased with a single terse invocation? Hurriedly, I begin again, cobbling together a litany from Ruven's recitation and my memory of Nin-

Anna's prayers: "O knife of the gods, hear me. O judge of hearts, bless me. O bloody silence, hearken to my prayer. O final word, speak to me. O breath of night, I praise you."

But my words fall limply into dead silence, and Mor-Iva doesn't answer.

I begin to chant psalms from memory, praises for all and any gods. When my voice cracks and grows hoarse, I pray silently.

Nothing works. No one answers.

What am I doing wrong? I think desperately. *I made a pact. I did everything right. What more can Mor-Iva want?*

And if I can't speak to her, how long will the royal family let me live?

I wake to the solemn, graceful notes of the nuns chanting Lauds around me.

I fell asleep in choir again, I think, and open my eyes to a painful dazzle of light. Blinking back tears, I sit up, trying to recall if today I was supposed to chant a solo part—

Then I remember that I'm not in the convent anymore. I'm in Ir-Atsakha, I belong to Mor-Iva, and I fell asleep failing to speak with her.

It's morning now. Sunlight streams through the slit windows of the chapel and pours across the black-and-white stone panels of the floor. On the steps before the altar burn a hundred little candles, and what seems like a hundred nuns are crowded into the chapel to sing.

At the front of the crowd stands Anabekha, psalter in hand. She sings with note-perfect joy, her voice rising above the rest of the choir. Her gaze is fixed on the paintings of the eight gods, and I feel as judged and ashamed as if she'd been staring right at me.

Anabekha found me dozing in the convent chapel when I tried to keep vigil too. It seems like she's always there when I'm most unworthy.

Then I notice Araunn.

He isn't kneeling in prayer; he sits cross-legged behind me, golden hands resting on his knees, eyes closed. There's an expression of peaceful delight on his face that I've never seen before.

Light dances around him.

There's sunlight, of course, falling across his shoulders and picking out the ruddy gleams in his golden-brown hair. But there's another kind of light too: white-gold sparks that shimmer and dance across his shoulders, through his curls, down his arms. The morning sunshine looks drab beside it, and I know—this is the power of Nin-Anna.

For one moment, Araunn is the most beautiful and remote thing I have ever seen outside of two goddesses, and I hate him for it. I hate him for the peace on his face, for how effortlessly he has taken everything I ever wanted.

I did everything right, I think despairingly. *I did more for the gods than he ever did. What is wrong with me?*

I look down at my hands, which now rest on my knees; without thinking, I've drawn myself into the same position as Araunn. The claws and the long fingers and the charred, cracked skin all prove that Mor-Iva made a pact with me. I remember her wanting me. And yet now—

Was it all a trick? Was this her judgment on me, to make me hers and then make me fail at being hers? Or am I just so worthless that I can't even pray to one goddess properly?

"If I were you," Ruven says conversationally—I twitch and catch a glimpse of him seated beside me—"I'd be much less worried about your goddess and more about your princess. Since they started chanting, she's been watching you with eyes like a hungry knife."

The skin between my shoulders prickles. I don't doubt him for an instant. Of course Varia would follow her brother to see his first morning prayer to Nin-Anna. Of course she would scrutinize me.

It's her job, after all, to kill me if I fail. While Araunn might hesitate, Varia never would.

She *cannot* see me fail.

The thought echoes inside my skull as the nuns chant the final benediction. *She cannot see me fail. She cannot see me fail.*

And not just for my own sake. The realization dawns on me with sickening clarity. Five hundred years ago, Queen Imvada could kill her brother and sister before the court without shame. But now? Even *I* was horrified to hear the story, and I've loved the royal family all my life.

If Varia kills me, nobody will understand. The papers will scream the news in lurid headlines: "GRISLY MURDER ON THE ROYAL PROGRESS! MAD PRINCESS HACKS COMPANION TO DEATH!" Faithless clergy like Reverend Coldren will say this is why we must temper our primitive piety and ignore the will of the gods. The prime minister and Parliament will claim that the royal family is barbaric and unfit to rule.

They will stop the Royal Progress. The gods will be left unawakened, and there will be no saints. The Red Death will continue killing families like mine unchecked.

I cannot let that happen.

Gods and saints, what am I going to do?

121

As the last note fades away, Araunn's eyes open. He rises to his feet and looks around the room.

"Servants of the goddess I serve," he says, a strange solemnity in his voice, "which of you desires sainthood? Nin-Anna spoke to me as you sang her praises, and she will allow me to grant any of you that blessing."

Instantly, Anabekha steps forward and drops to her knees before him. "Your Holiness," she says, and there is an admiration in her voice that I would have done anything to receive, back when we were in the convent together. "Please, allow me—"

To my utter surprise, Araunn cuts her off. "No," he says. "You are faithful and true, but you have other duties than sainthood now."

Anabekha's cheeks flush, and I can't help feeling a crumb of triumph that she finally knows what it's like to fail. But then she says calmly, "As Your Holiness desires," and rises to her feet with a serene expression on her face.

Even in failure, she's perfect.

"Is there anyone else?" asks Araunn, raking his gaze over the choir.

There's a moment of silence, and then a scrawny girl no older than me, with olive skin and dark eyes, bolts forward. "Your Holiness," she says, falling to her knees before him, "please, I—"

Araunn seizes her by the hands and draws her to her feet. His eyes flicker shut for a moment, and then he smiles at her.

"Iramna, who was cursed by her mother," he says, and I realize with a chill that the goddess is speaking to him *right now*, "receive the blessing and the sainthood of Nin-Anna."

Iramna makes a little choked noise, her eyes growing wide. From where Araunn grips her, gold seeps across the skin of her hands, coating wrist to fingertip. She draws a shuddering breath, and then she smiles radiantly.

"And so your prince becomes a murderer," Ruven mutters in my ear.

It's not like that, I think at him. *It's holy.*

Mortal flesh, without the Royal Gift, withers beneath the searing weight of divine power. Of course all saints are eventually consumed by it.

"Like the mark of judgment?" he asks.

Nothing like it, I tell him.

The end that comes for the saints of Nin-Anna is easy enough: a fever that burns them out of life, while every surface they touch sprouts with flowers. Saints of the other gods have more painful deaths. But for all of them, that is simply what it means to be filled with divine power. Sainthood is exaltation, not murder.

"Even the sainthood of Mor-Iva?" Ruven asks dryly, and my heart thuds as I remember that when Araunn is done, people will wonder if I spoke to *my* goddess.

Now there's an old nun with pale, sagging cheeks holding out her hands to Araunn. He smiles and says, "Nerann, who buried four husbands before she took the veil, receive the blessing and the sainthood of Nin-Anna."

As the old nun's hands turn gold, Araunn sways slightly. His hands drop from hers, and he looks around in what seems like confusion until his gaze lands on me.

"Lia?" he says softly, as if noticing me for the first time.

A torrent of panic crashes over me. Everyone is looking at me now. Everyone is about to find out I have failed. I'm going to die for it, and then the royal family will pay for my death in the worst possible way.

I don't want to die.

If I want our country to have saints again, I have to live.

With every bit as much desperation as when I sat on Ruven's lap, I stare down the whole room and say, "Mor-Iva spoke to me as I slept. She wants me to create saints as well. Do any of you desire it?"

For one moment there is silence and stillness, and my heart throbs with painful doubt. If any of them call my bluff—

Then Varia laughs from behind me. "I'd say that's a no."

I turn to see her leaning against the wall by the door, her smile mocking and her pose one of insolent disdain.

A strange indignation pricks at me. "Mor-Iva is a hard goddess to serve," I say. "That doesn't make her less holy."

"Of course not," Varia agrees. "But so long as *you* serve her, I think we're all right."

"I do," I say without hesitation.

Araunn's hand drops onto my shoulder. "*We* do," he says warmly. "Every god of the royal family belongs to all the royal family, right?"

Varia's mouth curves in a razor-sharp smile that might be skeptical or might be conspiratorial.

"Then let's go wake the other shrines," she says.

15

I'VE LIED ABOUT MOR-IVA TO SAVE my life. I deserve the mark of judgment more now than I ever did when it was on my skin.

As the stagecoach rolls away from Ir-Atsakha, I tell myself that my sins and lies will all be worth it if I can just survive to see our country filled with saints again. Even if I'm not the one who makes saints of Nin-Anna, even if all I do is avoid disrupting the Royal Progress—surely that will be enough.

But it's hard to accept being useless. Every day we stop in at least one town or village, and Araunn works miracles. He makes saints. He heals sickness. He lays his hands on an infertile woman's stomach and tells her she will conceive within the week; he takes the hand of a paralyzed man and raises him up to walk.

I . . . watch.

And lie.

Nobody asks me for a miracle because nobody wants to die. But every time we are greeted by a town council or village leaders, I smile and raise my hands and promise that I am granting them the blessing of Mor-Iva.

I feel so wretched and false, I could weep. But what else can I do?

Nothing has changed from that first morning in Ir-Atsakha: Varia killing me would be a dreadful scandal. I've already ruined the Royal Progress enough with my failure to talk to Mor-Iva; I can't give the royal family's enemies an excuse to seize power. Surely it's better to wait and confess my sins once I'm back at the palace, when nobody will notice if I disappear.

I try not to think about that inevitable reckoning. I'm still so very afraid to die.

Every night, I kneel beside my bed for hours, praying to Mor-Iva. But no matter what I say, or how desperately I praise her, she never responds. I never feel her presence. I cannot use her power.

"Clearly she's not interested in prayers," Ruven says to me on the fourth night. "Maybe she wants you to kill for her first."

"I already *did*," I snap, shivering. The chill of the night air has crept into my bones, but I stay kneeling by the bed, not ready to give up.

I still have nightmares about killing him: the blood, the smell, the jagged ruin of his neck. His breath on my wrist, and the awful sound of him choking on his own blood.

"And she talked to you once," Ruven points out, faintly mocking. "Maybe it's one speech per death, no exceptions."

"That's disgusting," I say. "Blasphemous too. The sort of thing that only a heretic would imagine."

"Is it?" He tilts his head. "What *else* is holy to Mor-Iva, besides killing?"

And the answer is right there, heavy on my heart.

"Judgment," I whisper.

I lied about Mor-Iva. I falsely claimed to speak for her. It's no wonder she has judged me unworthy of being heard.

126

But why didn't she listen to me before that?

The thought haunts me when I finally give up and crawl into bed to shiver under the covers and cry into my pillow.

Why didn't Mor-Iva answer me when I still deserved her, when I *needed* her? Did she know I would become a lying coward, and abandon me in advance? But what sort of justice is that?

I fall asleep with dried tears itching against my face and no answers at all.

The next morning, as Jaríne is combing out my hair and I'm trying not to cringe from the tickle of fingertips against my neck, Varia strides into the room. I see her face in the mirror—fierce, but no more than usual—and I dare to hope that she's just here to complain about the prime minister. That my secret is still safe.

As I turn to face her, though, Araunn also enters the room. He looks sorry, and he won't meet my eyes.

They know, I think bleakly.

"We need to talk," Varia announces.

I nod to Jaríne. "You can go," I say, my stomach twisting with a cold nausea.

As the door closes behind her, I gather my courage for one final lie.

"What is it?" I ask, lifting my chin.

"What is wrong with you?" Varia demands bluntly.

My heart thuds against my ribs, but my voice is steady. "Nothing's wrong."

"I'm not stupid," says Varia. "Neither is Araunn, though he's a bit of a fool—"

"*Varia*," Araunn interrupts.

"What? You know it's true. Just like you know she can't talk to Mor-Iva."

I'd thought I was afraid before. I'd thought I knew what was coming. But hearing Varia say those words out loud—it feels like the floor has given way beneath me, dropping me into the churning waves of an endless, icy ocean of fear.

"I can," I protest numbly, thoughtlessly. "I do."

Varia snorts.

"Of course you do," Araunn says quickly, smiling at me and then turning to his sister. "Didn't I tell you? Didn't you see her hands? She obviously made a pact with Mor-Iva, so—"

"So?" Varia demands. "What does that matter, if she can't make saints and work miracles?"

There's a short, awful silence.

"I—of course I can't work any miracles *right now*," I say. "There's nobody to kill."

"There's always something to kill," Varia says. "What about that village with the plague of mice? They didn't ask you to kill them because nobody dares ask *anything* of somebody who serves Mor-Iva. But it was well within your powers. Or should have been."

I can't speak. I keep trying to think of a lie, but I can't imagine anything good enough.

Varia heaves an annoyed breath. "You fool, we are trying to help you. Araunn can't kill you and I would prefer not to. Wouldn't you rather tell us, who will help you to live, than wait till we return to the capital and you're discovered by our mother?"

I gape at her, dumbfounded. It had never occurred to me that Varia, of all people, might want to help me.

Or is this just a comforting lie, to coax the truth out of me?

"Lia." Araunn is suddenly kneeling before me, taking my hands without flinching. "I know Mor-Iva spoke to you that first night. You were ready to make saints then. Please, tell us what went wrong so we can help you." Behind him, Varia nods in agreement.

Everything suddenly feels very cold and remote, my mind working very quickly. Because there are suddenly two things I'm certain of: Araunn, at least, truly wants to help me. And neither of them knows yet that I lied at Ir-Atsakha.

So I still can't trust them.

If I die, then Ruven will win. If Varia kills me, the Royal Progress will fall apart. And I will never see anyone cured of the Red Death. Even if I can't work the healing myself, I still want to be there the first time that somebody waiting to die like my family stands up and lives.

Isn't that reason enough for me to lie? To be wicked and cursed and wrong?

Maybe. Maybe not. But my body thrills with the hot, shameful knowledge that I'm going to do it anyway.

With a quavering voice I don't have to fake, I tell Araunn, "I'm just so frightened. That morning at Ir-Atsakha, it seemed easy to belong to Mor-Iva. But since then—I keep thinking that if I touch her power for a moment, I'll kill someone."

"Yes, that is a great problem whenever somebody is fool enough to make a bargain with Mor-Iva," Varia agrees.

Araunn throws a warning look over his shoulder. "*Varia*," he says again.

Before they can argue, I go on quickly, "Everywhere we go, every time I'm asked to use Mor-Iva's power, there's always a great crowd stuffed with little children and old women. I can't have an accident there. I *can't*. But—if we could stay somewhere a little while, if I could practice for a week or so in peace . . ." I trail off hopefully, the lie sour and stiff in my mouth as I meet Varia's eyes.

She nods, and relief cascades through my body. "Fair enough. I've been meaning to commission us all new clothing anyway, so that these baseborn lords and ladies will have less excuse to treat us as children. We might as well stop in the next city and do it there." Varia fixes me with a merciless stare. "One week. That's enough time to stop being scared of your goddess, isn't it?"

"More than enough," Araunn says eagerly. "Isn't it, Lia?"

One week to make a goddess pay attention to me is nowhere near enough time. But it's better than dying tonight.

"Of course," I say, smiling. "Thank you. Thank you both."

Araunn stands. "Promise you'll tell me if you need any help?"

"I promise," I lie.

He kisses my forehead and leaves the room.

Varia stays.

After a few moments, when I realize she isn't about to follow her brother, I say, "Well?"

"It's not that I don't believe you," says Varia. "Only . . . Araunn has always loved dogs."

"What?" I say blankly.

"Not just any dogs," Varia goes on. "Strays, mongrels. The more pitiful and abused, the better. He believed he could cure every one of them with his love . . . and he almost always did. But once, when he was fourteen, he came home with a dog that was half-starved

130

and bleeding in five places. He'd bought it from a man who set his larger hounds on it for sport."

I still can't understand why she's telling me this story, but I believe it. That sounds exactly like something that Araunn would do.

"Araunn nursed that dog back from the brink of death," says Varia. "He swore it loved him and was kind, but it growled and snapped at anyone else who approached. Three times it bit men who worked in the kennels, but Araunn cajoled them into forgetting. Then one day—I still don't know exactly what happened, because he won't speak of it, but the dog mauled him. By the time the guards dragged the creature away and killed it, he was bleeding in a dozen places." Varia laughs bitterly. "A saint of Nin-Anna died healing him; how's that for divine providence? It's the only reason he can use his hands now. Probably the only reason he's alive."

I try to imagine Araunn—his kindness and easy faith—so hurt and so betrayed. I can't.

"I'll give you a week," says Varia, after a few moments of silence. "I'll let Araunn save you if he can. I'll try to help. But it seldom ends well when somebody makes a bargain with Mor-Iva. And I won't let you become his cur."

"I won't," I say, but Varia is already turning away to leave the room, and my words fall weakly into the widening gap between us.

The door shuts, and I'm alone with Ruven. He grins at me as he leans against the wall.

"You can't deny," he says, "that was quite an elegant way to call you a bitch."

My hands are shaking; I clench them into fists, relishing the bite of claws in my palms. "Of course you'd like her."

131

"Oh, she's as much a monster as the lot of you. I just admire her claws."

I hate him. I hate that he thinks there's anything funny about this mess. I hate that he has ruined my life. That even though I killed him, somehow he still has the upper hand.

I hate Araunn too, for kissing me yet not caring enough to stop his family from killing me. And I hate Varia for being so much stronger, and for knowing exactly how much of a failure I am.

Mostly I hate myself, for being just as wretched and desperate as a mad dog, willing to do any evil thing if it will only save my life.

"Even now?" Ruven shakes his head. "You're *still* hating everyone but the gods who have destroyed you?"

I look down at my hands, at the charred, flaking skin that never stops itching, the needle-sharp claws that grow back overnight if I trim them. I remember Nin-Anna's serenity as she struck me with the mark of judgment, and Mor-Iva's suffocating silence ever since.

I remember the first time I looked at a painting of Nin-Anna and felt like I was not alone, and the first time I chanted the psalter with the nuns and felt like I was afloat on a river of solemn praise, and the first time I saw a patient I'd helped nurse walk out of the hospital, healed.

"No," I say, looking back up at Ruven. "I don't hate the gods. I love them. That's the one thing you can *never* take from me."

16

VARIA TALKS TO THE PRIME MINISTER at once, and by the time we climb into the stagecoach the plans are set. We will skip three towns we had planned to visit and drive straight to Moranda, a city with no shrine but a wealth of factories—and, according to Hézoraine, dressmakers. She spends almost the whole drive chattering to me and Varia and even Araunn about exactly what we will need for our wardrobes.

I barely hear a word she says. With every mile, dread lies heavier on my chest. Another week isn't going to make me less of a liar, nor Mor-Iva less vengeful. I'm as doomed as I was before; I just have another seven days to dread Varia's knife.

"It's not the worst way to die," Ruven says lightly, and I have to strangle the bitter laugh that wells up in my throat.

How would you know? I demand silently. *You've never died another way.*

"I saw you get halfway through dying from the mark of judgment," he says, the words suddenly clipped and bitter in a way I didn't expect. I look up, startled, but he's already vanished from his seat in the carriage, and I don't see him for the rest of the day.

When the road takes us through the woods, I stare at the tree trunks rushing past and pretend for a moment that I could run away and hide myself in a forest. But I know what would happen: if they didn't track me down with dogs, I'd certainly starve, or else poison myself eating the wrong berries.

At least then the papers would blame me instead of Varia or Queen Imvada, so it might cause less of a scandal.

We reach Moranda after dark. I plead a headache to get out of a candlelit dinner with the richest businessmen of the city, and spend two hours kneeling beside my bed, desperately praying first to Mor-Iva and then to any god who will listen.

Nobody answers.

When I wake the next morning, my fear has turned into a sort of light-headed irritation, as if I'd had one glass of wine too many. At breakfast, I gobble down the eggs and fried mushrooms and blood sausage with relish. For the first time in what seems like forever, I don't worry what anybody is thinking of me. I don't even feel lonely when I see Anabekha sitting serenely in her immaculate habit.

It doesn't matter. Nothing matters. The gods have abandoned me, and I'm going to die.

When Hézoraine asks if I would like her to take me to the best dressmaker in Runakhia, I don't care that Varia is making the dressmakers come to her as a princess should. I don't care that Hézoraine is a foreigner and a brazen atheist. I don't even care if the people in the dressmaker's shop gawk at my hands.

I'd never imagined that despair would feel so much like freedom.

"Thank you," I tell Hézoraine, smiling politely. "I would be delighted."

I might as well die wearing the prettiest possible dresses.

At first, it's exactly like I dreamed of when I was a little girl dawdling on my errands to stare wistfully into dressmakers' shops. Better, even. The shop Hézoraine brings us to is exquisite, its name painted in gilt letters on the huge glass windows and the display dresses made from shimmering cascades of silk ruffles and lace. When we go inside, Hézoraine has only to introduce herself, and we're instantly whisked away to a private dressing room. A minute later, the senior dressmaker—a tall, exquisitely coiffured woman wearing a rose-colored dress that glows against her golden-brown skin—bustles into the room and says, "Well, my ladies, what can we do for you?"

"My friend," says Hézoraine, "requires a new wardrobe. Within the week."

"Ah," says the dressmaker, turning to me. She doesn't even blink at my hands, just looks me up and down as if estimating my measurements. "And for what sort of occasions are we preparing you?"

My own execution for the sins of blasphemy and failure.

For an instant, the words tremble on my tongue. I picture the horror that would spread across the faces of everyone in the room— Hézoraine, Jaríne, and the dressmaker—and crazed laughter bubbles up inside my chest. I push it back down, swallow the truth, and say meekly, "Going into shrines. And . . . formal dinners?"

The dressmaker and Hézoraine exchange a look.

"She was raised in a convent," Hézoraine says tactfully.

"Ah," says the dressmaker. "Well, everyone is going to realize what a shame it is you were hidden away for so long."

After that, she and Hézoraine carry on the conversation between them. I stand still and silent as a mannequin at the center of the room while they try dresses on me, hold up swatches of fabric to match my complexion, and stand paging through ladies' magazines and discussing the engravings of fashionable gowns.

It's while they're poring over a magazine that I notice Jaríne trying to catch my eye. She's standing in the corner, very still but twisting her hands, and as soon as our gazes meet she hurries forward.

"If you please, my lady," she says quickly and under her breath, "might I ask a favor?"

There's a nervous meekness to her voice that's never been there before, not even when my claws were new.

"Of course," I say, curious.

"Might I step out for just a few minutes?" Jaríne asks. "I only— there's an errand I thought I might run, and you surely won't need me to carry things back for hours yet—"

She glances at Hézoraine and the dressmaker, who are still completely absorbed by the magazine.

"I surely won't," I agree wryly. "Go on, then."

Jaríne bobs a curtsy and slips out through a plain little door at the back of the room. I wonder idly what "errand" could make her so nervous—does she have a sweetheart in this city?

As the minutes wear on, I start to wish I had gone with Jaríne. Neither Hézoraine nor the dressmaker have looked at me for a quarter of an hour; they're too absorbed in a debate about the relative merits of different crepes. The fitting room, which was charmingly cozy when we arrived, is beginning to feel stuffy and hot.

I look longingly at the door that Jaríne used. If only I could slip out as well.

And then I think: *Why not?*

That sense of dizzying, heedless freedom descends on me again—the feeling that since I'm utterly ruined and doomed already, I can do as I please. What can they do but kill me?

The image of Hézoraine and the dressmaker attacking me with shears flashes through my mind, and I have to stifle a giggle.

They don't notice as I slip quietly to the door, nor as I carefully turn the knob and silently ease the door open. I take one final glance—neither of them turns—and I'm through.

On the other side of the door is a narrow, empty hallway that ends with an outside door clearly meant for deliveries. There's a bell that can be rung from outside, but nobody watching. I step outside.

Sunlight dazzles my eyes, and a gust of cold wind scrapes my face. I suck in a greedy breath, not caring about the dirty, metallic tang to the air. This freedom can't last more than five minutes, but it is *glorious*.

The place I'm standing isn't particularly glorious, though. It's a dingy alleyway running behind the row of glittering shops. On the other side of it are what mostly seem to be tenements, as well as a wall hiding what must be some sort of garden. Through the loops of the iron gate I can see grass and rosebushes.

Curious about the garden, I step closer—and catch my breath.

It's a graveyard.

There's no mistaking the stone slabs standing side by side, inscribed with names. I've never seen one before, but I've heard the nuns discuss them in hushed, horrified whispers.

Here in Runakhia, we burn our dead and scatter the ashes, freeing them from the mortal world to seek the gods. In the old days, the bones of the saints were boiled and scraped and cleaned so that they could be kept in shrines and chapels.

But the heretics who follow the Magisterium . . . they bury their dead in the ground to *rot*.

The gate is unlocked; it swings open easily at a touch of my hand. I step through onto a little dirt path that winds through the grass.

A shiver, at once horrible and delicious, runs up my spine. There are bones in the ground beneath my feet.

I remember, suddenly, the skeleton that I found in the briar. Here are more bones hoarded by heretic power, and yet . . . The breeze flutters against my neck and ruffles the buds of the rosebushes. There is a peace here that was not in the briar.

"Because this is a holy place," says Ruven, "and my briar was, at best, a necessary curse."

I look back. He stands just outside the gate, the iron swirls of the latticework screening his face.

There's something so instinctively *wrong* about a wall between us that I take a step back—then stop myself. But even just one step closer, I can see there's a strange longing in Ruven's eyes that I've never seen before.

"Why don't you come in?" My voice is soft, and as I speak the wind rises and gusts, drowning out my words with the rattling of leaves.

But Ruven hears. Ruven knows. His mouth twists bitterly, and when the wind lulls again, he says, "I worked that curse every day for five hundred years, and I died still feeding its wretched power, and now my body hangs unburied and profane in a courtyard of your heathen palace."

I shudder. I haven't seen it, but I've heard all about how Queen Imvada strung up his corpse, part of the traditional punishment for a traitor. She was furious that the remnants of his sorcery still clung to him, preserving his body from rot as he had preserved a summer afternoon for five hundred years.

But Ruven seems to feel no triumph. His voice is low with vicious misery as he says, "What have I to do with a holy place such as this?"

"You've walked into the realm of the gods," I say. "I don't see why you should spare a mere graveyard."

He stares back at me without speaking.

"Well," I say, "stay there if you can," and turn away to walk farther down the path. When I glance back a moment later, he's gone. Perhaps he lingers invisibly by the gate; perhaps he has been dragged along with me but wants to hide himself.

It doesn't matter if there's desperate, shattered longing in his eyes. He's a heretic sorcerer, and I am—I am—

No better.

The thought curdles in my stomach as I walk through the graveyard. As I go on, the gravestones grow larger; instead of standing slabs with a single name, there are family graves covered with great coffin-shaped stones, lists of names written upon them.

Then I see the girl.

For a moment I almost think she's a statue: she kneels so utterly still at the side of a huge gravestone, leaning forward to rest her forehead and clasped hands on the stone, a rosary trailing out from between her fingers.

Then she raises her face to look at me.

It's Jarine.

I stare at her, blinking stupidly. The bright, sensible daylight feels like a betrayal—because *Jarine*, of all people, follows the Magisterium? She's always seemed so respectable.

I've seen heretics before, many times. Some have been like Mr. Akharyn, successful enough to bear the fines of not attending chapel; most have been poor, ragged factory workers, scurrying into their shabby little churches as if their twisted, tortured god could save them from their debts.

But I've never really talked to one—besides Ruven—and I've never let one braid my hair and dress me for dinner.

Except Jarine.

As I think this, she bolts to her feet. "Your Holiness," she says, not quite meeting my eyes, "what are you—why—they're going to miss you."

"They won't," I protest automatically.

"Of course they'll notice you gone, *Your Holiness*," Jarine snaps. She strides forward and seizes my arm just above the elbow. "Do you have any idea how much trouble you'd be in if you were found here?"

Not as much as you, I think, but I don't say that. Instead I start to ask, "Why were you—"

Jarine's grip on my arms tightens like a vise. "Later," she says, dragging me back out through the gate of the cemetery. "I'll answer any question you want tonight."

Jarine's right about two things: I have been missed. And I am in *so* much trouble.

Hézoraine is the closest to furious that I've ever seen her, chattering a hundred words a minute about how worried she was and how many terrible things could have happened to me. Eventually she calms down, but for the rest of the visit she relentlessly draws me into the process of ordering dresses, asking my opinion on every seam and scrap of lace. I don't have a moment to think about what I've learned.

But that evening, when I finally go back to my room to get ready for bed, I see Jaríne standing by the dresser with her hands clasped, her mouth in a flat line.

"If you keep this secret, I'll keep any of yours," she says fiercely, the moment the door closes behind me. "Not a word to my mistress, no matter what she pays me."

This is not how I expected the conversation to start. Warily, I ask, "Did Hézoraine hire you to spy on me?"

Jaríne rolls her eyes. "That lady worships her husband like all the gods the Zémorine don't have; of course she wanted a maid who would tell her if you conspired against him. What sort of wits did you learn in that convent?" Her mouth snaps shut with a grimace, as if regretting the words, but she doesn't take them back.

I feel like a fool for not having guessed it before. And yet, what does it matter? Varia's going to cut my throat in a week, and then it won't matter how much gossip Hézoraine knows about me.

"Why were you in the graveyard?" I ask.

Jaríne lifts her chin. "Because I'm a heretic," she says bitterly. "You're clever enough to tell *that* much, certainly."

I shake my head. "But why did you go there today?"

No lady of high society would hire a heretic for a maid, not even a foreign-born atheist. Jaríne must have been desperately careful to keep her secret for years. Every time Reverend Coldren holds a chapel service for the Royal Progress, she is right there singing hymns to Juni-Akha and Ithombriel with the rest of us. Why would she risk it all now?

Jaríne's shoulders slump a little. "Because my whole family is under that stone," she says softly. "Mama and Papa and my little sister. It's been six years since I left them here, and I didn't know when I'd get another chance to kneel over their bones and pray for them again."

Six years. She wasn't much older than me when she lost her family.

A strange mix of pity and resentment twists through my chest. It doesn't seem fair that Jaríne's false, twisted god can comfort her for the death of her family, as Nin-Anna never did me.

"They're just bones," I say. "Unless the heretic god leaves the souls of his followers to rot in the cold, wet ground?"

"No," says Jaríne, her chin jutting forward. "He died so he could find us even in the darkest tombs."

Any god who can die is not a god, I want to snarl. But when I open my mouth, what comes out instead is: "And you think he's going to come find you? After you've spent years denying him?"

"I'm a sinner," says Jaríne, "but never an unbeliever. He's still my god, and he will punish me but not forget me."

I realize that I have taken two steps closer to her. My heart is pounding with jealous fury. I want to carve Jaríne's faith out of her with a knife and trample it under my feet. I want to make her admit that it is folly to trust so blindly.

Oh, I think. *Oh, no.*

This is how Ruven feels, all the time.

However else I have fallen, I can resist him in this.

"I'm not going to tell anyone about you," I say, meeting Jaríne's eyes. "This Royal Progress already has a Zémorine atheist and a vicar who's the next thing to one, so why not a heretic as well?"

Jaríne stares at me a moment, and then her mouth crooks up. "And to complete the set, a saint who shows mercy to heretics."

Laughter rips from my throat. "You were never taught catechism, were you? I'd only be a saint if I'd been claimed by a god. But I made a bargain with one."

And I broke that bargain. I can blame Mor-Iva all I want, but that morning in Ir-Atsakha, I lied and blasphemed to save my life. I broke faith with her first, and I deserve to be abandoned now.

I brood on that thought as Jaríne brushes out my hair and dresses me for bed. But as I lie curled under the covers afterward, I begin to see things from a different angle.

I have already betrayed Mor-Iva, irrevocably and unforgivably. I can never be the princess that the royal family wants me to be. I can never be what the *gods* want me to be.

So I don't have to keep trying.

All that matters now—all I can let myself care about—is making sure that the Royal Progress is a success, the saints are restored, and the Red Death is ended, no matter what lies I have to tell. And if someday the mark of judgment blossoms on my skin again, what of it? What have *I* ever mattered, compared to all Runakhia?

Jaríne's not the only one who can love a god she knows will punish her.

Once I let myself think that way, the answer is obvious: I need to fake miracles. It's the only way I'll get to live.

And there's only one power that could accomplish that, and one person who could teach me to use it.

If I ask Ruven to help me, he'll laugh in my face. But my conversation with Jaríne has stirred an old memory: Mother Una telling me that priests of the Magisterium claim their funeral ceremonies offer rest to the dead, so their followers are desperate not to die without them.

Ruven has had no funeral, nor any burial. Queen Imvada was adamant about following the old tradition that the bodies of traitors should be hung up to rot and be devoured by crows. When Parliament protested her having hung Ruven's body from the palace's front gates, her only compromise was to move him to a palace courtyard instead.

I remember the lonely desolation in his eyes this morning.

"Ruven!" I call softly, sitting up.

In the shadows of the room, his golden eye glows very bright. "What is it?"

"Don't you already know?" I ask.

"I do not actually enjoy hearing every vapid piety that runs through your head. I ignore your thoughts whenever I can."

The floor is cold against my bare feet as I slip out of bed. A shiver runs up my spine, but my voice is steady as I ask, "Then tell me— what if you could amend your fate?"

Ruven snorts. With the shutters closed, the room is pitch dark, but still a faint light clings to his face. "Even if you could bring me back to life, you wouldn't."

144

"Never," I say, stepping toward him. "But I can give you something else . . . for a price."

We're barely a handspan apart now. Despite the chill, my skin feels hot beneath my nightgown, and my heart pounds as a guilty, curious energy runs through my body. I'm about to do something terribly wrong, and this is the last moment I could turn back.

But I know, with a certainty sharp as the knife I used on Ruven's throat, that I won't.

"What do you mean?" Ruven sounds uncomfortable now, his back pressed against the wall as if to escape me.

Oh, Nin-Anna, I am sorry, I think, but I don't repent.

I reach up to lay a hand against Ruven's cheek. No solid surface meets my palm, only a chill in the air. His eyes go wide, his breath hissing in, and for a moment he looks very young.

Just a boy who spent one hour as a weapon and five hundred years so terribly alone.

"When we are back in the capital," I say, my voice sweet and tempting as honey, "I can steal your body and take it to the heretics for proper burial. You can have that much of the paradise your monks promised you."

His mouth quivers slightly; then he draws a breath and asks grimly, "What's the price?"

"Teach me sorcery," I say. "Teach me how to use it to fake miracles, so that the royal family will believe I'm a worthy princess and let me live."

Ruven stares at me for a moment, then laughs. "So this is the reason for which you'll throw away your god-kissed sanctity."

A guilty thrill ripples through my stomach, but I meet his eyes steadily.

"Yes," I say. "To make this Royal Progress a success, end the plague, and see Runakhia filled with saints, I will commit any sin. The same as when I sat in your lap and cut your throat."

"Oh, very well spoken." Ruven smiles as his cold hands close over mine. His grip is no more than a cold breath of air, and yet I don't resist as he brings my hands together. I feel like my bones have turned to wax that he can mold as he wills.

I've already given him leave to reshape my soul. To make me into something blasphemous and accursed, like him. There's not much point in resisting him over anything now.

But I still make my voice hard and defiant as I look up at him. "So? Do we have a bargain?"

"Yes, my little apostate," he breathes, "we do."

17

THE NEXT MORNING AT BREAKFAST, WHEN Hézoraine starts chattering about the day's plans, Varia fixes me with a severe look as she scoops jellied eel onto her toast.

I know what that look means: *This is day three of seven.*

Fear rolls through my stomach. She's probably suspicious already because I did nothing but visit shops yesterday. But she can't possibly suspect I've made a blasphemous bargain with a heretic sorcerer's ghost.

I lift my chin and say meekly, "I would love to, Hézoraine, but first—I was hoping I could spend this morning in meditation somewhere quiet?"

"Of course you can," says Araunn, his voice all relieved warmth. "I'll arrange it myself."

An hour later, I'm kneeling alone in a small meditation chapel at the cathedral of Moranda. The wooden door behind me is locked and bolted; through the crack between door and tiled floor seeps the faint sound of the cathedral choir chanting psalms.

Before me is a wall covered in a vast mural of the gods, its colors garishly bright. Eight candles sit burning on the floor, one at the feet of each god.

"Well?" I say aloud. "Are you going to teach me?"

Ruven sighs in my ear; I turn and see him sitting beside me, legs crossed.

"You're ready to learn sorcery before the eyes of all eight gods?" he asks.

"Only two of them are awake," I say. "And yes, I am ready."

"Then tell me," says Ruven, "when your nuns were training you to cut my throat, did they teach you anything about the Royal Gift?"

A strange ache lodges behind my ribs. Ruven's voice is calm, unruffled, yet I feel accused.

"Of course they did," I say. "They taught me the same catechism they'd teach anyone."

His eyebrows lift. "And what was that?"

I feel almost naked as I start to recite the familiar words, but then the comforting rhythm takes over, and I remember what it was like when the world was simple and good because I thought I could please the gods forever.

"Why is my heart sad? With longing for the gods. How may I see them? If I please one enough to claim my soul and bring it to the divine realm after I am dead. Can anyone see the gods in this life? Yes, those whom the gods have given the Royal Gift—marked by the golden eye—that lets them enter the divine realm and live."

My heart is still sad with longing. I belong to the gods even as I sin against them.

That thought gives me the courage to meet Ruven's gaze as I continue, no longer quoting the catechism but condensing a thousand lessons, "The gods love those who serve them, and we serve those whom the gods love. So the royal line began, and so it must continue."

"Well," says Ruven after a few moments of silence, "not *every* word of that was wrong."

But he's smiling as he says it, and I can't help smiling back at him. "Well, not every word of *that* was insulting. So tell me, what wisdom does a heretic sorcerer have to give?"

"Ah," says Ruven. "Well, this first: there's very little difference between miracles and sorcery."

He rolls the words between his lips as if he expects them to shock me, but they don't. The nuns told me long ago that sorcerers steal divine power by unholy means.

"You think of the gods as granting you their power," he goes on, "but it would be more accurate to say that they grant you the power of their homeland. There is a potency to the divine realm that can accomplish wonders in our world. The gods can grant power to members of the royal family because the pacts create a channel between their world and ours."

Now he sounds more like Reverend Coldren than the nuns, and my stomach twists with an awful, lurching uncertainty. I don't want Coldren to be right about anything.

I also don't want to trust Ruven about anything, but right now I don't have a choice.

"What's that got to do with sorcery?" I ask. "Because I'm sure the gods never willingly granted *you* anything."

"Of course not," says Ruven. "Sorcerers don't speak to the gods. They cross to the divine realm, carrying relics that they fill with the power of that world, and then they return."

"You went to the realm of the gods? *Before* I brought you there?"

Ruven grins, pointing at his golden eye. "Why did you think the monks chose me?"

"But—the shrines—"

"Were not always so well-guarded as the devout might have hoped five hundred years ago. That doesn't matter now. If you want to use sorcery, you must carve yourself a relic and take it into the divine realm. The next shrine will do nicely."

The next shrine belongs to Zumariel, the god of love and war. He's a kind and generous god, but he's no less holy than Nin-Anna, who judged and nearly destroyed me. I can't imagine slipping past his vigilance to steal power from his realm.

But I must if I want to live and see the Red Death ended.

If Ruven did it, you can too, I tell myself.

"How do I make a relic?" I ask.

"Oh, come now," he says. "Don't be willfully dense. What do you think I could possibly mean when I say 'relic'?"

It takes a moment for me to realize what he means, and then I recoil, surging to my feet. "You want me to *defile the body of a saint*?"

"Honestly," says Ruven, "I thought you were well-versed in your heathen theology. What other object in this world do you expect to hold the power of the gods?"

"You told me about relics two minutes ago, forgive me for not leaping immediately to the most blasphemous conclusion," I snap.

When I walked into this room, I was determined to commit this sin, but now horror and shame crawl over my body in hot-cold ripples. I remember the precious single bone in the convent chapel, and the skeletons hanging in the shrine of Ir-Atsakha, and I think nauseously, *I cannot do this.*

"What if I went to the divine realm and brought something back?" I ask desperately. "A pebble, or a flower, or—"

"Impossible," says Ruven. "Sorcerers have tried, though not for that reason, and none ever succeeded. Even if you did, it would remain an object of the divine realm only. It could not become a channel of that realm's power."

As the saints are, their bodies having been reshaped by the gods and used to work miracles. I can see the logic, even as it turns my stomach.

I'm just not sure I can do this.

Perhaps my scruples are foolish; I have already decided to commit the blasphemy that is sorcery. But I'd thought that sorcery would only be taking a power that should have been mine, had things not gone so terribly wrong. Plundering the bones of a saint—forcing that saint, even by proxy, to be a party to my sin—is unthinkable.

And yet I am thinking it.

I look down at my claws, at the charred skin endlessly crumbling off my hands. The sign of Mor-Iva's blessing turned into a reminder of how I failed.

How the gods failed you.

I try to ignore the treacherous thought. But it's hard not to feel betrayed, when Mor-Iva made the pact with me, when she promised me her miracles, then left me with nothing but—

These hands.

I look back up at Ruven, my heart quickening with hope. "What about me?" I ask. "I've been transformed by the power of the gods. Why couldn't *I* be the relic?"

"You mean, why can't you work miracles?" Ruven asks dryly. "I don't know, I never studied your theology that well."

"But . . . even if Mor-Iva won't talk to me, I'm still . . ." I flex my clawed fingers, almost relishing the sting as the charred skin cracks in new places.

Ruven shrugs. "I suppose it's possible that someone else might use your flesh for a relic. But it's against the nature of sorcery for you to use yourself that way. The relic must be something you *take*, in the same way that you take the power of the divine realm." He cocks his head. "Really, now. If you haven't got the stomach to steal the bones of a saint, how will you steal power from the gods? Did you think there was a holy way for you to sin?"

"No," I say miserably, "but I don't want . . . I can't . . ."

I don't know how to end that speech.

"I resisted it too, you know," says Ruven. "Damning myself to save my people. The Holy Father—you know him as the Heresiarch of the Magisterium—forbade sorcery a hundred years before I was born. When I read that encyclical, I wanted to give up." His eyes are dark, staring into nothing. "But I was persuaded to sacrifice even my soul. To be a *hero*," he says, spitting the final words.

The bitterness in his voice splits me open. Because in this way we are the same: we both angered the gods we loved because we thought it was our duty. And neither of us can stop loving what we have blasphemed against.

At least I don't have to hate the people who made me into a weapon.

I sink to my knees. Without thinking, I catch at his hands—they feel like a cold fog in my grasp, but I still cling to them.

"You aren't damned," I tell him. "You won't be. I'll get you a heretic burial, remember?"

His laugh is harsh and jagged. "My unburied body is not why I fear damnation. But yes, make me promises. You can't break them more than you did the promises in your eyes and hands when we met."

When we met.

152

When he tried to save me from a fate that I'm only now beginning to comprehend.

When I sat in his lap, caressed his face, and cut his throat.

"I'm sorry," I whisper. I touch his cheek as I did then, but now he has no breath that can stir against my wrist. "I'm sorry. I wish I hadn't . . . I wish I hadn't had to kill you."

Ruven turns to meet my gaze, a rueful resignation in the lines of his mouth. "You don't wish it," he says gently. "You're glad that you got to do one holy thing for your goddess before she rejected you."

I feel naked under his gaze, at once humiliated and understood. My breath shudders in my lungs.

"Yes," I say. "But I do regret hurting you. I regret killing you. I—" My voice cracks as our eyes meet, as I feel the ferocious gap between us. "Whatever my catechism says, I *regret*."

"Hmm." Ruven's cold phantom hands tighten on mine. "But are you going to learn? Enough to steal a relic?"

I have no answer.

For the next three days—perhaps my *last* three days—I have no idea what I'm going to do.

I go to the cathedral every day and stare up at the skeleton hanging from the ceiling of the sanctuary. It's a saint of Ithombriel; I know this because of the smooth, round hole in the center of the skull's forehead.

If I could somehow steal even one of those bones, I would have my relic. I could become a sorceress and save my life. But how? I can't exactly ask Araunn to kindly procure me a ladder so I can climb up and desecrate the holy relics.

And even if I did find a way to commit such a crime—could I? Even to save Runakhia from the Red Death, and myself from Varia's knife?

The worst part is that Ruven is kind to me about it. Oh, he still delights in heresy and mockery; he prods me to swallow my scruples and steal a relic. *Isn't Mor-Iva the goddess of judgment?* he asks. *Judge that a few bones of the saints belong in your hands, then.*

But he doesn't ever throw my weakness and apostasy in my face. Ever since that first morning in the meditation chapel, something between us has changed. I can't forget how it felt to touch his ghostly hands and tell him the truth: that I am sorry. Perhaps he can't forget how he confessed that he had sinned against his faith as much as I am now sinning against mine.

Whatever the reason, there's a new gentleness between us. We sit side by side, I ramble about what doctrine I learned from the nuns, he replies with tales of sorcery, and the question of what I'll do sits unspoken between us.

Ruven's kindness weighs on me like an iron cloak, burns me like glowing coals. Because what am I, if the worst of heretics is kind to me? Who am I, if I am grateful for his consideration? (If I sometimes, some mornings, look at the ghostly lines of his face and mouth and almost think I want—)

In the afternoons, Hézoraine takes me to shop after shop, watching me like a hawk the whole time. I try to enjoy the process, but while the first dressmaker was fearlessly calm, others . . . are not. The haberdasher trembles as she sets a new hat on my forehead; the shoemaker cannot stop staring at my hands even as he fits a shoe on my foot. The city's best glove-maker ruins three pairs of gloves trying to fit them over my hands, then goes away grumbling to himself.

154

I feel like I am those gloves: stretched, torn, completely unsuited to the task I have been given.

On the morning of the seventh day, I go to the meditation chapel. It's the last day of the week Varia gave me, and I have to make a choice, find a way—*something*.

I should at least try, one last time, to pray to Mor-Iva. But all I can bring myself to do is stare, weary and resentful, at her face in the mural.

Somebody knocks at the door and I start, my heart pounding with guilty alarm.

"Yes?" I call out nervously, looking back.

The door swings open to reveal Araunn on the threshold.

"Lia?" he says. "Are you . . ."

"I'm fine," I say instantly, scrambling to my feet and fixing a smile on my face. "Just meditating."

"Oh," says Araunn. "I'm sorry, I didn't mean to disturb you, I just—"

"You didn't," I say, and then quickly amend: "I mean, you *did*, I was deep in meditation on the beauty of Mor-Iva, but I'm happy to see you."

The words feel like ash and worms in my mouth. Ruven, still sitting beside me, rolls his eyes and heaves a derisive sigh.

Then he vanishes, and I am left with only Araunn, who smiles as he steps forward and puts his hands on my shoulders.

"Lia," he says. "You don't have to pretend with me."

My breath freezes in my throat. I'd thought that if anyone would see through my lies and get me killed, it would be Varia.

"I know you don't want to serve Mor-Iva," Araunn goes on. "Nobody ever has. Well. Nobody who was sane."

155

I hardly dare to breathe. Is he saying . . . does he only think . . .

"I know you wanted to serve Nin-Anna," says Araunn. "It's not fair that I have her pact instead, just because you saved us from Ruven. I'm sorry. I can't fix that. But . . ." He lets go of my shoulders and takes my hands instead. "I'd like to do what I can to make things easier for you. Please. Tell me what I can do?"

I stare into his eyes and wish that my heart were as kind and honest as his.

"Take me out of here," I say. "I just . . . need *one* hour where I'm not thinking about all this."

And that's how we end up in one of Moranda's parks, eating a picnic lunch of jellied duck and pastries, and drinking wine as we watch living ducks swim on the lake.

"You know," says Araunn, "of all the things we've seen on this Royal Progress, I think those ducks might be my favorite. Even more than the trains."

"Why?" I ask, honestly curious, because Araunn has babbled about the wonders of our modern trains almost every day.

"When I was a child," says Araunn, "we spent our summers at a country house. It had a duck pond, and I fed them every morning." He tosses a crust into the lake. Instantly two ducks lunge for it. "Everywhere we go, everything in Runakhia has changed. It's marvelous—the gas lamps, the sewer system, the trains—but it's also strange. Whatever I remember about the places we visit isn't so anymore. But the ducks? They're just the same."

His voice is soft and heavy. I straighten, turning to look at him, and I see the somber set of his mouth, the sorrow in his eyes.

Until this moment, I haven't really considered what it would be like to fall asleep one afternoon and wake five hundred years later. To lose an entire world in the blink of an eye.

I'm so ashamed that I have never tried to imagine what he's suffered.

"I'm sorry," I whisper.

Araunn turns to look at me, smiling softly. "At least I got to meet you."

And there's no answer I can give to that, except to lean forward and kiss him.

Again that strange thrill of touching, *taking*; again the awkwardness of lips and teeth and tongues jammed together in such a small space; again the slow, steady unfurling of desire. I can't be a princess, can't love Mor-Iva, but I *can* kiss Araunn. I can delight in him and hear his breath coming faster as he delights in me too.

Suddenly he draws back. He stares into my eyes, his golden hands cupping my face.

"You're beautiful," he says. "Don't ever doubt that. Even—"

He stops, biting his lip. The unspoken words hung between us: *Even with your hands.*

Even though you're a murderer, Ruven would say. But he isn't here.

I raise a hand to Araunn's cheek. He twitches slightly, but he doesn't draw back. He's willing to endure my monstrous holiness, and I am deeply, desperately grateful.

For a moment, it doesn't matter how much I am defiled, or how little Araunn knows the truth about me. He is willing to hold me in his golden hands. He is willing to bear my touch, he who has been touched by Nin-Anna.

He who has been *transformed* by Nin-Anna.

In one blazing instant, I understand. This is the answer. This is how I can get a relic without having to steal it.

I can become a sorcerer. I am going to live.

"Araunn," I say breathlessly, "would you give me a lock of hair?"

He draws back a little in surprise, dropping his hands from my face. "What?"

"To put in a locket," I say in a desperate rush. "It's a thing that girls do nowadays, when they—" My face heats.

"Oh, like a token," says Araunn. "Of course." He draws out his pocketknife and reaches for his hair.

Two hours later, I have purchased a heart-shaped golden locket at one of the finest jewelers in the city. That evening, alone in my bed, I grip the locket as it hangs around my neck. I grin into the darkness and say, "Now tell me how to use my relic."

There's a moment of silence. Then Ruven says from behind me, into my ear, "Very clever. You betray your prince instead of a saint."

"I'm not—" But I can't finish the protest. Because I *am* betraying him: Araunn would never want me to work sorcery.

But Araunn and Varia and the gods themselves have left me no choice.

"At least it was a gift," I tell him. "Teach me how to use it."

18

"WELL?" SAYS VARIA THE NEXT MORNING in the breakfast room. "Your week is up." Her voice is low, as if she fears being overheard, though she and Araunn are the only ones in the room with me right now. "Can you wield Mor-Iva's power?"

It's my last chance to confess the truth.

"No," I say, lifting my chin. "But I'm ready to go. Last night, Mor-Iva came to me in a dream. She said that I must speak to her in the divine realm. The easiest way to do that is at the next shrine."

My voice doesn't waver. I rehearsed the lie, word by word, for half of last night.

"That's wonderful," Araunn says warmly.

I don't dare meet his eyes. Varia I can deceive without any real guilt, but Araunn? He helped me. He trusted me. And I am betraying him.

"Good," says Varia. "We'll leave as soon as our clothes are delivered. At the next shrine I'll make my pact, and then you can enter to speak with your goddess."

I swallow dryly. "That sounds perfect."

Three days later, we arrive at the shrine of Nan-Darakh.

Like Ir-Atsakha, it is a shrine that gave its name to the thriving town around it. But while Ir-Atsakha is a town of tourists and traders, Nan-Darakh is home to the Royal University of Runakhia. When the Royal Progress rolls into the town, young faces throng the narrow streets as the best students of the country forsake their studies and lectures to see their new-yet-old rulers.

I stare out the window of the carriage, my stomach roiling with fear and hope at once. Today I will enter the realm of the gods for the second time. I will become a sorcerer or die in the attempt. I will risk everything to see our country filled with saints again, and I wish, I *wish* I could feel more noble about it.

"Not so different from our day, is it, Varia?" says Araunn.

Varia smiles at the crowd outside, but her words are acid. "Indeed, the students are just as eager for an excuse to ignore their classes."

At the doors of the shrine, we are greeted not only by a group of assembled clerics, but also by the most senior professors of the university, one of whom launches into a speech that seems like an attempt to demonstrate all the rhetorical devices he has ever studied at once.

Varia cuts him short. "Thank you for your wisdom," she says, smiling prettily enough to take the sting out of her words, "but my brother and I have travelled very far, across both miles and centuries, to reach this shrine. Would you kindly permit us to enter?"

"We will gladly hear all of you speak after. I'm sure the eloquence of the Royal University has only increased with age," Araunn adds, as smoothly as if he and Varia had planned the interruption.

And so we are led inside.

Nan-Darakh is the shrine of Zumariel. In the mosaics that glitter between the shrine's pillars, he is a slender young man with a pale face and golden curls, forever dancing, naked except for the thousand red ribbons swirling around his body. His saints, also depicted in the mosaics, are faithful spouses and shameless whores, honorable warriors and ruthless killers, for Zumariel is the god of every violent passion. The one thing that unites his saints are the red ribbons that grow from their bodies, and which they will eventually die vomiting. When we come to the sanctuary, it is hung with the skeletons of saints who have those same red ribbons—faded and stained—sprouting from their bones.

Fear shivers down my spine as I look up at the skeletons. Nin-Anna is the gentlest of the gods, but she didn't hesitate to strike me with the mark of judgment; if he realizes what I'm doing, Zumariel will be no kinder.

Can I trick my way past him, to walk undetected as I fill my relic with the power of the divine realm? It seems impossible, and yet it's my only hope.

The innermost shrine is once again a cave, but instead of a pool, there is an eternal fire. Varia strides into it without pausing; fifteen minutes later she stumbles out again, red ribbons growing from her scalp and neck and wrists.

Then it is my turn.

Help me, Nin-Anna, I pray to the goddess who now hates me, whom I have forsaken, and then I plunge into the flames.

The pain lasts for only a moment. Then there is darkness and a feeling like wind, and I am once more in the world of the gods.

This time, the divine realm is a desert. Cracked, parched earth stretches away from me, utterly flat all the way to the merciless horizon. Scorching sunlight pounds down upon me, a heat so intense it's like a physical weight.

Worse than the heat is the light. It doesn't make my eyes water, and yet there's an impossible *sharpness* to it and the shadows that it casts from every pebble and every crack. Beneath this brightness, it feels impossible for any secrets to exist.

And yet, so far, Zumariel has not found me.

The locket—my relic—is heavy around my neck. "Well?" I say aloud. "What now?"

Ruven's teeth gleam in a smile. "Take out your relic."

I seize the chain and pull it off my head. I snap open the locket, revealing Araunn's strand of hair—

Which glows with a pale, unearthly light, brilliant even in the scorching sunlight. I stare at it, speechless in wonder.

"It's drinking up the power of the divine realm," says Ruven. As he speaks, the glow fades from the hair in the locket. "And now it has taken all it can."

"That's all?" I ask, feeling a strange disappointment. Sorcery cannot possibly be this easy.

"That's all it can take *here*," says Ruven. "The deeper you walk into the divine realm, the more power will drain into the relic."

I examine the locket in my hand. Now it looks like any other trinket. "How will I know when it's full?"

Ruven sighs. "Here is your second lesson in being a sorcerer: there is no fixed limit to the power you cram into your relic. There is only what you risk and what you dare. What the gods allow, and what you survive."

He intones the words as if he's pronouncing my inevitable doom, but the posturing only makes me feel more confident.

"How far did *you* dare?" I ask, snapping the locket shut.

He laughs dryly. "Halfway up the mountain of Nin-Anna," he says. "Whose cruelty you know full well."

Gods and saints, halfway up the mountain. The thought of that sacrilege is staggering, but I shove it away. I can't feel angry at him, or I'll start to really think about what *I'm* doing, and—

"You seem to have come out with your hands intact," I retort as I turn away from him and stride forward into the desert.

"Well, I was a little less devout than you," says Ruven, falling into step beside me.

It's dizzying to walk into this featureless expanse of desert. I can feel myself walking, but when I look forward, I don't seem to be moving. Like the ground is sliding under me, and all my effort is only keeping me in place.

I stop, my stomach lurching, and look down at my relic. Now the whole locket is glowing with a soft, pearlescent light that reminds me of Araunn's smiles, his gentleness, and for a moment I am comforted—

Who comes into my kingdom?

The voice sears through the air, driving me down to my hands and knees. Shudders run through my body as my heartbeat pounds in my ears.

Then I manage to sit up. My eyes are blurred with tears, but I can still see quite clearly who has found me.

It's not Zumariel.

A tall woman stands before me. She wears swirling robes the same brown-black shade as her skin, while her tightly curled hair is bone-white, forming a halo around her head. Her golden eyes glow with a blinding light, her hands are wreathed in fire, and there's a swirling vortex of flame at the center of her chest. This is Im-Yara, the goddess of loyalty and devotion, who like Mor-Iva has no shrine.

And I am a traitor.

I feel dry and hollow, like a husk about to drift away on the wind. But I cannot give up now; before I've fully realized what I'm doing, I'm lying to a goddess.

"I am Lia Kurinava, of the royal house," I say. "I have a pact with Mor-Iva. I came here hoping to speak with her."

As soon as I say the words, a new fear clutches at me: what if she can summon Mor-Iva to judge me?

Why bring you a sorcerous relic into my kingdom?

There's a sudden directness to Im-Yara's burning gaze that was not there before. For a moment, there's nothing in my head but a white-hot blaze of fear.

"I—I didn't," I stammer. "I don't know what you're talking about."

I cringe at the whine in my voice. I sound like a child caught stealing sweets from the kitchen.

Are you faithful to your sorcery?

"I'm not—what?" I stare at Im-Yara in bafflement.

The gods don't offer second chances. She cannot possibly be asking if I want to repent of my sorcery.

Are you devoted? Are you loyal?

The goddess is suddenly closer to me, though I didn't see her move. Her burning hands cup the air just inches from my face; the sweat dries on my nose and forehead.

If you are faithful, you are holy.

Faithful to sorcery? It doesn't make sense. But I know that what is holy, the gods will accept.

"Yes," I gasp, miserably, desperately. "I'm faithful to my sorcery. I'm loyal, I'm devoted, I need it to serve the gods—"

Will you burn?

"What?"

You want sorcery to serve us, says Im-Yara. *Burn for me, and I will let you.*

"That is not a thing you want to dare," Ruven says quietly.

I flinch, expecting Im-Yara to turn her wrath upon him, but the goddess's burning gaze remains fixed on me only. It's as if, having chosen to speak with me, nothing else in the world exists for her.

"Whatever she's offering," Ruven goes on urgently, "it isn't love or mercy."

I know that. But if I refuse her, then she will surely judge me as harshly as Nin-Anna did.

"Yes," I say to Im-Yara. "I will."

Her mouth curves in a smile, and her hands cup my face.

The world is instantly fire and pain. I scream, and liquid fire pours down my throat to scorch my bones and eat me up from the inside out.

It feels like I'm being annihilated. But as moment after agonizing moment crawls on, I slowly realize that I'm not going to die. This isn't going to stop. I'm aware of my body now, and I'm not crumbling to ash, just shuddering in Im-Yara's implacable grip.

Suddenly the flames dim. The agony becomes a bearable pain, and I sob in relief.

Ruven is shouting something, but I can't concentrate on his words. It doesn't matter. I passed the test.

You may end this, says Im-Yara, stroking my cheek. *If you renounce me and your sorcery, the flames will cease.*

I whimper as the full horror crashes down on me. I'm not done yet. Im-Yara wants more agony of me, this time willingly and knowingly undertaken.

If I renounce her, she will probably kill me. That's not so frightening anymore. I think I might rather die than face that fire again.

But then I won't be able to end the plague.

I sat by, untouched, while Mama and Papa and Colan all died in agony. Surely I can bear a little pain for their sakes now.

"You *idiot martyr*," Ruven snarls, and somehow his anger gives me strength.

I manage to lift my head a fraction, to meet Im-Yara's fiery gaze. My voice is already nearly gone from screaming, but I manage to force the words out: "I . . . will burn."

The fire returns.

I can't stop myself from thrashing—the mindless, animal instinct to escape is too strong—but Im-Yara's grip is stronger. And it seems to be enough for the goddess that I made the choice, that I don't beg her to stop.

I think dizzily that I couldn't beg my way out now even if I wanted; I have no control over the wordless moans working their way out of my throat.

Then I stop thinking at all.

Awareness returns slowly. First I notice only that I'm no longer burning, and for a while I drift, content in that blissful lack of agony.

Bit by bit, more of the world returns to me. There's a miserable, exhausted ache all through my body. My eyes are wet with tears. I have the distinct feeling that I was just now whimpering, though I'm not making any noise at the moment.

And I'm lying in somebody's lap. A hand gently strokes my fore-head and my hair.

Im-Yara has accepted me, I think, dazed with sudden joy. At last, one of the gods has offered me kindness. With a sigh, I open my eyes—

And look straight up into Ruven's furious ones.

It's so utterly unexpected that for a moment I can't believe what I'm seeing. Even though now I'm remembering the coolness of the touch on my forehead, which could not have come from Im-Yara's burning hands—but it's unthinkable that Ruven of all people would want to cradle and comfort me—

"Finally done whimpering?" he asks flatly.

Well, that feels a bit more real. But my voice is still quavering as I say, "You . . ."

"I'm sorry, did you think your goddess would condescend to lift your twitching body off the ground?" He jerks his head to the side. "She's waiting. Sit up and say whatever holy words you must so we can take your relic and go."

"Are you really mocking the gods in their own kingdom?" I ask.

My voice isn't as hoarse as I'd expected, and the ache in my body is fading fast. I sit up; my vision swims for a moment, and Ruven puts a hand against my back, steadying me.

The hand braced against my spine feels so solid and *alive* that a shiver runs down my spine, and I feel a strange impulse to start crying again. I'd never thought I would feel his touch again, and for a moment it's almost as if I never cut his throat and have no blood on my hands.

But the black claws on my fingertips won't ever let me forget what I've done and what I've chosen. Nor will the locket, now hanging as heavy around my neck as if it were made of lead, wreathed in a corona of shifting light.

I lift my head and see Im-Yara standing before us, serene as before, her flames still endlessly dancing.

You are faithful to your thieving, says the goddess, *so I will allow you to live. Go with my blessing.*

She raises one hand, palm outward, and the divine realm fades away.

19

ONCE MORE, I'M FALLING THROUGH DARKNESS.

This time, when my feet touch the ground, I stumble forward into somebody's arms. Hands clasp my shoulders, steady me, and I lean against his shoulder thinking, *Ruven*—

But the next moment, I realize that the hands are a fraction too small to be his, the voice a shade too soft. My face is pressed not into dark robes, but the jacket of a finely tailored suit. It's Araunn who is holding me and saying my name.

I straighten and force myself to meet his eyes.

"I'm all right," I tell him.

But my voice sounds subtly strange in my ears. As Araunn leads me back up the stairs, I realize there's a new weight in my bones, a fullness pressing against my skin. My teeth ache and my scalp prickles.

Is this sorcery?

Then we emerge into the sanctuary, and I look around in amazement. The glittering mosaics of the shrine have faded—no, the whole *world* has changed, color leeched away as if I've passed from an oil painting to a delicate watercolor.

A watercolor painted over sketched lines.

The thought catches at my mind, and I feel a sudden conviction that there *are* lines in the world all around me, borders of being and probability that I could shift with only a touch.

Entranced, I raise a hand. The air shimmers, and barely visible lines of golden thread wind about my charred fingers—

A cold hand seizes mine.

"Don't," Ruven whispers in my ear.

The glowing lines vanish, and I feel a sudden, irrational burst of fury. How dare he rip me away from that beauty?

"You are tasting sorcery for the very first time," Ruven says quickly, softly. "There will be few times in your life when the power comes so easily and strongly, and believe me, a wave of your hand will topple this building unless you are very, *very* careful."

His quiet vehemence shocks the anger out of my head. My heart pounds with a mix of fear and wonder. I think, *I am a sorcerer. I have stolen the power of the gods and made it mine.*

And right now, I realize, everyone is staring at me. Varia's face is grim, her feet planted as if prepared to weather a storm; the prime minister's composure is unruffled, but his gaze is sharp. Behind them, Anabekha's brow is furrowed with worry, her hands clasped in prayer. Coldren stands protectively at her side.

In an instant, I realize what they all just saw: the new princess stumbling out of the inner shrine, raising her hand without explanation and then staring into nothing like a madwoman.

"Lia?" Araunn asks softly, unease in his voice.

He's wondering if I've been rejected and broken by the gods once again. Varia probably already believes I have been. In another moment, everyone else will too.

Unless I give them a sign.

Around me, the world still pulses with urgent power. No—my *relic* pulses, and its power flows through me as easily as blood through my veins.

Tell me how to work a miracle, I ask Ruven silently.

"Sorcery is not a miracle," he says.

Tell me how to fake *a miracle, you heretical pedant*, I snap. *I'm doing it with or without you.*

Ruven sighs loudly. "Well, if you must."

He presses his cold palm to the back of my hand, his arm running alongside mine, his chin nestled in my hair. A shiver runs down my spine. It's strange to feel him as a cold shadow, when he was so solid and alive in Im-Yara's realm.

"Feel it," he whispers. "The gaps between every strand of the world. The power that can fill those spaces, if you let it."

I gasp, because I do feel it. And I *see* it: the shimmering network that fills the mortal world, being after being held in glittering tension, and in the gaps between them—

Not power. But possibility, almost within my reach.

"Will you allow me," Ruven murmurs into my hair, "to help you?"

Yes, I answer with all my heart.

Ruven's fingers close, lacing between mine to grip my palm. His touch tingles and then it burns and then—

The chain around my neck is heavy. Through all the layers of my dress and corset, I feel the searing power hidden in the locket. Every nerve in my body flares as the golden, white-hot lines of the world suddenly flow through me, drawn in and spun out again by Ruven's sure, steady grip.

For one moment, it's like I have all the heat and power of the sun rolling under my skin. Then I'm cold and empty, hunching over as I gasp for breath. But Ruven's ghostly fingers are under my chin, urging my head up, and when I look, I see our handiwork.

All the bones of the saints hanging from the sanctuary's ceiling are now coated in glittering gold.

I force my spine straight and sweep my gaze about the room as I say, "Behold the power of Mor-Iva."

Then I realize there's something wrong. Anabekha is smiling, clearly delighted to see the power of any god. But Araunn looks strangely shocked, as if he'd never expected me to come back working miracles, as if it's *wrong*, while Varia's face has gone utterly blank.

Can they tell that was sorcery?

There's a rushing noise in my ears, and the ground rocks slightly under my feet. I swallow, suddenly nauseous.

At the same moment, Varia bursts into action. She turns to the cleric of Zumariel standing next to her—a kindly looking old man—and slaps her hand to his wrinkled forehead.

"Receive the sainthood of Zumariel," she says, and he staggers as red ribbons grow out of his white beard.

The professor standing closest to them recoils. "Your Holiness, what—"

Varia takes his hand. "Receive the sainthood of Zumariel," she declares, and ribbons surge from between his chubby fingers.

There are gasps and exclamations from all around us as people back away, leaving Varia at the center of a little circle. Araunn catches the arm of the newly sainted old man, steadying him and whispering in his ear. I alone am still, rooted to the floor in shock.

There was no reverence to the way Varia slapped sainthood into the two men. It feels almost *blasphemous* to fling about a holy gift so lightly—but Varia does nothing lightly. She would never risk offending the gods, I'm sure of it.

Unless she thought it absolutely necessary.

But why?

"As if the royal family ever needed an excuse," Ruven growls.

At the same moment, Reverend Coldren thrusts himself in front of Varia. "Your Holiness! You *cannot* keep sainting people without permission!"

Varia stares him down, her eyes like chips of ice. "Zumariel has waited five hundred years for saints," she says. "I could not deny him honor any longer."

She's breathing hard, nostril flaring, like she's just run a race. Or like she's afraid.

Then I notice the prime minister watching us with cool calculation, Hézoraine clasped to his side. And I know he is going to use this against us. He will talk to the papers and make it a scandal.

I chose to become a sorcerer so I could *stop* that from happening.

But I don't do anything. It's Araunn who steps forward, supporting the old cleric that Varia first sainted.

"Zumariel's honor is satisfied now," he says. "You can feel his joy, can't you?"

Then the old cleric says, "Your Holiness . . . *thank you*," and kisses Varia's hands.

And suddenly everyone is delighted, as if the old man has given them permission to stop being afraid. People crowd back around us; I see the newly sainted professor laughing and showing off his ribbons.

But the prime minister is still watching us carefully, and I know the danger isn't over.

The rest of the day goes by in a blur. There are speeches and ceremonies with the professors of the university, and then their choir sings solemn Vespers in the shrine. At the end of it all, there's a feast in one of the university dining halls.

I know what I'm doing. I smile and nod at all the right moments. But all I can think of is Varia's sudden, violent sainting of those two men, and the way people cringed away from her use of divine power.

It isn't right for people to dread sainthood, but it wasn't right for Varia to force them into it either. Why would she do that? Why didn't Araunn stop her?

Why did Zumariel allow her?

"Because your gods are monsters," Ruven growls as I pick at my dinner, "and sainthood is their favorite cruelty."

His anger is comfortingly familiar, a certainty to brace myself against.

Is that what you told yourself in the palace? I ask, and spear a pickled green bean, even though I feel no hunger. *Year after year, while people died with no saints to heal them?*

But there's another question weighing on me, one that's even more terrifying. That evening, when we have retired to our rooms and Jaríne has left me, I finally allow myself to think about it.

Im-Yara knew I was a sorcerer.

So why did she bless me?

It makes no sense. She is the goddess of devotion and faithfulness and single-minded choices. If I had been devoted to any other grim or terrible thing, I could accept her blessing.

But sorcery is not just a sin—it's blasphemy. It is spitting on the gods by stealing their power. How could any god forgive such a thing?

"Is that what's troubling you?" Ruven asks. "Your goddess's sanctity? I doubt she needs you to protect it."

"Im-Yara isn't my goddess," I mutter, pulling my knees up under my chin.

"As if that matters," he growls. "You worshipped her, and she tortured you like a child pulling legs off a spider. And you *don't care*?"

I flinch at the banked fury in his quiet voice. "Of course I care," I say, lifting my head to meet his gaze. "I've only ever wanted the gods to love me. But I can bear it if they hurt me. Even if they hate me. Only . . ."

What I can't accept is that Im-Yara didn't seem to think my blasphemy so very sinful.

Ruven laughs harshly. "What? You don't mind the gods torturing you, but you can't accept them forgiving you?"

"What's it to you?" I demand, surging to my feet in sudden fury. "I cut your throat. I worship the gods you hate. Shouldn't you be happy those gods also hurt me?"

Ruven flinches, and then the harsh line of his mouth wavers and drops open, like a wound.

"I should," he says quietly. "But I am not. You're too good for your gods, and when Im-Yara tortured you . . . I wanted to destroy her."

Heat rushes to my face. I can't meet his eyes. I want to crawl out of my skin to escape his reluctant concern, and yet it's sweeter to me than honey, knowing all that concern is just for *me*.

My claws bite into my palms. "Enough," I say. "It doesn't matter what you wanted. Just tell me how to use sorcery for *myself*, instead of letting a heretic sorcerer work it through me."

"Very well," says Ruven. "Take my hand."

I start to reach for him but pause. Earlier today, I was so desperate to touch the glimmering power of sorcery, I didn't care that Ruven was the one wielding it through me. I didn't think about how much I was trusting him, or what terrible things he might have used that sorcery to do.

Ruven laughs.

"Of course," he says. "If you were in my place, and I were in yours, not even death would make you stop trying. You would have slaughtered me along with all the royal family, razed that shrine to the ground, and likely found a way to kill the gods as well."

I grimace, unable to tell if he's mocking or praising me. "Death hasn't made *you* any less heretical either."

The laughter drains from Ruven's face.

"No," he says bleakly. "But five hundred years alone in the palace—that *life* was enough to break me of devotion. If you can call how I spent those years living."

And I see it again: the agonizing loneliness that I glimpsed when we first met, that made me pity him and nearly stay my hand.

"However much I hate your gods, I've no stomach left for martyrdom," says Ruven. "And I'm not sure I could wield your power again even if I tried. This morning you were just arrived from the realm of the gods, brimming with newborn power; you will never be so easy to use again."

He holds out his hand again, and the thought slices through me that as much as I'm trusting him, he is trusting me far more.

If I refuse to keep my promise and give him burial, he has no recourse. If I use my new power to persecute the heretics, he cannot stop me. Persuading Nin-Anna to reject me and using my sorcery this morning—those were both chances that he had one time only.

Gently I reach out for his hand, and his cold, ghostly fingers wrap around mine.

"The power of sorcery comes from your relic," says Ruven. "But the working of it comes from this: you have seen the realm of the gods. You know that things *can* be as they are not here."

A strange weight drags at my eyelids, and yet I feel the world sparking to life. I sigh, and Ruven's cold grasp burns against my skin, and I watch the golden threads of power blossom into being around me.

"There is an order to the world you cannot break," says Ruven, "for all that the gods may crack it. But what *may* be, in the natural order, you can summon and command."

"What was natural about the sleep you cast upon the royal palace?" I ask.

"Did you not hear the stories?" His voice grows sweet and singsong. "I came upon a summer's day, in the most drowsing hour of afternoon, when the sunlight is drugged honey, and every breath a lullaby."

As he speaks, I see it: that summer day, so long ago, and the sleepiness in every corner of the palace—dragging at the eyelids of the queen on her throne and the scullery boy peeling potatoes.

"A hot summer afternoon is already halfway out of time," says Ruven. "I took its nature and made it more. Made it truly timeless. That is the trick of sorcery, and its power: to make a thing more and more itself, until it becomes something else entirely."

A glowing net of power surrounds us. Ruven's eyes gleam at me, one gray and one gold.

I meet his gaze. "You loved the summer, didn't you?"

The confidence in his eyes falters. "That is hardly—"

"You couldn't speak of it as you do, unless you loved it dearly." A strange, sparking certainty and understanding has filled my mind, and I grin at him for the pure joy of it. "You couldn't command it as you did unless you loved it. That's the real trick of sorcery, isn't it? When you love a thing, you can change it."

I think of the herbs I grew in the convent garden, the sharp joy I felt at each new sprout. I spread my hands, brushing my fingertips against the golden threads of power, and I remember the damp, warm smell of newly planted earth.

Grow, I think, and curl my fingers into fists.

For a heartbeat, the room is silent and still. Then I see a green haze on the floor, and know it is seedlings. The next moment, the seedlings have grown into full plants, leaves opening, flowers blossoming.

Feverfew and basil, wormwood and comfrey—all the herbs I carefully tended as a novice are here, stretching their leaves defiantly toward the ceiling. They were all made through blasphemous, sorcerous power, yet when I look at them, I feel nothing but delight.

"Oh, very well done." Ruven looks from the seedlings to me. "You truly loved your convent garden, didn't you?"

The memory of my dream during the vigil rushes back: digging in the garden's soft, damp earth, and the ecstatic shock of warm hands wrapping around mine. To my absolute surprise, I open my mouth and say, "Once, I—"

Then I snap my mouth shut, face heating. For a moment, telling Ruven about my dream had felt absolutely natural; now all I can think is how he would mock me for it.

"I felt closest to Nin-Anna there," I say instead. "And it made me feel . . . powerful, to imagine all the people I could someday save with those herbs."

"And instead you were made into a weapon," Ruven muses, then meets my eyes. "I'm sorry, truly. Your nuns should have let you be a healer."

Indignation sparks along my spine—I don't want his pity. "Herbs can kill in the correct doses," I inform him. "I really wanted to kill you, as well."

He laughs—a sudden, unguarded sound, more beautiful for being awkward. "Perhaps you were worthy to defeat me."

Our faces are only a handspan apart. His lips are open in a smile, and my mouth opens too as I lean toward him—it feels like there is a weight between my shoulders and at the base of my spine, pushing me toward him—

The door slams open.

"We must talk," says Varia, each word ice.

I cringe back against the wall, and for a moment I almost start to babble excuses. But then I remember that Varia can't see Ruven, that she cannot possibly know about my sorcery. So I manage to say, in a level voice, "About what?"

Varia doesn't respond. She's staring at the carpet of herbs growing on the floor.

"Mor-Iva is teaching me to work more kinds of miracles," I say, hating myself for the lie.

Varia looks up, her mouth a grim line. "Perhaps too many."

"I can remove them before we leave," I protest.

Varia shakes her head, gesturing at the floor. "I don't mean *that*." Her nose wrinkles. "Do you not know?"

I stare at her in bafflement.

"The shrine," Varia says slowly, as if speaking to a dim-witted child. "Your miracle. Didn't you feel it? The moment when the ground trembled as Zumariel's wrath awakened?"

Horror rises in me like a slow, freezing tide. "I thought . . . I was just feeling faint."

"Gods and saints." Varia heaves a sigh. "You really *are* that ignorant nowadays."

I bristle automatically. "The nuns—"

Varia waves a hand. "Loved the gods dearly, I doubt it not. But they clearly didn't know the truth of holiness, which is this: we are aliens and abominations to the gods' eyes."

There's was a strange, hollow feeling in my chest. Childishly, I want to plug my ears.

"The Royal Gift is to walk into the divine realm and meet the gods," says Varia. "But the gods hate what they do not recognize. When the royal house awakens them to look on this world, they judge it. Only the presence of saints who conform to their power persuades them not to destroy it."

"But . . ." I can't finish the objection. I don't even know what I was going to say. It can't be true—the gods *love* Runakhia—and yet there is no deception in Varia's face or voice.

"You did something holy to Mor-Iva," Varia goes on. "But what does not belong to Zumariel is an abomination to him. And you did it in *his shrine*. If I hadn't sainted those two men, his wrath would have been kindled against the whole city. Thousands might have died."

I can't speak. My mouth and throat are suddenly dry as I stare at

Varia, as I remember Ruven curving his fingers around mine and using a power far worse than the wrong god's miracle.

I'd thought I was only risking my own soul. Instead I nearly destroyed us all. And those two men, sainted against their wills—I'd thought it was Varia's sin, her callous misuse of divine blessings. But it was all mine.

I know what I should do now: confess to Varia and accept punishment. Remove the danger of my blasphemy from this world.

And yet.

Im-Yara did accept my faithfulness.

Waking the gods and returning the saints to Runakhia is too important. I can't let anything disrupt the Royal Progress, not even the punishment I deserve. I can't give Parliament any excuse to turn against the royal family. Not when I know that the gods can be appeased as they were today.

Gods forgive me—though they should *not* forgive me—I am going to keep using sorcery.

"I'm sorry," I say finally, breathlessly.

Varia raises her eyebrows.

"I cut a man's throat for love of the gods, of *course* I'm sorry to offend them," I snap, then draw a slow breath as I fight for control of myself. "The nuns never taught me this. There's so much we have lost. But I will try."

Varia snorts. "You must do more than *try*." But then she seems to take a second look. "Truly?"

"Truly," I say, and I mean it, for all my sins and secrets. "Please. Teach me how to please the gods."

20

ONCE I'M A SORCERER, EVERYTHING CHANGES.

Now that I'm working "miracles," Anabekha and Coldren look at me with new reverence, the prime minister with a new respect. Araunn smiles at me more easily, more gladly—only now do I see how worried he has been—while Varia remains as prickly as ever.

But she also teaches me.

To please the gods, you must reflect the gods.

There's no secret ceremony. No easy way out. This is what Varia explains to me as the Royal Progress travels through the next three towns. Humans can love and forgive, but the gods can only *know*. And their knowledge is of two kinds only: *this is mine*, and *this is not*.

To put it more devoutly: the gods are holy and beautiful, and they love what is in accordance with their own particular holiness and beauty. Whatever is not—even if it is sacred to another god—they hate.

And so I am hateful to all the gods. Even if I had never learned sorcery, every part of me would still be hateful to them, except for whatever corner of my heart belonged to Mor-Iva. And that corner would be hateful to every god but Mor-Iva herself.

I want so badly to believe that Varia is lying. I grew up praying every night to all eight gods, and the thought that each of them hated seven of those prayers sends a dreadful, hollow pang through my stomach.

But when I remember Nin-Anna's rejection and Im-Yara's strange acceptance, I cannot doubt Varia's teachings.

"A strange sort of judgment," Ruven observes to me one night as I sit up in my bed practicing sorcery. "To condemn you not for your sins, but for the wrong perfection."

"Your god would do the same," I retort, twisting my hand. The glowing tendrils of power in the room shiver and curve in response. "Even though I'm the perfect apostate."

"You are the *worst* apostate I've ever seen," Ruven says wryly. "You know your gods are monstrous and you've turned against them, but still you can't stop loving them."

"Because they're holy," I tell him wearily, wishing the words didn't feel so hollow in my mouth. "It's not my fault you call holiness monstrosity."

"Eight different kinds of holiness that all hate each other," says Ruven. "That's why the Magisterium says there is only one god. Because there is only one goodness."

Those last words have a strangely rehearsed tone, like when I recited words from my childhood catechism.

"Is that what the monks taught you?" I ask, and then can't resist adding, "When they were promising you'd be a hero?"

Ruven's face goes very still. When he speaks again, his voice is cold and quiet.

"Let me tell you what *your gods* taught me when I was only a child. I was orphaned too young to know my parents, so the closest I ever had to a father was a monk named Brother Yaren. He worked in the infirmary, and he was kinder than anyone else in the monastery. For this, Nin-Anna forced her sainthood upon him. He never worshipped her, never used the power that she gave him—and yet he died of it. He burned with fever for three months, until he had withered to skin and bones, and then Nin-Anna was finally kind enough to let him die." Ruven draws a shuddering breath. "I was ten years old. The day we buried him, I swore I would break the grip of your gods upon this country if it killed me."

All my life, I've heard stories about people who tried to keep the saints from following the gods. I've always despised them, even the ones who claimed they were acting out of love. Keeping someone from the gods is the worst kind of cruelty. But now, as I look at Ruven, all I can feel is pity.

It's clear enough what happened: Brother Yaren *had* loved Nin-Anna, must have prayed to her in secret, and was chosen for sainthood in return. But he'd been too afraid of the other monks to reveal his devotion, so he had died silent.

And Ruven, bereaved the same way I was, swore the same kind of vengeance I did.

"Spare me your pity," Ruven snaps. "Your delusions too. I knew Brother Yaren and you did not. And I regret *nothing* of the harm I did to your gods. I would do it all again if I could."

But he can't, because I killed him.

I feel a sudden, wretched wave of regret. Not that I broke his spell upon the palace, nor that I killed him, but that now he can't be saved. He'll never renounce the lies the monks taught him, and he'll never have a chance to live in freedom. I can give him a heretic burial, and maybe that will even lay his ghost to rest. But I can never teach him to love the gods.

Ruven growls low in his throat and then vanishes. I don't see him again until the next evening. And by then everything has changed.

Because Varia has taught me the second half of my duty.

"You must start making saints of Mor-Iva," she tells me once Jaríne has left us alone together. "As soon as possible."

Fear lurches inside me, because that's the one miracle that sorcery can't allow me to fake.

"But," I say nervously, "nobody wants to be a saint of Mor-Iva—don't you remember when I offered at Ir-Atsakha?"

"Then you will have to saint them anyway," says Varia. "As I did at Zumariel's shrine."

"But that was *wrong*," I say before I can stop myself.

Varia raises her eyebrows. I flounder for a moment, and then find the courage to go on. "I know you had to, because of what I did. But . . . when there isn't such necessity . . . isn't it wrong to pour divine power into a heart that despises it?"

And it would make Ruven's horrible story about sainthood almost *true*.

"Whatever makes you think it's not still necessary?" Varia asks, sounding almost amused.

"Because I'm not working miracles in Zumariel's shrine anymore," I say.

Varia laughs. "And just what do you think we're doing on this Royal Progress?"

"Awakening the gods," I say. "Drawing their gaze back to our world, so they will inhabit their shrines again."

Varia nods sharply. "And what do you suppose they see, when they look at our world?"

And in one horrible, heartbreaking instant, I understand.

"They see us," I whisper.

I remember a phrase from the catechism I was taught by the nuns: *it is the essence of divinity to disdain mortality.* The words had always seemed like a promise that Nin-Anna hated the deaths of my family as much as I did—but now they suddenly have a darker meaning.

Varia nods. "In our day, the gods made their own saints, and were well pleased with Runakhia. We hardly had to help. But now, when they're still only half awake, newly aware of this world . . . we must make saints as fast as we wake them."

"But . . ." I try to find a way out of her logic. "But I can only make saints for Mor-Iva. Won't the other gods hate her saints as much as they hate mere mortals?"

"If you made them in their shrines, yes," says Varia. "But in the wider world . . . they are still touched by divinity. They will help to pacify the other gods until they start making saints of their own." She steps forward and grips my chin, forcing me to meet her eyes. "You were allowed to live for the purpose of hallowing Runakhia. You cannot fail."

I am going to fail, I think to myself that night as I lie miserably curled under the blankets. *Gods and saints, I am going to be the destruction of Runakhia.*

And if, somehow, I do find a way to create saints . . . I will have to take them unwillingly. It will be like I am making the gods into monsters, the same kind of monsters that Ruven thinks they already are.

The bed doesn't shift as Ruven sits beside me, but I still feel his presence. I squeeze my eyes shut, not wanting to see his expression. I wait for him to say something—mocking, triumphant, pitying, no matter what, I don't think I can bear it.

But he's silent. After a moment, he lays a hand on my head; I feel the chill of his touch sinking through my hair.

And that gentleness undoes me. I finally start sobbing, hot tears sliding down my face and into the pillow.

"It's all my fault," I whisper. "I'm going to destroy us, and—and the gods have *always* hated me."

That should not be what hurts the most, but it is.

"I don't believe that," says Ruven. His fingertip traces the edge of my cheek, and though his touch is nothing but a cold current in the air, it sends a flicker of warmth through me. "Weren't you always monstrous enough to cut my throat?"

I choke on a laugh.

"And you couldn't have used sorcery to make those herbs unless some part of you was like to Nin-Anna."

"Not enough of me for her to accept," I say with familiar bitterness.

"Well, then I suppose we're back to how lucky you are that you're also bloody enough for Mor-Iva."

I sit up suddenly, turning to face him. "Why are you being kind to me?"

He shrugs, for once not quite meeting my eyes. "You've left me with nothing else to do."

"You hardly seemed busy before," I say.

I remember the terrible loneliness I glimpsed in him the first time we met, and suddenly I realize how little has changed for him. He can see the world outside the palace, but he cannot touch it. He can do nothing but follow me wherever I go.

Nobody can see him but me. He can speak to no one but me.

I'm his prison and prison-keeper alike, and perhaps I should feel guilty, but I am only deeply, desperately grateful. Because he could have kept trying to torment me, but instead he is kind to me. And because I'm not alone anymore.

I can tell nobody about my sorcery, my fears and my doubts and my hate, except for him. I can trust nobody else, not even the gods.

So nobody knows me but him.

I touch his hand; my fingers sink into the phantoms of his.

"If you're that bored," I say quietly, "will you stay with me? To-night?"

He snorts. "It's impossible for me to leave you."

"When you disappear, though . . . I know you're not *gone*, but it's not the same for you, is it?"

He shakes his head. "No. I can feel your presence, but all I see is darkness."

"Then stay," I tell him. "Here. Tonight." Heat prickles across my face, because I know how the words sound, but it's not the same as asking a living man to spend the night with me.

And I don't want him to be alone.

This night, I don't know if *I* can bear being alone.

Ruven raises his eyebrows. "Are you asking a heretic to share your bed?"

I can feel the blush flaming across my face, but I glare at him and say flatly, "You are already sitting in my bed and looking at my nightgown. I think propriety is far behind us."

He laughs softly. "Then lie down, my virtuous apostate."

I do. I feel him settle at my back, his face in my hair, his hand on my waist. At first his presence is cold, and I shiver under the blankets. But then it changes, or perhaps I grow used to it—there's no more chill, only a soft, bodiless pressure, like a breath upon my back. Only the knowledge that the one person who truly knows me is tucked into bed beside me.

I should be ashamed, with even the ghost of a man in my bed. I should be afraid, with a heretic sorcerer at my back. I should feel *anything* but safe and comforted—

And yet I fall asleep more easily and sweetly than I have in weeks.

21

WHEN I WAKE THE NEXT MORNING, Ruven is gone. Sunlight streams through the window, and my tears are long dried. I can almost imagine last night was only a dream. It's hard to believe that I ever turned to him for comfort, that I begged him to spend the night beside me as if—as if—

With a groan, I cover my face in my hands. I don't know how I'll ever look him in the eye again.

It's normal for Ruven to avoid me while I'm dressing, but when I'm halfway through breakfast and still haven't seen him, I start to hope that maybe he's just as embarrassed as I am. Maybe he won't laugh at me for my weakness.

Maybe we can both pretend last night never happened.

Halfway through the day's ride, Ruven still hasn't returned. I try not to stare at the empty seat where he likes to appear, but my eyes are continually dragged back to it, as if by looking I can make him appear. As if by wishing, I can know what he's thinking right now.

Then I remember that he can hear what I'm thinking right now, and my face goes hot. Hiding from me today is perhaps the kindest thing that Ruven's ever done for me.

It's nearly two o'clock by the time we arrive in Morvenn, the town where we are supposed to have lunch. All of us are hungry; there's a strained edge to even Araunn's smile. But what we find when we arrive makes us forget food.

The welcoming committee is much smaller than any we've seen before: just the mayor flanked by two old men and a gray-robed nun of Nin-Anna. Instead of welcoming us at the center of the town, they stand waiting outside the gates.

On the wall above them hangs a red plague flag.

Dread roils through my stomach. After all that we have done—all that I have sinned—the plague is still here. There still aren't enough saints. People are still dying just like my family did.

The prime minister looks grim as the carriage rolls to a halt. He's out the door the moment it's stopped, not even waiting for the footmen.

"How many infected?" he calls out, his voice pitched to carry.

"A dozen households," says the mayor. "We think—we hope we have it contained now. But it's been only two days since the last quarantine started. We can host you if you wish, but we cannot advise it."

Contained. Such a quiet, bloodless way to describe a dozen families walled up in their houses to die. I shudder as I remember the grim sound of the nails pounding into my family's door.

Then I realize that Varia is scrambling out of the carriage. "Varia, wait!" Araunn calls, but she ignores him as she strides past the prime minister, right up to the nun standing beside the mayor of the town.

Araunn follows her out of the carriage, and after a moment of stunned hesitation, so do I.

"Take us to the sick," says Varia. "Immediately."

The nun looks shocked. "Your Majesty, I'm not sure you understand—"

"This is the Red Death, isn't it?" says Varia. "Of course I understand. We had it in our day as well. And as the royal family, it is our duty to heal it."

"But you don't have a pact with Nin-Anna," I say blankly.

"And you're still ignorant," says Varia. "This is the one illness that anyone who's made a pact with the gods can heal."

"What?" I stare at her, utterly baffled. "*Why?*"

Varia grimaces. "It is a privilege of the royal family," she says stiffly.

"Regardless of whether you can heal it or not," the prime minister cuts in, "I cannot allow you to risk yourself in such a way."

"It's our duty," Araunn says earnestly.

"It's not a risk," says Varia. "Nobody with the royal gift can get the Red Death. I've accompanied my mother a dozen times as she went to lay hands on the sick, and I've never taken ill."

Her words seize me by the throat. For a moment I can barely breathe; I can taste again the awful stench of sickness and blood, feel the weight of my little brother's body in my arms.

I remember waiting to die.

I remember wondering why I wasn't sick yet.

"What?" I whisper.

"If you won't take us," Varia says impatiently, "we'll find them."

Without waiting another moment, she strides through the gate. The prime minister and the town's mayor look at each other, and I see them both realizing there is nothing they can do to stop Varia without bodily hauling her back and facing the consequences of assault on her person.

"You heard the princess," the prime minister says to the mayor with dry resignation. "Go on, obey her holy commands."

The next few minutes are a bustling chaos as the townsfolk rush to assemble workmen to break down the nailed-shut doors of quarantined houses. Varia takes me aside and quickly teaches me the exorcism prayer. It's a short, simple thing; after I've repeated it back to her four times, she nods in approval.

"You'll do," she says. "This isn't like working any other miracle. It's not hard at all."

"Why not?" I demand. "What is the Red Death, really? Why do you say it doesn't touch the royal family?"

"Because it doesn't." Varia arches an eyebrow. "Feeling a little nervous?"

For once, I'm not afraid of her sharp words and sharper smiles. I meet her gaze and say evenly, "My family died of the Red Death. I sat with their bodies for the whole quarantine, waiting to sicken as well, but I never did. I want to know why."

Varia grimaces. "It's not a pretty tale," she says. "But you're one of us now, so you have a right to know—more than the rest of us, even. Because it started with the last member of the royal family to make a pact with Mor-Iva."

She tilts her head, as if waiting for a reaction. When I say nothing, she goes on, "It was seventy years before my time. Perhaps my mother heard the whole story, but all I know is this: Princess Yarekha made a pact with Mor-Iva, and in the process lost her mind. She started to judge unworthy all who were not royal and cursed them with a strange new sickness. The royal family put her down, but her curse remains. We can lay hands on the afflicted and exorcise them individually of Yarekha's judgment, but we cannot purge the curse from Runakhia."

I stare at Varia, dizzy with horror. "I'm surprised you let me live after my pact," I say finally.

"Lucky for you," says Varia, "right now we aren't in a position to be picky. Besides, you seem to bear Mor-Iva's power well enough."

Because I don't use it. Because I'm a failure at making a pact with a goddess.

Because I won't be able to heal anyone of the Red Death.

The thought knifes through me, and I want to cry. I learned sorcery so I could stay alive and help *end* the Red Death. But that sin means I will never be able to heal it.

"But if you breathe a word about Yarekha to anyone else," Varia continues, "I'll kill you with my own two hands."

"Of course," I say numbly.

"Your Holiness," calls out the mayor, approaching us. "We're ready."

He stops a good three paces away; in his mind, we're already infected, and I can't find it in me to blame him.

Varia nods sharply. "Good," she says. "Lead us."

They've opened three houses, one for each of us.

I walk through the doorway of mine and into a nightmare.

The stench makes me gag: blood and vomit and human waste, and beneath it all a strange, sweet rottenness that I never smelled in the convent infirmary, no matter what disease our patients had.

It's the smell of my family dying.

I look around, my eyes slowly adjusting to the dim light. The downstairs room of the house is a mess: a pot abandoned on the cast-iron stove, chairs knocked over, and—my heart shudders in my chest—a lump in the darkest corner that might be a person.

I should go to him or her and check for a pulse. But my feet won't move. I feel the same way I did in the middle of Ruven's briar: lost and helpless in an endless, shifting maze of dark horror.

Beside me, Ruven snorts. "Helpless," he says. "You were never *that*. Don't you remember how that night ended?"

I turn to him, my bones melting in relief. "But all I had to face was you," I say, breaking into a smile.

I know him. I know this dance between us, the push and pull of mockery that is almost kindness. And with him here, now I have something to steady myself against. Now it feels like courage is possible.

I take one step forward, then another. Then I run to the person—a boy, ten or maybe twelve years old—and feel at his throat.

The instant I touch his cold flesh, I know he's dead.

"May Nin-Anna bless you and gather your soul into her kingdom," I whisper—the same prayer we always said in the convent infirmary when somebody died in our care.

I remember the weight of my little brother in my arms, and how it felt when *he* turned cold. For a moment I let the tears sting my eyes and tighten my throat. I let myself feel again that infinite, lonely grief.

Then I stand up. Ruven is staring at me, his eyes dark and wide. "You had a younger brother?"

"I thought you knew all my secrets already," I say, making my way to the stairs.

"You hardly ever think of him," says Ruven.

"He died in my arms, weeping blood and choking as his own throat melted," I say flatly. "I missed him—I missed all my family—so much I thought I would die."

So I put all the memories, good and bad, behind a glass pane in my heart. I knew they were there, but I never took them out. As much as I could, I thought only of serving Nin-Anna and killing Ruven.

"I see that I've been a comfort to you all your life," says Ruven.

I laugh shakily. "Truly, your haunting me has not been that much of a change," I say, and start dragging myself up the dark, narrow stairs. If there are any people left alive in this house, I have to find them

"Hello?" I call out when I reach the top. "Is anyone there?"

From behind the door to my left, I think I hear a faint moan. In a sudden frenzy, I wrench the door open and spring into the room—then stagger to a halt.

The walls are coated with blood, and blood also pools on the floor inches deep, warm and wet around my ankles. The scent is overpowering, like in the moment that I killed Ruven, and I stare and stare, unable to move or think.

In the center of the room is a bed. The woman lying on it, her red hair tangled across the soiled pillows, is motionless and waxy pale—I'm sure she must be dead. But the two children nestled beside her are twitching and moaning, one flushed with fever, the other frighteningly pale.

I shudder, and then all at once the blood is gone. The sheets of the bed are still filthy, crusty in some spots and slick in others, but the walls are clean. My ankles are dry.

I can still smell it.

"What a curse," says Ruven with bleak admiration. "This place is so filthy with divine power, it's practically a shrine."

His words are blasphemous, but I can't disagree. This curse is the royal gift horribly misused; it's the one holy thing I won't hesitate to destroy.

Slowly, carefully, I sit down on the bed and put my hand on the forehead of the nearest child, a little girl with flaxen hair.

I take a deep breath. I am a sorcerer, an apostate. And yet I still belong to the royal house. I made a pact with Mor-Iva, and even if I did not succeed, at least I survived it better than Yarekha did.

I can do this.

The exorcism that Varia taught me was simple enough: a chant of four notes, bidding the Red Death to depart in the name of whatever god the one chanting it serves.

But don't expect it to be easy, she had warned me. *Most of us need to chant it nearly half an hour before the curse submits.*

I draw a breath. "O—" I begin, but my voice cracks on the note.

Did I just hear a whisper in response?

The skin on my back prickles as I try again. "O Nin-Anna, I bid this illness—"

The song crumples in my throat. That's the wrong goddess, I had meant to say *Mor-Iva*, I must say—

"O Nin-Anna—"

With a gasp, I bite my lip. *What is happening to me?* I wonder desperately.

Nin-Anna, the blood whispers, running down the walls again. *Nin-Anna.*

The floor is awash again—no, the bed is afloat, bobbing up and down on an infinite sea of blood beneath a coal-black sky. The walls of the room are gone, the whole world is gone, and there's nothing left but blood.

Did my family see this as they died?

A thin mist swirls over the surface of the blood and hisses, *You love Nin-Anna.*

"Yes," I say, my voice shaking. "I do. In her name, I bid you—"

You loved her you loved her loved her you you you loved you

KILLED

And I am back in that moment, Ruven's throat parting under my blade, his blood pouring into my lap. I am back in Nin-Anna's realm, rejected by my beloved goddess with the mark of judgment blossoming across my skin. I am back in my family's house, sitting with my back against the nailed-up door, wondering why I haven't died and knowing that *I should have.*

I should be dead. I should die right now.

Understanding rolls through my body, warm and soft like the thrill of wine. I lean down and dip cupped hands into the ocean of blood. I will drink and I will die and then everything will be all right.

Fingers seize my wrists and wrench them apart. The blood I had scooped up spills from my parted hands.

"You really are a pious idiot," Ruven says, his voice low and ferocious. Our eyes meet, and I realize with stunned amazement, *He wants me to live.*

Then Ruven lets go of me and straightens, his eyes raking the dark, bloody realm around us. "I'm a heretic sorcerer," he calls out, fire in his voice. "I hate the gods and would kill them if I could. By what right does a servant of Mor-Iva try to avenge my death?"

Guilty, the mist and the blood whisper from all around us. *Guilty, guilty, guilty.*

But it's not just the mist and the blood—the remnants of Yarekha's power—that are whispering. In a sudden rush, I understand why the royal family has never broken the curse: because Yarekha herself remains, caught in the prison of her power as Ruven was in his. Every time somebody sickens of the Red Death, she is there, helplessly judging over and over.

I square my shoulders and call out, "Yes, I am guilty. So are you. By the guilt we share, *show yourself.*"

And Yarekha appears.

She's my age, but prettier, plumper. A girl who tasted all the fine things of the world and knew no misery until she met the gods. Now bloody furrows run down her face, and her dark eyes weep blood.

Her hands are charred and clawed like mine.

"You are guilty." She says the words like a prayer. "You brought bloody hands into Nin-Anna's kingdom. You turned from Mor-Iva to sorcery. You betrayed the gods, so now you must die."

Every word she says is true. And yet as I stare at Yarekha, hatred and disgust ring through my body like the clanging of a bell. However right she may be about me, Yarekha is the reason my family died. She was meant to protect Runakhia, but instead she became the gangrenous rot at the heart of our kingdom, poisoning our people for year after year.

I want to tell her that *she* is guilty and cursed and wrong. I want to see her break beneath the weight of what she's done. I want to summon sorcerous fire and burn her out of this world.

But then Yarekha draws a ragged breath. "I cannot stop until everyone guilty is dead," she says, and now her voice is small and wretched. "Then Mor-Iva will love me. Then I will finally love her."

And against my will, my heart breaks for her. Because she is just like me: yearning for the gods to love her, wishing she could love the goddess who chose her.

Mor-Iva is the goddess who judges guilt, while Nin-Anna is the goddess who grants healing. A strange thought slides into my head: *Perhaps I have a place between the two of them.*

I reach forward and—shuddering, but not hesitating—take Yarekha's monstrous hands in my own.

"You are a murderer," I tell her. This is true.

"You are dead," I continue. Also true.

"Your name is Yarekha and I command you to be free," I say, and the blood on Yarekha's face fades away as she smiles. Then she sighs and disappears—and with her vanishes the ocean of blood, and every last trace of her power.

22

AT FIRST I DON'T REALIZE WHAT I've done. All I feel is a quivering relief that makes every bone of my body heavier and lighter at the same time. All I know is that Yarekha finally has peace.

Then I hear a tiny, quavering voice say, "Mama?"

I look down and see the two children sitting up. Their color is normal, and their eyes are clear, and they're both staring in horror at the dead body of their mother.

"Come with me," I say quickly, reaching for the nearest one's wrist. She cringes away, and I realize how I must look: a clawed monster standing over their mother's body.

"It's all right," I say. "I serve Mor-Iva, but I'm only here to kill the Red Death. Not you." I take a step back, hoping it will make them feel safe. "You're not sick anymore, so you can leave this house. Come with me. Please?"

After a moment, the older of the two girls nods and grasps her sister's wrist. "Will we see the prince and princess?" she asks.

"Yes," I say. "They're waiting for you. Just come with me."

The two little girls stumble out of the house after me. What we find outside is chaos: people rushing about, shouting and crying—

Araunn and Varia are both outside as well, surrounded by a cluster of thin people in rumpled, bloodstained clothing.

The people they had gone to visit, I realize. All of them healed.

Varia sees me from across the town square and instantly bears down on me, her stride ferocious.

"Was this your doing?" she demands as soon as she's close enough to be heard without raising her voice.

"Why do you think that?" I ask, tensing for an accusation.

"Well, I know my brother and I didn't try anything new," Varia says impatiently. "So if anyone found a way to heal the whole town at once, it must have been you."

She isn't angry. The sharpness in her voice, the glint in her eye— Varia is *eager*. She knows what this could mean for Runakhia.

Araunn has caught up with Varia now and stands at her shoulder. "Lia?" he breathes.

"I saw Yarekha," I say slowly. "I told her to rest. I *judged* her."

"And because you belong to Mor-Iva, she obeyed," says Varia. "Oh, very clever."

It hadn't felt like I was using the power of my relic. It hadn't felt like I was working a miracle either.

"And the Red Death went away with Yarekha," says Araunn, his eyes wide with wonder. Then next moment he's caught me in an embrace and kissed my cheek. "Oh, Lia. You're a hero."

Then why don't I feel like one?

I stare over his shoulder at the chaotic town square. People are breaking down the doors of the quarantined houses, eager to drag out survivors.

This was my dream: the power of the Red Death broken, quarantine doors thrown open and people staggering out of the houses where they had thought they would die, dazed by sunlight and fresh air and sudden hope.

It's too much and too sudden, I tell myself. The joy will come later, when I've had enough time to feel what I've done. When Yarekha's soft, desolate voice has stopped ringing through my head.

I pull back a little, so I can meet Araunn's eyes and return his smile.

"I can't believe it's really over," I say.

The celebration lasts well into the night. The decorations are hastily thrown together, as is the food, but the joy of the people is passionately real. They have lived all their lives in fear of the Red Death—they had given up family and friends as already good as dead—and now against all hope, the sick are cured and they are free.

I did this. The thought echoes through my head, over and over, as I eat roast lamb with mint jelly and pastries stuffed with cream, as I drink sparkling wine. It's starting to feel real now. *I did this. No one else could have done this.*

It's still ringing through my head late that night when I wander away from the press of the celebration into a little grotto—part of the public garden in the center of the town—and throw myself onto a stone bench.

I did this, I think again, and laugh out loud.

Perhaps my sins were actually worth it. If I had confessed my failure to Varia and died, the Red Death would still be ravaging Runakhia. If I had made a successful pact with Mor-Iva and never learned sorcery, Yarekha would not have judged me, and I would not have been driven to exorcise her.

Ruven flickers into sight, standing by my side with his arms crossed, and I nearly laugh again at his stormy expression.

"What's wrong?" I ask aloud. "Disappointed that an apostate found a way to serve the gods?"

I'm vaguely aware that I should be worried about someone over-hearing me, but the wine is humming through my body and I can't be afraid.

Ruven doesn't rise to the bait, but only looks grimmer.

"Did you?" he asks.

"I laid Yarekha to rest," I tell him. In this moment, all my doubts and self-hatred are nothing to me. "I ended the Red Death." I lean toward him, my hands pressed against the cool stone of the bench. "Everything I've done is *worth it*."

I grin recklessly. The look Ruven gives me in return is all somber hatred, and I bristle.

"What?" I ask, stung with a strange sense of betrayal.

"Your precious gods *caused* the Red Death," he says. "Don't deny it. That was divine power Yarekha wielded."

"Power she misused," I snap. Ruven's blasphemy is not remotely surprising, yet it stings.

"Semantics." Ruven crosses his arms. "It was Mor-Iva's nature that drove Yarekha mad. Those who love your gods will always be corrupted. That's why their power must be broken."

"No, that's why we need saints," I say. "So they can heal curses like the Red Death, so they can soften and tame . . ." My voice trails off as I realize what I'm saying.

"Tame the gods?" says Ruven, sounding amused. "Remind me again, why do you worship wild animals?"

"That's not what I said," I mutter, face heating. "They are *holy*, they just—they just—"

They just don't love us.

The thought crashes through all my carefully constructed joy. The god don't love us, not the way I thought they did, not the way we need them to.

Mor-Iva never answered Yarekha's prayers as she desperately killed and killed. Nin-Anna didn't care how much I loved her when I came begging before her. None of the gods care for us unless we make them; that's what Varia has been teaching me since the last shrine, and I know too much now to deny it.

When Mother Una promised me Nin-Anna's love, it was a lie. Just like when she promised that the convent would always be my home.

I realize there are tears sliding down my face. Memories bleed through my head: how afraid I was, when the nuns brought me to the convent, that they would send me away again. How afraid I *always* was, every day of every year that I lived there. I survived by telling myself that everything would be different once I killed Ruven and proved myself.

But nothing's changed. I'm still afraid. I'm still alone. I'm still desperately trying to earn somebody's, *anybody's* love.

Did I ever even love the gods, or did I just love what I thought they could do for me?

Ruven makes a noise of disgust and sits down on the bench beside me. "Congratulations, you're still far too good for the creatures you worship."

"I'm not—"

"I live in your head," he interrupts. "I know what they are to you. And I know what loving gods is like." His voice goes even more soft. "Because I, too, once loved mine."

"Did your monks promise the heretic god would love you once you carried out your mission?" I ask bitterly.

"Worse than that," says Ruven. "They promised he would love me regardless." He laughs, soft and bitter. "All those long years in the palace, I would think to myself, this is what his love is really like. Silence and darkness and loneliness, world without end."

His shoulder is brushing mine, a chill presence in the air, but now there's a little seed of warmth inside my heart. Because he is here. And he knows what it is like to love the way I have. To be betrayed as I have been.

To remain loyal even after betrayal, as I do.

I sigh and tilt my head against the chill of his shoulder. He can't support the least fraction of my weight, but it's soothing to feel his presence against my cheek.

"Then you know why I can't turn on my gods," I say. "Because you, too, still love yours."

He snorts. "I most certainly do not. Weren't you listening just now?"

"Yes," I tell him. "But I saw your eyes at the graveyard. I know that you have no reason to help me except to get a heretic burial. So *yes*, you love your weak and broken god as surely as I love all my powerful and monstrous ones."

"Did you really just call your gods monstrous?" Ruven asks, wicked delight in his voice.

"Are you ready to admit I'm right?"

He laughs, this time fondly. "Perhaps. But you're wrong about one thing: I do have a reason to help you, besides wanting a heretic burial."

"What?" I ask, genuinely curious.

"Spite, of course," he says. "Against the nuns that raised you, and the monks that raised me. Teaching you sorcery spits in all their faces."

I remember the pure, piercing notes the nuns sang in the choir, and Mother Una's hand pressed against my forehead in blessing, and how earnestly I trusted all of them.

"Do you think . . . they ever really loved us?" I ask softly.

Ruven considers that, and as I wait for his words, I realize that I trust him to tell me the truth as he sees it. I trust him, in that one respect, as I do no one else—for despite what he's done to me, however much he may still hate me, there's nothing he's trying to make me become. Even sorcery, he only trained me in because I asked him.

It's a strange sort of trust, as strange as his kindness to me the night before, and just as comforting. The warmth in my heart is starting to grow and blossom.

"I think they did love us," Ruven says finally. "Only . . . not enough."

And I believe him.

But I still say, a hollow echo of a thousand catechism lessons: "It's right to love the gods more than anyone."

"It is," he agrees, and my heart thuds with sudden surprise. "But even so, it wasn't right how little those nuns loved you."

There's an odd note in his voice, and I turn to look up curiously at his face. He's staring at me with the strangest expression, his brow furrowed and his mouth half open.

My own lips part, as if there's some mysterious force driving me to mirror him. Again I feel that strange tug, in my throat and my spine and my stomach, making me want to lean toward him and—and—

The next moment he vanishes. I flinch; it's no more sudden than so many other times that he's left me, but my heart is beating very fast.

"Lia?"

It's Araunn's voice. I surge to my feet, my face heating with guilt.

"I'm here," I call out.

He comes around a curve in the path, smiling that easy, generous smile of his.

For the first time, it leaves me cold.

23

WHEN I WAKE UP THE NEXT morning, I feel hollow and raw and new. I can't unknow the things that Ruven made me face last night, but I don't know how to bear them either.

The nuns loved me, but not enough. Just as I loved the gods, but not enough to keep me from turning to sorcery, and just as the gods . . . well, they have never loved me even a little.

If I'm not the girl who was loved and saved by Nin-Anna and her nuns, then who am I?

As I sit at my dressing table, watching in the mirror as Jaríne combs out my hair, I wonder if it's any different for the heretics who follow the Magisterium—if all of us are equally lonely and abandoned, and I'm the only fool who ever thought it could be otherwise.

"Can I ask you a question?" I ask her.

"Yes, and whip me too if you don't like the answer." Despite the harshness of the words, Jaríne's voice is light, her fingers not slowing in the slightest as she weaves my hair into the braids that she will pin up on my head in a crown.

"Does the god of the Magisterium love you?"

Her fingers still. "Yes," she says finally. "He does."

I shouldn't care, and yet the confidence in her voice feels like needles sliding between my ribs. "Even though you deny him in order to be my dressing maid?" I ask sharply. I've seen Jaríne attending chapel with all the other servants, and I know the Magisterium considers that a terrible sin.

An instant later I'm ashamed to have lashed out. But Jaríne doesn't seem to take offense.

"Well," she says calmly, starting to braid my hair again, "a heretic god can't be too picky. All the respectable worshippers are already taken."

I flex my right hand, feeling the charred skin crack and split into new fissures—an itchy, maddening, yet strangely satisfying pain.

"Mor-Iva doesn't want respectable," I say.

"Well, then all the ferocious worshippers are taken too." Jaríne actually sounds amused now. "Our god became weak for us, and so he loves everything helpless and broken."

A wave of fury crashes through me as I remember Nin-Anna's serene rejection and Mor-Iva's silence, the way that the nuns only wanted me if I could kill, and the royal family only wants me now if I can work miracles.

I wouldn't want to worship the heretic god even if he were real. A god who is helpless and broken, who became infected with humanity and died when men hanged him on a tree, is not anything that deserves reverence.

But it would be . . . *something* . . . to have a god who did not disdain me.

It is the essence of divinity to disdain mortality.

What would be the point, I remind myself, of a god who wasn't *better* than me? If Nin-Anna could have accepted me with blood on my hands, she wouldn't have the beauty that I loved so desperately.

"The nuns once told me," I say, "that your heresy began when people were so ashamed of their weakness that they created a god in their own image. That's why you're able to believe that anything divine could die."

Infuriatingly, Jaríne grins into the mirror, her fingers practically dancing as they pin up my hair. "Well, our priests say that your gods were made to serve ours, but they forgot him and their mission. That's why we call them the Fallen."

The name catches at my curiosity. "Fallen?" I echo.

Jaríne nods. "They fell from heaven and forgot whence they had come, and so Our Lord fell farther still, to remind them and to save us."

"They don't seem to have remembered," I say dryly, thinking of Nin-Anna's serenity, Im-Yara's ferocious purity. I can't imagine either goddess acknowledging a master.

An instant later, guilt drags at my heart. *Because there is no god above them*, I remind myself. *Because they are greatest and most beautiful. Because they are the gods, and it is all* your *fault if they do not love you.*

Two days later, our carriage crests a hill and I see the spires of the next shrine, Zal-Enda.

Once, I would have said that this was the shrine I most wanted to see after Ir-Atsakha. There's no town surrounding it, only a vast monastery that houses the monks and nuns devoted to the goddess Nem-Una, ringed with a ragged jumble of houses for common folk who have somehow made a living there. The nuns told me it was an idyllic refuge, the one place in Runakhia where people still lived in true harmony with the gods.

Now, when I see the spires of Zal-Enda, all I feel is . . .

Heavy.

That's all I can call it—I can't truly tell if what I'm feeling is anger or sadness, weariness or dread. I just know there's a terrible weight on my chest. I'm still determined to serve the gods, and I know I've made the right choice. But I can't seem to *delight* in them anymore.

We arrive at the shrine in the middle of Vespers, as the air shakes with a chorus of honeyed voices. There's no grand welcome for us; the door of the shrine is opened by two white-robed postulants, a girl with a white veil and a boy with his head shaven. They bow low before us, but do not speak.

Zal-Enda belongs to Nem-Una, the goddess of secrets. Outside of the prayers they chant seven times a day, her monks and nuns keep a strict, holy silence.

There's no law that binds *us* to silence. But as we walk into the shrine, the complex notes of the sixteen-part chant roll over us. The vastness of the shrine—taller than any other—swallows us. Even the great beams of afternoon sunlight pouring in through the tall windows feel heavy and ponderous.

So we walk in silence through the shrine, past choir after choir of monks and nuns who do not raise their eyes from their books; past glittering mosaics and murals glowing in the afternoon light. From a dozen domes and angles, Nem-Una stares down at us.

The goddess of secrets, she wears no clothes, but a hundred gray rags swirl around her body to shield it, and one hundred knowing eyes grow across her skin. In imitation, her saints sprout eyes upon their palms and cheeks before they finally die of the visions that consume them.

As at Ir-Atsakha, the heart of Zal-Enda's shrine is a pool within a hidden cave. There's a little comfort in that familiarity. Araunn gestures, Varia grimaces, and I step forward to fling myself into the dark water without hesitation.

But as I sink down, something feels different. Wrong. The water isn't just cold; it prickles and burns against my skin with a strangely heavy pressure—as if it wants to eat away my skin and crush my bones at the same time. Then I realize that I've been sinking far too long—why haven't I reached the realm of the gods yet—

What if I'm not allowed in anymore?

My heart pounds and my lungs burn as I thrash and struggle against the water. *I cannot die here, I* will not *die here*—

My lips part helplessly, and for one instant the water burns in my mouth and my throat and my lungs.

Then I'm sitting up, gasping for breath, my body a leaden weight, my clothes hanging on me wet and heavy.

I'm here, I think. *I made it.*

The first thing I notice is that the world is entirely gray around me: a silver-gray sky, and a steel-gray plain stretching away toward the outline of ghostly gray hills on the horizon.

The next thing I notice is that I'm in chains. My wrists and ankles are all cuffed, weighed down by heavy links of pale gray stone.

She knows, I think with sick, miserable fear. *She knows and she is going to punish me for my crimes.*

Why else would Nem-Una bind me with chains the instant I entered her realm?

"Don't tell me," Ruven drawls, "this is the goddess of grateful slaves."

I turn. Ruven is kneeling beside me, chained in exactly the same way, grimacing in furious distaste like a wet cat. I can't help smiling at his expression, and I can't help feeling a rush of warmth that he's here. I may be condemned, but I'm not alone.

"No, it's the goddess of secrets," I tell him. "Of course she knows why we deserve chains."

Truly it has been very long time, says Nem-Una, *since anyone bound by such lies and secrets has come into my realm.*

Her voice is whisper-soft, but it makes my head ring and buzz. Suddenly afraid again, I look up.

Nem-Una stands before us, long dark hair billowing around her as if suspended in water. Her pale hands are spread to the sides, cupped upward to face the silver-gray sky; her face is also tilted up, but not so sharply that I can't see the light of her golden eyes staring blindly into some unknown infinity.

The rest of her eyes—scattered all over her pale body, visible in the gaps between the sinuous gray strips of cloth that float around her nakedness—are every color of the rainbow, and they all stare at us with a terrible, ruthless attention.

My heart is pounding in my throat, but I still manage to meet those many eyes. "O goddess of secrets," I say, "I am not worthy to ask you this, but—for the sake of your people—"

They are not mine.

The words drift from Nem-Una's mouth indifferent and relentless as falling snow, and for a moment I'm frozen by them. Then I find my voice and say, "I know they aren't your people *now*—but if you return to your shrine, then—"

All secrets are mine, but no people.

"Then it seems *we* are your people." Ruven lifts his wrists and jangles his chains. "Since we are uncommonly bound by secrets."

"What are you doing?" I hiss at him.

"Attempting to speed the resolution of this farce," he says, not lowering his voice in the slightest, his gaze still fixed on Nem-Una. "Truth is what you want, isn't it?"

As he speaks, the chains hanging from his wrists shudder and writhe. For a horrifying moment, I think they're going to strangle him; then they go still again, and I realize the links have become thinner.

I do desire it, says Nem-Una. *And I will awake and inhabit my shrine if you tell me a truth known to none but you, and not even by you.*

A nauseating wave of fear and shame washes through me, hot and cold at once. I know what I have to tell her.

"I . . . I am a sorcerer," I whisper, and instantly my chains begin to writhe and thin.

Beside me, Ruven snorts. "That's no secret from *me*," he says, because he has no idea what I'm about to say next.

I lick my lips and fix my gaze on Nem-Una's hundred eyes, a refuge from having to look at Ruven.

"I am a sorcerer," I say more strongly, "and I doubt the gods. I love them, but I doubt them, and—and sometimes I hate them too."

Just shaping the words in my mind is like flaying the skin from my hands. Speaking them aloud is like scraping flesh from bone. But they are true, and a truth I've never dared speak to anyone— and I have to awaken Nem-Una, if everything I've suffered and sinned is to be worth anything—

That is true, says Nem-Una. *And it has been unspoken by you. But not unknown.*

The soft words feel like a kick to my chest. For a few moments, I struggle to breathe.

"What?" I finally croak.

You have known this for weeks, says Nem-Una. *You could not speak all the words to yourself, but you knew.*

It feels like the air has been sucked out of my lungs. Without meaning to, I look at Ruven—who must surely be exulting in how thoroughly he's turned me against my gods—

But there's no joy in his face as he meets my eyes, then turns to face Nem-Una.

"You contradict yourself," he says, "O lady of the Fallen. You want a truth she has known and not known. What can that be, except the truth she has not yet spoken to herself?"

There is strange mirth in Nem-Una's inhuman voice as she asks, *You defend her? Is she so dear to you?*

"I hate her," Ruven snarls, "but I hate you and yours more."

The next moment he gasps and groans as his chains triple, wrapping over his shoulders and around his neck, dragging him to the ground in a parody of obeisance. And yet he still glares at Nem-Una, defiant for the sake of—of—

For my sake, I think, but that is not even the whole of it: he is defiant and angry on behalf of truth and fairness, all the things he

216

claims to hate and *does* hate, but also cannot help loving, the same way that I cannot help hating the gods, cannot help—

—*loving*—

Oh, I think. *Oh, no.*

But once I have thought it, known it, I cannot make myself forget. Helplessly, the truth rings through my head: *As I cannot help loving him.*

Blood rushes to my face, hot and heavy. I feel Nem-Una's attention swinging to me like a pendulum, see Ruven turning his eyes to me, full of loneliness and fury—

And it's not my duty to the gods and Runakhia that makes me speak. It's Ruven's eyes, so hateful and so wronged, that I look into as I say, "Here is a truth that none but I know, and that I have not known until now: I love Ruven. I love the heretic who hates my gods and burned my kingdom down. He hates me, when he does not pity me, and I love him."

The ground shakes beneath my feet. The chains at my wrists shudder and writhe and crumble to dust. I strand, tottering under the sudden freedom, and wonder if I'll ever dare to meet Ruven's eyes again.

But as I think this, I notice how Ruven's head and shoulders are bowed. The next moment, he beings to shake with a great, hollow laughter.

Then he says aloud: "This is the truth I have known for days but dared not think: I love the girl who cut my throat. She hates everything I hold dear, and I love her."

His own chains shiver to dust, and he stands. I turn instantly to Nem-Una, because I can't bear to look at his face yet.

For these truths, I will render truth, says Nem-Una.

I realize that her two blank, golden eyes are trained on me. So are her hundred other eyes, and for a moment I nearly collapse beneath the weight of her divine attention.

All other gods have forgotten what I know, says Nem-Una. *For of all that they chose to love, none of them chose truth; and I chose knowing only, not revealing.*

My body is numb and my head is reeling, but the goddess's words are clear and deliberate as the tolling of the convent's funeral bell.

"What . . . do you mean?" I manage to ask.

We were tasked to love the world, each in our own way, but we each loved only what was ours.

The words, so terribly like what Varia told me, ring through my head. I see the mortal world as if I were a god: an impossibly strange and myriad thing, haunted with flashes of beauty but crawling with horrors like a swarm of ants on rotten food; and every mortal life is the world in miniature, a thing of beauty and rot that demands to be rent apart until it is clean.

Each one of us is one thing only and the same, ourselves we speak and judge, and destroy what is not according to our own particular word.

I see the sky turn first bright crimson and then the color of dried blood as the wrath of the gods clots to a single intent: to destroy this world that is a mockery of what they loved. And I see tiny, crawling humans wiggle into the divine realm and miraculously spark and take flame with sudden holiness, sudden *semblance* that lulls the divine wrath.

I am Nem-Una, the lady of secrets, and this is the truth I hold behind my hundred and two eyes.

The vision releases me and I stagger, gasping for breath. Hands squeeze my shoulders and steady me—Ruven.

And now I shall awake, says Nem-Una, and fades like the smoke of a snuffed candle.

I expect the divine realm to vanish along with her. But for heartbeat after heartbeat, the strange gray world remains steady around us, and when Ruven's hands release my shoulders, I realize that I can't escape this reckoning.

With a feeling of inevitable doom, I turn around and meet his gaze. I feel terrified and raw and naked, already cringing from what he'll say, how he'll surely throw all my foolish cruelty and faith in my face—

But he is silent. And there is no more anger in his eyes, only a terrible question.

I remember his words: *I love the girl who cut my throat*, and I look at the wound that is raw and weeping red, a violent challenge to any peace between us.

"You—" I falter, my voice breaking.

"You," he breathes, agreement and challenge and caress in that one syllable.

There's only one way I can respond. I close the space between us in a single stride, grip his shoulders, and stand up on my toes to kiss the bloody gash in his throat.

It changes nothing. For all that I'm sorry I hurt him, I can't be sorry I defeated him. But I can offer him this penance: to kiss the wound I created, to feel the slip of blood on my lips, to gag at the sensation of two sliced edges of flesh moving against each other, and again at the taste of blood on my tongue.

Beneath my hands and my lips, Ruven shudders and goes still—

And suddenly there's unbroken skin beneath my lips, no blood seeping into my mouth. I release him and stumble back a step.

The wound is gone.

Ruven lifts a hand to his throat, and wonder spills across his face as his fingers trace the healed skin.

"You do nothing by halves, do you?" he says.

I shift on my feet. There's a curious feeling almost like fear sparking through my body.

"What about you?" I ask.

Ruven raises his eyebrows but does not reply, and after several moments of silent frustration I burst out, "Will you kiss me back or not?"

My face instantly heats, but it's worth it for the grin he gives me in return.

The next moment, he pulls me into his arms. There's a strange sense of both safety and danger at once in the embrace. I close my eyes as I tilt my face upward.

His lips press against mine. The slight, soft pressure sends a shiver through my whole body—then a moment later, it's gone.

I open my eyes. Ruven is staring down at me with an expression I can't read.

"Is that all?" I ask.

Red flushes across his cheeks, and I suddenly realize that he's embarrassed. "Forgive me for not having had the opportunity to practice kissing with a convenient prince," he says.

I laugh. I should feel guilty that I'm betraying Araunn, or that Ruven isn't the first man I've ever kissed, but all I feel is delight that he doesn't fear to show me his sharp tongue, that he trusts me to understand.

I put a hand to his cheek, and marvel that he doesn't just accept the charred, clawed touch but leans into it, as if even my monstrosity were dear to him.

"I'll show you," I say.

But when our lips meet again, I feel like I know nothing either. I've kissed Araunn at least a dozen times, and always enjoyed the strange sensation; but I'd never guessed, until this moment, what it would be like to kiss someone I desperately wanted to delight. To coax his mouth open not from curiosity, but because I want him to know he is loved. To curl my claws into his hair, my heart pounding with the need to protect and cherish, my breath ragged with wonder that he is *mine*—

And to know he feels the same way.

It's everything. It's too much. And it is nothing.

We've sunk to the ground now, with me sitting nestled on his lap. With a ghastly shudder, I realize that we've re-created the moment before I cut his throat.

"I killed you," I whisper hoarsely.

Ruven nuzzles at my throat. "Really?" he says, and presses a little kiss to the base of my ear. "I hadn't noticed."

"You're *dead*, and when we leave here—"

"I know." He presses his forehead to mine, solemn now. "I know."

Around us, the gray landscape has begun to shimmer and shift, tendrils of smoke or fog drifting up from the ground. We're running out of time.

"We are both still weapons," says Ruven, "and only one of us is broken beyond use."

"Not to me," I say fiercely.

"Oh? I'd say I've been *very* useful."

I roll my eyes. "I mean, you are not a weapon to me. You never should have been one. Not to *anyone*," and I snarl the last words in sudden fury at the monks who used him five hundred years ago.

His gaze is dark. "Neither should you," he says, and traces a finger across my cheek. "At least *you* learned to turn in your wielders' hands. My little apostate."

Then everything is shadows and falling, and I'm back in the shrine, secrets and lies and stolen kisses heavy upon me, and Araunn is smiling trustingly at me as he holds out a hand.

24

PERHAPS I SHOULD HAVE TRIED FOR *a pact with Nem-Una*, I think several times in the days that follow.

Because now I seem to be made of secrets.

I am not the devout, loving girl that Araunn thinks, though I smile at him every morning just the same. I am not the competent princess and miracle worker that Varia thinks, though I flex my fingers and cause a tumor to fall dead from a woman's breast. I am not the saint that Anabekha believes I am, though I kneel in every chapel we visit.

I am not even quite the girl that Ruven thinks I should be, but at least *that* is no secret.

"You heard the truth from the mouth of your own goddess," he says to me one evening as I sit alone in my bedroom, practicing sorcery. "How can you not see it? How can you not *act*?"

"What truth?" I demand. The golden swirls that wreathe my hand spark and flare. "Certainly not the doctrine of the Magisterium. Nem-Una spoke of no god above her. She did not name herself 'Fallen.'"

"She described her own fall," says Ruven. "She spoke of being given a task that she failed to accomplish. And who tasked her?"

"Not some useless weakling of a god who died screaming and nailed to a tree, that's for certain."

My words are harsh, but Ruven doesn't seem angered by them.

"You know, you're not the only one who's ever doubted," he says gently.

"And yet I don't ask the one I love to change," I growl, twisting the light that dances between my hands. I don't want to argue with him—

I don't want to remember Nem-Una's words: *We were tasked to love the world, each in our own way, but we each loved only what was ours.*

It's not quite the heretical doctrine that Jaríne told me—that our gods are no more than fallen servants of their god—but it's far too close. When I try to think of what Nem-Una's words could mean, I feel like a soap bubble stretched over a cold, infinite void.

Ruven sighs and sits beside me. The bed doesn't shift as he settles, but I feel the cold, incorporeal shiver of his lips against my hair.

"Why would you ask anything of me?" he says. "Between us, you're the only one unbroken."

I look up at him, my gathered sorcery winking out unheeded. "I told you before, you're not broken. Not to me."

His mouth curves up. "As your gods are truly gods?"

Cold shudders through my stomach, but I don't let myself look away from his eyes.

"As they are *holy*," I tell him. "Whatever they are, however they came to be, they are holy enough to disdain mortality. That makes them worthy of my love and loyalty. That means I can trust them to be godly."

"Trust them, lie to them, be killed by them," Ruven muses. "Truly, I think you must have loved me *because* you hated me."

The quiet teasing in his voice is familiar ground, and I feel my shoulders relaxing as I fight a smile.

"Truly," I tell him, "I did not."

"Then for which of my sins did you love me?"

I loved him—had been doomed to love him—the first moment I saw that bleak loneliness in his eyes.

When he'd asked, *Who promised you?* he had claimed me for his own.

"For all of them together," I say lightly, stretching out a hand. He takes it, his fingers wrapping around mine in a cold, ghostly grip. "But for which of my virtues did you love me?"

His teeth are bright in the moonlight as he smiles. "Whichever one allowed you to cut my throat."

I've always known I wanted to be good, but I never realized how desperately I had tried to please everyone until now—now, when I'm loved by the one person I never tried to make love me, who loves me in spite (or perhaps because?) of all my worst moments.

And yet Ruven, too, is a secret. A burden. Almost a thing that I hate. Because I am still engaged to Araunn. And oh, I hate *him* too.

I know it's cruel and unfair and wrong. The words for what I've become are ones the nuns would never let me say. But I do love Ruven; I do hold his cold hand at night as he lies beside me in my bed, and press my lips to his icy, phantom mouth—

And in the morning, I still smile at Araunn, and let him take my hand and kiss me on the cheek.

He's so sure that I love him; that I'm good and I'm his. I loved that about him once, and now I hate it, but neither love nor hate can make me tell him the truth.

"If it troubles you so much to be a halfway traitor to him," Ruven says to me one evening, "then be traitor all the way."

I stiffen. "I've had enough of cutting people's throats."

"I'm not asking you for revenge," says Ruven. "If that boy lives or dies, it makes no difference to me."

"It will if you're both haunting me together," I say . . . and then wonder when I became the one of us who used mockery for a shield. "Even if you remain a heretic," I say, more slowly, trying to be honest, "surely—surely you can understand that I want Runakhia to be safe and happy."

"I do." There's a strangely earnest tone to Ruven's voice as he kneels beside my bed. "Lia, I do."

Hearing him say my name sends a shiver down my spine. I reach out a hand and lay it against his cheek; beneath my palm, there's a chill and a not-quite-solid pressure. I think of what would happen if I curled my fingers inward, clutching and carving through his brain, and I'm ashamed of the pleasure sparking in my stomach.

I should not *like* to be stronger than the man I love, but I do.

(I should want to destroy the sorcerer who hates my gods, but I do *not*.)

"You've seen the gods," Ruven goes on. "You've seen their work, the way they seize people and twist them into saints that must die for them. You've heard their monstrous nature from Nem-Una's own lips. How can you still help them rule Runakhia? How can you not want them sent back to sleep?"

There's no pride or mockery in his face now, only simple earnestness. He is *begging* me, and he has never looked so young or so vulnerable. My heart aches to give him whatever he wants, even as it revels in how he kneels before me.

My heart is a wicked and selfish thing. I've known that for a long time, much as I tried to deny it.

My catechism, at least, is sure and solid.

Why is my heart sad? With longing for the gods.

"They are my gods," I whisper, letting go of him. "And I love them."

Slowly, Ruven nods, a bleak resignation in his eyes.

The next day we arrive at Undanna, the last stop on the Royal Progress. It is the shrine of Sarriel, the lord of endings.

He's not a god many people love, but he is very feared and much invoked, so the town surrounding his shrine has always remained small but prosperous. When we roll into it, we are greeted by a choir of twelve children singing a hymn, and there's a new-minted saint of Nin-Anna making flowers sprout beneath our feet.

I don't meet her eyes. Instead, I stare up at the shrine. It's small and very old, a wooden building with a high-pointed roof painted gold.

We will go inside and, as we discussed at the inn this morning, Varia will have the honor of awakening the shrine. Then we will return to Anazyr, and I will—

Live, if I'm lucky.

I will keep using sorcery and pretending to work miracles. I will fear every day that I am earning the wrath of the gods, and I will *know* they do not love me.

I will also know that I ended the Red Death. I'll see saints walking our streets, the city's chapels and cathedral thronged with worshippers. And that's enough. It has to be.

On the inside of the shrine, every surface is painted with Sarriel's image: a young man with silver skin and bone-white hair, his four arms ending in stumps, a blindfold covering the bloody sockets of his eyes. It's not shown in most of the paintings, but I know that Sarriel also lacks a tongue; his saints, who strangely aren't painted here, lose first their hands, then their eyes, and finally their tongues.

"And whom would you bless with that delightful sainthood?" Ruven asks as we walk through the shrine.

I don't answer. I can't help the wave of revulsion that shudders through me when I look at the paintings of Sarriel any more than I can help my love for Ruven. But I can make myself stride toward the sanctuary. I can make myself *do* what my heart cannot want anymore.

The heart of Sarriel's shrine is underground: a long, narrow chamber carved out from dark gray rock, at its center a round well filled with shadows. The priest who has guided us proudly declares that law-abiding folk of the town have their ashes thrown into it.

I stare into the dark maw and can't help a shiver of fear.

But I have a duty. We all do. Varia steps forward, her face both heartless and serene—

And Ruven breathes into my hair, "I can't be sorry for this. But I do regret."

He is standing behind me, his chin nestled atop my head, as he did the first time I used sorcery. I have barely a heartbeat to notice this before his cold hand wraps around my wrist. There's a terrible, wrenching pull inside me, as if all my blood were trying to pump backward through my veins. I choke and stagger, but Ruven is holding me up—

How can he hold me, he's just a ghost here, I have barely enough time to wonder.

—and then sorcery roars like a fire through my body, just like in Zumariel's shrine. When my vision clears, there are flowers blooming everywhere in the heart of the shrine, tiny white and bloodred flowers sprouting from a thick carpet of moss, all over the floor and walls and ceiling.

It is beautiful and it is new life and it is an abomination to Sarriel.

I think this, in the first numb moment of my surprise. Then I feel it. Sarriel's attention is like the turning of a vast, ponderous wheel, like the slow-building heat of a thousand banked coals.

In a voice that rings out so clearly I think that everyone must hear it, Ruven cries, "O lord of endings, behold the royal house that has abused your sanctuary, and much deserves your ending."

Betrayal is like a cascade of ice-cold water. I sputter and shiver and go numb, and then I spin to meet Ruven's eyes. I can't find my voice, but he knows what I want to ask:

How could you?

"Oh, my dearest saint." His eyes are sad, his mouth resolute. "The same way you killed me."

Of course. I remember how he called out to Nin-Anna and condemned me. I remember how he begged me to turn against the royal family last night. Of *course* he would try to destroy them when I wouldn't.

I was such a fool to ever trust him.

Varia seizes my shoulders and spins me around. "What did you do?" she demands, her voice harsh.

"Nothing!" I yelp. "I didn't do this. I don't know how—I'll fix it."

I reach out a hand, summoning the power of my relic to destroy the flowers, to make this shrine into a place of endings once again. But it's too late—the stone walls are glowing a dull red, and though there's no heat, the moss and flowers crumble to ash.

For a moment there's no sound but our ragged breaths and the whimpered prayers of the priest who accompanied us.

"Run," Varia says grimly.

I bolt up the stairs. I'm the first one who gets up into the sanctuary, which looks just the same as before—candles and paintings and incense, Anabekha and Coldren praying together, Hézoraine daintily holding the prime minister's hand. I feel like a madwoman as I shriek, "Everybody, get out of here now!"

The next moment, every painting of Sarriel bursts into flames.

I hear shrieks and realize that one of the panicked voices is my own. Then we're all pounding out of the shrine into the cool evening air.

I skid to a stop and bend over, gasping for breath. My heart is pounding in my chest like I've run for miles and miles. Ruven's betrayal and Sarriel's judgment are horrifyingly tangled together in my mind; I wrench up my sleeves and find only smooth skin, but I can't stop staring at my forearms, waiting for the mark of judgment to appear.

"Lia. Lia!" Varia has grabbed my shoulders again, and she gives me a shake. "Don't say that wasn't your fault. Don't lie to me now. You're the only one who could possibly . . ."

Her voice trails off. I raise my head and gasp in horror.

The sky has begun to glow a dull red. Not the golden-red of sunset: this is a deep, bloody crimson that covers the sky in every direction. Like the vision that Nem-Una showed me of the gods judging the world and wanting it to die.

What did you do? I demand silently, and Ruven appears before me, his face pale and grim.

"What I had to," he says, "to stop the Royal Progress." He steps closer, a strange pleading in his eyes. "Until you loved me, I thought I was useless. I believed in nothing, could hope for nothing. But then you changed me. You made me believe again."

Varia is right, I think numbly. *I did this.*

Through my apostasy, my weakness, my selfishness, *I did this*. And now all Runakhia—no, the whole world—will suffer for it.

Ruven doesn't seem to realize it yet. He must not have seen the vision that Nem-Una showed me. But I did, and I can *feel* what is happening.

The sky that is now crimson will soon turn the dull red-brown of dried blood. Sarriel's wrath will fall upon the whole world, and all the gods will follow him, sensing Ruven's blasphemy even though it was not enacted in their shrines. There are not enough saints to pacify them, not nearly enough. The gods will destroy Runakhia, and then they will destroy the world. And it will all be my fault.

My fault, and Ruven's.

I stare at his still-pleading eyes and I feel a wrath, a pure and absolute *rejection* I have never felt before, not even when I cut his throat. For the first time I hate someone as much as I hate myself, and oh, it is *glorious*.

The world is ending, the gods are angered, Runakhia is lost. But I am going to make one last—and first—act of piety.

"O Sarriel," I say aloud. "O lord of final endings, watch me as I wield the power of Mor-Iva."

I hold aloft my hands, palms outward to face Ruven. It feels like a new chamber has opened in my heart, connecting *wrath* and *judgment* and *rejection*. With that sudden wave of surety, I push—and Ruven is gone.

In his place stands a god: four-armed, un-handed and un-eyed and un-tongued.

Sarriel.

I bow deeply. From the corner of my eyes, I see Varia and Araunn do likewise.

Is this an ending? Sarriel asks.

"Yes," I say with absolute conviction, because I will not accept any world where Ruven continues to exist.

I am satisfied, says Sarriel. *I shall love you, and awake for you.*

Then he is gone. The crimson sky is fading to blue. And I am—

Alone.

25

IT ALL HAPPENED SO FAST.

I stare numbly at the chaos of the town around us. Half an hour ago, I loved Ruven and I was a sorcerer. Now I hate him and I've used my pact with Mor-Iva to kill him a second time. In between, the world nearly ended.

It would have been my fault if it did.

"We are going to speak of this later," Varia mutters in my ear. It takes me a moment to register the words, another to parse the threat; when I turn to look at Varia, she's already striding forward into the frightened chaos of the main square.

"Behold," Varia cries out, her voice ringing across the square in a way that feels more than mortal, "Sarriel the lord of endings has looked on this world, and considered its end, and allowed it to continue. In celebration of this, he allows us to make saints of Nin-Anna, Zumariel, and Mor-Iva, here on his very doorstep." She spreads her hands, the late afternoon light glowing through her golden hair, making her scarlet ribbons gleam. "Those who love the gods and would have their favor, come forward. Those who would win blessings for their kith and kin, come forth."

Perhaps it's Varia's solemn conviction; perhaps Undanna is more devout than other towns. Most likely it's the terror of Sarriel's judgment. But the people flock to us, in numbers such as I have never seen before. They drop to their knees and they beg for sainthood.

And we all grant it.

Even me.

I didn't think I could do it—didn't even think I would be asked—until suddenly an old woman drops to her knees before me and says, "Make me a knife for the sake of my family."

I stare down at the pale, papery wrinkles of the woman's face. I can still feel the echo of the old fear that used to rule me: the familiar thought of, *If I can't do this, I will die.*

But another voice is much louder in my head: Ruven saying, *We are still both weapons.*

Once I was fool enough to think he meant those words in tenderness, not warning. Now there's a murderous heat in my heart as I look down at the old woman, as I think, *I will be a better weapon than he ever imagined. I will make all the weapons he feared and hated.*

In that hatred, there is peace.

And the presence of Mor-Iva.

I lay my hands on the old woman's shoulders. With a jolt, I feel her fragile bones beneath my fingers, the weak flutter of her old heart, and the slow pulsing of blood through her half-clogged veins.

I feel the woman's mortality, and I hate it as the gods hate it, and I *judge.*

"Izanya, who poisoned the man who used to beat her daughter," I say, and know it is the goddess speaking through me, "receive the blessing and the sainthood of Mor-Iva."

As I speak, divine power shudders through my body and rips out through my hands. It's a strange combination of pain and perilous delight that feels like it is unhooking all my bones from each other, yet also filling up all the gaping, painful holes within me.

The old woman—Izanya—moans softly. She raises her hands, and I see their skin shrivel and crack and char, fingers lengthening as the nails sharpen to claws.

The river of divine power is gone as suddenly as it appeared, leaving me dizzy and trembling. When I look at the saint I have made, my stomach turns. I've turned this old woman into a monster like myself.

But she was already a killer, a monster, and a weapon.

Just like me.

The truth crashes over me in waves: I killed Ruven. I chose, again and again, to lie and blaspheme. I have never been anything but a ruthless weapon, and when I tried to hide from that—when I imagined I could love somebody the gods hated, when I believed that person might love me—the world nearly died for it.

Never again.

I will wade up to my neck in blood if I must, but I will *never* try to be anything but the knife of the gods again.

I hold up my twisted, charred hands. "Who else desires Mor-Iva's favor?" I cry aloud.

Eight more people do, and I give it to each of them. With every sainting, I feel more hollowed out by the rush of divine power. My hands begin to shake, even between saints. But I don't slow down.

This is holy, I think as I watch the hands of a ten-year-old boy twist and lengthen and char. *This is holy.*

I can't feel it. But I can no longer feel much of anything right now, except for my anger at Ruven. That's the one way left in which I'm disobedient: as I make saints for the goddess Mor-Iva, I am still thinking of a heretic sorcerer.

I loved him. I *loved* him. I, the girl chosen by the gods, who always believed she loved the gods best of anyone, still loved *him*. And he used that love against me.

I wish I could kill him all over again.

At last, after nearly an hour, Varia declares that we have made enough saints. With a gasp of relief, I stagger back from the pregnant woman I just sainted. She's still gasping and moaning with the pain of her newly changed hands.

Will her child be born with charred claws? I wonder, and then my legs give out.

Araunn carries me to the inn. I'm not aware of much, but I do know that I feel his arms around my body, I lean my face against his shoulder, and I inhale his smell.

He shouldn't be so gentle, I think fuzzily. *I'm just a knife.*

Once I'm in my room, there's a great deal of fussing from Jaríne and Anabekha and even Hézoraine. They give me tea and a hot bath and then even more tea, combined with a meal.

It feels like I'm suspended in a vast ocean of numb exhaustion. I want to lie down and never move again, but resisting orders is utterly beyond me. So I do what they tell me, sit and eat what they give me.

At last the fussing ends. For a while, I don't notice anything except the quiet. Slowly, though, I become aware of the world around me again: the dark brown dregs of tea at the bottom of my cup. The ash my fingers have shed on the lacy white coverlet.

I'm sitting in bed, leaning back against pillows, cradling a half-empty cup of tea in my lap. There's a damp cloth on my forehead. Anabekha is sitting beside me, lips moving silently as she prays from the psalter open in her lap.

She looks as perfect as ever, and I feel a twitch of resentment, the first real emotion I've felt in . . . hours?

I try to sit up, and the teacup jostles in my still-numb fingers and spills across the coverlet over my lap. Anabekha instantly snaps her book shut and takes the empty cup from me.

"How are you feeling?" she asks.

"I'm fine," I say, wishing she weren't there.

Anabekha's mouth flattens. "You are not. I spent too many years studying the signs of divine exhaustion not to know them when I see them."

"Divine what?" I ask, surprised out of my resentment.

"Divine exhaustion." Anabekha sits up a little straighter, her face falling into the perfect decorum she always has when reciting catechism lessons. "It was a rare malady in the ancient days, but not unknown. When those who are new to wielding the divine power use too much at once, they can tax both spirit and body beyond endurance. From the way you were brought in, I'm surprised you can even talk again so soon."

My shoulders hunch with familiar shame. Of course Anabekha knows about it, was prepared for it.

"You should have been the one with the Royal Gift," I mutter.

"It's not our place to question the will of the gods," Anabekha says primly.

Anger suddenly sparks inside my chest. "Well, it's a sin of which the whole convent was guilty."

237

"What?" Anabekha's eyes are wide and innocent, and that only makes me angrier.

"They all wished you had been the one! Surely you heard them say so often enough; *I* did, and I think they meant to hide it from me. You were their perfect daughter who did everything right. They wanted so *desperately* for you to be the one." My voice wavers on the last words, and I snap my mouth shut.

After a moment, Anabekha says quietly, "Of course I was perfect. That was my job. That's why they let me stay and take the veil."

"Well, then." My voice shakes. "You said it, not me."

Anabekha's brow furrows. "You must know, don't you, that they only wanted me as your handmaid? Your servant in the service of Nin-Anna? That's why they trained me so thoroughly, wanted me so perfect. That's why they gave me a home."

I stare at her, feeling like the whole world's turned upside down. "That's not—"

"Mother Una told me," says Anabekha. "Often. It's not their way to take in orphans, you know that. They didn't keep me on account of my father's money, they kept me because they knew that you would have to join the royal family and they wanted someone there to guide and help you."

There's no bitterness in her voice, though I think I can hear a shadow of pain in it.

Slowly, my voice very small, I ask, "Then why did you stay?"

I only stayed because I thought they wanted me, I think. *What did they promise you?*

"Because I fell in love with Nin-Anna," Anabekha says, very

simply. "And I would have done anything for a chance to serve her, in any way."

"Oh," I whisper.

For the ten thousandth and yet the very first time, I think, *I wish I could be like her.*

"What happened in the shrine?" asks Anabekha. "I thought we were going to die. There was such—such *wrath* in the air, even before the sky turned red."

The truth is too complicated, too shameful, too . . . *much* for me to tell her. And yet—also for the first time—I really want to tell her something true.

"I wasn't good enough," I say. "Sarriel judged me. And then he started to judge us all, until I called on Mor-Iva." I drop my gaze to the bedside table. "I'm sorry."

"It is the essence of divinity to disdain mortality," Anabekha says wryly, and I smile from the simple relief of having someone else here who has learned the same lessons, repeated the same catechism day after day.

At least I'm not *completely* alone.

But Anabekha can't protect me from the reckoning that's coming any more than Ruven could have.

The sun has barely begun to set when the door of my bedroom bangs open and Varia strides inside, Araunn trailing behind.

"They tell me you're well enough to speak now," says Varia. "So. What happened in the shrine?"

I sit up straighter, taking a deep breath. I've thought a good deal in the past few hours, and I think I'm ready.

"It was Ruven," I say.

They both stare at me. "What?" Varia asks sharply.

"There's something I haven't told you," I say. "Ruven has been haunting me. I've seen him . . . at least a dozen times since I killed him. Always telling me I was vile, unworthy of the gods, doomed to fail. It's why I had so much trouble learning to use Mor-Iva's power."

I'm deceiving them, yet I'm saying nothing but the truth. Ruven *did* tell me I was a monster. He told Nin-Anna herself that I was unworthy. And he tried so hard to make me fail.

When I gave him my trust, when I started to hate the gods at his command—how he must have laughed in secret.

I know that Ruven loved me. He said so when Nem-Una was forcing him to tell the truth. But he *used* me too, and I was so desperate for any affection that I was happy to let myself be used. As I think of it, my skin crawls with humiliation.

"I hoped that making a divine pact would send him away," I go on. "But then, in Sarriel's shrine"—and there are tears in my eyes and my voice, suddenly, real ones that I don't have to fake—"he *used* me, somehow. He used my power to work a miracle of Mor-Iva as I did in Zumariel's shrine, only this time . . . the god I offended did not forgive me." My shoulders slump. "I'm sorry."

"You banished him, didn't you," says Varia. "When Sarriel appeared to us all."

I swallow, remembering Ruven's face in the last instant before I destroyed him: his eyes widened, but without surprise. He knew what I would do to him in return.

"Yes," I say, my voice low and rough.

240

"As you banished Yarekha's ghost," says Varia. "So why didn't you send Ruven on his way earlier?"

"Varia," Araunn says warningly.

"It's a question that needs to be asked," says Varia.

To my surprise, Araunn replies, "No, it is not."

Varia turns to him, eyebrows rising.

"Lia has more than proved herself," Araunn goes on. "She killed Ruven. She made a pact with Mor-Iva. She *ended the Red Death*. And when Sarriel's judgment was about to doom us all, she satisfied him." He stares his sister down, more determined than I've ever seen him. "Lia has earned your trust. She's earned all our trust."

There's a short, taut silence. Then Varia says, "Let's hope she keeps it," and sweeps out of the room.

As the door shuts behind her, I release a quiet breath of relief.

Then Araunn turns to me, his face soft with care. "Lia," he says, and my breath shakes with a sudden, wretched grief.

He believes in me. He defied his sister for me. And I deserve nothing of his kindness.

An instant later Araunn is by my side, wrapping me in his arms. "Don't blame Varia," he whispers. "Mother wanted her to be the strong one and taught her very harshly. But she is wrong about you."

"How do you know?" I ask. The words taste bitter in my throat, but they come out soft and trembling from my lips.

"Because I know *you*." Araunn traces the line of my cheek. "I know you, Lia, and I know how you love the gods. How you love *us*, though we have done nothing to earn your loyalty."

"Ruven—"

My throat closes up as soon as I've said the name. I'm not sure what I was going to say anyway.

"He lied." Araunn presses a kiss to my forehead. "He was a heartless monster and he lied to you, Lia. And you gave him Mor-Iva's judgment as he deserved."

A sick thrill runs down my spine. *You're wrong*, I want to say. *He wasn't heartless.* Even though I hate him and everything he did—I know that he was never heartless.

But I don't say it. I sob, then I tilt my face up to kiss Araunn, as tenderly as I once kissed Ruven. I melt into his arms and accept his comfort, as if I were exactly the girl that he thinks I am.

This was what I do. This was what I *am*: a girl who can tell any lie, play any part, be anything at all that somebody wants of her.

I was the dutiful weapon that the nuns wanted. I was the apostate that Ruven wanted. Now I am the damaged princess that Araunn wants and Varia is willing to tolerate.

I close my eyes, leaning against Araunn's shoulder as a wave of cold despair washes over me. All my life, I thought I loved the gods more than anyone, but truly, I only ever loved pleasing the people around me.

I belong to Mor-Iva. I am a monstrous weapon, just like she is. I've accepted that now, as I never did before. But this is what it means to be a weapon, no matter how holy: to obey the hand that wields you, without caring about anything else.

Without ever choosing or being brave enough for anything, *anything* else in the world.

I once thought I was going to be a hero, but I have only ever been a willing puppet who begged for somebody to pull her strings.

"Oh, Lia," Araunn breathes, and I kiss him in perfect, monstrous obedience.

Late that night, when I am alone—the same hour when, last night, Ruven curled beside me and pressed ghostly kisses into my hair—I slide out of my bed and kneel on the cold floorboards.

O Mor-Iva, I pray silently. *O knife of the gods. O final breath. I have killed and sainted with your power. Please, finally, speak to me.*

The night air is cold and silent around me. All I hear is my own weak mortal breaths, the pounding of my foolish mortal heart. I'm a fool for expecting anything else.

As I think that, heat prickles along my fingers and hands. Silently and yet very clearly, I hear a voice inside my head: *Kill in my name and be mine.*

The voice is so soft and natural, like a blend of my breath and heartbeat, that I could almost imagine it was my own thoughts. And yet I tremble, because I know this is Mor-Iva speaking to me outside the divine realm for the very first time.

All she has to say to me . . . are the same words she used to claim me.

Because I have always been a weapon. Because I was always a fool hoping to be loved by anyone, nuns or gods or Ruven.

I crawl into bed, my throat aching but my eyes dry. It's a long time before I fall asleep.

26

FOUR DAYS AFTER SARRIEL'S SHRINE, WE finally return to Anazyr. When we first see the gleam of the river and the jagged line of buildings and smokestacks on the horizon, I feel a desperate surge of relief.

These last four days, I've been consumed by a cold emptiness. I know that I *should* be happy, for now I have done everything I ever dreamed of and more. I have completely defeated Ruven. I'm a true princess of Runakhia, able to wield Mor-Iva's power at will. And I have utterly destroyed the Red Death. But my heart remains cold and heavy in my chest. When crowds cheer for us—when Araunn kisses my fingers and smiles for me—I feel nothing but a dreary chill.

But when I see the capital city on the horizon, I start to hope that maybe things will be different. Maybe, once I'm back in my childhood home, I'll be able to feel my sacrifices were worth the price.

Then, as our carriage rolls closer to the city, I start to feel a reverent wonder.

I grew up in Anazyr; the capital city was the only world I knew. So for all my life, my world was rimmed in smog. Sometimes the refuse of the factories was only a brown band on the horizon; sometimes it was a thick, noxious pea soup that mixed with the river fog to crawl through our streets, blinding everyone and strangling the sickly. The winter I was twelve, three nuns died for no reason but that the air had become poison to their weak lungs.

But now as we drive toward Anazyr, the horizon is blue and clear. The air is piercingly sweet. The smog is gone as if it had never been.

I feel as if I'm falling into a dream. The world, my childhood city, cannot possibly be so sweet and pure. But it is. As we drive through the city gates, I see moss and white flowers growing over the lintels.

It's beautiful and it's surreal and it is as if everything I suffered—Nin-Anna's rejection and Im-Yara's torment, Nem-Una's secrets and Ruven's betrayal—never happened. As if I've gotten everything I wanted when I left on the Royal Progress, dreaming that I would learn to know the gods and save my country. Now that I have returned . . .

Knowing your gods too well, Ruven would have finished the thought, but he's not here anymore.

My eyes sting, and I blink hard. I don't miss him. I can't. He is, despite everything we shared, my enemy. So I put him from my mind and stare out the carriage window.

We are greeted by a vast crowd, larger than I have ever seen on the Royal Progress. That's not surprising; Anazyr is the largest city in Runakhia. There are also more beggars than I've seen anywhere else, but that is also no surprise; the richest and the poorest of Runakhia live together in the capital.

But then one of the grubby, crouched figures catches my eye

and I straighten in my seat, a cold shock running down my spine. There's no mistaking it: the beggar woman who kneels by the side of the road is a saint of Juni-Akha, her head bowed under the weight of golden horns like Queen Imvada's.

A saint. And yet she sits in the dirt with a tin cup, like every other beggar I've ever seen.

"What is it?" Varia asks sharply.

"Look—" I point, but the carriage has already rolled on, the woman lost behind us.

Now everyone in the carriage is looking at me instead.

"There was a beggar," I say, feeling somehow embarrassed, "but—but she was a *saint*."

"Ah yes," says Coldren, his voice heavy. "I've already gotten letters about it from my colleagues at the royal shrine. Is it not beautiful that the gods touch even the lowest among us?"

I stare at him. I can't seem to find the words to explain how shocking it is that a woman chosen by the gods is still so despised and abandoned that she must beg for her dinner.

But Anabekha has words enough for both of us. "Is it beautiful," she asks, "that our faithless people do nothing to support the saints who make our kingdom pleasing to the gods?"

Coldren jolts in his seat. "Of course it's not *good*," he says, a fire in his eyes that I've never seen before. "But that woman was poor and abandoned before she ever was a saint. Does she only matter now because she has grown horns?"

Anabekha draws herself up. The air seems to crackle between them. "No," she says. "Do you only care about her because you think *we* don't?"

"Stop the carriage," Varia interrupts, her mouth a grim line.

Both Anabekha and Coldren stare at her, but it's the prime minister who speaks. "Your Holiness, we cannot stop the in middle of the procession. The security precautions—"

"Stop the carriage," Varia repeats, her voice louder. "That is an order from your princess."

"I'm afraid," the prime minister says apologetically, "that I promised our queen I would deliver you home safely. I must do that."

Varia's nostrils flare, but she says nothing. She is realizing, perhaps, what I am too: that this is the prime minister's city, which he has been ruling for years, and right now we are surrounded by the procession he has organized. In Morvenn Varia got her way by surprise, leaping into action before the prime minister could stop her. But here, there is no way we could defy him.

Unless one of us worked a miracle.

As I think that, Mor-Iva's voice rings through my head: *Does he deserve death?*

It's only the second time she's spoken to me since I became hers. I tremble and I shudder and I want to obey.

But she wants to kill.

Tell me, Mor-Iva says again, more insistently, *does he deserve it?*

And for one instant, I can see myself doing it: reaching forward and ripping my clawed fingers through the prime minister's neck as though it's no more than tissue paper pressed over soft butter. His blood would fountain so beautifully, the very smell a hymn to my goddess—

And then I am pressing back in my seat, clawed hands clenched tight, as I think and pray, *No, no, no.*

Killing him might stop the carriage, but it would only cause more chaos and violence. And I don't want to kill again—not anyone. I'm a little surprised by how much I do not want it.

So be it. Mor-Iva sighs in my mind. *Mercy it is, then.*

For now.

There's a ceremony to greet us at the palace, of course, attended by half of Parliament and all the court, alongside two dozen clerics and nine saints as well. At the center of them all stands Queen Imvada, fierce and splendid in a red gown, her golden horns gleaming in the late afternoon sunlight.

"Welcome," she says, "child of the gods and children of my body. Have you done your duty and awakened the gods?"

"We have," says Araunn, his voice ringing across the palace steps as he drops gracefully to one knee. "Permit us to return, O holy queen."

Imvada inclines her head, a soft smile touching her lips. "I do."

Afterward there is a grand banquet, very much like the one at which the queen first announced the Royal Progress and my engagement. It's a glittering, tense affair; I know that I'm a mere child when it comes to politics and social niceties, but I can still hear how brittle the laughter is, how rigid the courtesy.

By the time we're able to leave the great hall, it's nearly one in the morning. I can't stop yawning, but there's no going to bed for us yet: Queen Imvada wants to speak with me and Araunn and Varia privately. So we climb the winding marble stairs to the royal apartments.

After dismissing the servants, the queen sits down at her dressing table and begins combing out the long red waves of her hair.

"So," she says, staring at us in the mirror. "Tell me what you learned on the Royal Progress."

"We should have the prime minister executed," Varia says instantly.

I told Mor-Iva I didn't want that, and yet for the first time, I feel a rush of sympathy for Varia. When we first saw the beggar saints through the window of our carriage, he was the only one whose heart remained truly cold.

Imvada shakes her head. "Don't talk like a foolish child," she says, and to my surprise, Varia flinches. "All Runakhia would be better off without that man," Imvada goes on, "but for the moment, he can't be removed. In which lies half our troubles. But how did he offend *you*?"

"There was a saint of Juni-Akha begging on the streets as we arrived," says Varia, sounding meeker now. "I wanted to stop the carriage to help her but he would not let us."

Imvada snorts. "Of course he would not. If the church is powerful and respected enough to give sustenance to all the saints, that benefits him nothing, and hurts him not a little."

"Then—" My voice fails as everyone turns to look at me.

"Well?" says Imvada after a moment. "Out with it."

"Then we must help the beggar saints," I say. "It's our duty as the royal family, isn't it?"

"Oh?" Imvada rips viciously at a snarl in her hair. "And why is that?"

"Because—we are meant to please the gods," I say, my heartbeat pounding in my throat. "And that means we have to be holy. Doesn't it?"

"Oh, indeed, we must be holy," says Imvada. "But we are the royal family. Before all else, we serve Juri-Akha, queen of the gods. Our only holiness is to rule and command. Whatever undermines our rule is unholy and obscene to us. Do you understand that, daughters?"

I can't answer, But Varia speaks for both of us.

"Yes, Mother," she says, her face and voice leeched of emotion.

"I've told you again and again, haven't I? Don't presume to speak on a situation before you know the facts." Imvada combs her hair in silence for several moments before she goes on, "Parliament has passed several resolutions urging me to sign a constitution that will make the royal house no more than a bit of pious mummery, brought out at festivals to decorate their *proceedings*."

She spits the final word, and I take a step back.

"The gods are awake now," Araunn ventures hopefully. "And we have ended the Red Death—everyone is talking about it! Surely Parliament will reconsider?"

Imvada raises her eyebrows, but her voice is gentler than when she spoke to Varia. "While they leave saints to starve on the streets? I think not."

"Then we use the saints against them," says Varia. "Lia made saints of Mor-Iva in the last town; she can do it again, and they can dispense judgment, even if she's not brave enough to do so herself."

I can't speak. My mind is a welter of emotions, fear and shame and horror. I see hands curling, fingers twisting and charring, as I brought the blessing of Mor-Iva down upon them.

I don't want to do that again. Yet I must . It is *holy* to do it again and again, forever and ever.

"Of course not," says Imvada, as ruthless and cynical as Ruven. "What sort of fool are you? Do you imagine that the favor of the gods will safeguard you from all dangers? It will not, else Ruven would not have laid his spell upon us."

My heart bangs against my ribs at the sound of his name. I don't know if it's longing, anger, or regret.

"We will play their game," says Imvada, laying down her comb. Her fingertips drum against her dressing table. "We will be more effective and more terrible and more clever than they could ever expect. And we will use the power of the gods to make them pay."

She's so passionate and so sure that for a moment I almost believe her. I *want* to believe her, much as I'm starting to dislike her, because she's a queen from the golden age of Runakhia. She is blessed by the gods and she's supposed to set things right.

But as I silently follow Araunn out of the room, I think, *What about all the beggars who are saints?*

What about all the beggars who are not *saints?* I can imagine Ruven saying, and my throat aches with heretical tears.

27

THAT NIGHT I LIE AWAKE FOR hours, staring up into the darkness, Imvada's and Ruven's voices ringing through my head in terrible harmony.

They both believe there's no more to the royal family than survival, no greater holiness than power. They're both wrong.

They have to be.

At last I fall asleep—a long, heavy sleep. Jaríne doesn't wake me in the morning, because the Royal Progress is over. There's nowhere I am needed. When I do wake, it's slowly and groggily, sitting up and yawning in my bed and then asking for tea.

Anabekha comes to see me when I'm halfway done with my cup.

When I hear the knock at my door, I answer it myself—and stop in horror, the breath freezing in my throat as I stare at Anabekha's golden hands.

"You're a saint," I whisper.

Anabekha nods. "Yes."

She walks into the room. Numbly, I close the door and turn to watch her.

I should be glad, or at least jealous. But all I can feel is dread. For the first time, the inevitable deaths of the saints are *real* to me.

Anabekha is going to die. She will work miracles, maybe for months, maybe for years, but sooner or later she will be consumed by fever and die coughing up flowers from dry, cracked lips.

I don't want that for her.

I feel a horrible suspicion that I don't really want that for *anyone*.

Anabekha raises a hand, gleaming fingers half curled, and stares at it thoughtfully. Then she meets my gaze. "Aren't you going to congratulate me?"

"But you'll *die*," I burst out.

"I'm no longer needed for the Royal Progress," says Anabekha, her voice as quietly perfect as always. "And you seem to have found your footing. I don't think you need me any longer." Her mouth curves slightly. "And the prince agreed."

As if that means anything. As if Araunn has any idea of what it means to suffer under the power of the gods. I know it's treason and heresy both to think those things—but I do.

"How could you ask him for it?" I demand.

"This morning after Lauds in the royal chapel," says Anabekha, willfully misunderstanding. "Coldren was there too, and I thought he would lose his voice shrieking at me. He refused to believe I could possibly want sainthood."

"He talked to you about it?" From the way they argued on the Royal Progress, I hadn't expected that either of them would willingly speak to the other again.

"Yes." Anabekha shifts, looking a little uneasy now. "He said . . . he wants me to live. I told him the gods were my life, and that I would not turn away from them for anyone, least of all a faithless clergyman who gives the gods no reverence."

There's an entire story in the way that Anabekha flushes as she says the words, and in the awkward longing that flickers across her face. I stare at her in blank surprise. The thought of either her or Coldren having such feelings for each other seems absurd, and yet—and yet now I remember all the times I saw them standing together in the shrines. The way that Anabekha could ignore anyone's disbelief except his, and he could condescend to everyone's faith except hers.

For a moment, I can almost hear Ruven saying dryly, *Good thing she never cut his throat, because then a romance would be* really *impossible.*

"And I'm already a nun," says Anabekha, her voice a little defensive now. "I'd never break my vows."

I swallow down the lump in my threat. "Of course you wouldn't," I say. "But—but why did you have to become a saint? You're going to die."

She nods. "Yes. So will you. None of us live forever. But I—" Her voice cracks, and she struggles a moment for control. "I have seen my goddess. And I am going to heal people whom we might once have buried." Her voice is low and fervent, like a prayer. "That is more than worth it."

She really is as good as the nuns always said, I think. *She really should have been the one the gods chose.*

"Why are you here?" I ask softly. We might understand each other a little better now, but we are still not friends.

"To say goodbye," says Anabekha, meeting my eyes. "And to ask for your blessing."

"I don't serve Nin-Anna," I say, feeling the horrible lurch of guilt again. I don't serve *any* god, not truly.

"I saw you serve her all your life," says Anabekha. "And you are the chosen of the gods, who saved us all from Ruven." She drops to her knees. "Please, give me your blessing."

So, with my eyes blurring, I lay my hands on the crown of her head and whisper a blessing. A moment later, I can't remember what I said, but it seems to have pleased Anabekha, who smiles radiantly at me before she leaves.

For a few moments I stare at the closed door, unable to identify the cold, numb feeling snaking through my gut. A moment later, as I turn away to face the little ornamental table holding a delicate porcelain vase of roses, I realize: I am *angry*.

I don't know why. I just know that I want to scream in anger, and I shouldn't, but the pressure inside me keeps building and building until finally I pluck the vase off the table and throw it at the wall. It shatters with a gloriously loud crash that does nothing to release the knot of tension in me.

Neither does the guttural shriek I finally allow myself a moment later.

I snuffle, and then I sob, and then I can't stop. I stand at the center of my room, crying hot, messy tears and shaking with a vast rage at the whole world: the nuns, the gods, Anabekha, Ruven, and most of all myself.

I don't like this.

The childish thought rings through my head over and over as I sob. I don't like what I've done. I don't like the person I've turned into. I don't like that the royal family is so ruthless, that the gods are so cruel, that the whole world is *like this*.

I can work both miracles and sorcery, but I can't seem to change anything that matters.

All I want is to go back to being the simple girl who knew she loved the gods. Except now I'm not even sure that it's right to love them.

Finally I run out of tears. I dry my face, blow my nose on an embroidered handkerchief, and sit exhausted in the window seat, knees pulled up to my chin.

What am I to do? I think.

I don't want to keep on being a puppet, dancing to the tune of whoever will keep me alive. I want to start doing what's right, not just what feels necessary. But I'm no longer sure what that is.

I wish I could talk to Ruven, even though I know he'd just tell me again to kill the royal family and defy the gods. Or maybe not: his plan did nearly destroy the world, after all. Even the most famous of heretics might have learned from that.

Stranger things have happened, I can imagine him saying. *Like a holy princess turning to sorcery.*

I smile faintly. It's true that I do have a power that no one expects. But what can my sorcery possibly be *for*, besides faking miracles?

Do I even have it anymore, now that I've been accepted by Mor-Iva?

Curiously, I raise one of my hands and concentrate on the power of my relic. For a moment there's nothing—but then I feel it stir to life, and faint golden strands of light appear around my fingers. I laugh in relief and send the lights swirling into the form of a rose.

This power, however cursed it is, has not been taken from me.

The door opens. I start, instantly quenching the luminous flower. Then I realize that it's only Jaríne, who would certainly not be able to tell sorcery from miracles if she saw it.

Jaríne gives me a narrow look, her mouth flattening. For a moment I think she's about to say something; then she simply shrugs and sets about cleaning up the remains of the vase.

"I'm sorry," I say quickly.

"It's no matter," she says, none of the sharpness I remember in her voice.

With a slow, lurching sensation of dawning guilt, I realize how silent she's been in the days since our last stop in Undanna, how . . . meek.

She's afraid of me now, I think miserably. And don't I deserve it? I've become a maker of saints; I'm what the Magisterium most hates and fears. How many sermons must Jaríne have heard preached against people like me?

Suddenly I remember the day when I found Jaríne praying in the heretic graveyard. And the following night, when I promised Ruven I would steal his body and give him a heretic burial.

I made a promise.

The fact is so simple and pure, I could almost sob in relief. Whatever monsters the gods may be, whatever liars the heretics may be—surely it is still good to keep a promise.

There is, after all, one good thing that I might be able to do.

I take a deep breath. "Jaríne."

She turns to me slowly, caution in her eyes. For a moment I hesitate; then I plunge forward, deciding to get the worst over at once.

"I've decided it's wrong for Ruven's body to be hung up in a courtyard," I say. "So I'm going to steal it and see him buried by a priest of the Magisterium. I need your help."

Jaríne stares at me, utterly blank. I wait, but when she still hasn't responded, I ask, "Will you help?"

"Those people you sainted in Undanna," Jaríne replies quietly, "did *they* need your help?"

I go hot and cold at once with mingled fury and shame. For a moment, I imagine myself saying, *Does Hézoraine need to know you're a heretic?*

Jaríne would bow to the threat, I know. She would nod her head and help me. After all, she's a survivor just like me.

But.

But the problem with trying to do *one* good thing is that it makes you desperate to avoid ruining that goodness along the way. If I blackmail Jaríne now, then keeping my promise won't be worth much of anything. Certainly Ruven wouldn't thank me for it.

"A good priest would bury anyone who needed it, even Ruven," Jaríne goes on, "and your queen would see him hanged for it. I won't help you make that happen."

"But I don't—" I fall silent. Of course Jaríne thinks I've embarked on some bizarre scheme to further persecute the followers of the Magisterium. She's watched me do what they think most cruel and most vile.

For a few moments I stare at Jaríne, trying to think of a lie that will persuade her to help, to believe this isn't a trap. But I can think of nothing—except threats, which would *make* it a trap—

Unless I tell the truth.

The wave of fear is awful and nauseating. But I'm so tired of being afraid. I only wanted to do this one thing, and with everything else ruined—

What have I got to lose, really?

"I'm a sorcerer," I blurt out. "I couldn't work miracles, so I got Ruven's ghost to teach me sorcery so I could fake them. I promised him that in return I'd get his body a proper burial. I exorcised his ghost after he tried to kill us at Sarriel's shrine, but I still want to keep my promise. To do that, I need your help."

Jaríne stares at me, her mouth open in frank surprise.

"A sorcerer?" she asks finally.

"Yes." I nod, sick with dread and yet unutterably grateful to be finally, *finally* telling the truth to somebody. "I stole power from the realm of the gods. I am a blasphemer against everything holy. You can destroy me if you tell anyone. Will you help me?"

"Nobody would believe me," says Jaríne, her voice dubious and dazed and thoughtful all at once.

A ragged laugh bursts from my lips. "Varia already half suspects. The queen has promised to kill me if I fail as a princess. You would find it very easy to convict me."

For a few moments more, Jaríne studies me. Then she asks, "Why?"

"Because even the royal family is not—" I stop. "Why what?" I ask.

"Why do you want to bury Ruven?" asks Jaríne. "Even if you made him a promise—don't you think our rites are blasphemous?"

The simple honesty in her question takes my breath away for a moment.

"I do," I say finally.

You want to think you do, the phantom voice of Ruven murmurs in my head, but I ignore it.

"You blaspheme the gods with your beliefs and your rites," I say. "But I have blasphemed them too, and in worse ways. And I want . . . I think it is holy for anyone to keep a promise. Even for me. Even to one of you."

For an endless, excruciating moment, Jaríne holds my gaze.

"Then I'll help you," she says at last. The side of her mouth quirks up. "But you'll have to steal the body yourself."

28

STEALING RUVEN'S BODY TURNS OUT TO be the easy part.

Before we left, I took care to learn exactly which of the palace's inner courtyards Queen Imvada had used to hang his corpse from the walls. I wanted to make sure that I never, ever saw it. When I go looking for the spot now, I'm afraid that I might have forgotten it, but my feet find the route easily.

I stop outside the door into the courtyard. For a moment I can't move, my heart pounding and my stomach churning. Then I think, *I have to face him*, and push the door open.

It's a small courtyard, walled in white stone, with a chattering fountain at the center of a swath of bright green grass. Ringing the courtyard is a luxuriant line of rosebushes, red flowers open, their scent heavy and sweet on the air.

And strung up on the wall above them, hanging from a noose about his neck—

Ruven.

For a little while, it's all I can do not to weep or vomit. To my relief, there's still no sign of rot in his body, no swelling or discoloration in his hands or his face. The remnants of his spell continue to preserve him. But the ragged, gory ruin of his neck—visible just under the noose—is enough to make my head swim.

I remember sitting in his lap, touching his face, carving that jagged canyon in his throat. I've thought often enough, even as I learned from him, even as I kissed him, that I would do it again. And yet now—

—*now*—

It feels like a miracle that I keep from screaming.

There are no guards in the courtyard, because nobody who is not trusted can get so far into the palace to begin with. So it's easy for me to walk back down the corridors late that night, carrying first one chair and then a second. I stack them, and I climb them, and then—my heart pounding at every creak and sway—I saw through the rope with a knife, trying to ignore the scent of blood that's as fresh as when I first killed him.

Ruven's body falls to the floor with a meaty *thunk*. A heartbeat later I jump down, the stacked chairs falling after me in a clatter. I catch my breath and then—

It is *him* lying before me that is the problem. When I promised to bury his body, I had known that he hadn't decayed, and yet somehow I'd still pictured a skeleton, or . . . *something* strange and inhuman.

But it is Ruven himself who lies crumpled at my feet in the moonlight: the wavy black hair I once combed my fingers through, the soft lips I kissed, the jawline that I traced with my mouth.

My throat closes up, and I drop to my knees. I want to scream at him. I want to kiss him one more time. I want, more than anything, for him to open his eyes and speak to me, to be the ruthless, acerbic companion I grew to love.

But he does not. His body is cold and still. He is dead twice over, both times at my hands, and I have only his corpse left.

Gently, I lean forward and press a kiss to his forehead. The skin is cold and clammy, but I don't let myself flinch.

This is the man I love. This is what I have made him.

Then I set about trying to move him.

The thing about the dead body of the only man you've ever loved, I realize after a few moments, is that no song or story prepares you for how *heavy* he is. I've managed to drag him only a few steps, holding him by his collar, and I'm already out of breath.

Jaríne is waiting for me with a donkey cart by one of the servant doors. The path from here to there took me nearly ten minutes to walk, unburdened and in daylight.

You are laughing, aren't you, I think resentfully at Ruven's cold, lifeless face. Then I seize his wrists, wrench them over his head, and start dragging.

After all, I think as I stagger toward the doorway, tugging the weight of his body behind me, *he won't mind if he gets a few bruises*.

It feels like an hour at least before I arrive, sweaty and sore and breathless, at the door where Jaríne waits for me. She raises a judging eyebrow, but she still helps me haul Ruven's body into the cart and starts the donkeys on their path as soon as I've climbed in beside her.

"Are you sure this priest will help?" I ask once I have my breath back. We're already well into the city, Ruven's body covered with a simple drop cloth.

"Yes," Jaríne says simply. "He promised."

I find that hard to trust, but I'm doing all this for a promise myself, so I hold my tongue.

The heretic church is tucked away in a maze of narrow streets near the docks. Jaríne knocks at the door only once, and a moment later the priest comes out. He's a tall, bony man with dark skin and tightly curled hair; there are plenty of native-born Runakhians—including the prime minister—who look like that, so it's a shock when he greets Jaríne in a lilting accent that clearly comes from not just overseas, but beyond the Continent.

I knew the Magisterium had no seminaries in Runakhia, but I had still imagined that all their priests in our country had been born here, and only left for their studies. Clearly not, though.

"I wasn't sure you'd come," says the priest.

Jaríne is smiling, a lightness in her eyes and shoulders that I've never seen before. "My lady took longer than I thought, but we're here now. You're ready?"

"Of course," he says, nodding. Then he looks at me. "You should leave now, princess," he says gently. "You will consider what follows to be blasphemy."

I raise my chin, feeling a rush of pride and shame at once. "Yet I will stay."

He's right that I should leave; the gods will hate me for this. But I'd feel like a coward if I left now.

I don't understand the ceremony that follows—literally, for it is offered in the sacred language of the Magisterium, a ponderous tongue that the priest chants in a droning half-melody. Instead, I look around curiously at the chapel. It's a small, cramped wooden building with a pointed roof, full of narrow pews. The walls are covered in paintings that must have once been garishly bright but now are dimmed by many years of candle smoke.

Behind the altar looms a portrait of the Magisterium's only god, writhing and dripping blood as he hangs nailed to his tree. I know his story—vaguely—but I'm surprised by how wide the branches spread and how luscious the golden fruits half-hidden in the leaves are. Why is there a naked man and woman eating the fruit in one corner, and why does a baleful snake twist about the roots of the tree?

The rest of the walls are painted with the heretic saints, or so I assume: they all have round, golden halos about their heads, which I know is their symbol for holiness. But while a few of them do have wounds in their hands and feet, many others do not, as if they defied all reason to find some gentler kind of sainthood. And who is that weeping woman with her heart floating in front of her chest, ringed with flowers and pierced with seven swords, like a gentle-eyed Mor-Iva?

None of it makes sense. But it is fascinating, and wondering at it is easier than looking at Ruven's body as it lies on the steps, or at Jaríne's veiled head bent in prayer—Jaríne, who is almost as unfaithful to her faith as I am to mine, but who doesn't seem to doubt if her god is holy or monstrous.

Then the priest beings a slow circling of Ruven's body, swinging a thurible to incense it, and I can't look away anymore. As the clouds of fragrant smoke drift out to touch me, I stare at the lines of Ruven's face, the mouth I kissed and the throat I gashed open, and my heart aches with an infinite grief.

In whatever place there may be for heretics, I pray, *please be safe. Please be happy. Please, do not be alone.*

When the ceremony is finished, Jaríne and I help the priest

carry Ruven's body out to the churchyard, where graves are huddled together from one corner to another. There is no more room here, the priest explains, for new graves, but as Ruven's luck would have it, the stone mausoleum at the far end has just been emptied, when the rich immigrant family who commissioned it decided to take their dead back to their homeland.

So we lay Ruven to rest in a stone coffin, sealed by a lid with someone else's name. The priest says more prayers over the grave, but I hardly hear them, too busy staring at the cold stone and trying not to cry.

For the first time, it's truly striking me that he is *gone.* I've looked on his face for the last time, and then stone closed over him, and I will never see him again.

Never, never.

I try to think of facing the days and years ahead without him, without his voice and his blasphemies and his grim smiles, and I can't imagine it. Can't want it.

But this is the choice I made. When I killed him, and when I killed him again, and every step in between. I always tried to escape and extinguish him, so it's foolish to complain now just because I finally got what I wanted.

When it's over, we stand by the grave for a few moments in silence. Then Jaríne says quietly, her voice raw, "Father? Will you hear my confession?"

"Of course," says the priest. He looks at me. "Is there anything else I can do for you?"

"No," I say, trying not to feel rejected—but why would I want to be part of blasphemous ceremonies any more than I can help?

I stride out of the mausoleum and the churchyard without looking back. It's better to return to the palace without Jaríne anyway, I tell myself as I march down the narrow street. That way, if I'm caught, at least she won't be in trouble as well.

"Truly, I didn't think you'd keep your promise."

Ruven's voice rings through my mind and sets every inch of my body alight with fearful wonder. Slowly—heart pounding—I turn, and there he is, standing a pace behind me, exactly the same as always, his mouth crooked in a wry smile.

"You," I whisper.

Ruven sounds very smug as he says, "Yes. I."

"But—I killed you—"

"Some time ago. I know."

"At the shrine of Sarriel! Don't pretend you don't remember, you were there and you had just tried to kill *me*."

"Yes," says Ruven. And for the first time I can remember, the arrogance leeches out of his voice and his shoulders completely. "I tried to turn the gods against the royal family. Instead I turned them against the whole world."

"Don't expect me to pity you for it," I say tartly. I felt grief for him half an hour ago, but now that he's alive again, the acid pain of betrayal is twisting through my gut.

"I don't," he says simply. "But I am sorry for it."

My hands clench. "I'm not sorry for killing you," I say.

He shakes his head. "Don't be. Such complete rejection, such murder of me in your heart, was likely the only way you could have satisfied Sarriel." His mouth curves up. "And surely you were *born* to kill your lover so that you might save the world."

My eyes blur. "Surely you were born a fool," I whisper.

266

A moment later, I feel the bodiless chill of his hands on my shoulders, his lips kissing my forehead like a breath of cold air, and I sigh in relief. He is here. He is *here*—ghostly but real—and all my anger and confusion feel like nothing in the face of that one fact.

For a little while.

"But how are you still here?" I finally ask, stepping away from him.

Ruven shrugs.

"I think," he says slowly, "that when you killed me—while I was the center of a sorcerous spell that held all around me in thrall— you bound me, not unlike the way I had bound the court. While I lived, they slumbered. While you live, I haunt. When you rejected me so utterly, I could no longer speak to you, but I was not gone. Only silenced."

Not gone. Only silenced. I shudder with sudden horror and shame, but I make myself meet his gaze. "So you know what happened next."

"Yes."

"Are you going to tell me I should be sorry for making saints?"

"No," he says gently. "Because you already are."

Tears prickle at my eyes. I am sorry. I am not sorry. I am both at once, but most of all, I am . . . not Ruven.

And it seems he hasn't accepted that.

"I loved you," I tell him, my voice cracking, "because I thought you loved me. Not a girl who would obediently hate the gods at your command. *Me.*" I swallow, wishing my throat didn't ache this way. "But you didn't."

"I did," says Ruven. "I do. Lia—"

I turn away from him and stare at the cobblestones as tears spill

267

from my eyes. "I'm glad you're here," I whisper. "I was lost without you. But please—*please* don't talk to me just now."

When I finally look back over my shoulder, the street behind me is empty. There's silence inside my head.

It should feel like victory, but it does not.

29

QUEEN IMVADA IS ABSOLUTELY FURIOUS THAT Ruven's body is gone.

I expected it, yet her anger still shakes me. She gathers us—me, Araunn, and Varia—shortly after breakfast, and tells us for twenty minutes how Parliament hates her, the people of Runakhia don't deserve her, and the gods will surely avenge her.

I feel the pressure of Ruven's hand on my shoulder, but he says nothing. Perhaps he has grown a little considerate. Perhaps he's still cowed by what I said to him on the streets of Anazyr.

I never meant to be a traitor or a liar, and yet—

Here I am, meekly nodding along in time to Imvada's wrath as if I shared it, completely unrepentant in my heart.

She has made me a traitor, I think, my throat tightening as I remember my first glimpse of Ruven's body strung up on the wall. *They all have. Even the gods. None of them needed to be so cruel.*

I know I will repent of thinking such things about the gods soon enough. I doubt I'll change my mind about Queen Imvada. Even by the ruthless standards Varia taught me, she's a bad queen. The royal family exists to protect all Runakhia from gods and men alike;

Imvada seems to care about Runakhia only insofar as it can protect her own family.

I suppose that makes her not so different from me. But at least I'm trying to change.

The next evening, we are the guests of Parliament at a grand gala hosted once a year by the prime minister. We drive to his house in the same glittering, spacious stagecoach that we used for the Royal Progress.

It's strange to see familiar streets through the gilt-edged windows—also now familiar—of the stagecoach. It's stranger still when we draw close to the prime minister's house. I know what it looks like; I have been more than a few times to his neighborhood, pushing my way through the busy streets to gawk at the pale pillars and arches of the houses where the richest and mightiest live.

But now, the streets are not just busy, not just thronging—they are *crawling* with people. And not with the rich or almost rich who usually stroll down those streets. There are people from every walk of life here.

Some of them are saints.

I see light glint off golden horns and hands. I glimpse a girl with eyes growing all across her face, and a boy without hands or tongue.

As our carriage rattles to a halt, the noise from outside grows from a murmur to a shout. When the footman opens the door of our carriage, the noise is like a blow to the face:

"Give them back. Give them back!"

The chant rings through the air, from the mouths of saints and commoners alike. I shudder in a mixture of horror and guilt, but I cannot hesitate. Queen Imvada already thinks me weak enough.

When my turn comes, I square my shoulders and step out, chin held high. The prime minister is waiting to greet us while blue-helmeted policemen hold the protesters at bay.

"I apologize for the noise," says the prime minister, smiling politely. "It won't last long."

Imvada gives him a sour look. "It would not have lasted a moment, in my day." She snorted. "And to think, it's only been weeks since we freed them of the Red Death. The ingratitude."

Once we are inside the prime minister's house, we're in another world: a grand ballroom decorated with hothouse flowers. Musicians play elegant melodies from the far corner, and the tables are laid with a profusion of tiny, exquisite delicacies. All the richest and most powerful of modern Runakhia are gathered, men in perfectly fitted black suits and women in brilliantly colored ball gowns with sweeping skirts. They cheer and clap, bow and curtsy as we enter. It's as if neither the angry crowds nor the schemes of Parliament exist.

"I'm so delighted to see you again," Hézoraine declares, greeting us with a curtsy. "Allow me to present to you Runakhia's newest saint: Miryakhel Corbatton, daughter to one of my husband's dearest friends."

Is she newer than the saints in the streets? I want to ask, but hold my tongue. The girl curtsying beside Hézoraine is my age; she has a pale, narrow face, and red ribbons growing out of her dark hair. She's well fed and her dress is fine, but I know that nothing could have prepared her for the gods.

At least the nuns *tried* to prepare me. I look at Miryakhel and wonder what it would be like to wake up one morning, claimed by the gods without any warning.

"I am honored to meet you," Miryakhel murmurs, smoothly and softly obedient.

Whatever she feels about sainthood, she clearly doesn't want to share it with me. I retreat to a corner, where I eat the pastries and tarts, the roast sparrows and the tiny mousses molded in the shape of minnows, and I listen to the music and watch the swirling dancers, and I try not think of the people chanting, *Give them back.*

Was it also like this in Runakhia's golden age?

"Not in my day," Ruven says softly, "for all that we had no penal laws. The royal family was much too strict to allow it."

I find that I can't rebuke him for speaking. We both look at Queen Imvada, who is holding court among a circle of guests. The only one clothed in the ancient style, she's a bolt of crimson among all the dark suits of the men and the pale flower-blossom dresses of the women.

"May I have this dance?" Araunn asks from over my shoulder.

I startle, turning to look at him. "I . . ."

"Please," he says quietly. "We've hardly talked this past week."

We've hardly talked since Undanna. When I killed Ruven a second time and chose to be the perfect princess Araunn has always believed me to be, and somehow became even more heretical and more Ruven's.

I can't help myself: I look to where Ruven stands by my shoulder, feeling a strange need for permission even though I haven't fully forgiven him.

He grins. "I promise not to be jealous so long as you don't cut his throat," he says, and disappears.

I look back at Araunn. "I don't know how," I blurt out.

That seems to surprise him. "To dance?" he asks.

I shrug. "I was raised in a convent. And there wasn't time to teach me before we left on the Royal Progress."

Araunn laughs suddenly, a fresh, disbelieving sound that makes me remember why I nearly loved him.

"What?" I ask.

"Sorry," he says hastily. "Only . . . I was so afraid you'd laugh at me."

"Why would anyone laugh at *you*?"

"I don't know how to dance either," says Araunn. "Not the dances they do today." He holds out a hand. "Would you like to pretend together that we know how?"

The warmth in his smile is so simple and genuine that I can't resist. I take his hand and smile back. He's always been kind to me, and for all that I don't love him, for all that I'm betraying him—I am still grateful.

Araunn draws me into the center of the ballroom, dancers swirling out of our way. He's a quick study; after only a few minutes, he is drawing me through a soft, rocking step that is something like the dance performed by everyone else—not exactly the same, but close enough that I don't have to feel any shame.

Enough that I can stop worrying about the movement of my feet and notice the way Araunn smiles at me, the gentle pressure of his hands as he grips me.

"Lia," he murmurs. "I wanted to thank you."

"Why?" I ask, startled into honestly. And then hastily, to cover my guilt, I add, "I only did as I was taught. As the gods demanded."

Araunn shakes his head. "No. I don't mean—of course I'm

grateful that you woke us. *Saved* us. But I wanted to thank you because . . ." His voice trails off, and for a few moments we sway silently to the music. Then he goes on, "I grew up hearing stories of miracles. I saw them performed sometimes, by my mother and the saints."

I shiver, reminded again how old he is, how he was born and raised in another world.

"But they were no miracle to me," Araunn goes on. "They were only . . . the way the world was. The way the world would always be. And then Ruven came."

I stumble, my heart pounding. "Yes?"

"He destroyed us," Araunn says, his eyes distant as his hands still rock me through the motions of the dance. "He laughed at my mother, and instead of suffering her wrath, he cast sleep upon our court. It wasn't instantaneous. I struggled—I don't know how long—trying to move, trying to speak. It felt like dying when I gave up and let the sleep take me."

I can't speak. Ruven is blessedly silent in my mind. I spent so long hating him and his works, yet I never imagined what it would be like to suffer them.

Now I don't *want* to imagine it. But I still do.

"But you woke," I say, my voice breathless and trembling.

Araunn smiles suddenly, brilliantly. "You woke me," he says, and I can't help smiling back, despite all my sins and doubts and secrets.

"And in the days that followed," Araunn goes on, "you strove so hard for the gods' favor, and were so changed by it—and let me see the changes to all Runakhia because of it—" He shakes his head. "I always wanted to be a good prince, to fulfill my duties. But I do not think I ever truly loved the gods until I saw you love them."

There's a strange, powerful warmth thrumming through my stomach, my cheeks, my limbs. I've taught someone to love the gods. I have taught a prince from the golden age of Runakhia to love the gods.

It's been a long time since I imagined I could do anything so *good*.

The music swells. Araunn drags me—clumsily, earnestly—into a series of dizzying turns. Then we are dancing normally again, and he is gazing into my eyes as he says, "I always knew I would marry for the good of Runakhia, not love, but Lia—"

Suddenly the warmth is gone, replaced by a queasy chill. Araunn thinks I am a saint, not a sorceress, and he's convinced himself that somehow—

"—when I look at you, Lia, I lo—"

Somebody shrieks.

We both spin around to look. In one glance, I realize that who-ever shrieked doesn't matter.

What matters is Miryakhel, a saint of Zumariel, staggering back as Varia glares at her. Though I didn't see it, I'm absolutely sure that she just slapped Miryakhel across the face.

"I cannot believe you would ask such a thing," says Varia, her voice ringing across the room in a clear bell peal of fury and loath-ing. "I cannot believe that any saint would ever *want* such a thing."

"I am *dying*," says Miryakhel, her voice shaking. "If you do not heal me—"

"Miryakhel, darling," interrupts an elegant, middle-aged

woman, laying a hand on her shoulder in a gesture that is clearly motherly, "I know you are overwhelmed by the honor of the gods, but—"

"*I never wanted their honor!*" Miryakhel shouts, wrenching herself free of her mother's grip. She staggers slightly, panting, as she looks about the room that has gone completely silent. "I never wanted to be a saint," she says in a small, miserable voice. "I never wanted to suffer and die at the gods' pleasure. But I woke up growing ribbons from my face, and—and please, I just want to—"

She shudders and suddenly vomits a tangled mass of bile and crimson ribbons. Her mother cringes back from the mess, as do several of the nearest guests.

"Your Holiness," bleats a plump, worried man who must be Lord Corbatton. He grabs Miryakhel by the shoulders as he goes on, "Please forgive my daughter. She is not well. The blessing of the gods lies heavy upon her."

Varia stares him down in silence for a few brittle moments—while Miryakhel coughs and gags—before saying, "Blessed are they who accept the favor of the gods."

"Blessed are they," Lord Corbatton agrees fervently as Miryakhel sags in his arms.

"I am going to faint," Miryakhel's mother announces, and swoons to the floor in a suspiciously graceful swirl of petticoats. Instantly there are servants and guests running to attend her; in the hustle and bustle, Miryakhel is whisked away without any fanfare.

Minutes later, the music starts up again, and with it the dancing. The murmur of conversation and the clink of glasses resume.

The only sign of what's happened is Varia's grim face; the rest of the party spins on unbothered, as if it were completely normal for a girl to vomit ribbons while she hates and fears the god who changed her.

I can't move. I feel cold and heavy, as if I've turned to stone.

I learned to dread and doubt sainthood when I saw it laid upon Anabekha. But I never imagined it like this.

How can what has happened to Miryakhel even *be* sainthood? Saints love the gods so much that they die conforming themselves to the divine natures. That's what the nuns taught me. That's what I saw at Undanna, and in the eyes of Anabekha.

But Miryakhel's transformation has nothing of love or trust or even reverence, only pain and fear and hate.

Like what Mor-Iva did to you.

I'm not sure if it's Ruven whispering in my mind or my own treacherous thoughts.

"Lia?" Araunn asks softly, taking my hand.

"Please take me outside," I blurt. "Not—not out of the house, I don't want to cause more commotion, but—isn't there some kind of garden here?"

There is. Araunn leads me to a marble bench beneath an arched trellis of blooming roses. I suck in breaths of the cool, damp night air and try not to remember the awful gagging sound that Miryakhel made.

"Did you ever see anything like that?" I ask. "Before?"

Was sainthood like this in the golden age? I wonder.

"Once," says Araunn. "A very old saint of Zumariel. He had come to bless my second cousin's wedding, but he could barely say the words of the prayer for gagging. It was . . . strangely beautiful, to see his devotion in the midst of agony."

I pull back from him, feeling cold. "No," I say sharply. "I mean, did you ever see a saint who didn't *want* to be one?"

"Oh." Araunn's shoulders slump a little. "That. No, I never did."

His voice makes the words into an apology, but I only feel a strange flicker of anger. "You knew what I meant. Why did you pretend you didn't?"

"Lia, I wasn't—" He breaks off, and looks away for a moment. When he looks back, his voice is quiet as he says, "I was afraid."

"Of what?" I ask, more gently this time.

He lets out a strangled, nervous laugh. "I don't even know. There are stories of apostate saints, it's not a thing that's impossible. But that girl—she was like the worst lies of the heretics come to life, and I . . . panicked."

"If our words are come to life, that makes them not lies," says Ruven. My eyes flicker from Araunn's face for a moment, and I see Ruven standing in the corner of the garden, his arms crossed, his face set in a grim challenge.

"What lies?" I ask Araunn. I know what Ruven likes to say, but I don't know what the other heretics of the golden age did.

"Do they not proclaim it in the streets anymore?" Araunn asks.

"They don't proclaim much of anything nowadays, with the penal laws."

"Oh," says Araunn. "That's good." My surprise must have been evident in my face, because he goes on, "My grandfather was much too kind to them. My mother tried to set things right, but Parliament was reluctant, and by then there were preachers on every street corner, it seemed, proclaiming the sins of the royal house and the cruelty of the gods. The . . ." He grimaces, then blurts it out: "The rape of the saints. That's what they called it, that is the *only* way they could imagine the holy union between humans and the divine." There's a sudden, furious energy in his voice. "That's why my mother had her guards arrest them when they spoke in public. Not for their blasphemies against the gods—they would have been allowed that, if they said it in private. For their insults against the saints, who suffer and die so we may know the gods."

"Were there . . ." I grope numbly for words. "Were there people like Miryakhel in your day?"

"The gods chose her for a reason," Araunn says soothingly. "If she hates them, surely it's her father to blame. It seems most of the rich and powerful have been raised that way. But things are changing now. She'll learn to love the gods." He smiles. "Like I did."

I stare. Araunn's face has become as foreign and frightening as Ruven's was the first time I met him. How can he think those words will comfort me? How can he comfort *himself* so easily?

Araunn grew up in the golden age of Runakhia. He knows why Miryakhel's sainthood is its own kind of blasphemy, a wretched parody of what sainthood should be. Either he is unutterably callous, or—

Or sainthood was never what the nuns taught you.

Or the golden age was never what you believed.

Or the gods are even more cruel than you thought, and holiness even more bitter, and Ruven was right to turn on you.

"Lia," says Araunn, taking my hands, "I was trying to tell you something earlier. Do you want to hear it?"

I swallow. I see Ruven looming behind Araunn like a tall shadow, his arms crossed. There's no anger in his eyes, and that feels worse than any reproach.

"Yes," I say, though I dread what I know I'm going to hear. "Tell me."

His smile grows wider, his hands tightening on mine. "Lia Kurinava, who saved us and gave me hope . . . I love you."

I feel like a dark hand is closing around my heart. Araunn is my betrothed. I will marry him. I must, if I want to live and keep helping Runakhia as one of the royal family.

And I do want it, so very badly. I've already destroyed the Red Death and brought saints back to our cities. Whatever's wrong with how things are now, it's better than what we had before.

But I can't say *I love you* back to him. I've only ever said those three words to Ruven, and that's one kind of honesty I want to keep.

There's more than one way to lie, though. I smile at Araunn and tilt my face up. When he kisses me, I work my lips and my tongue against his exactly as I have before.

I squeeze my eyes shut so I can't see Ruven. The shiver that goes through my stomach is more shame than lust.

When we finally part, Araunn sighs. "Oh, Lia." I don't know if I pity or hate him more as he rests his forehead on my shoulder.

I realize that Ruven is still there, still watching me. And there's still a terrible understanding in his eyes.

"I would have done anything," he says. "To achieve my mission. I wouldn't have spared my body any more than my soul."

My throat tightens. *This isn't my mission*, I think at him. *I kissed Araunn because I want to stay alive.*

The words make me feel even more horribly traitor than before, to both of them. The next moment, I cannot sit there any longer. I push Araunn away and surge to my feet.

"I should go back inside," I tell him, pasting a smile on my face. "It's my duty."

And I flee—out of the garden, through the ballroom, and into the vestibule where we entered the prime minister's house.

I'm looking for solitude, for a moment where I can be only myself, and not a liar.

What I find is Miryakhel. And Hézoraine.

They sit at the bottom of the stairs, Miryakhel with her head in Hézoraine's lap. She looks as if she has been sobbing, but now she's still. Hézoraine is stroking her hair with a strangely maternal air.

I stop, suddenly feeling like an intruder. After another moment, Hézoraine looks up to meet my eyes.

"Do you need anything, Your Holiness?" she asks, and she doesn't sound any less elegant and proper than before, but—

I realize that I want to cry. I swallow and try to get control over my voice.

"I doubt her parents or their doctors know anything about treating a saint," I say.

Hézoraine's mouth thins. "They do not."

"The Convent of St. Eruvaun," I say, "they have a saint of Nin-Anna there, and they—are prepared to care for saints, I think. If she needs a place to stay."

Hézoraine searches my face for a moment, and then, as regally as Queen Imvada, she nods. "Thank you."

30

I NEVER THOUGHT I WOULD MISS the Royal Progress, but in the week that follows, I do. There I had a purpose, however often I failed, however many lies I told.

Now the shrines are all awakened and the gods themselves are making new saints every day. My only use is to be a symbol, holding hands with Araunn and smiling to show everyone that the royal family is beloved by the people of this era. Night after night, there are dinners and dances, trips to the opera and the public gardens, visits to the halls of Parliament.

I do my duty, smiling until my face aches. But I hate it, because it feels like every lying, deceitful moment from the Royal Progress times ten.

Because I can't ignore what the gods are doing—what *we* are doing—to Runakhia.

The streets of Anazyr are restless with penniless saints: men and women who made their living by working every day in a shop or factory and were beggared when they could not go to work anymore. Their families are often with them on the streets, ruined as well; and meanwhile there are also protests from the families who are rich enough to support their sainted loved ones but hate the death sentence that has been handed down to them.

Miryakhel's father and mother are not among the protesters. But that's because they are rich enough that they have something to lose by blasphemy.

I still cannot hate the gods. I don't know if that makes me holy, or foolish, or broken. I cannot hate them, nor wish them back asleep. I cannot feel it's anything but blasphemous when a riot breaks out around the cathedral and people throw horse dung at the windows. And yet I cannot hate their fury. However wrong they may be about the gods (and I am no longer sure how wrong they are), I cannot dismiss them the way Imvada and Varia and—worst of all—Araunn do.

Araunn means to be a comfort. He *tries* to be one. He sits with me at breakfast, and takes me for walks in the palace gardens, and smiles at me during the terrible length of royal dinners.

Once it would have been enough. Once it would have been *everything* that the heir of the royal house, that anyone was so concerned for me.

But now, when he smiles at me, all I can think of is how easily he forgot Miryakhel's pain. How he smiled when he made saints at Undanna. How it doesn't matter what I think of him; I will have to marry him and bear his children anyway.

"You're a sorceress," Ruven tells me. "You can escape him. You can kill all this monstrous royal family. You're strong enough."

But I *can't.* Because I can't give up loving the gods either. Oh, I doubt them, and sometimes I hate them; but without them, I don't have a language to love anything. I want to see the sick healed and protected, and I can't want that without thinking it's a way to honor Nin-Anna. I want to see the people profiting off the plight of the beggar saints punished, and I can't separate that from Mor-Iva's yearning for blood.

In the end, it's Varia who changes everything.

A week after that terrible party at the prime minister's house, we are all standing in Queen Imvada's bedroom, watching her comb the long red strands of her hair. I'm no longer listening to the conversation but staring at the arches of the ceiling and wondering how I'll occupy myself tomorrow. What I'll do with the terribly endless space my life has been reduced to when I'm not performing a part with Araunn.

Then I hear Varia say, "The convent of Nin-Anna was nearly burned last night, I cannot see why—"

"What?" I demand, coming instantly to attention.

Imvada arches an eyebrow. "Ah, you care at last to listen?"

"There was a mob outside your convent last night," says Varia, fixing me with a gimlet gaze. "They were offering food and shelter to saints who had nowhere else to go, but rumors had started that they were holding them prisoner, forcing them to work miracles in the hospital. And that," she says, turning back to her mother with her chin raised, "is why we *cannot* wait to do something for the new saints."

A mob. The convent, nearly burned. I feel sick. I've done my best to put my longing for it out of my mind—I'd been so furious at the nuns for sending me away, for never wanting me to stay at all—

But that old wound hardly seems to matter now, when I think about Anabekha laboring to heal all the people that I never will. And Miryakhel, who I promised would be safe within those walls.

"I should go see them," I blurt out.

Everyone looks at me—Imvada skeptical, Araunn concerned, Varia opaque—and for a moment I panic and nearly apologize. Then I gather my courage and say, "Surely it would be good for one of the royal family to show concern for such faithful subjects who love the gods and honor the saints."

Imvada considers this a moment. "Very well," she says finally. "It is, at least, an action that will not disturb our other goals. Unlike *some* proposed this night." She slants a weary, contemptuous glance at Varia.

"Really?" says Ruven, from his corner of the room. "So eager to go whining back to your masters with your tail between your legs?"

Though I still haven't forgiven him, I don't take offense as I once might have; I know that his fury is not at me, but on my behalf.

Would you do any differently, even now? I ask him silently. *In Sarriel's shrine, did you not hope at least a* little *to finally please the monks who raised you?*

Ruven's mouth flattens, but he nods in acknowledgment.

And the next day, I go back to the convent.

This time, I go in a royal carriage. But when I'm shown into Mother Una's study, and as I wait for her, I can't help feeling like I'm a foolish runaway again. Like I'm still a little girl wanting nothing but her approval.

I hear the door open, and I turn to see Mother Una and Anabekha entering the room together.

My first thought is an astonished, *She's so old.*

Not just old: frail. I know that for all the troubles in the city, Mother Una cannot have aged much in the couple months since I last saw her. The change must have been creeping through the wrinkles of her face, slowing her steps and weighing down her shoulders, for the last several years at least. But I had never noticed it before. Always, when I looked at Mother Una, I saw only the strong, decisive woman who looked at a little child and declared her Nin-Anna's chosen.

Beside Mother Una, Anabekha is radiantly young and beautiful—and worried. She is biting her lip as she enters the room, a gesture I've never seen from her before; when our eyes meet, she smiles, but smooths her skirt nervously.

"The blessings of Nin-Anna upon you, child," says Mother Una. She sits down in her chair with a sigh. "What brings you here?"

"I—I heard about the riot," I say. "I was worried. Is everyone all right?"

"Of course we are," says Anabekha, her eyes haunted. "Nin-Anna protects us."

With an awful wrench, I realize that Anabekha no longer quite believes that. Or no longer finds it fully comforting. And as much as I might have once wished for Anabekha to feel even a fraction of the doubts that torment me—

Now I don't. I hate that someone else is suffering the way I have, just because the world and the convent and the gods are all so cruel.

The thought is blasphemy, but I can't feel sorry for it.

A knock hammers on the door.

"Yes?" Mother Una calls out.

The door creaks open. "I'm sorry," a girl wearing the habit of a novice says, "I told him to go away, but—"

"Excuse me," says Reverend Coldren from behind her. "But I was hoping to have a word with you, Reverend Mother."

Anabekha's expression doesn't twitch, but her body is alight with sudden tension.

With an asthmatic huff, Mother Una hauls herself to her feet. "I have told you already," she says as Coldren enters the room, "in this convent we are faithful to the gods and we have no use for your apostate schemes."

"I'm not here to scheme," says Coldren, looking at Anabekha. There's a rawness to his voice that I've never heard before. His dark hair, always so perfectly slicked back on the Royal Progress, is a rumpled mess. "I see now I was wrong to suggest that the saints leave your infirmary," he continues. "I am only here to . . . bring some gifts from their families. Fruit baskets and favored toys and the like."

"Nin-Anna's saints are not children," says Mother Una, and there's a peevish tone to her voice that is new, or that I never noticed before.

"Yet many of them are young," says Anabekha. "Please, Reverend Mother." She lays a golden hand on Mother Una's arm. "I think it would do some good—not just for the saints but for their families as well. You know how hard this has been on them."

"Lord Corbatton was *most* desirous," Coldren adds.

"Surely we should give the saints every comfort," I put in. I don't fully understand what's going on, but this feels too much like the problem of the beggar saints for me to be silent. Besides—I realize, suddenly—I trust Anabekha far more than I do Mother Una.

For a few moments, Mother Una's face is taut with suspicion. Then she sighs. "If the two of you accompany him to make sure he does nothing improper," she says, "I suppose it would be all right."

"Thank you, oh, *thank you*," Anabekha cries. She kisses Mother Una's cheek, and I cannot help a spurt of jealousy when I see the affection and delight that soften Mother Una's face.

287

"You were always such a good child," Mother Una whispers, and the way she gazes at Anabekha makes it seem like there is no one else but the two of them in the whole world.

For a moment I feel like I'm choking alone in a dark ocean of despair: *Now she has the saint she always wanted, that I was never good enough to be.*

Then I notice Ruven's grim gaze from the corner of the room, and the way Anabekha's golden fingers tremble, and I cease to be jealous.

Coldren left his presents stacked in a handcart out in the hallway. He pulls the cart himself as we walk to the infirmary in awkward silence, Anabekha staring straight ahead and Coldren staring at Anabekha and I glancing uneasily between the two.

I wonder if I misinterpreted what Anabekha said at our last meeting. They'd certainly shown no tenderness for each other on the Royal Progress. And how could anyone love *Coldren*, of all people, even as humbled as he seems to be now?

Ruven murmurs in my ear, "I'm glad there is *someone* you would have been more horrified to love than me," and despite all that's between us, I can't help smiling.

Then we reach the infirmary and I forget everything else.

I've entered this hall many times, to clean floors or bring meals or empty chamber pots. I'm used to the rows of beds filled with patients—mostly the impoverished of the city, but sometimes the devout rich who want to be treated by Nin-Anna's nuns. Usually no more than a third are strong enough to sit up, turn, and look at anyone who enters.

Now, almost every person in a bed sits up to look at us.

Most have golden hands. But some have the golden horns of

Juni-Akha's saints, or the terrifying hole in the middle of the forehead that signifies Ithombriel's chosen. In the nearest bed sits a girl with crimson ribbons growing through her dark hair.

Even before she raises her head to look at me, I know who it is: Miryakhel.

When our eyes meet, her mouth twists as if she's swallowed something bitter. But her expression eases when she sees Coldren.

"Did my parents read my letter?" she asks hopefully.

"I'm not sure," says Coldren. "But I have gifts regardless." As he steps to her bedside, there's a gentleness to his face and voice that I've never seen before, and suddenly I can understand why Anabekha loves him.

"Look," he says, and gives Miryakhel an orange. "Just as I promised."

Her smile glows as she takes the orange, her fingers curving around it. She's grateful for it the same way I was once grateful for the nuns: because, like I did, she thinks that she deserves nothing more.

That gratitude touches me in a way that her fear and my horror never did. I hardly realize I'm moving before I'm at Miryakhel's beside.

"Hello," she says warily.

"I'm sorry," I tell her, and then I lay a cracked, charred hand on her forehead.

This is wrong. This is *all wrong*. Somehow Zumariel seized this girl who never loved him, never wanted to be his saint. He plundered and changed her body and condemned her to an early death. And it is wrong. It is so wrong, and my mind and body alike catch fire with a pure, wrathful judgment.

The gods should not do this.

This kind of sainthood should not exist.

I'm no longer a single girl, doubting and alone. I am wrath and judgment and inevitable consequences. There is only one way that the world can, should, *must* be allowed to exist, and I beg and command Mor-Iva at once, *End this.*

She responds with a rush of satisfaction like blood sliding down the back of my throat.

Power thrums down my bones and set my skin alight. The world is glory and judgment and melting wax around me, and then it is a cold, quiet space again.

I realize that my hand has dropped from Miryakhel's forehead. We're both shaking and gasping for breath.

The ribbons growing from her face are gone. As I watch, the ones in her hair shiver and fall to dust.

The power of Mor-Iva is still pounding in my veins, roaring in my ears. I hardly understand what's happening as Anabekha and Coldren rush Miryakhel out of the room. It's only after, as I stand staring at the empty bed, that I start to understand. Start to wonder.

I unsainted somebody. I took the blessing of the gods away.

That should not be possible.

"All judgments are possible to the beloved of Mor-Iva," says Ruven, appearing beside the bed. "Why do you think she was neglected for so long by the royal family?"

I take a ragged breath, and say silently, *Don't tell me that you reverence her now.*

"No," he says. "I reverence the one who heals what none of us ever could." He kneels and stares up at me in desperate adoration. "I reverence *you*."

And before I can fully absorb the full import of those words, he seizes my monstrous hands. His grasp is lighter than a breath of air, but I yield to it like I am grass swaying in the breeze. He draws my hands forward, and he kisses my charred, cracked palms.

My breath stops in my throat. My heart flutters against my ribs like a captive moth straining toward the light. All I can think is that Ruven shouldn't say those words, not when I am everything he thinks blasphemous and vile, and that I shouldn't delight in his reverence, not when he is a heretic who hates the gods and who I still have not forgiven—

And yet, oh, my heart is singing, and for the first time my body feels like a holy place.

Then I hear a boy's voice call out cautiously, "Please, ma'am . . . can you heal me too?"

My head snaps up. The chubby, tow-headed boy two beds over is looking at me.

Everyone in the infirmary is looking at me.

In the back of my mind, I feel a sensation of stirring and stretching, claws flexing, and I hear Mor-Iva say, *If this is the only judgment we have to make, then get on with it.*

Isn't it blasphemy? I ask cautiously. *Aren't you angry?*

Mor-Iva chuckles, small and soft like blood clots. *I am the knife of the gods. I judge and cut as I will. You may too.*

And so I heal the saints in the infirmary.

Not all of them. Some, when I come to their bedsides, beg me to pass on. A balding man with ruddy cheeks tells me, "I thought nothing could be better than gin, and then I found Ithombriel." A young woman, her stomach swollen in pregnancy, says, "The babe never moved until I was a saint. I'll gladly give myself to Nin-Anna as repayment."

But most of them want to be delivered. Most sob, or smile, or gasp in relief when I lay hands on them, judge their sainthood wrong, and carve away the invisible hooks of the gods' power.

As I labor on through the infirmary, I think that perhaps I should be feeling wretched that I have turned against the gods who were my first love, and whose favor is necessary for the world to continue; or perhaps I should be triumphant, that I am stealing saints from the gods who rejected me.

But all I feel is a sense of solemn rightness. I am cutting what needs to be cut, I am a blade justifying my own existence. And I love it.

When I have at last attended to the final patient, I turn to look back at the doorway into the infirmary—and there stand Anabekha and Coldren, their mouths dropped open in identical expressions of slightly horrified shock.

"They did not want to be saints," I say, walking toward them. "So Mor-Iva judged them unworthy of it, and took the honor away."

My voice sounds calm and confident to my ears, but inside I am quaking. The serene assurance I felt moments ago has faded away, and now I'm just a foolish apostate girl who has revealed to everyone how little she ever loved the gods.

"Did you heal them all?" Anabekha asks slowly.

"No," I say quickly. "Only the ones who didn't want sainthood."

I reach for Anabekha—to take her hand, pat her shoulder, I am not sure. But she flinches.

"Don't touch me," she says.

A cold shock runs through me. "What?"

"I want to be Nin-Anna's saint," says Anabekha, her voice breaking. "It's all I've ever wanted. Healing people is all I've ever wanted. Please don't take it from me."

There's a strange pressure in my chest. *Please don't make me lose you*, I think—but that isn't quite true. We grew up together, but we were never close. I would feel more bereft if I lost Araunn or Varia, despite the short time I've known them.

Anabekha is only . . . everything I ever wanted to be, and a girl I never fully understood, and now a saint who loves the gods as I cannot.

My eyes blur as I look at her.

"You should go now," says Anabekha, her words low and quick. "I can make sure Mother Una doesn't know you're part of this, or at least doesn't dare name you. But you have to *go*."

I hesitate. *Will you be all right?* I want to ask. *Is this really what you want?*

"Can you get Miryakhel home?" I ask instead.

"I can," says Coldren, arriving behind Anabekha. "And, Your Holiness . . . if you will permit it, I will bring you more saints for healing. But you need to go now."

I nod. "May Nin-Anna and Mor-Iva bless you alike," I say to Anabekha. And then I leave.

31

THAT NIGHT, I DREAM OF MOR-IVA.

I am standing in a dell that is surrounded by trees but filled with nothing but lush grass and little white flowers. It's late afternoon; the honeyed sunlight dapples the grass, glowing emerald bright through the stems. At the center of the little valley is a round pool of still, dark water.

On the other side of the pool, Mor-Iva sits with her legs crossed, fidgeting idly with the stubby severed ends of her aorta.

"It took you long enough," she says, not looking away from the heart she holds in her hands. I recognize her voice as the one I've heard before, yet it's strangely more human and easier to bear.

"What is this?" I ask, unable to restrain my bitterness. "Why are you speaking to me *now,* when you wouldn't before?"

Mor-Iva's head snaps up, and her golden eyes burn as she says, "You were never so willing to be a knife before. To choose and judge and cut. You were never willing at all. I called and called, but you never listened."

My voice cracks as I say, "I *begged* you to hear me."

"I did." Mor-Iva shrugs. "It's a weakness of the pact: you are the only mortals we cannot compel to listen to us, the only minds we cannot master. Because we have bargained with you, and so become indebted."

I stare at her, fear worming through my gut. I still remember the troubling words of Nem-Una: *We were tasked to love the world, each in our own way, but we each loved only what was ours.* This too sounds like heresy, and yet once again, I cannot doubt that I am truly speaking to a goddess.

"For what are you indebted?" I ask slowly. "What do we have to give you?"

Mor-Iva stands; her fingers flex, and the heart is gone from her grasp, instead throbbing once more in the jagged ruin of her chest.

"Do you not know? Each one of us loves eternally just one thing, and that thing only you mortals can incarnate. *We* have no power to wrench it into the world, unless we write it in your bodies. Unless we make pacts with you, and saints through the channels of our pacts."

There is a wrathful, desperate earnestness to Mor-Iva's voice, like a fire that could engulf the whole world, and I shrink back.

But I have to know.

"What were you before?" I ask. "Before you concerned yourselves with us, *what were you*?"

Mor-Iva shrugs even as she leans hungrily forward. "That's no concern of mine," she says. "All I see is you. All I know is you. All I am is *you*."

I want to protest. Our only duty is to conform ourselves to the gods we love. The nuns taught me that; no matter how much I've sinned and failed, my heart still beats to that rhythm.

And yet . . . the part of me that loved to read theology, the more hairsplitting the better, cannot help grasping at this new doctrine and turning it over.

All I am is you. What does that even mean? I am not a goddess, whereas Mor-Iva is immortal and unchanging.

I think of how Sarriel went from judging the whole world in one moment to accepting it the next, simply because he witnessed an ending that pleased him. Perhaps it's not that we can change the gods, but simply that we can change what they see.

Perhaps this is what it means to be part of the royal house, instead of merely a saint: to redirect the gods, these ruinous storms of power and might, into something humans can bear, can live with . . . can even love.

I draw a shaky breath and decide to try my luck.

"I don't want to kill people," I say, all in a rush. "I want to release all those who were unwillingly sainted. I will make saints of whoever truly wishes it. But I don't want to kill. Not again. Not ever again."

Mor-Iva tilts her head. "Truly? Is that who you are?"

A moment later, the backwash of her power slams into me, a tidal wave of questioning: *Is that what we are now? Is that all we are?*

I gasp and shudder under the weight of Mor-Iva's wondering as memories dance through my mind and burn across my skin. I see girls slaughter warlords, men slay sorceresses, and queens execute beloved traitors. I see every bloody, ruthless judgment that anyone who's ever made a pact with Mor-Iva has rendered.

I see, and I judge, and I think, *Yet I refuse to kill again.*

Ruven's blood is still hot upon my hands. The saints I made at Undanna are heavy on my soul. And I want no more. *No more.*

Eventually the storm fades. I realize that I'm on my knees, leaning forward on my hands.

A clawed finger catches my chin and tilts my head up. I look into Mor-Iva's serene golden eyes.

"You are strong," she says. "And you are determined. And you hate what you judge to be wrong. That is what I love. That is all I have ever loved."

She bends down and presses a burning kiss to my forehead.

I wake with a gasp, bolting up in my bed. It's not quite dawn; I'm alone in the dark blue half-light of my room.

Sweat beads on my face. I can still feel the burning imprint of Mor-Iva's kiss on my forehead.

She loves me, I think, hardly believing it.

But the gods don't lie. And Mor-Iva said that she loved me. She looked at my willful choice to refuse killing like a proper saint of hers—my heretical determination to heal saints—and she said, *That is all I have ever loved.*

It's like the first time I saw the golden eyes of Nin-Anna's portrait, but a thousand times more. I'm completely overwhelmed by the sudden, gasping relief of realizing that I don't have to be hated, that I'm not something abhorrent and wrong, that I am *wanted*.

I raise my hands. In the dim light, they're like shadows, but I can see their shape clearly enough: the long, spiderlike fingers, the sharp claws.

For the very first time, I don't hate my hands. I have healed with them, Ruven has kissed them. And Mor-Iva, who gave them to me . . .

Is *my* goddess now.

The next moment I'm sobbing, all the misery of the past weeks ripping through my chest alongside the dizzying relief of knowing that it's over. I'm angry and doubting and—yes, half apostate still—but I'm no longer sundered from the gods. Not as I was before.

Eventually I run out of tears. I rub away the worst of them with my forearm—I can't use my hands unless I want ash in my eyes—and then get up to wash my face with the cloth that lies folded next to the bowl and pitcher on my bedside table.

The cold water stings and tingles on my skin, and I grin wildly into the darkened mirror. I belong to a goddess. I'm no longer just myself, meek and lonely and afraid. I can do *anything*.

"It seems to me," Ruven drawls from the corner of the room, "you did quite a lot before."

I turn to him, confident delight sparking down the length my spine. "Then you haven't seen anything," I say. "When I killed you, I still thought I was beloved of Nin-Anna. But after . . ."

"After, you became a girl who could love me?"

I am suddenly solemn as I step toward him. "After, I became afraid. Of everything, because I had hardly any faith left. But then I found you to love, and now I've found Mor-Iva. And *now*"—I take his ghostly hands, feel the chill of his fingers curve around my own—"I'm going to heal every saint who wants it, and laugh as I do it."

He laughs softly under his breath. "Of course you will," he says, bending his cold forehead down to press against mine. "My dearest apostate."

I tilt my face up and find his ghostly lips. "Also," I whisper between cold phantom kisses, "I am going to forgive you."

Healing all the saints is easier said than done.

So is loving Mor-Iva.

I still don't like the word *healing*. I still can't believe it's true, that the gods are a curse and a plague upon us. I am only adjusting; I am setting things right; I am making—

Heresy incarnate, Ruven supplies helpfully, and I glower at him. But I'm not truly angry, because I know that he's wrong.

The gods are not like that. I will make them not like that.

Mor-Iva, at least, I can make to be not like that.

She doesn't like it when I start, despite her promise in my dreams. The first time I meet Coldren in the shabby rooms he has rented for our purposes—the convent will not have us anymore—and see the sniffling girl whose hands have gone gold for Nin-Anna—

In that first moment, Mor-Iva whispers viciously, *She is a coward. She deserves to suffer. Judge her, and let her die in the service of the goddess she doesn't love enough.*

I shudder, suddenly stiff with the feeling of divine disdain.

I look down at the young woman whose golden hands are clasped with my own. Her stomach is swollen with a baby that cannot be more than one or two months from birth. Coldren told me that she's from his parish, a girl who was never devout until her lover abandoned her unwed and she needed the charity. He'd arranged a place for her to stay, and she was doing well until Nin-Anna chose her for a saint.

Do you know, Mor-Iva whispers in my ear, *she nearly swallowed drugs to scour the babe from her womb?*

She'd hardly be the only one tempted, I reply silently. Sometimes, at the convent, we would treat women who had poisoned themselves as they tried to escape pregnancy. There was always a story of desperation behind their eyes.

But she was too much of a coward to do it, Mor-Iva hisses in my ear. *If she doesn't have the nerve to kill, she doesn't deserve to live.*

I feel suddenly queasy as I realize why Mor-Iva hates the girl so much. As I remember that the gods love only what is according to their natures, and motherhood is not of Mor-Iva's.

"Miss?" the girl quavers, because she doesn't know who I am; there are thick knitted mittens covering my hands. "Can you help me?"

She judged that the child should live, I say fiercely to Mor-Iva. *I judge that she should too. Surely you understand that?*

"Yes," I say aloud.

She's unclean, Mor-Iva thinks rebelliously. *Worthless, mortal, without the slightest teeth to justify her.*

But I can hear a slight hesitation in her hatred. Perhaps it's just my imagination, but even so, I can make it real. I can choose not to hate those who are hated by the goddess whom *I* once hated.

"Yarilana," I say, knowing her name by the power of Mor-Iva, "live and hold your child in human hands."

As I speak, I brush my hands over her face, strengthening the child in her womb with all the power I rip away from her golden hands.

That night, I sit up in my bed, staring sleeplessly into the darkness. I think and pray: *It is not wrong to be human. It is not filthy to be weak, and it is* human *to be kind as well as ruthless. I am kind as well as cruel, and you have judged that you love me.*

Slowly, Mor-Iva starts to listen.

And the world starts to change.

I don't notice it, at first. I am so busy smiling to Araunn and obediently nodding to Imvada and secretly slipping away to meet with Coldren or Anabekha and all the wretched, faithless saints they have managed to find. Every time I strip away somebody's sainthood, my stomach churns with Mor-Iva's disgust, and my skin crawls with divine revulsion. Every evening when I stumble back into my bedroom, I'm dizzy with exhaustion. Jaríne has to take charge of putting me into my nightgown and pushing me into bed.

Then I lie awake for what seems like hours, praying to Mor-Iva. Telling her that I'm not wrong, that mortality is not obscene, that ripping the divine power from these human creatures is good and holy.

Sometimes I see Ruven sitting by the side of my bed. He never prays with me, but he lays a hand on my shoulder, as if to encourage me.

Does he think I'm corrupting the gods with heresy?

Perhaps I am. The nuns taught me that I should never question the gods. They never told me that one day Mor-Iva would whisper into my mind, *Is this who we are? Is this what we are?*

The gods are ancient beyond imagining, and yet she sounds so young and fragile.

Yes, I think as I heal another saint. *Yes, this is what we should be. Yes, I make this judgment. Yes, it is right to do this.*

Sometimes I think Mor-Iva might be starting to believe me.

Sometimes I dream of fire and blood and claws, and I wake feeling glad.

I know that I'm becoming famous. If Imvada didn't rant about

301

the tales of a saint-destroyer, then I would have heard the rumors from Anabekha when she met with me. Anazyr is a city boiling over with ambition, terror, and wonder—of course the people trade stories of the nameless phantom girl who can free any soul from the grasp of the gods.

I know this, and I'm confident the rumors cannot touch me.

But then comes the day when Hézoraine invites me to dinner.

32

I'M SITTING LISTLESSLY IN THE WINDOW seat of my bedroom when Hézoraine arrives. Last night I healed five saints, and now I feel like my bones are lead and my brain is a lump of clay.

Imvada and Araunn spent the evening making a dozen more saints. I know this because Araunn told me and Varia about it at breakfast, his eyes alight with hope and wonder.

"They were so happy," he said. "I know you both are worried, but we are changing this world for the better. We are bringing people back to the gods."

I had to suppress both a wince and a gag of revulsion. And yet I know that once I would have thought the same. Once—and not so long ago—I would have wanted nothing more than to serve the gods in exactly the way the royal family dictated.

I can't hate Araunn for believing what I once did. But I've seen too much—too many reluctant, agonized saints, writhing with pain and out of their minds with fear—to feel any joy in what he's telling us.

As I sit in the window seat, I keep returning to that moment at breakfast. In my memory, the moment twists, Araunn's delight becoming a lurid glee, his words all obscenities.

And yet I know he is kind. And yet I know what he has done. And yet—

"A visitor, Your Holiness," Jaríne calls out, startling me from my daze.

"Oh," I say, sitting up straight as Hézoraine strides into the room.

"My dear!" Hézoraine cries and kisses my cheeks. "I can't stay long. I only wanted to ask you to dinner tonight at our private residence. Just you, me, and my darling husband."

The words are utterly unexpected. "I can't—" I falter, then fall silent.

"Don't worry, I've spoken to our queen already and she can spare you for an evening," says Hézoraine. "The carriage will come to fetch you at six. I can't wait, it seems so long since we were all together."

Without waiting for a reply, she sweeps out.

I've been given orders, I think with a sort of numb surprise.

Hézoraine's orders are not the only ones I get. Queen Imvada speaks to me later that afternoon, pacing restlessly back and forth in my bedroom.

"Of course she believes that she is going to flatter and cozen you into taking Parliament's side," says Imvada. "Be as pleasant as you can but promise them nothing. And remember everything that's said at the table, because I *will* ask you."

As she delivers that last sentence, she turns on me a piercing, critical gaze just like the old nun who once drilled me on history, and I have a wild urge to laugh.

But there's no laughter in me that evening when I arrive at the prime minister's house. Ghostly white in the evening light, the facade of pillars and arches and cornices looms over me, like a threatening echo of the palace.

For years I hated and feared the prime minister, because I knew he stood against the gods. Now . . . I still serve the gods, but I stand against what people have always believed them to be. Against what the nuns always taught me was right and holy. I can't help fearing that my rebellion means I will somehow *have* to submit to the prime minister's whims.

And yet I'm only judging according to the rights that Mor-Iva gave me, with no thought for what Parliament wants.

I'm no longer a little girl in the convent. I'm a princess who's made her own pact with the gods, and whatever happens tonight, I have the right to judge the prime minister as I please.

I get out of the carriage, lifting my chin and squaring my shoulders to face the evening.

At first it's fine. Hézoraine is remarkably adept at moving a conversation no matter the circumstances. The food, served on fine porcelain that gleams in the candlelight, is exquisite. I smile and nod as I eat my roast partridge, and I think that perhaps everything will be all right.

But eventually, Hézoraine beckons one of the footmen to her side and whispers something in his ear. He nods, and a moment later, he and all the servants who were waiting on us file out of the room.

A prickle runs up my spine, though a moment before my eyes were growing heavy, lulled by the food and wine.

The prime minister is looking at me with a grave, focused attention he's never shown me before.

"I hope you won't take it as an insult," he says, "if I confess there is a reason we invited you here besides the pleasure of your company."

"That depends on what the reason is," I say, proud of how my voice doesn't shake.

"The reason, I fear, is the queen." The prime minister sighs. "She is . . . a remarkable lady," he says with a gentle sadness that makes my skin crawl. "No one admires her virtues more than I."

I hope he doesn't notice the grimace that briefly tugs at my mouth.

"But she is a lady of an earlier time, and I fear that not all the ways she seeks to honor the gods are . . . prudent. Or kind to some of our people. Have you seen the suffering caused by this"—his voice stirs with a sudden ripple of anger—"this *plague* of sainthood?"

"Of course you have," says Hézoraine, smiling gently. "Else why are you healing them?"

Cold shock binds me in place.

They know, I think in horror. *How many people know?*

"My dear," the prime minister says, gently reproving.

"It's no use pretending we aren't aware, darling," Hézoraine replies. Then she looks back to me. "I promise you we haven't told—"

"I promise *you*, I've done nothing of the kind!" I snap, my voice tight with barely leashed panic.

One distant little part of my mind thinks, *Oh. Now I've made a false promise. Add that to my sins.*

"You've been very careful," Hézorine says gently. "Not even Jaríne suspected; I quite respect that. But I do charity work among some of the . . . respectable poor, and one old woman, bless her heart, couldn't help describing the young lady who saved her grandson."

"There are, after all," says the prime minister, "a limited number of young ladies with dark hair and one golden eye. No matter what kind of gloves they wear."

The faint humor in his voice is more humiliating than a slap to the face. I want to snarl at him, but I remember the lesson I learned in the convent as a child, when I had secretly broken or spilled something and Mother Una informed me that there was only one girl clumsy enough to have done it.

"You mean, there's only one *that you know of*," I say steadily, meeting his gaze.

If he had better proof than one old woman's description, he'd have trotted it out to begin with. He might feel certain, but he doesn't *know*.

"Consider this a message for your long-lost twin, then," says the prime minister, again with that infuriating humor. I open my mouth to protest, but he raises a hand. "No—just listen. You don't trust us, of course you don't. So hear this: there are more reasons to be worried about the queen than the plague of saints. She desires that the crown should have all its ancient powers—and more, according to the scholars I've consulted—which I hope that you, as a child of this age, might agree would be bad for Runakhia. It was my hope, and that of Parliament, to persuade the queen that her role should be to lead us in honoring the gods. What does she know of the wars we have fought, the dangers we now face, and the glories we hope to find in the future? Why—" He checks himself. "But I'm not giving a speech to Parliament; please excuse me. The real point is this: we desire to negotiate fairly with the queen, and yet between her status in the eyes of the faithful and the power she commands through the

Royal Gift . . . it's not possible." He fixes me with a piercing gaze. "Unless, perhaps, you were to help us."

"You are a hero to the people twice over," Hézoraine says warmly. "To those who love the gods and those who do not. If you proclaim a new way . . . they will listen."

"And you have the Royal Gift," says the prime minister. "That special threat of the queen's is matched by you."

They're asking me to commit treason, I think in stunned amazement.

"Isn't that what you've been doing for weeks?" Ruven asks dryly from behind my shoulder.

I press my lips together, fighting a smile despite the circumstances. *I mean new treason.*

"Oh, well, a *new* treason. That's utterly shocking and depraved."

I focus on the prime minister. "I would never, ever do anything to hurt the royal family," I tell him.

"Oh, no, no, no, of *course* not," Hézoraine says quickly. "Nobody wants to harm them in the least! But surely you have also feared, as we have, that they will harm themselves beyond saving? And all the country with them?"

I sit back in my chair. Is that a *very* carefully worded threat, or actually something they fear?

It makes no difference, really. I still have a decision to make: help them or not. Rebel or not.

I take a deep breath. "I hope you don't expect an answer tonight," I say.

The prime minister nods. "Of course not. But think on it. That's all we ask."

My voice is heavy in my throat. "I will."

And I do think about it, all the way back to the palace. I stare through the window of the coach at rain-spattered streets glittering under the gas lamps, and I think of the beggars who must try to find shelter from the rain tonight. I think of Queen Imvada, combing out her hair and complaining how nobody gives her proper honor. I don't really know what it means to be a good queen, but I feel reluctantly certain that she is not.

And yet . . . to depose the rightful queen? That's the dream of heretics and traitors, and despite all my sins and treacheries so far, the thought of it makes me nauseous with dread. And in this new world the prime minister wants to build, what will become of Araunn and Varia? Or Anabekha and Coldren?

But if I say no, that won't stop the storm that is coming. I think of the bitter desperation I saw in the crowd chanting their demand to have the saints returned. I've answered that cry—but not fast enough, and only in one city. And I know that people are angry with the royal family for more reasons than just the unwilling saints.

With or without me, the prime minister will make his move. The people of Runakhia—not all of them, but far too many—will follow him. And the whole country will be torn apart.

Unless the royal family changes.

Queen Imvada will never listen to me. But she dotes on Araunn, and he says that he loves me. More important, he has still kept the secret of the morning I tried to run away. He's the only one of the royal family who might possibly have sympathy for the people plotting against them.

So when I get back to the palace, I go to find him. Araunn is in

309

the same place he's been every evening for the past week: hidden in a corner of the palace library, surrounded by books over five hundred years old while reading one published last year about trains.

"Lia!" he exclaims, looking up as I approach. "You're back already?"

"Yes," I say, kneeling beside his chair. Araunn's forehead creases in mild puzzlement—I know he's not used to seeing me kneel before him like a petitioner.

I know, also, that he thinks I am especially pretty in the soft glow of lamplight. As I take his hand, I know that he's going to blush when he feels my skin against his. And I know that I am using myself as a weapon to pierce his kind heart—but I don't hesitate.

For Runakhia, I have to do this. I have to make him listen.

"Please," I say quietly, "I need your help."

"What's wrong?" he asks.

"Do you remember the crowd of people protesting outside of that party?" I ask him. "The riot that nearly burned down my convent?"

"It's horrible," Araunn agrees softly.

"It's only getting worse," I tell him. "That's what the prime minister wanted to talk to me about tonight—so many people are unhappy with the royal family. They're glad the Red Death is gone, but they still don't want their whole world to change overnight."

Araunn stiffens. "We didn't want that either," he says, a new edge to his voice.

"I know," I say guiltily. "But . . . then you understand, don't you, how desperate that kind of change can make people. And your mother wants to change everything so quickly."

"She has a vision," says Araunn, "of what Runakhia could be."

I nearly wince at the raw faith in his voice.

"There's going to be a rebellion," I tell him. "That's where her vision will lead us—if she doesn't change, if we can't change the minds of the people who are angry. But she doesn't listen to anyone . . . except you." I squeeze his hand. "Araunn, if you talk to her, you can make her understand how perilous things are. You can find a way to make her vision real—to make everyone else see it the way she does. I believe you can, truly."

I don't know if I'm lying or not. But I want it to be true, and I need Araunn to trust me, so I stare up at him with all the willful faith I can muster.

Araunn stares back down at me, strangely tense. I can't tell what he's thinking.

"Lia," he says finally. "The prime minister . . . he's one of the people who's going to rebel, isn't he?"

Terror jolts through my chest.

"You can't tell the queen," I say quickly. "She'll have him executed for treason, and then there really will be a war. And I know it *is* treason for him to say such things, but it was also treason when I tried to run to the convent—I think everyone's just afraid, the same way I was. You knew that, didn't you? That I didn't mean any harm? I think . . . it might be the same for all those people." I bite my lip. "Some of them, anyway. And I don't want to see anyone hurt."

"Of course you don't," says Araunn, his face softening. He leans forward and kisses my forehead. "I'll talk to her, Lia. I promise."

I've done all I can, at least for now. It's a strangely weightless feeling. I float back to my bedroom, I let Jaríne put me in a nightgown and comb out my hair, and then I lie down in my bed and sleeplessly wonder for hours if I've done the right thing.

Until the palace guard burst through my door.

One moment my room is dark and still, and I've finally started to drowse.

Then there are bright lights and people shouting. I bolt upright, my heart pounding, but I'm too dazzled by the sudden light to really see anything—

Hands seize my shoulders and slam me back down to the bed. I shriek, trying to twist out of their grip. I think, *Mor-Iva*, but I get no further before something cold and heavy snaps around my neck and the world turns into a cold white haze.

When I come back to myself, I'm on my feet, each arm gripped by a palace guard. There must be a dozen of them at least crowded into my bedroom: men in red doublets, glittering swords at the hips, all of them more than five hundred years old. The thought feels funny, but I can't laugh.

There's a cold weight around my neck. I manage to raise one hand and touch it: a necklace of braided metal. There's something wrong in the shape of it, in the way it presses against my collarbone, something *wrong*—

Nausea roils through me. I grip the necklace convulsively; the next moment I'm doubled over vomiting, my hand falling away numb.

One of the guards swears, but another laughs. "Didn't you know, Your Holiness? That's what happens if you touch an anathema collar."

I blink up at him. *Anathema collar.* I'm too dazed to remember if I've heard the name before or not.

"Time to go," the guard says, addressing his fellow men. "The queen wants her. Daven, put that back or I'll cut your hand off."

They drag me out of the bedroom, footsteps clanking and echoing in the hallways. It's so empty. So very empty.

"Because it's the middle of the night," Ruven says, walking beside me. I open my mouth to reply, but he instantly shushes me. "Don't talk, you fool. You really aren't taking the collar well, are you?"

It feels very unfair that Ruven is dead and yet has a better idea of what's going on than I do. While I'm trying to think of a way to tell him this without saying it out loud, the guards haul me into the queen's bedroom, and then I forget everything as they shove me down to my knees.

The shock of that clears my mind a little; I manage to raise my head and meet Imvada's gaze. Still dressed for a formal dinner, but with her hair falling loose about her, she stares down at me with an expression of wrathful disappointment.

"So briefly you were faithful." She sighs.

"What?" I manage to say. "I'm not—I *am*—"

"Araunn told me what the prime minister said to you," says Imvada, and even with my mind scrambled, I can still feel the horrifying import of those words. "And I know from my own spies that you are the apostate who unmakes saints. I know that you have betrayed us. The prime minister is being dealt with now. His career of grubbing for power is over." She pinches my chin, raising it up as she stares balefully down into my eyes. "You, though. You will do one thing more for your gods and your queen. You will serve as our

Great Sacrifice. You will break open all limits on divine blessings and drench us with the power we need to restore the old ways."

Great Sacrifice. I *know* those words from long-ago history books, but though I can feel the ominous weight of them, I can't quite remember what they mean.

Imvada lets go of me. "Take her away," she says.

33

THE DUNGEON CELL IS SMALL AND cold, with only a tiny barred window in the door. The guards shackle me to the wall by one ankle, and then they leave me.

It's a relief to be alone again. To sit still. I huddle against the wall, my head resting on my knees.

"They don't know you're a sorcerer," says Ruven.

"What?" I raise the weight of my head to stare at him blearily.

"They don't know you're a sorcerer," Ruven repeats. "There are ways to restrain us from using our power, but that anathema collar? Not one of them. It only cuts you off from the god with whom you made your pact." He grimaces. "Unfortunately, you seem to be reacting to it much worse than most."

"Oh," I say. I can tell that he's saying something important, that I'm supposed to care about it, but my mind keeps sliding away into the cracks between the flagstones.

He makes a sound of disgust and hooks cold hands around the back of my neck, pressing the tips of his thumbs to the hollows behind my ears. "I won't apologize for this," he says—

And brilliant, sorcerous power wrenches through me, burning away the cold fog of the anathema collar, leaving me gasping and awake.

I straighten as Ruven backs away. It's like the other times he's used my power—but worse, more painful. The inside of my mind feels scraped raw and bleeding. There's an ache just below my collarbone—no, a burning—

With a jolt of panic, I realized it's the locket that holds my relic growing hotter and hotter. I fumble at the clasp for a few moments before I give up and just wrench at the chain, breaking it.

The locket falls and skitters across the floor—not a moment too soon. Its golden surface is already glowing a dull red; then it begins to twist and bubble. I stare in horror, wondering if it's going to melt. Instead it starts to char—like burning flesh, I can't help thinking—until it's no more than a little pile of ash.

"Well," says Ruven after we've stared at the ruin of my relic for several moments, "I *will* apologize for that."

I shake my head. "No, don't. I feel better now." The rush of sorcery that cleared my mind is gone, but the terrible fog has not returned. "That collar can't have been forged for somebody who was a member of the royal house *and* a sorcerer. Perhaps that's why I reacted so badly."

I'm still a sorcerer, but now one without a relic and hence without power. The anathema collar is no longer addling my mind, but I also have no way to escape.

Where could I go, anyway?

Araunn won't help me now. I don't know if he tried to persuade Imvada as he promised, or if he simply denounced me to her as a traitor—but it doesn't matter, because she knows that I've been healing saints. And Araunn won't forgive me that. No true child of the royal house could.

The prime minister would likely help me, but Imvada must have sent men to arrest him as well—unless he started his revolution as soon as I left his house, in which case I suppose he'll come free me in the morning.

And if there's anyone else who might have the power and the will to intercede for me with Queen Imvada, I simply have no way of knowing.

With a sigh, I roll onto my side, pillowing my head on my arm as best I can.

"You're going to sleep?" Ruven asks, his voice sharp. "Just like that?"

I yawn. "What else can I do? Bite through the chains?"

I can't work sorcery and I can't ask the gods for a miracle and . . . perhaps I am very foolish, or only very tired, but after months of desperately trying and failing and trying again, it is curiously comforting to be caught up in a disaster that I can do absolutely nothing about.

"They're probably going to kill you," Ruven says impatiently.

"I know. I'll panic in the morning." I look up at him. "Sit with me, please?"

He huffs indignantly, but then sits beside me and lays a cool, ghostly hand on my shoulder.

"Sleep then," he says. "I'll keep watch."

I don't panic in the morning. But without darkness and exhaustion wrapped around me like thick blankets, I do worry.

I *fear.*

I don't want to die, I don't want to be imprisoned, and now my helplessness is not so comforting anymore. I feel like a tiny lost doll swept away on a vast dark current.

I wish that I could hear Mor-Iva again. She would probably rage and demand to know why anyone who touched me is still alive—but I miss her.

It only gets worse when Araunn and Varia come to visit me. Araunn is the first in the door; he rushes across the cell and pulls me up into an embrace.

"Lia," he whispers desperately into my shoulder, "I'm so sorry. I told Mother you weren't a rebel, that you refused to listen to the prime minister and you couldn't possibly be the apostate who claims to heal saints—but with so many enemies, she has to be very careful. I promise we'll get you out."

I'd started to relax into his embrace, but now I go rigid. He still thinks I'm innocent, that I'm faithful and devout and have never sinned, and the guilt is suddenly too much to bear another moment.

"Araunn," I say, and then wrench myself away from his grip. "Araunn! Listen to me."

He looks at me, listening, trusting, and I hate myself.

"I am the apostate," I say, quietly but clearly. "I've spent the last three weeks healing people of sainthood and I regret none of it. I only wish that you and your mother would have listened."

"What?" says Araunn, his voice stunned and soft and broken.

Too late, I realize that perhaps I've provided evidence against the prime minister that I shouldn't have. But then Varia says from her place beside the door, "Well, it sounds like Mother picked a good time to arrest half of Parliament."

Half of Parliament. I feel dizzy. This is far more than my personal treason or the prime minister's plotting. Imvada is making a conquest of Runakhia and she seems to be winning.

"So tell me this," says Varia. "Did you ever have a pact with Mor-Iva at all? Or was it sorcery from start to finish?"

"Have you *still* not seen my hands?" I demand.

"Sorcery could do as much," Varia says coolly, and Araunn gives a horrible flinch.

My throat hurts. "No," I tell them. "I did have a pact. Until your mother took it away, apparently." I gesture at the anathema collar around my throat, careful not to touch the metal. "I didn't know that was possible."

"Really?" Varia sounds curious. "What did you think, that no one in the royal family has ever disagreed before?"

Araunn rounds on her. "This isn't a joke, Varia!"

"Of course not," Varia says flatly. "Your betrothed is a traitor and an apostate and she's going to die for it. Mother was quite serious on that point."

A wave of nauseating fear washes through me. I don't want to die.

"Lia," Araunn says, turning back to me, "please—I don't know why you'd say these things, but—I can't believe you're really guilty, I *know* you're not. Just tell me the truth and I'll help you. I promise."

He doesn't believe me, I realize despairingly. He still loves me. And he is going to try to save me, and probably get himself killed.

I think of the story Varia told me about the dog that once savaged him.

At least, I think bleakly, *I know what it will take to make him give up.*

"The truth," I say slowly and clearly, "is that I have looked the gods in the face and I have hated their works. I would unseat your mother if I could. And I have never, *ever* loved you."

Araunn stares at me, his eyes wide and haunted. Then he spins around and flees the room, the door slamming behind him.

"Well, now you've broken his heart," Varia says conversationally. She sets the basket she's carrying on the floor and steps forward.

"I—" My voice breaks; I press a hand to my mouth.

"Oh, I certainly approve of lying to him," says Varia. "It's the only way to keep him safe, sometimes." She looks me up and down. "But you truly are an apostate, aren't you?"

"Yes," I croak, hating how I'm on the edge of bursting into tears.

It is true, also, that I have never loved Araunn, at least not in the way that he came to love me. And yet—and yet now that he is gone, I regret driving him away.

"I'd hoped you were innocent of at least one crime," says Varia. "But I knew . . . probably not." She shrugs. "It's an ugly business, serving the gods. Not many can bear it."

"Why do we have to bear it?" I burst out. "Why does loving the gods have to be . . . *like this*?"

"Wouldn't we all like to know," Varia says bitterly. "But it is what it is. For us, there's only one way we get to live."

I want to rail against those words, but I know Varia won't listen. Instead I say, "The queen said something about a Great Sacrifice."

Varia nods. "She's been planning it almost since we awakened. Told me and Araunn about it as soon as we got back from the Royal Progress but thought it best to wait on telling you. She was planning to draw lots from among the three of us—that's tradition—but now that you're a traitor?" Varia's mouth curves in a humorless smile. "You get the honor."

"But what is it?" I ask. I've been racking my brain since I woke up, but though my mind is clearer now, I can't recall anything but vague references in the oldest histories. "The nuns never told me about it."

"Oh, of course they didn't," says Varia. "I don't think most folk knew about it in our time either; it's a very old tradition, and hardly cheerful. But did you ever hear the story of Prince Irazaunn, who prayed so passionately for deliverance from invaders that he died of it? And in answer the gods wrecked the Zémorine armada?"

I nod. It was a favorite story of mine as a child.

"That was a Great Sacrifice. Irazaunn walked into the divine realm with his sister and she cut his throat before all the assembled gods. In repayment they gave her such astonishing power that she could set a ring of storms around Runakhia at will. So you see why Mother is eager to make another one."

I try to imagine Imvada with that kind of power, and I feel numb with horror. I've never heard her speak of whom she wants to help, only the enemies she wants to kill.

Varia sighs. "Well, I've done my duty and more now, so I might as well be going. The basket is courtesy of Araunn. I suppose he isn't as desperate for you to have it now, but you might as well enjoy it all the same."

"Varia." I hadn't meant to speak again, but the name rips out of me, and when she pauses by the doorway to look back, I plunge on, "Do you—do you really think that your mother should have that kind of power? Do you think she'd use it kindly?"

"No," Varia says quietly. "But those arrayed against her are just as bad or worse. So I'll live and bide my time. That's the way of our family." Sadness flickers across her face. "I do wish you could have learned our ways, truly."

Then she's gone.

I stare at the closed door, feeling utterly wrung out—and terrified. Imvada ruling the country with that much power, that much ruthlessness—what will become of Jaríne and Anabekha and Coldren? Of all the former saints who came to me for healing, and the families who brought them?

I'd wanted the old ways and the worship of the gods restored, but not like this. Even before I'd started to doubt, I hadn't wanted it like this.

"Then you must stop it," says Ruven.

"I'm chained up in a dungeon," I say bitterly. "What can I possibly do about it?"

"They're going to take you into the realm of the gods," says Ruven. "They have to remove the anathema collar for that. Of course they'll bind you and threaten you and rely on the power of their own pacts. But you're a sorcerer even without your relic, and you have a pact with the knife of the gods."

"And?" I ask, knowing what he's going to say and dreading it.

"Kill them," Ruven says quietly. "Then renounce your pact with Mor-Iva. End this perverse connection between mankind and the gods, once and for all."

I'm standing with my back pressed against the wall now as he looms over me. Memory flickers through me of that first night, when his power slammed me into the wall of the palace, and I realized that I could use his loneliness against him.

Even then, I had belonged to Mor-Iva. So now I tell Ruven what I've already told the goddess: "I don't want to kill again."

"Your beloved royal family doesn't have such scruples."

"Which is why I will stop them if I can," I say sharply. "But I won't turn into them. And I won't renounce the gods."

His voice is caustic. "Still hoping for a return to your beloved convent?"

I shake my head. "No," I say quietly. "What the gods are doing right now, the way they are making saints, it's wrong. It has to stop. But . . . I can't renounce them."

"Still? After all this?" His voice seethes. "What kind of cruelty would it take to break your idiot adoration?"

I swallow. I remember the sky turning dull red with Sarriel's wrath, and Miryakhel's agonized fear. But I also remember sick children healing under Araunn's golden hands, and Mor-Iva's judgment laying Yarekha's ghost to rest. I remember how just a glimpse of Nin-Anna's portrait made me desperate to help everyone.

"You were right," I say. "They are monstrous gods. But . . . they are beautiful monsters." I look up into his eyes, willing him, *begging* him to understand. "And I love them, as I love you."

Ruven lets out a little strangled noise and sinks to his knees, laughing bitterly.

"Oh, my little saint," he whispers, clutching at his hair. "What have we done to each other?"

I kneel beside him and touch the ghostly chill that is all I can feel of his face. "We have loved. At least we have done that."

Jaríne comes to visit me later that day. She isn't allowed to close the door as Varia and Araunn did, but I'm just surprised she was allowed to come at all. In fact, for the first awful moment, I think that she's been arrested as well.

But then she stops a pace away, hands twisted together, and says barely above a whisper, "I didn't tell them. No reason for you to believe me, I suppose, but I swear I never told anyone."

Desperate relief washes through me. "I know you didn't," I say, just as softly, rising to meet her. "Is Anabekha—"

"Fine, so far as I know. And that vicar has more than a few connections; I think even now he can protect her."

"Will *you* be all right?" I ask. Jaríne worked for the wife of the prime minister, after all.

"I'm not arrested, am I?" Jaríne shrugs. "Nor is my old mistress. She's too important back in Zémore. I think she'll get shipped back there, and like as not I'll go with her." Her mouth quirks. "I suppose a country full of atheists can't be worse."

I nod. It's hardly good news for Jaríne that she will be exiled, but it's probably for the best—especially if Imvada succeeds at the Great Sacrifice.

"Could you take a final message to Anabekha for me?" I ask. "Not if it's dangerous. But if you can, tell her—tell her I said thank you. And that I pray she has many years to serve Nin-Anna."

Jaríne nods. "I can and will."

"Thank you, Jaríne," I whisper.

"You know that's not my name," Jaríne says after a moment. "I don't have a drop of Zémorine blood. My mistress just thought it sounded more elegant."

"I . . . am not surprised," I say, a little baffled by the shift in subject.

Jaríne reaches forward and takes my hands, fingers wrapping

around fingers. "My real name—the one I was baptized with—is Mareya. After the lady who became the mother of our god." She smiles waveringly. "I wanted you to know."

It's a farewell gift; more than that, it's an act of trust. To share with me something that Jaríne—no, Mareya—holds sacred, in the confidence it will not be disdained.

I squeeze her hands. I think, *Even if I die, at least I did some good. At least I made some friends. At least someone is happy I was once alive.*

"Thank you, Mareya," I whisper.

34

TWO DAYS LATER, THE GUARDS COME at sunset to take me out of my cell for the Great Sacrifice.

I'd half expected to be dragged through the streets in a cart, like a criminal for execution in the old days. Instead I am bundled into a carriage with the curtains drawn, a guard sitting on either side of me.

Of course I'm not going to be marched publicly through the streets, I realize as the carriage rattles forward. Imvada hasn't yet gained the power she desires. There are still people who think of me as a hero, or who at least wouldn't like the idea of the Great Sacrifice.

Briefly I consider trying to pull back the curtains or wrench open the door. But how likely is it that somebody would notice the brief commotion before the guards have me subdued? And even if somebody did notice—what could one person do? It would take a whole angry mob to stop one carriage, and I have no way to stir one up.

Briefly, I imagine a world in which I'd been quick-witted enough to ask Jaríne for help escaping. Perhaps Jaríne could have told Anabekha about the sacrifice, and Coldren could have used his contacts at the cathedral to find out when it would happen. Then on the appointed day, Anabekha could summon a crowd with miracles and tell them what was happening, and the whole city would rush to save me—

"But you didn't," Ruven says softly. "So they won't."

He's seated across from me, so I'm able to glower at him as I think, *You're very comforting today.*

He sighs. "I did it often enough myself, all those years in the palace. Dreaming of one thing after another that I might have done differently, so that I might have cast that spell without trapping myself. It's a good enough pastime when your fate is set. But yours is not." He leans forward, his voice burning with intensity. "Not yet."

I close my eyes. *Not yet,* I think. I'm not in the realm of the gods *yet,* and so I don't yet need to make my choice. But soon.

I don't want to break my promise to myself and kill again. But I can't let Imvada wield the power of the Great Sacrifice.

And I still, selfishly, do not want to die.

When we get there, I whisper silently to Ruven, *don't leave me.*

"Never," he promises. "No matter what."

When we finally reach the cathedral, it feels like a fever-dream parody of the Royal Progress. Once again I am entering a shrine—but this time there's no extravagant welcome, only guards surrounding me. I barely have a glimpse of white bell towers before I'm hauled inside.

The nave of the cathedral is dark and cavernous, lit only by occasional little clusters of candles; all I can see of its famed beauty is a little curlicue of white stonework here, a tracery of gold leaf there.

Not that I have much attention to spare for such things, because waiting inside the front doors of the cathedral—flanked by more guards and six acolytes with candles—are Imvada, Varia, and Araunn.

They are all dressed in the old style, gold and silver embroidery glinting on their robes. I'm still wearing nothing but my grubby nightgown, and I feel hideously ashamed even in the dim light.

Imvada looks me up and down but says nothing; Araunn won't meet my eyes; Varia's face is a scornful mask.

"Let us begin," says Imvada, her voice low and solemn.

And so we do. It's the strangest procession I could ever have imagined: a dark, empty cathedral; six acolytes, chanting in voices that sometimes tremble; the ancient royal family, arrayed in splendor; and me, clad only in my nightgown and the anathema collar, dragged along behind them by guards.

"And me," Ruven adds dryly. He's walking beside me now.

And you, I agree.

I remember how furious I was the first time he followed me into a shrine—how much he had despised me—and now he is my only comfort. Ruven, the heretic sorcerer who serves the Magisterium. What would Mother Una think?

I can't help a little snicker at the thought, and once I've started laughing, I can't stop. Nothing about this situation is funny, but it's all so bizarre and surreal, and now everyone is pretending I'm not laughing, which just makes me laugh harder.

When we reach the sanctuary of the cathedral, Imvada turns and, without any warning or ceremony, slaps me across the face.

The shock strangles the laughter in my throat. I blink at her and try to catch my breath.

"You won't like what happens if you go laughing into the realm of the gods," she says.

I'm not likely to enjoy it anyway, I think, but I say nothing and do not resist as they open the little sacred door and drag me down the narrow stairs.

The heart of this shrine is a sacred fire. Varia walks into the flames without even pausing.

Araunn does. He stops, and wavers, and looks over his shoulder.

"Lia," he says softly, and my heart lurches as he almost meets my eyes.

"Go on," says Imvada.

Araunn swallows, and without another word, he obeys.

Imvada turns to face me again. "Hold her," she says, as if I weren't being held already. Then she reaches around my neck and unhooks the anathema collar.

It's like daylight suddenly blazing through my brain. I hadn't realized how much the thing still weighed on me until now—now when my body feels lighter than air and the power of Mor-Iva is singing through my mind—

As I think this, I'm already stumbling forward, pushed from behind. The next instant, the flames swallow me up.

I fall and I burn and then I am in the world of the gods once again.

This realm is the home of Juni-Akha and Ithombriel, king and queen of the gods: the lady of the sun, of daylight and glory and triumph; the lord of the moon, of darkness and stars and wisdom. So it is a mountain between daylight and night.

To the left is a soot-black sky glittering with ten thousand stars, far more than I have ever seen in mortal skies. To the right is a sky of flame-bright blue, an azure more intense than I have ever seen beneath the mortal sun. The two halves of the sky meet in a seam of mottled purple and red, gold and cream, and at the apex of that twilight band burns a sun whose flame is purer and nearer than the mortal sun's, and yet bearable to look at.

The mountain itself is a vast, crumbling spike of pure white rock that reaches up into the sky. A narrow path of stairs winds up the slope; from where I stand at the base, I have no idea where it ends.

All this I have only a heartbeat to notice, for the next moment Varia has seized me with an iron grip, and the moment after Imvada is holding me as well.

"Oh, no you don't," says Imvada. "There's nowhere for you to run here, apostate."

Only Ruven is allowed to call me that, I think, and wish I had shoes on so I could at least stomp on the queen's foot.

Where is Ruven, anyway? I crane my neck, but he's nowhere to be seen. Has he somehow been left behind? Or is he remaining hidden?

"Let me make you a bargain," says Imvada.

I stiffen under her grip and turn a scornful look over my shoulder. "What do you have to offer?" I ask, not trying to sound meek now, because what does it matter?

From the corner of my eye, I see Araunn flinch. Let him be shocked. I don't need him to think I'm good now either.

"Walk with us to the top of the mountain," says Imvada. "Submit to the sacrifice. Die with honor, and all your sins will be forgiven."

"Or?" I demand.

"Or else you try to run, and we hunt you," Imvada says flatly.

"And when we return to the mortal world bearing all the power of the gods, it will not go so well for the convent that raised you."

I won't let it come to that, I think fiercely.

But I let my shoulders slump and I say, "Very well."

Whatever I choose to do in the end, I'm not ready to fight them yet. And I'm not quite desperate enough to kill myself right away before they can use me. So the only answer is to pacify them and bide my time.

Until the top of the mountain.

It seems that is farther away than I thought. We climb for—there is no way to tell time in this strange day-and-night world, but it feels like hours. When Imvada finally calls for a halt, at a little flat place where the stairs briefly ease into a platform, Varia slumps to the ground without a word, like a puppet with her strings cut.

I collapse at one end of the platform, as far from Imvada as I can manage. I lean against the rock and close my eyes. For some trackless period of time I simply rest and breathe, but finally I call silently: *Ruven?*

"Lia?"

My eyes snap open. Araunn is kneeling before me, looking terribly unsure.

I feel like my heart is two stones grinding against each other, aching with guilt.

"What?" I ask quietly.

"Did you . . ." His voice trails off; then he visibly gathers his courage and plunges ahead. "Varia says I should stop trying to fool myself, but I can't quite believe it unless I hear it from you again. Did you ever love me?"

I bite my lip. I can imagine myself saying, *Yes, I love you, I'm sorry I lied.* Araunn would believe me. I could pull him into a kiss, and he would melt. If I did that—now, here, with the knife hanging over my head—he might very well turn against his mother to help me.

But that would be using his longing for affection the same way the nuns once used mine.

If I can't love him the way he deserves, I can at least give him the truth.

"I don't know," I say, the words slow and painful. "I liked you. I trusted you. I could have happily married you. But—"

But there was Ruven.

But I learned too much of the gods, changed too much, and now I am no longer the girl just rejected from the convent who asked him for a kiss. I am something strange and jagged, half apostate and half holy, who can no longer fit into his arms.

And right now, I have to stop his mother, whatever the cost to myself. Or him.

"But *I* love *you*," Araunn says hotly, with more anger than I've ever seen from him. "Lia, don't you—can't you, please—" He stops, struggling for words. "I know you're more than a pawn of my mother or the heretics."

"What do you want?" I ask. "Even if I did love you, your mother is still planning to kill me. Unless you want to make her take Varia's life instead?"

". . . No," he admits miserably. "But—perhaps she would take mine." The idea must have come to him that instant; I can see it take root and possess him. "I'm not as clever as Varia, certainly I wouldn't be as good an heir, so—"

"She'll never let me live," I say flatly.

And she loves you far more than Varia, I think, but if Araunn still hasn't noticed that, then perhaps it's just as well not to tell him.

"There doesn't need to be a Great Sacrifice," I say. "Runakhia doesn't need to be ruled by fear. You know that, don't you?" I grip his hand, looking deep into his eyes. "Help me. We can stop this madness together."

For one moment, I think he's going to say yes. Then he drops his eyes and pulls his hand free.

"I'm sorry," he says. "She's my mother."

My throat aches as he walks back to Imvada's side.

We climb again, and rest again. Climb, and rest. I begin to feel as if we've been there for days, and I wonder if Parliament will take the opportunity to seize back their power. Perhaps everything in the mortal world has sorted itself out, and all I need to do is make sure that the royal family never leave. I could cast them into an enchanted sleep and then lie down beside them, or maybe sit and play cat's cradle with Ruven *if he ever bothers to show up.*

I realize that I'm getting light-headed, and I pause to lean against the side of the mountain and gasp for breath. Varia has also paused, looking winded.

"Hurry up!" Imvada calls from around the corner, her voice ringing out without the slightest hint of exhaustion. "Araunn and I have reached the top!"

For one moment, Varia and I share a look of mutual, miserable resentment. Then we both push away from the wall and trudge up the final flight of steps.

The top of the mountain is a flat circle crowned with broken columns. In the air above the peak flat is a half circle of eight vast thrones. Six are carved of the same white stone as the mountain; but the two at the center are different, one silver and one gold.

This is it, I think, my exhaustion washed away with fear and excitement and resolution. *This is the end.*

Imvada steps forward, tall and proud. "In the name of Juni-Akha, lady of sunlight and triumph, I call upon all the gods. Come to witness my sacrifice."

For one moment, light and shadow flicker around the eight seats.

Then the gods are with us.

I don't see them, because I've already felt their presence: an enormous, crushing weight that crumples me to the ground where I lie gasping for breath, my vision swimming.

Gods and saints, I think numbly, half praying, half blaspheming. *Gods and saints.*

"Eight gods," Ruven grits out, "and four saints."

I open eyes I hadn't been aware of closing. Ruven lies beside me, at last revealed, crushed to the ground beneath the same terrifying weight of divine perception.

His hand lies near mine; gasping with effort, he reaches forward to touch my fingers. Here in the divine realm, his hand is solid and warm, and I feel an answering warmth in my chest.

We will fight Imvada together. We will win.

Grunting, I manage to push myself up onto my hands and then my knees. I'm surprised to realize that I am the first to rise; even Imvada is still doubled over, hands pressed against the ground. This can't possibly be what she had planned.

What have we done? I think as I climb laboriously to my feet.

Then I finally look up at the gods.

They are like their paintings, or like the way that they were when I met them in their shrines, but now they sit on their thrones wearing long white robes that trail down into the air below. Their majesty is dizzying; I want to fall back to my knees.

There are too many of them. There are far too many. No mortal resolution can defy them. How could I ever have hoped it?

But then I realize that none of them are looking at me—none except Mor-Iva, who grins fiercely at me as she cradles her heart in her hands. All the other gods stare far into the distance, as if what happens at their feet is nothing to them.

It *is* nothing to them, I realize, my heart aching with a vast pain that began when Nin-Anna rejected me—no, before that. I felt this same hurt years and years ago in the convent, longing for the nuns to look at me, love me. Now that I have met all the gods, have seen their beauty and monstrosity, I want them to love me too.

But they cannot.

Each one of us loves eternally just one thing, Mor-Iva had said to me.

Nobody who is not one of their saints, who has not forged a pact with them, can be noticed by them.

As Ruven struggles to his feet beside me, strands of dark hair falling messily into his face, it occurs to me that the gods have missed so much. Their realm, though lovely and unearthly, is still so very small, and they understand so little of what lies outside it.

Then Imvada's voice rings out: "Let the glory of Juni-Akha be chains to those who defy me."

Instantly there's a weight on my wrists and neck: golden chains, warm as if they had been lying for hours in the morning sun. They tighten, dragging me down to my knees; I barely have enough slack in the chain to keep my head up. Beside me, Ruven is bent double.

I open my mouth to call on Mor-Iva, to try to fight, but I find that my tongue won't move. I can't speak. When I try to pray silently, to feel the goddess's power in my mind, there is nothing.

Despairingly, I realize there is nothing left that I can do. In this realm, the glory and the triumph of Juni-Akha—queen of victory and power—reign supreme, and so Imvada, as her chosen, is inevitably supreme as well.

Slowly, gracefully, Imvada draws a knife. The hilt gleams with gold and jewels that catch the unearthly light of the divine realm; I wonder if this is the same knife that she used to kill her sister and brother.

"O gods," she says, "accept my sacrifice."

"Wait!" Araunn cries out. "Mother, wait!"

It's the last thing that I had expected to hear; from the look on Imvada's face, she hadn't expected it either.

The next moment Araunn has flung himself between the queen and me.

"Don't kill her," he says urgently. "Whatever she's done, she loves the gods, I know it—"

"Then she should be glad to die for them," Imvada says calmly.

"—and you don't need the Great Sacrifice, I know that too. You are the greatest queen to rule in centuries." He smiles up at her as he catches her hands in his own. "Please."

Imvada half smiles at him in return. "Oh, Araunn. You were always too gentle to be one of us. Step aside. You don't need to watch."

"I won't let you hurt her," he says stubbornly. "Mother—"

"Let go," she says, more sternly now.

"Never," he says, and then he tries to pull the knife away from her. Imvada's fingers nearly let it slip, but then she wrenches it back with a grunt of effort, and for a moment they struggle—

Then Araunn staggers back at the same time that Imvada makes a dreadful, hollow moan.

For a moment, I can't understand what's happened. Then the crimson stain begins to spread across his chest, horribly fast, and I realize that the knife Imvada still holds is now painted red.

It was an accident—that much is clear from the shocked agony on Imvada's face. She drops the knife and lunges forward to catch Araunn as he crumples.

"No," she whispers, "merciful Nin-Anna, please, *no*—"

Already the blood is everywhere. The blade must have gone straight to his heart.

Araunn manages to raise his head. His eyes meet mine and I think my heart will break from the peace in his gaze. Then he slumps forward into his mother's arms and is gone.

The entire tragedy has taken less than a minute. As Imvada begins to weep, cradling her dead son in her arms, I stare at the spreading pool of Araunn's blood in a daze, not quite able to believe it really happened.

Varia is not dazed. Her face is grimly focused as she picks up the knife that killed Araunn and steps behind her mother.

My throat is tight and soundless. I'm not sure if I cannot cry out or if I simply don't want to warn Imvada.

Varia seizes a handful of Imvada's hair—right between her

337

golden horns—as she puts the knife to her throat. But Imvada doesn't struggle. She doesn't even flinch as Varia slices her throat open. She dies still staring at Araunn's body, and then she crumples over him.

"O gods," says Varia in a voice of dreadful calm, "accept my sacrifice."

The chains that Imvada put on me are suddenly gone. I gasp, nearly toppling over, and then stagger to my feet.

Just in time to see the power of the Great Sacrifice descend upon Varia.

On their thrones above, all eight gods raise their hands as one. Varia raises her hands as well—not victoriously, but as if they are being drawn up by a power beyond her control. Her fingers claw and writhe; drops of blood seep out of the places where Zumariel's ribbons sprout from her skin.

A great gust of wind rushes down on the mountaintop from on high; my hair blows into a tangled veil over my face. When I can see again, Varia's hands are lowered. A strange, shimmering radiance clings to her, soft yet fathomless. It's like the light of the sun here in Juni-Akha's realm—it does not dazzle, and yet in its softness lies a terrifying power.

Varia has received such power from the gods as no king or queen has wielded in hundreds of years. She can reshape Runakhia at will, if she wishes.

My heart is beating very fast, and I hardly dare to breathe. I half hear, half feel Ruven start to move beside me, and I grab his wrist to stop him.

I still don't know the princess well, but I know that she truly loved her brother. Whatever is in Varia's heart right now, it is surely balanced on the edge of a knife.

"I once believed that our family was more blessed than any other, because we loved the gods and they loved us." Varia's voice is utterly calm and collected, but when she looks at me, there is a terrible, fragile grief in her eyes. "Tell me there is a way to stop this from happening again. Or I swear by all the gods that none of us will leave here alive."

"That's hardly the worst thing you could do," says Ruven, apparently no longer able to keep silent.

Varia ignores him, her eyes staying on me. "We both tried so hard, Araunn and I," she says. "But he was doomed, because he loved the gods. As my mother was doomed, because she was *like* the gods." Her voice turns harsh and bitter on the last words.

I remember what I said to Ruven while I was in the dungeon, and now the words reverse themselves in my head: *They are beautiful monsters, but oh, they are* monstrous *gods.*

As I think that, I remember Ruven kissing my monstrous hands, and the way Mor-Iva's disgust had slowly turned to wonder. I remember Jaríne saying, *Our god became weak for us, and so he loves everything helpless and broken.*

The gods of Runakhia have never known weakness or pain. But—

"What if we could change the gods?" I ask.

"What?" says Varia. "That's impossible. What would it even mean?"

I'm not sure. But I know this: the gods cannot change themselves. They have each loved one thing and changed for that love so completely that they cannot remember how to even imagine loving something else.

I know this also: they change when they make their pacts with humans, with people they have judged worthy of themselves but who are still in some way *not them*. Mor-Iva showed me that.

It's a very small kind of change. Nothing of the sort I am starting to imagine now. Those who wield the power of the gods through a pact cannot do something so against the nature of the gods.

But I am also a sorceress. The first, perhaps, who has ever loved the gods from whom she stole.

"Will you let me live long enough to try?" I ask Varia. "Will you *trust* me to try?"

Slowly, Varia nods.

I turn to Ruven. "Will you help me?" I ask.

His mouth curves up. "For this sort of blasphemy? Always."

I draw a deep, shaky breath. "And you, O final word? Will you help me?"

As suddenly and softly as breathing, Mor-Iva stands beside me, golden eyes alight with curiosity.

What is it you are planning to rend? the goddess asked.

"Everything," I say. "If you ask them, will Juni-Akha and Ithombriel come down from their thrones?"

Oh, you are an ambitious knife, says Mor-Iva, a wicked grin spreading across her face. *I think I can bring your prey.*

She shimmers away into the air.

Silently, I say to Ruven, *I know what I have to do, but I don't . . . have the skill to do it. Can you wield me again, one more time, if I guide you?*

"Of course," he says, stepping behind me. His hands fit to the sides of my throat, and he presses a kiss to the top of my head. "My dearest apostate."

You shouldn't use that word here, I'm about to say—but then Juni-Akha and Ithombriel appear before us.

Again their presence is a crushing weight, but this time I manage to stay on my feet. I look up—the gods are very tall, and they hover a few feet above the ground, the trains of their robes swirling slowly in the air as if washed by invisible currents of water.

Juni-Akha is terrifyingly like to Imvada: a tall, imperious woman with golden horns growing out of her long red hair. But a flat gold sheath covers her face from hairline to mouth; no mortal has ever seen her features. Her robes are shimmering gold and cream and rose, all the colors of triumphant dawn.

Beside her, Ithombriel stands yet taller and far stranger: a slender, pale god with no face. Atop his neck sits not a human head, but a great ring of unearthly, opalescent flesh. His robes are silver and gray and violet, all the colors of contemplative twilight.

What victory have you to report? asks Juni-Akha.

What wisdom have you to share? asks Ithombriel.

"This," I say, my voice ringing like a bell as I boldly take first Juni-Akha's hand, then Ithombriel's. "And this."

Juni-Akha's hand is hotter than the worst fever patient I've ever nursed, while Ithombriel's is cool as a corpse. A shudder runs through me, but I don't let go.

I think of my conversation with Ruven about the nature of sorcery, and the kind of love it takes to know something well enough to enchant it. Ruven loves the warmth of summer days, and he twisted that into a noonday drowse that lasted five hundred years.

I love the gods, and I am going to twist that into hope.

Ruven's hands are warm on my throat, gentle with absolute trust, and I relax into his grip with equal trust.

Now, I tell him silently, and we begin to work.

Sorcery in the divine realm is not the same as in the mortal world. There, I worked by feeling the gaps between the filaments of the world, the places of emptiness that left room for power. Here, every thread of the world is bursting with power, singing only one of two songs: Juni-Akha's or Ithombriel's, triumph or wisdom.

So I work by prying the threads apart, by casting silence into that chorus, a bittersweet half harmony into that chord, so that— for the first time in nearly an eternity—a change in key is possible.

I work, and I shudder as the power of the divine realm flows into me and fills me up. But Ruven is behind me, holding me, using me to drain away the wave of divine power that would otherwise have drowned me.

I work and he wills, and he works and I will, and together we rewrite the gods. We dare to touch the divine flesh of Juni-Akha and Ithombriel, to dent and mark and change it with mortality, so that the queen and king of the gods become something like saints of mortality.

The golden plate over Juni-Akha's face cracks down the center, the right side falling away to reveal a brown eye with no trace of divine light. Mortal wrinkles and wispy white hairs spread across half the ring of strange flesh that is Ithombriel's head.

The gods are infected with mortality now, as their saints are infected with divinity.

I understand this and let go. The next moment I'm staggering back, then sinking to the ground, darkness speckling my vision and a ringing in my ears. It's several moments before I'm able to sit up straight. Then I look back to ask Ruven why he didn't catch me—

But he's gone.

Where are you? I call silently, fear trickling through me. When he doesn't reply, I croak aloud, "Ruven?"

Ithombriel turns his now half-wrinkled ring of flesh to face me.

Your sorcerer channeled away too much of the power that would have killed you, he says. *The bond that tied his soul to you is broken now.*

The words don't make sense. I stare up at Ithombriel, willing him to speak again, to explain how he hadn't meant it—*wishing*, so desperately, that Ruven would appear to tell me I'm a fool for being so scared—

But Ithombriel has turned away from me, back to Varia and to Araunn's body.

I am the lord of wisdom, and yet I do not know this, he says. *What is this? Is it grief? Is it fear? What is this?*

I have been defeated, says Juni-Akha, kneeling by Araunn's body. Her skirts pool in the air two handspans above the ground. *The royal family is my triumph, and he is dead, and I am defeated. How am I defeated?*

My eyes blur as I watch them. Their confusion feels like my own grief, like the dark abyss that is suddenly threatening to swallow me whole. So I can say nothing, do nothing to give them comfort.

It is Varia who rises and kisses the foreheads of Juni-Akha and Ithombriel, who promises that she will comfort their sadness as I watch mutely.

Is this truly the object of your devotion, then?

I recognize Im-Yara's voice and I shudder with remembered pain. But I still force myself to turn and face her.

This bloody, broken weakness—these creatures that cannot help themselves—is it for them *that you burned in my arms?*

"Yes," I say. "It is."

Im-Yara nods solemnly. *Then we shall burn for you*, she promises, and disappears.

In her place stands Nin-Anna, her golden hands gleaming as perfectly as when she set the mark of judgment on me.

You have brewed us a bitter medicine, she says.

I can't speak. Even after everything that has happened, all the ways I have changed and rebelled, I still want to crawl to her, kiss her feet, and beg forgiveness. I still want, so much, for her to love me.

She cups my face in her golden hands, and my heart stutters at the soft warmth of her touch. But there is no love in her gaze; she examines me as a surgeon would a tumor, and I close my eyes in grief.

The gods cannot love me, not the way I love them.

You are not entirely unlike me, says Nin-Anna, and presses her lips against my forehead in a kiss.

It's not love. But it is a promise.

The next moment, I feel like I am falling. When I open my eyes, the divine realm has vanished. Varia and I stand before the sacred fire in the great shrine. The acolytes are still waiting for us, and more clerics beside; incense and chant alike hang on the air.

"Queen Imvada gave her life for Runakhia," Varia proclaims, looking down at them as if she were a statue on a pedestal. "I am now the queen."

There is a terrible, nervous pause, and then—

"Long live the queen," they chorus, bowing low.

But your sorcerer will not live long, Mor-Iva whispers in my ear.

I straighten suddenly. *What?*

You know, says Mor-Iva. *In his coffin.*

A cold feeling, half fury and half fear, washes through me. *No*, I say. *I don't know. Tell me.*

He broke the bond that held him to you, says Mor-Iva. *So he was returned to his body, and with enough breath of the divine realm on him to heal his wounds. But I think you left him in a coffin, didn't you?*

My heart is ice in my chest.

"Did Mor-Iva just say what I think she did?" Varia asks under her breath.

I jerk in surprise, and then say, "Yes."

"He's nothing to me, and in fact I'd enjoy seeing him dead," says Varia. "But hadn't you better run?"

35

BY THE TIME I REACH THE heretic chapel, my breath is wheezing in my throat and sweat slicks my back. I stagger into the churchyard, and when I get to the mausoleum, I have to stop and lean against the wall as I gasp for breath.

A terrible doubt works its way into my mind: what if Mor-Iva was wrong? The gods are not all-knowing when it comes to mortal things. *Especially* when it comes to sorcerous things.

For a moment I want to turn back. If I wrench that coffin open only to see him lying still and dead, I know my heart will break all over again.

But I can bear that if I must. What I can't bear is the chance I might have left him to suffer when he could still be saved.

As I think this, I find the strength to stand again and walk into the mausoleum, to kneel by the stone tomb where Jaríne and I helped lay Ruven.

For a moment there's only silence, and I think despairingly, *He's dead, he's really dead—*

Then I hear a faint, desperate pounding from within the tomb.

I slam my fists into the stone as I scream, "Ruven!"

Then I start scrabbling at the edges of the tomb's lid. My claws snap and fingers bleed, but I hardly notice the pain. My heart is cringing in horror. He must have been in there for an hour at least, with no hope that anybody would come for him. How much time does he even have left?

And I can't move the lid. I'm not strong enough. I start sobbing even as I continue to struggle. Ruven is going to die all over again, inches away from me and in agony, because I'm not strong enough, because I didn't think to bring any help with me, because—

Because you've forgotten me, Mor-Iva interrupts, her voice coolly amused.

I sit back, tears still running down my face, and feel like the greatest fool in the world.

I lift my charred, monstrous hand—the broken claws are already growing back—and strike the tomb with the power and judgment of Mor-Iva.

Cracks blossom across the smooth surface of the stone, and it crumbles into dust. Ruven sits up, coughing and gagging, but alive.

He's *alive*.

Suddenly I can't move, only stare at him in frozen wonder. I fell in love with him when he was already dead. I kissed him, knowing I could never hold him in the daylight world. I never had the slightest hope, and now—

"Lia," he rasps, meeting my eyes, and then I fling myself forward into his arms.

"I'm sorry," I whisper, not sure if I'm apologizing for killing him or for getting him buried alive. "I'm sorry, I'm so, *so* sorry—"

"What did you do?" he asks, and my heart jolts in my chest with dread, but then he pulls back from my grip and I see reverent wonder in his eyes as he asks again, "What did you *do*?"

"Nothing," I say, absurdly near to laughter. "It was an accident."

"Or grace," he whispers, and I want to ask him what that means, but then he kisses me and I forget that words exist.

Eventually, we stop kissing. For a little while we lean against each other, staring out the doorway of the mausoleum into the sunlight.

I tell Ruven what happened after he disappeared. When my voice wavers and cracks, he presses his face into my hair and whispers comfort.

Finally he asks me, "What now?"

"What do you mean?"

"You've done what you set out to do, haven't you?" he says. "Restored the royal family, awakened the gods, rid yourself of a heretic ghost, and escaped the queen. And you've become a sorceress and made a pact with Mor-Iva besides, so I doubt that either Varia or the prime minister could hold you to anything you don't want to do. Whatever sort of hospital you want, I think they'll build you."

I frown, wanting to protest . . . and realize he's right.

I've thought of myself as helpless for so long. But there's no anathema collar on me now, and I'm no longer locked up in prison. I know the prime minister thinks he needs me, and Varia likely does too. Even if all my secrets were revealed, I don't think I would have to fear either one of them.

It's almost impossible to imagine making a choice without fear. But Ruven sitting alive beside me is more impossible still.

"So," Ruven says, "what now? What do you want?"

I think of the day before my birthday, when I went into the city with Sister Zenuvan. When I thought I would do my one heroic deed and then spend the rest of my life in the convent, expanding its mission but never leaving. So much has changed since then, I barely feel like I'm the same girl anymore.

One thing is still the same: I want to heal people. I want to help.

Even if that means unmaking saints, and befriending a ruthless yet grieving queen, and teaching gods what it means to be human.

"Well," I say, "I think perhaps I don't want to be a nun after all."

He laughs. "That's all it took to change your mind? Several deaths and blasphemies and miracles?"

"And working sorcery on the gods," I say, smiling back at him. "Don't forget that." Then I stand up. "I'm going back to the palace," I tell him. "I'm going to find Varia and pledge her my loyalty."

Ruven looks up at me quizzically. "I didn't realize you liked her that much."

I think of Varia threatening to hurt me if I caused Araunn harm, and slicing her own mother's throat. I remember how she promised two gods that she would teach them to bear the sorrow of mortality and told me that I should run to save Ruven.

"I don't," I say. "Not yet, anyway. But . . . I think I trust her. And I want to help her be a better queen than her mother." I pause a moment, then gather my courage and ask, "What about you? What do *you* want?"

"Well," he says, and rises to his feet in one smooth movement, "I seem to have fallen in love with a princess. So I suppose I'll have to give up on destroying the royal family." He holds his hand out to me. "Besides, I'm sure your new queen will trust you better if she has a hostage to use against you."

I laugh, because that does indeed sound exactly like Varia. Then I take his hand, wrapping my charred, clawed fingers over his smooth skin. Memory flickers: the dream I had during my vigil, of warm hands clinging to mine, of somebody choosing and holding me.

"I do love you," I whisper.

He kisses my forehead. "It's no more than you deserve for your sins."

As we walk out of the graveyard together, I feel a strange lightness, as if this sun-drenched morning were the first of all mornings, and the world around me is new made and strange.

Maybe it is. After all, the gods themselves have changed. How can that help but change the world as well?

I hope it can be a kinder world now.

I will *make* it one.

Hear me, O gods, who are no longer silent, whom I have made to listen: I have one love, one queen, and one homeland. I am going to protect them all. You are going to help me protect them.

And I will teach you to love them, just as I have learned to love you.

Acknowledgments

This book took a very long time to write, so there are a whole lot of people I need to thank. Absolutely number one would be my dog, Mssani's Lunafreya Nox Fleuret, aka Luna, who entered my life in 2018 and has made everything so much better. I love you, my darling little dum-dum princess, and I would happily pile the bones of your enemies in front of you (but you're too sweet to have any enemies).

In 2021, my grandmother Dolores Ramirez died. I don't think I can properly describe her, but I'm going to try. She grew up not only poor, but without a stable home because her mother was dying of tuberculosis in a sanatorium. Her dream was to someday create a clean, beautiful home with happy children—and she did. She was also an artist who loved to paint rocks for her garden, and later in life she became an iconographer. And while she was not a great reader herself, she always encouraged my mother's love of reading, and my mother passed that love on to me. So she's part of why I'm writing books now. Thank you, Grandma Dee.

Anyone who grew up as a nerdy Catholic homeschooler (as I did) will probably recognize that the "heretics" of Runakhia are inspired by the situation of Catholics in Victorian England, and they might even realize that Ruven was inspired by Guy Fawkes. I want to credit Alice Hogge's excellent book *God's Secret Agents: Queen Elizabeth's Forbidden Priests and the Hatching of the Gunpowder Plot* as well as Bill Cain's incredible play *Equivocation* for feeding a lot of my interest in Guy Fawkes specifically.

When I set out to create the gods of Runakhia, I knew that I wanted them to be alien, beautiful, and terrifying. And for many years, my gold standard of the near-monstrous numinous has been the art of Peter Mohrbacher's Angelarium project. I *think* I made my gods unique enough to be more than rip-offs, but there's no question I owe him a heavy debt of inspiration. Please check out his art at Angelarium.net and consider supporting him on Patreon.

My agent, Hannah Bowman, has continued to be the best support and advocate that any writer could hope for. And I am also extremely grateful to my editor, Kristin Rens, for her patience as I flailed my way through this project.

Brendan Hodge, Bethany Powell, R. J. Anderson, Suzannah Rowntree, Maria Farb, Marie Lewis, Mathilda Zeller, Jennifer Danke, and Claire Trella Hill all read drafts of this book and offered invaluable advice and/or encouragement. Thank you all so much!

Meanwhile, Sasha Decker did not read any drafts, but she lived with an author drafting under deadline, so she deserves a medal.

Shout-out to Mogus, Yevelda, Eunica, Nemmy, and Sami for being excellent friends IRL and also the best party members that anyone learning to play D&D could hope to have. Taliri is going to name the baby after all five of you.

Finally, I have to acknowledge above all the author of my own life. I went through some very dark times while writing this book, and I made it out safely only because God is the father of mercies, who will always give my life back to me. It is through His loving kindness, and the precious blood of His only son, and the breath of the Holy Spirit—with the prayers of blessed Mary, ever virgin, and all the angels and saints—that I have hope. Jesus, I trust in You.